PAYBACK

By Janet Periat

Payback

Published 2013 by Madison Avenue Press

www.janetperiat.com

First Edition: 2013

ISBN 978-1-937813-04-8

Cover Art: © 2013 Randy Cleveland

Book Design: Frank Higgins

Edited by: Ann Fischer

For Ann Fischer

For saving Rollin's life—and my ass, too many times to count

ACKNOWLEDGMENTS

Firstly, I'd like to thank my critique group, The Phoenixes: Ann Fischer and Anne Maragoni for their support, guidance, astounding editing skills, and for always challenging me. You ladies keep me on my toes and keep me afloat. I have no idea what I would do without you.

Thanks to Google for being a reliable porthole to the millions of answers to questions that arise while writing a book. Like about guns and Stinger missiles, tanks and bullet wounds. Thanks also to Google Maps so I could study Concord, New Hampshire and Washington DC down to street level. Saved me a lot of airfare and time.

I'd like to thank Linda Sullivan for inspiring the character of Sam. While Sam's background has almost nothing in common with Linda's, they share the same heart, loyalty, charm, ebullience and ability to light up a room. We'd already been friends for years when Linda began caring for my stroke-victim sister Judy. I don't know what I would have done without her. And at the time of this writing, she's still helping my sister. Not only is Linda always there when you need her, she is one of the funniest and most fun people alive. Just like the character she inspired. And her nickname just happens to be Sam. So thanks Real Life Sam! You rock!

Thanks to my therapist, Delores DeAlba, for continually providing me with a solid reality check; for helping shape my character's psyches; for slapping me upside the head when I need it, and for being my compass when I get lost. Thanks my dear, for helping me on my journey to enlightenment. Now all I have to do is take your advice.

Thanks to my neighbor and friend, RN Marisa Parsons, for her medical expertise and advice. Thanks to another neighbor, Julie Strider-Cook, for the expression: "Ah, pickles!"

Thanks to my cousin Diane Castle for always being there for me and encouraging me. Love you, girl.

Thanks to Randy Cleveland for his amazing artistic talents, his unrelenting sense of humor, and for generally being a wonderful person.

Thanks to all my friends who support my career by buying my books, reviewing my books, and selecting my books for their book clubs. Especially Victoria Skinner, Carol Little, Jeanne Simari, Maryfrances Charney, Joan and Elinor McCormick, and Marianne Smith. You guys ROCK!!!

Thanks to the members of the Silicon Valley Romance Writers of America for their help, guidance, support and inspiration. You ladies (and gentleman) have been instrumental in my career. Especially Teri Bradburn who helped with the editing of this book.

And last, but not least, I'd like to thank my husband Frank for his steadfast support and love. I can't say enough good things about him. When I was in the hospital recently with mysterious seizures and terrified to my core, every time I woke up and saw him there, I knew I was going to be okay. Not only has he supported me and my career forever—and been my computer and book formatting guru—he's funny as hell and HOT. And he bakes awesome life-size skull cakes for me, complete with raspberry mousse brains. Here's to twenty-five more great years with you, honey, I love you!

PREFACE

About halfway through writing *Caught*, I fell for Burke Cherlenko. Hard. I originally wanted him to be a short-lived villain that would only appear in *Caught*, but he had his own plans. Normally, characters take time to mature, but Burke was one of those rare characters that popped off the page and came to life, fully developed. Once I realized how special he was, I knew he needed his own story.

Originally, when I began *Payback*, I wanted Burke and Emma to be together. I mistook their chemistry as material for a long-term relationship. But the only way to get them together cleanly was to kill off Rollin. I wrote the first three chapters featuring the two and had a completely different storyline. At the time, I honestly thought they belonged together.

However, my editor and critique partner, Ann Fischer, was convinced that killing Rollin was a mistake. She suggested that Burke hook up with Sam. She argued that Emma was too nice for Burke, but that Sam was strong enough to stand up to him. But no matter how well she presented her ideas, I wouldn't listen to her. No way was I changing my mind. Rollin was a dead man. Finally, after six months straight of impassioned pleas, Ann got through to me.

At the time of this writing, I can't imagine how I ever thought that killing Rollin was a good idea. While his end would have been very heroic—dying while saving the lives of his friends and Emma (kinda like that scene in *Star Trek, Wrath of Khan* where Spock gives his life for his friends and everybody's crying)—it was an incredibly shortsighted idea. Rollin is a treasure. He has become such an important resource, such a dependable character—really the heart and soul of the Patriots—I can't imagine the series without him.

But it was when I brought Burke and Sam together that I realized Ann's true wisdom. The scenes wrote themselves. The two were a great match. Perfect foils. Ann had been right: Emma was far too nice for Burke. Sam will never let Burke get the best of her and Emma would have let him walk all over her.

This is why authors need critique groups. So they don't make mistakes they will kick themselves for later on down the road.

You can also thank Ann Fischer for *Payback* being the second of the Patriots' series instead of *Marked*. Originally, I wanted *Caught* to be first, *Marked* to be second and *Payback* third. But after I finished *Caught*, Burke was living fully formed in my brain and before he left (characters will depart if you neglect them) I decided to write his story. I planned on writing *Payback* and shelving it until I finished *Marked* and then publishing them both within a month of each other. But yet again, Ann came to the rescue and said, "If *Payback* is almost done, why don't you publish it? How hard would it be to make it the second book? Do you really want a wait a year to publish another book?"

I argued with her at first, of course, because that's what I do with Ann, especially when she makes sense. I thought I'd have to do a lot of editing to make *Payback* work as the second book. I also wanted to address the issue of Rollin and Emma's mysterious tattoos as quickly as I could. But as it turned out, all I had to do was edit a couple lines about Zane—the hero of *Marked*—and that was it. *Payback* was clearly meant to be the second in the series.

So please enjoy *Payback*: a story about revenge, love and redemption.

-Janet Periat, March, 2013

ONE

The barrel of the gun seemed three feet in diameter. Blood splattered all over her white Backstreet Boys sweatshirt. Drenching, sick, warm, meaty-smelling blood. The disbelief and shock in her father's eyes. Larry's psychotic leer.

Her body shuddered violently, breaking her out of the daymare.

"How ya doin'?" Paul asked from below her on the trail.

Samantha Murdock looked around, half-surprised to find herself hiking in a redwood forest, following her date down a steep trail. Covered in cold sweat, she forced a smile. "Great," she said, sounding shakier than she would have liked.

Paul sent her an easy, sexy smile. "Beautiful out here."

"Fabulous." Sam descended the single-track trail toward Paul. Grabbing a root on the moss-covered rock wall next to her for support, she stepped over a small boulder, and tried for some upbeat patter. "I couldn't believe it when we drove past Pescadero and the fog disappeared. In summer, Butano State Park can get as socked in as the beach. We hit a perfect day."

"We sure did." Turning, he continued on.

Thank God, Paul had asked her out on this date. A week ago when she'd accepted his invitation, she'd had no idea how much she would need a nice tranquil walk surrounded by gorgeous scenery—Paul being the best scenery of all. He outshone the entire Santa Cruz

Mountain Range. With his steel-blue eyes, aquiline nose and square jaw—not to mention his astounding buff body and broad shoulders—the man was a HUNK. Thank God for the Internet.

And thank God for the distraction.

Ever since she'd seen Ursula the day before to confirm the location of the murder weapon—and then stumbled across that wild evidence against Larry—the flashbacks had been intensifying. Last night, she'd hardly slept at all. She had to relax. Her mind had to be razor sharp to handle the next two weeks.

Sam took a deep sniff of the forest air, catching the musty and muddy hints of the sandy creek bed far below, the piney scent of the trees, and the intense lemongrass-like aroma of the sword ferns, nettles, and oxalis. Blue jays and woodpeckers chattered, the creek babbled, and the wind rustled through the branches and leaves of the tall, majestic redwoods. Stepping into a patch of bright warm sunlight, she let out a long breath and felt more peaceful.

Gunfire pierced the air and echoed off the ridge opposite them.

Sam's heart jumped and her attention snapped across the canyon. "What the hell? There's no hunting allowed back here. Oh, yeah. Probably coming from Ridge Road. I know some guys who like to do target practice up there."

Paul's eyes widened. "Let's hope they stay on target."

A shot rang out. The shale rock wall blew apart right above her head, spraying her with debris.

"Hey!" Sam yelled up toward the ridge. "There are people down here, you idiots! Knock it off!"

Gun blasts strafed the area. Trees splintered and puffs of dirt exploded in the ground near her feet.

Her heart rate quadrupled, adrenaline blasted her system, and she frantically searched for cover. Holy shit! This wasn't any accident! Larry had found her!

Someone heavy tackled her from behind. Screaming, she ate trail. Every muscle bellowed at her to run. Rocks and redwood leaves poked painfully into the exposed skin on her arms and legs while she struggled against the muscled mass on top of her. She turned her head as best she could, but couldn't see her attacker's face.

Paul leapt to his feet and charged with fierce expression. "Get away from her!"

Another volley of gunfire shattered the silence of the forest. Bullets pounded the area around Paul and he dove off the trail behind a small tree.

All at once, she was up and facing the other way and shoved forward.

"Run, Sam! Run!" came a male voice. "There's no good cover here!"

Gunshots blazed. Dirt and a spray of rocks peppered her left side.

The person wasn't attacking her, he was protecting her! Her heart slamming in her chest, her body jacked, Sam sprinted up the hill. "Where's my friend?" she shouted over her shoulder.

"Right behind us! Run!"

Sharp cracks of gunfire bounced off the two tall walls of the canyon above her. Rocks, dirt, and trees were torn apart as she flew by them. She crested the trail and jumped down the rocky path. Ursula must have leaked her identity. Damn it!

But Ursula wouldn't.

Unless Larry had kept surveillance on her old friend. That was it. He'd found out about their meeting. And now he knew Sam was still alive.

She should have brought the Glock. Her peashooter Smith and Wesson 314 revolver was no match for snipers.

Sam came around a corner and was shoved sideways into a clump of brush. The man protecting her tackled her again and covered her with his big and muscular body. Leaves, sticks, and rocks dug into her flesh as the man's weight pressed her to the ground. While he was clearly trying not to squish her, the forest floor against her bare skin hurt. Of course, getting shot would be a lot less comfortable.

"Who—"

He clamped his large hand over her mouth. "Hush."

A barrage of gunshots filled the air. No bullets impacted their area.

"Stay down for another second, then I'll let you up," he said quietly in her ear.

Wait a minute. She knew that voice. But it couldn't be. She turned around to see who it was and gasped.

Burke Cherlenko, a mercenary and ex Navy SEAL who terrorized her best friend, Emma. Notorious and dangerous. All her instincts told her to run and keep running.

She tried to throw him off, but he kept her pinned, his hand tight on her mouth.

But where the hell did Burke come from? And how did he know Larry was after her? She'd only met with Ursula the day before. What the hell?

She elbowed him in the ribs and scrambled to get away, but he stayed with her.

"Stop fighting me. I'm trying to protect you, you idiot."

Idiot? She nipped his middle finger.

"Ow!" Burke pulled away, shaking his hand.

Sam pushed off the ground with all her strength—Burke fell aside —and she jumped to her feet. Throwing herself further into the brush, she leapt bushes like hurdles until she reached a small clearing that seemed safe from attack.

She stopped and spun to face him. "Burke? What the hell are you doing out here?" she snapped in a harsh whisper.

Breathing heavy, he scorched her with his dark brown gaze. A flush raced over her skin and her body prickled with unwanted sexual awareness. She'd forgotten how fine he was. From his symmetrical oval face to his strong jaw and full sensual lips to his muscled, lean body, he screamed man. Real man. But his eyes mesmerized her. Sultry, mahogany, radiating self-confidence and power.

"What the hell is wrong with you? I'm trying to save you and you bite me?"

"Answer my question," she whispered. "What are you doing out here?"

"Who is this guy and why are those people shooting at us?" came Paul's voice from behind Burke.

"Thank God, you're okay." She brushed by Burke to embrace her hard-bodied date.

Paul crushed her in a hug. His warmth and strength reassured her instantly.

He let go and offered his hand to Burke. "Thanks for protecting her, I'm Paul."

Burke took his hand and shook it. "Burke Cherlenko. And you're welcome." He shot a disapproving glare her way before turning back to her date. "I was sent by Sam's best friends—Emma and Rollin—to protect her. Which she doesn't seem to appreciate," he said directly to her with a nasty twist to his lips. "I have to get you both out of here."

Sam stood her ground. "Wait. How did you guys know someone was after me?"

Burke stared at her and his brow wrinkled. "Bobby intercepted a message between a group of contract killers slash professional kidnappers we're tracking. Your picture and name were attached. Their orders were to kidnap you, but apparently, they've changed their minds."

Her fists balled, her teeth clenched, she wanted to scream. Damn it! That bastard! Now he had the money and power to deploy a team after her!

Paul paled and stared at her with his mouth slightly open. "Sam?"

Her insides burned. Holy bejeebus, she'd put her new boyfriend in danger! This couldn't be happening! "Paul, I swear, I—"

"It's not her fault," said Burke.

"But why would someone want to kill her?" Paul gestured toward her in quick movement.

Sam searched Burke's face. Why would he say it wasn't her fault? Unless it had nothing to do with Larry. Could this be about something else?

Burke turned to her. "Does the name Linda Anderson mean anything to you?"

She gaped. "Linda Anderson? This is about *Linda Anderson?*"

Her body flooded with relief and she let out a long sigh. The shooting wasn't about Larry? He still didn't know she was alive? Thank God! She could still bring down that murderer.

Wait a minute. Rollin was cheating on Emma with Linda Anderson. Why were contract killers after *her*? All she'd done was drop by Linda's house.

Her stomach twisted and she got goosebumps. This better have nothing to do with that box the mailman had shoved into her hands. The package addressed to Linda filled with evidence against Larry and several other high level politicians.

Please tell me I didn't just fuck myself.

Burke honed in on her with his laser-sighted gaze. "Who did you think was shooting at you? Is someone else trying to kill you?"

Holy shit. She'd almost let out her most precious secret!

Quick! Cover your reaction, girl!

She averted her attention. "No." She forced herself to make eye contact. "I'm just…shocked, that's all. Hard to imagine contract killers would target me."

"You look relieved," Burke said with a penetrating stare.

The bark on the trees above their heads splintered. Gunfire echoed through the forest. Every nerve ignited and Sam flattened to the trail.

Burke grabbed her and pushed her further into the brush. "Go! And keep down! Paul, hurry!"

She bolted into the dense shrubbery and realized that she was on a very old, overgrown trail. Maybe an old logging road. Keeping her head low, she raced forward, pushing aside branches and leaping over sticks and logs. The men crashed behind her.

The trail zigzagged around massive thousand-year-old redwoods. No one had used the abandoned road in years. Sam's boots crunched through a thick layer of duff. The soft mass slowed her and she picked up her legs higher.

She hopped over a fallen log, landed on a sword fern, and kept running. Twigs whipped her bare legs and arms. Her lungs and muscles burned. Taking a cobweb in the face, she clawed it off.

Burke grabbed her daypack and stopped her. Sweat glistened on his brow. She was happy he was breathing nearly as hard as she.

In full Navy SEAL mode, he surveyed the area. His sharp focus didn't miss a detail. "They can't get us from here."

Paul came up next to her and put his arms around her protectively. She leaned in to him. His scent, warmth, and the feel of his buff body made her feel better. Such a great guy. The way he was handling this whole crazy mess said a lot about his character. Give him a kajillion more points for that.

Burke headed back down the path. "You two stay here, I'll lead them off. I want them to think we're going another way." He disappeared into the brush.

A few minutes later, gunfire.

Her stomach reacted to every shot. Her shoulder muscles were so tight, they felt like a solid flaming mass. Sam sat on a moss-covered log and tried to distract herself by brushing the dirt off her shorts.

But her whole body felt like it was sinking in quicksand. This had to be about that evidence. As soon as she'd seen those photos and checked out the files on the thumb drives, she'd known the information was insanely dangerous.

Shit. Linda must have found out that she had taken the box. And now the woman was trying to kill Sam before the information got out.

Figures that Rollin would be sleeping with another spy.

Fuck! How should she handle this with the Patriots? She couldn't admit that she had the package. If they asked, she'd lie. But somehow she had to get them to keep protecting her from Linda.

Besides, if they found out she had the box of file and photos, they might connect her to Larry. Those guys were so true-blue if they found out she was preparing to destroy the most powerful man in the country, they'd use all their resources to stop her.

Sam picked moss out of her hair and released tension by jiggling her leg. Which barely helped at all.

Paul sat next to her and nudged her. "So who's Linda Anderson?"

As she cleaned off her clothes, she kept a keen eye on their surroundings. She still felt too open, too vulnerable. "Uh, this chick who lives in Seattle. She's sleeping with my best friend's boyfriend, Rollin. My buddy Emma found a bunch of love letters and the woman's address."

"I thought you went to Seattle on business."

"I did. After I picked up the shipment for Emma's store, I went by Linda's place to kick her ass, but she wasn't home." Sam decided not to volunteer the fact that she'd broken into the apartment with keys Emma had found with the letters.

His blue gaze sparkled. "Kick her ass?"

She shot him a grin. "No one screws with my friends."

"Looks like she wants to kill your ass," Paul said with a smirk. "Maybe you ought to find out who you're up against before you interfere."

"Yeah, I tried to find out all I could about her, but came up with nothing other than those letters. I have no idea how she tracked me down." Unless she'd been followed from the apartment. Maybe the woman had seen her with the mailman. Her stomach tightened painfully.

"If Emma's seeing Rollin, why would this Linda gal come after you?"

"Got me. I was just about to ask that same question," Sam said as innocently as she could.

"Ask Burke when he gets back. He seems to know all about her."

A chunk of cobweb was caught on her watch. She tugged at it and the gummy yet whisper light material stuck to her fingers. "I hope so. This is crazy," she said, flicking the spider adhesive to the ground.

"I'll agree with you there." He moved a few leaves off her shoulder, then smiled and gave her a squeeze. "Are you okay?"

She gave a small smile and sighed. "Yeah, but I feel crappy about bringing you into this disaster." Patting his wide, hard thigh, she looked deep into his sexy blue eyes. "I'm so sorry about this."

"Not your fault."

Oh, yes it is.

He rubbed her back and kissed the side of her head.

Despite her heightened sense of danger, goosebumps popped up all over. They had good chemistry. While they'd only kissed a couple times so far, she could tell they'd be a nice match. She'd hoped on this date that they'd ramp up the sexual connection. But at this point, having sex was the last thing on her To Do list.

"Such a great third date," Sam said with a roll of her eyes. "I won't blame you if I never see you again."

"Are you crazy? And miss all this excitement?" His eyes twinkling, he hugged her tight. "You stop worrying. This just makes me want to stay close to you and protect you."

His words stopped her. No man had ever said anything like that to her but her father. All her previous dates and boyfriends wanted her to take care of them. While some of the men had started off promising, they all degenerated into the same, whiny self-centered boy who wanted to sponge off her.

Was it possible? Had she finally found a man?

She smiled and leaned into him. "Thanks for that, Paul. You're a good guy." It was then she noticed that the forest had been quiet for a time. "Gunfire stopped finally. Thank God. Freakin' me out."

Paul ran his hand over her hair and moved a wisp from her face. "We'll be fine. I've got some old military friends who can help protect us, too," he said, massaging the back of her neck. "I won't let anything happen to you. I promise."

She gazed into his intelligent and kind eyes and her heart wrenched open. Mentally using both hands, she slammed it shut. This was not the time to make decisions about relationships. But he was being very sweet. "Thanks, hon. You're making me feel better."

Smiling, his attention went to her mouth.

Her body went warm and fuzzy and she tilted her head to receive his kiss.

"I took care of them," came Burke's voice.

Her hormone bubble popped.

Paul let go, stood, and turned to Burke.

Sam got up and brushed the dirt off her pants with a bit more vigor than needed. Goddamned Burke, ruining their kiss. He could have taken two more minutes. She could use a good kiss right around now.

Burke sent her a pissy look.

Why was he mad?

She gave him a nod. "You think they were fooled?"

"Yeah. We're safe."

Letting out a long breath, her body loosened a bit. "Thanks, Burke."

"You're welcome." He took off his small daypack and set it on a log. "We wait here for a bit, then we'll take another trail."

"Sounds good," Paul said.

Sam slid her backpack off her shoulder and laid it further down on the same log. "Burke, explain to me how breaking into some chick's apart—" She sent a guilty glance at Paul. "I mean, uh, how *visiting* someone's apartment made her put a contract out on me. And how did Linda find out I was there?" *Please tell me this isn't about the evidence against Larry. Please tell me that Linda didn't see me take that box.*

Burke shot her a glare. "Rollin wasn't cheating on Emma with Linda Anderson. There is no Linda Anderson."

"What do you mean there's no Linda Anderson? I was in her apartment. I read the letters she sent to Rollin."

Burke frowned and gave a wary look at Paul. His attention went to the forest floor and he sighed. He briefly raised his brows and gave a small shrug. Then he leveled his intense gaze at her. "Linda Anderson is a false person we created for one of our jobs."

Sam's train of thought veered off the rails and she took a step back. Linda Anderson didn't exist? That explained the anomalies in the apartment. She snapped her fingers. "No wonder there was that weird assortment of food in the cupboards. Didn't feel like anyone lived there, ever. Wait, this means that Rollin isn't cheating on Emma! Wicked cool! I mean, it didn't make any sense, the way the guy treats her, but damn, those letters were convincing." Her muscles went hard and her face heated with anger. "What the hell is he doing, leaving that crap around for Emma to find? She was devastated!"

Burke pursed his lips. "He thought he'd hidden them well. Apparently, Emma is a fanatical housecleaner."

"I still don't understand what's going on." Paul shifted his attention between her and Burke.

Burke said, "Rollin, Emma's fiancée, and I work for a security firm, Rampart—"

All the blood left Sam's head and her knees went weak. She hadn't stolen evidence from a stranger, she'd stolen evidence from her friends. Friends that happened to belong to a large, powerful spy organization. Sam's heart beat so hard, it hurt. She broke out in a full body sweat. Holy fuck.

Paul's eyes lit with recognition. "I know Rampart. I work for DAE, sold you guys some equipment. And you helped out a buddy of mine when you were Consolidated Security."

Burke did a quick double take at Paul, but continued. "A client of ours was in possession of sensitive information regarding a group of high-level criminals."

Here we go. Sam made a great effort to remain standing.

"Information which could expose them and ruin their business," Burke said in a grave tone. "We convinced these very dangerous and powerful operatives that Linda Anderson was in possession of the intelligence, not our client. This professional and well-funded crime organization believes that Linda Anderson is real, that she is our agent, and that she has information that could destroy their operation." He turned to Sam. "And now they've found her."

Sam chest contracted and she couldn't breathe. "Holy shit." How could she possibly keep the information now? How would she put

Larry away with hired killers after her? Especially when Larry belonged to the group that had hired them? Great. Now the asshole would try to kill her all over again, only this time without knowing her true identity.

And what about the Patriots? If they found out she had the packet, she'd have to fight them, too. Crazy!

Her pulse thumping in her ears, Sam stared into space, stunned, overwhelmed by how naïve and stupid she was and how badly she'd just fucked herself.

Burke nodded. "*Yeah, Miss Anderson.*"

She fought for equilibrium. Rubbing her forehead, she hugged her body with her free arm.

Samantha Murdock! Fight! Fight with every bit of your soul! God put that evidence in your hands! You prayed for help and He answered!

A crazy confluence of events took place that day in order for the information to land in her lap. Wouldn't have happened if she weren't meant to use the evidence. Right?

Paul's head jerked back slightly and his lips quirked. "Wait. Wasn't this a movie plot? Yeah. *North by Northwest.*"

"You're right." Her body trembled and she held herself tighter. "And I'm playing the Cary Grant role. Rollin's a Hitchcock nut. He probably came up with the plan."

Burke nodded.

Paul ran his hand down her back. "Jeez girl, when you step in it, you really step in it, don't you?"

"Unreal," Sam said, shaking her head. So hard to grasp. A day ago, she was safe in anonymity, now she had yet another death sentence on her head.

And if what Burke said was true, that meant Larry was now not only a Senator and Presidential nominee, he was also involved in organized crime. Great.

She gestured toward Burke. "So how did you get involved?"

"I was closest. I happened to be in Half Moon Bay when I got the call from Rollin. And I was in Seattle yesterday. I must have missed you at the apartment by minutes. Did you happen to pick up a package addressed to Linda?"

Her insides folded like Origami and she stopped breathing. Worst fear realized: they'd tied the missing materials to her. Thankfully, she had the wherewithal to hold his gaze firmly. She forced herself to continue breathing normally. "No, I was only there for a few minutes. What was in the package?" she managed to say with an ease in her voice that surprised her. *Good goin', Murdock. Keep it up.*

He looked away. "Something very important." His expression darkened. "Damn it. I was hoping you had it."

"Nope." Sam concentrated on keeping her face absolutely free of movement.

Now it was fifty million times more urgent that she get to Seattle and finish her plan of securing the evidence. But how was she supposed to get there with a team of hired killers after her?

Sam felt like she'd been transported unarmed and naked into the middle of an Afghani firefight. She'd known her life would probably be short, but not this short. Shit, she had to stay alive long enough to deal with Larry.

A spike of pain seared Sam's shoulder like someone had stabbed it with an icepick. "Ow!" She rubbed it out.

Paul massaged the area she worked.

She moved away from him. "Sorry, Let me get this, it's spasming." Digging harder into her shoulder, she eased the pain.

Paul asked, "Are you all right?"

"Fine. Shoulder's hurting from when Burke tackled me. Not that I'm complaining."

Burke sent her a half smile. The green and yellow filtered forest light played across his handsome face and illuminated the spark of playfulness in his dark gaze. How could this gorgeous man be the same evil jerk who kidnapped and tormented Emma?

Then like a glass of ice water in her face, the realization hit her. She had a score to settle with this bastard. Instantly, her belly turned to fire. She'd warned him what she'd do to him if he hurt Emma. "Oh, yeah."

She punched Burke in the face so hard, his head snapped back, he stumbled and almost went down.

Paul gasped and his eyebrows went high. "Whoa."

His eyes flaming with rage, Burke's face flushed bright red. "*What the hell was that for*?" he demanded, rubbing his jaw.

She pointed at him. "That was for what you did to Emma. No one hurts my friend. I warned you that night at the club. You're lucky you saved my life or you'd be holding your balls in your hand right now. Say *thank you, Sam, for not chopping off my nuts*."

Burke made an exasperated noise and gestured violently. "Emma didn't—"

"*Say thank you, Sam, for not chopping off my nuts*."

He squared his shoulders, his dark eyes blazing. "Sam—"

She stepped forward and got into his face. "Say it!" she snarled viciously, ready to kick him. She'd longed to have her moment with this man. Planned it carefully. And boy, did it feel good to channel all her fear into anger at the guy.

Burke's scorching dark gaze didn't waver. He seemed twice his size, all bristling muscles and wide shoulders.

Sam didn't move and kept her sneer firmly in place. No way was she backing down.

After a long few seconds, his fierce expression broke. His body relaxed and he sighed heavily. Fighting a smile, he said, "Thank you, Sam, for not chopping off my nuts."

She gave him a sharp nod. "Good. No one messes with my friends. Damn you. What the hell were you thinking?"

Stepping back, his face went hard. "I was under deep cover. Playing a role. That wasn't me."

"Bullshit. I hung out with you at your palatial penthouse in the City. I'll bet you still have that place and still shop at Burberry." Sam was starting to feel like herself again. Her anger and focus on Emma's defense was centering her.

He held her gaze with no apology on his even-featured face. Which made him twice as hot. "Despite my tastes, I'm no criminal and never was."

"No, but you're a smarmy, showy, smug bastard who uses anyone and everyone to accomplish his goals."

Dude didn't even react. "That was—and still is—a matter of national security. Through her actions, she put the country at risk. And I'm not going to argue the point with you any longer because we both swore not to discuss the situation. *Didn't we?*"

Narrowing her eyes, her mouth went tight. "I'm just about to cut your nuts off."

His anger broke, but his frustration was clear. "I have apologized. Profusely. Rollin forgives me."

"Emma doesn't."

"And I don't blame her. But I was doing my job to the best of my ability. Granted, I pushed her further than I meant to."

"Because you loved her."

"That was…unplanned," he said, looking down for a moment. A hint of pain flashed in his eyes and the line between his brows deepened. "I think that was most of the problem."

Sam's anger faded. At least he admitted to part of his game. "Rollin told me that you were okay and I shouldn't kill you when I saw you. But you deserved a good punch."

Much of the heated emotion left his face and he smirked.

Her fire gone, her beef with Burke aired, it occurred to her that she hadn't thanked him properly. Awkward timing, but so be it. "But you also deserve thanks for saving my life and Paul's. So thanks, Burke. Much appreciated."

He gave a small snort and the corners of his mouth twitched. "You're welcome. Brat. No wonder you're friends. Both you and Emma are trouble. But I knew the moment I met you in that club that you were fifty times worse."

Sam blinked innocently. "Me?"

Burke broke out into a wide smile. Her heart tripped and a zing went through her, electrifying the bottoms of her feet.

What the hell was wrong with her? How could she be attracted to this guy?

And why the hell was she thinking about being attracted to anyone when her life had just exploded into a bajillion pieces?

Burke stared at her for just that extra second longer. Damn, she hoped he hadn't caught the interest in her eyes.

He turned to Paul. "We should go. The assailants will assume they've flushed us out and will be waiting for us at the trailhead."

Paul asked, "What are our options?"

Burke jerked his head to his left. "If we double-back and take the other path, it leads to another trailhead. Earlier, I arranged for men to meet us at the end of each trail. We should be fine. But keep alert."

Sam grabbed her backpack from the forest floor, but had forgotten to zip it shut first and several items fell out. Including, unfortunately, her handgun. She tried to snatch it up before the men noticed, but when she checked their expressions, their eyebrows had shot to their hairlines. Damn it. She didn't want people knowing she carried. Especially these two guys.

Frowning, his focus sharp, Burke came closer and held out his hand. "Let me see that."

"It's no big deal." She stuffed the small revolver inside the pack.

He jammed his hand in front of her face. "Hand it to me."

"For crying out loud, here." Retrieving her weapon, she held out the gun, handle first, with the barrel pointed toward the ground.

He took the revolver and inspected it. Then he concentrated his piercing attention on her. "Where the hell did you get this?"

Sam's jaw and belly tightened. She let her gaze go cold. "The store."

Burke's eyes narrowed.

"Yeah, why did you slip that into your pack?" Paul demanded, coming closer.

She tried to look at them like they were mental. "Protection from mountain lions, hello?"

Burke examined her, his face full of suspicion. "On a busy Saturday? When there haven't been any sightings in a year?" He hesitantly handed the gun to her, butt first.

"I've always had a gun," Sam replied smoothly. "Sometimes I carry a lot of expensive stuff for Emma's antiquities store. I'm her manager, you know."

"I know. Still doesn't warrant a firearm." Burke challenged her with his harsh gaze and the set to his shoulders and mouth. "California has strict laws on carrying a concealed weapon. Do you have a permit to carry that?"

Damn this! She had to keep her cool. Had to be super careful about how she responded to this situation. No one could find out about her past. Maybe she'd blown it by visiting Linda Anderson's apartment and stealing that box of evidence, but she wasn't going to compound her mistakes by letting these guys know the truth about her.

"Of course, I have a permit." Ignoring the two men, she performed a check of the gun.

Paul stared at her little snubbed nose Smith and Wesson. "Sorry, but I agree with Burke. Not only are you putting yourself at legal risk, do you have training to use that, Sam?"

Her body went hot and she squeezed the grip of the gun until her hand hurt. Nothing pissed her off more than being patronized. She wasn't some weak female loser idiot. Glaring between the two, she snapped, "Why? Because I'm a woman?"

"No," Burke replied flatly. "This is not a gender issue, it's an experience issue."

"Exactly." Paul crossed his arms and his expression hardened.

Burke's shoulders bulked bigger. "More deaths are caused by amateurs than professionals. I have attitude about people who own and carry guns that shouldn't."

No way did she want to get into some stupid argument with these chauvinists. She tried to calm her reaction. Didn't need to be defensive, she could just be firm. "I've been shooting since I was a kid. Besides, look what happened today, will ya? Did we or did we not just come under fire? If you hadn't shown up, Burke, I would have at least been able to return fire and get us to safety."

Burke's focus on her intensified. "Interesting timing, isn't it? You just happen to be carrying a gun for '*protection*'," he said, and she could hear the air quotes in his voice, "and then you come under fire. Almost like you were expecting it."

She stared at him like he'd lost his mind. "What have you got in that canteen, Burke? Vodka? Expecting it? Oh, yeah, every time I take a walk, people shoot at me. Happens all the time. You are such an idiot. Mountain lions. That's why I brought it today. Why are you making this into a drama?"

Burke's mouth went even uglier. "Whatever. I'd prefer if you unloaded the weapon and allowed me carry it for the duration of the day."

Straightening her spine, she thrust out her chin. "No fuckin' way." She'd kill him if he tried to take it from her.

Burke scowled, but backed off. "Fine. Just don't shoot me."

She sneered. "If I did, it wouldn't be by accident."

Burke sent her a nasty smirk.

"I agree with Burke," Paul said. "Why don't you let him carry the weapon? He is protecting us. I'd feel safer."

Sam shot him the cold, powerful *do-I-need-to-kill-you* glare that normally made her men cower in fear.

Paul's eyes widened, then he frowned. Clearly surprised by her response.

She thought of and rejected twenty nasty retorts. Since all her replies seemed to include profanity, she chose to say nothing. But she didn't diminish her Death Stare, nor did she look away.

Paul's steel-blue eyes darkened, his thick brow flattened into straight line, and his mouth tightened. He stood taller and a flash of fire blazed in his expression. He looked like he wanted to slap her. A slight chill went through her. Dude had a menacing, authoritarian edge she hadn't seen before. But she wouldn't allow herself to flinch, nor shift her attention.

Paul finally threw up his hands and stepped back. But he wasn't happy and clearly didn't like her defiance.

Despite his hotness, the dude had better be careful about throwing his weight around or he might just throw himself right out of her life.

Both men kept their attention on her gun until she tucked it into her pack. Neanderthal morons. Why was she always attracted to cave men? High time she put out a fatwa on her sex drive.

Slipping on her pack, she followed Paul through the forest, Burke right behind her.

Sam mentally kicked herself with every step. She should have stayed in Seattle until she copied the information and returned the originals to Linda Anderson's apartment.

But how did the bad guys find her so fast? She'd worn a disguise to the apartment. Shit, this was crazy.

How was she supposed to trap or kill Larry while outsmarting a team of security professionals while avoiding a group of professional hit men? Absolutely insane.

She kicked a rectangular piece of shale and sent it sailing off the edge of the trail, down toward the creek far below. Would her life ever return to normal? Would she ever be safe again? Sam punted another rock off the single-track trail. A loud crash from below was followed by a *thoomp-splash* as the rock hit water.

"Sam? Could you please stop alerting the snipers to our location?" Burke bit out in a snide tone from behind her.

"Sorry," she grumbled without turning around.

Keep it together, Murdock. Maintaining her sanity and composure was paramount now. She needed a clear head to get to Seattle and cover up her theft. Once the Patriots had their evidence, she could disappear. Eventually, the bad guys would find out that the Patriots were in possession of the information again and would stop trying to find her. By then, she'd be mostly through her plan of attack on Larry. Chances that anyone would link her to the dickhead were slim to none.

Before he knew it, he'd be dead or in jail for life.

Looky here, Larry. Pretty photos of you and little girls frolicking naked together. But wait, there's more! A thumbdrive chockfull of evidence about your offshore criminal enterprises and bank accounts!

Sam grinned as she followed Paul up a steep incline. Couldn't wait to see the look on his face. *Yes, Larry, I'm still alive and see these objects in the jar I'm holding? These are your balls. They belong to me now.*

And if for some reason her new plan didn't work, she always had her original, assassinating the fucking deviant.

Burke followed Sam and her date on the trail, his attention torn between possible sniper vantage points and the tantalizing Miss Murdock. He loved the way her heart-shaped ass moved against her tight hiking shorts. Her long legs were perfect appetizers for the nirvana hidden between. And her gorgeous breasts should be in a museum. High, rounded, perfect handfuls. Not too big, not too small. Tight.

But it was the fire within her that made him hard as obsidian. Her hazel eyes, flashing with red-hot passion. That sock on the jaw she gave him. He should have been pissed. All it did was make him want to throw her to the ground and fuck her until she screamed.

Dangerous. He wanted her in a blinding, crazed sort of way. Every cell in his body wanted to possess her. Dominate her. Care for her. Keep her safe.

Insane talk. He couldn't lose his mind over another woman. It wasn't possible. Emma was the only one with that power. Or had been the only one. Last time he saw her, his lust and love had faded. Surprisingly fast.

But Sam was different. She wasn't afraid of him. In the least. He normally liked his women to be a bit fearful of him, kept them in line better. But Sam would constantly challenge his authority. Which for some reason, made him want her even more. She was a tornado disguised as a beautiful woman. Winning her would be pure poetry.

She glanced over her shoulder at him. He smiled.

Pursing her lips, she turned around with a haughty little toss of her head.

Blood surged into his cock. Sultry, wicked siren. He loved the way her wavy shoulder-length auburn hair fell loosely about her slim shoulders, the way her full burgundy mouth quirked when she was being sassy, and the way she sneered at him.

Smoldering. Defiant. And so very fuckable.

He smelled his hands. Sam's heavenly flowers-and-fresh-rain scent filled his nostrils. He got even harder and grinned. Just so happened she needed a bodyguard.

She turned again, did a double-take and frowned. "You'd better not be staring at my ass," she snarled.

"Wouldn't dream of it." He forced his face to go neutral. Had to watch himself. Didn't want to show his hand too early in the game.

"Yeah…" She sent him another glare, but as she turned away, she smiled.

He had to hold back his laughter. She wanted him, too. Badly and so soon.

This was going to be fun.

Well, the seducing-Sam part would be fun. Getting her to give up the package, not so much. Sam had a lot of fight in her, great for sex, not so great for coercion.

He was ninety-nine point nine percent sure she had the intelligence. When he'd questioned her, her pupils had dilated slightly and there'd been a flash of fear on her face before her obvious attempt to control her reaction. She must have gotten the box from the postman after she left the apartment building. The Patriots were in the process of verifying the delivery.

His gut burned and twisted, and his throat constricted. Holding a bleeding Joseph, the strained cough, the light fading from his eyes. "*Sent it…to…Linda Anderson.*" His stare had fixed and he'd stilled in Burke's arms.

Joseph better not have died for nothing.

Lying in a swamp with him. Sharing a cigarette. Joseph pushing him out of the way in that Iraqi back alley and taking a bullet for him. Only Rollin and he had been closer. Joseph had been a smart, loyal, strong man. To see what those fuckers did ripped him apart. Joseph hadn't deserved to die that way. Burke would make sure that the men who tortured him to death and the Cabal paid for that.

Ten minutes late. Ten minutes that cost Joseph his life. How would he ever forgive himself?

He only wished Joseph had stayed alive long enough to tell him *how* he'd sent the information to Linda Anderson. When he'd checked Joseph's pockets, he'd found no delivery confirmation slips, no paperwork of any kind. Nothing indicating Fed Ex, UPS, private courier or USPS.

But since no package had arrived at the apartment since and Sam had spent time with the mailman—plus her reaction—she must have it.

Strong turned around and checked on him.

Burke kept his expression passive. Strong was clearly behind the sniper attack. At first he believed the assailants were Cabal, but as the gunfire continued—by the pattern of hits: the trees next to Paul, the ground near him, but nothing close to him—and the fact that the bullets hadn't come within ten feet from Sam—it became obvious that the operation had been staged.

After Burke had sighted the two white men in camo, by their youth and because one kept taking phone pics of the other—who flashed some sort of gang sign—he'd pegged them as recently discharged Army grunts. Strong had said he worked for DAE, he probably had a military background and plenty of contacts.

To test his theory, Burke had ripped off a hit to the upper right arm of the more aggressive shooter followed by a quick shot through the top of the other kid's hat. The boys had erupted in screams and disappeared so fast, they almost left their weapons behind.

While relieved that the Cabal hadn't located Sam yet, why the hell would Strong stage an attack? More than likely trying to infiltrate the Patriots. Burke's news about her pursuers must have fed perfectly into

Strong's plan. Allowed him to comfort her and appear protective. The asshole. Poor girl was just a puppet.

Maybe Strong was trying to recruit her. He could have been sent after that evidence, but he and Sam had hooked up before it had come into play. She had thrown herself into the middle of events just the day before.

Maybe Strong was behind Sam's theft of the evidence. Why else would she have grabbed the box?

But if Paul hadn't put her up to it, he must be out of his mind with joy now that he knew she had the evidence. Unless he'd been up in Seattle and had seen Sam take it. Or had gotten word from his network that Sam was Linda Anderson.

Or perhaps he worked for another organization.

Whichever, as soon as Burke had determined that Paul was a spy, he'd made every effort to hide his suspicions. Which was why he'd had been so "forthcoming" with information when he was questioning Sam. He had to keep the man feeling safe so he'd drop his guard.

Burke would have a full report on him by that night. And assign a detail not only "protect" Strong, but to keep an eye on him.

Sam sent him another glance. This one guarded.

Seemed like everyone on that trail had secrets. If he was right and Sam had the information, why would she want it if she weren't a spy? Hadn't she been able to tell by the contents how dangerous it was? None of her actions made sense.

She hadn't been surprised when she'd come under fire; she'd been surprised the attack pertained to Linda Anderson. And she'd nearly gone rabid when he'd suggested he carry her gun—she clearly didn't feel safe without it. But who would want to murder Sam? From what he understood, she'd been a cocktail waitress at high-end clubs until taking charge of Emma's new store.

But Sam? A spy? With that sassy mouth and flamboyance? Did not fit the profile.

So who was after her? An ex-boyfriend? Did she have a stalker?

Wasn't a stretch to think some man got obsessed. Hell, he was almost there himself.

Whatever she was hiding, he'd find out. As soon as they cleared the woods, he'd call Bobby and get a full background check on Miss Sam Murdock.

He chuckled. Then he'd know all her weak points. He'd have her —and the packet—in no time. Protect her from the hired killers and that snake Paul Strong, find out who she was afraid of and help her defeat them. He'd come into her life at exactly the right time. She needed him. He'd keep her safe.

And fuck her blind in the process.

TWO

Sam stopped to rest after a particularly grueling uphill stretch. The men seemed relieved she'd taken a break. Neither would dare. The two were playing an Alpha Male/King of the Hill game. Idiots.

"God, I'm gonna get into shape with this hike," she said, patting her stomach. "What a great way to diet. You know, we should set up a company that follows people around and shoots at them to motivate them to hike faster. They could call it 'A Shot In The Park'." She broke out into loud guffaws. "The Gun Fun Run." She laughed harder.

The men didn't seem as amused by her idea, but she didn't care. Such a hilarious concept!

Burke finally snorted and smiled. "You really crack yourself up, don't you?"

"Yeah. I'm funny."

He shook his head.

"You have hair," she said, suddenly noticing. While it wasn't long, Burke now sported a short brown buzz cut sprinkled with gray. He'd been bald the last time she'd seen him. "I knew something looked different about you. And whoa, where'd you get that scar?" A thin, pink two-inch-long scar marred the perfect skin of his right cheek, next to his eye. Unfortunately, on him it looked good. "What happened?"

"Ran into someone's knife," he tossed off, turning his attentions to his water bottle.

"Why aren't you shaving your head anymore?"

"That was for my criminal persona."

Come to think of it, Burke was dressed completely differently. "I've never seen you out of a suit. You look…un-runway ready. What gives? Where's the Gucci? I didn't think you even owned a t-shirt or camo pants." He actually looked cute. Hella cute.

"I wasn't about to wear a five thousand dollar suit out here to the forest. Or the beach. I was at the Pillar Point Harbor when Rollin called."

"Why?"

"Picking up fresh salmon so I could make sushi tonight."

"Huh. That's right, Emma said you were a master chef."

"I like to cook."

"Guess it's better than being a masturbator." Sam laughed like hell.

Burke rolled his eyes. Paul shook his head and smiled, but there was more pity than amusement in his grin. Their reactions cracked her up even more. Any excuse to laugh was good for her. Especially today.

Thoroughly enjoying this mental break from terror, Sam examined Burke as he rummaged through his daypack. "You need a monocle, Burke."

"What?"

"Yeah, a monocle. You know, with that scar on your face, if you shaved your head again and wore a monocle, you'd look just like an evil German spy from the forties. Like Colonel Klink only actually menacing."

Burke's jaw tightened and his gaze went fiery.

She busted up. This was fun! Burke so deserved the harassment. Begged for it. Another benefit, it kept him off balance and off subjects like that evidence.

His hard expression broke and he reluctantly laughed. But it wasn't a friendly laugh. "So this is how you treat all the men who save your life?"

"No. Just you."

"I'd watch yourself. I don't take well to teasing," he warned with a flinty look in his eye.

A thrill went through her. Damn it. She liked him. "Tough beans. I'm not afraid of you."

"Maybe you should be." His voice was low and threatening.

"Sorry. And you need a monocle."

Paul chuckled and shook his head. "You two sound like siblings."

Burke sent her a penetrating stare. "If I was her brother, I'd be chasing her down and spanking her."

She formed her thumb and finger into an O shape, held it up to her eye and made a face at him.

Burke's anger broke and he finally started chuckling. "One wonders how you've made it this far in life without some man killing you."

She flashed back to that freezing, roiling water. *Her lungs burning. Terrified, clinging to a tree root, watching Larry through the murky surface of the water. His silhouette in the headlights from her father's car, standing on the bank of the river, searching for her. The gun in his hand. Her leg searing from the gunshot wound. Her mind foggy, then almost graying out.*

Her stomach convulsed, her eyes watered, and her throat swelled. If he'd stayed thirty more seconds, she wouldn't be alive.

Shuddering, she averted her gaze. "Yeah. A wonder." Damned sniper attack. Like she needed any extra help feeding her PTSD. Between her past, her scary day yesterday and today's fun, it was a miracle she wasn't babbling in a rubber room.

Wiping away a tear, she realized she was showing emotion when she didn't want to be. She couldn't be vulnerable in front of Burke. She was nearly sure he suspected she had that evidence and she had to make sure she didn't give herself away. She attempted to look tired.

"Is your leg okay?" Burke asked.

Startled, she focused on him. "Yeah, why?"

"You've been rubbing the side of your upper thigh for a while now."

Looking down, her body jerked with surprise. She'd been absently rubbing her gunshot wound! Shit! She moved her hand away like she'd been burned. "No. Nothing." Thankfully, her shorts covered the ugly scar.

Burke's attention on her sharpened. His gaze went to her thigh. "You sure you didn't hurt yourself?"

"Do you see blood? No."

"It's right under the leg of your shorts, why don't you check?"

"It's fine." Turning away, she opened her daypack.

She still hadn't come up with a good lie for the wound. The three-inch-long by half-inch-wide scar looked like a gunshot wound. She'd used various lies with lovers, but thankfully, by the time men got to that phase of lovemaking, their minds weren't on her scars.

Digging through her pack, she found a bag of trail mix. After popping some peanuts and raisins in her mouth, she glanced over at Burke. He was still staring at her. She worked hard at swallowing her food.

Damn it. Emma had said the guy was a mind reader. She'd have to be more careful. All this violence had rattled her.

Finally, she couldn't take Burke's intense focus. "What? Do I have a booger on my nose? Why are you staring at me?"

"Just wondering how one woman could cause this much trouble in such a short period of time."

She made an exasperated noise in the back of her throat. "Why are people always asking me that?"

Burke smiled, which lit up his whole face. A bell rang inside her sex, calling him to dinner.

Holy bejeebus, what was wrong with her? She liked Paul, not him.

Burke was just so smooth and sure of himself and hot and handsome and he'd saved her and his arms were amazing—the bulge in his pants intriguing—and she couldn't help but want his strong hands all over her.

SHUT UP!

She mentally picked up an imaginary rock and slammed herself over the head. Why was she noticing him like this? Her eyes seemed to be taking on lives of their own and kept wandering over to Burke. If she wanted any man, it would be Paul. He was super hot. And nice.

No! She didn't want either man. No time for fooling around.

Not wanting any more food, but knowing she needed some, Sam forced the trail mix down her throat. She tried to focus on Paul or the forest around her and not allow herself to look at Burke.

"So what happens when we finally get out of here? What's the plan?" Paul asked Burke.

"I'll be assigning a detail to protect you. We'll evaluate the threat and keep you informed. We'll guard you until the threat is gone."

"Thanks, I appreciate that. Been out of the loop for a while."

"The loop?" Burke asked.

"I was a Marine for years."

Burke brightened. "Me, too."

Paul's face lit and he peppered Burke with questions. They knew many of the same people. And they'd just missed being stationed together by a few months.

"No wonder your name sounded so familiar," Paul said. "But I'd only seen it written. Lt. Colonel Cherlenko." He gave a wistful sigh. "I mostly worked in D.C. Never saw the action the way I wanted to."

Myriad micro expressions flitted across Burke's face: pain and a haunted quality to his eyes, then sharp focus, then sorrow, and finally, neutral. He held his shoulders straighter. "Seeing action isn't all its cracked up to be. I twisted some arms, got transferred into the Navy so I could join the SEALs."

She'd have thought he'd be bragging, but there were hints of regret in his tone.

Admiration grew on Paul's face and he nodded. "SEALs, good for you. What rank did you reach?"

Burke's guarded expression didn't waver. "Captain. So why'd you leave?"

"I like money," Paul said with no apology to his tone.

Burke laughed. "Same reason I left."

He wasn't being quite honest with Paul. But the Patriots didn't advertise their good deeds. While they liked money, they were driven by more altruistic desires. According to Rollin, even Burke the Jerk had a noble heart. Not that she was convinced.

Paul picked at a stick caught in his shoelaces. "After I left the Corps, I got a sales job at Lockheed, and then moved on to DAE." Pulling the twig free, he tossed it. "We should talk sometime, Burke. I have some products you guys might like."

"Sounds good. Sam, you rested?"

"Yep." She stood and shouldered her pack.

After far too long of a hike, they neared the trailhead. Burke stopped and pulled them off the trail. He held his cell in his hand. "I finally have signal and need to make a phone call. Bobby? Yeah, tell Rollin and Emma I found her. And yes, we're under fire. Shit, when? Okay. Tell Rollin that we'll meet at Zane's as planned." Burke clicked off. "Cops have been alerted and we have to get out of here. But we could be walking into an ambush at the parking lot. I'm going first. Listen for my order. If I tell you to drop, do it. Got it?"

Her heart beating wildly, Sam nodded. Paul gave a casual salute.

Her legs wobbled, but the adrenaline kept her mind sharp. She cautiously followed Paul. Burke led, holding his gun in an isosceles pose, his attention focused on possible sniper locations.

They cleared the end of the trail and she recognized the two hulking guys hanging around the entrance to the tiny parking lot.

Burke nodded and lowered his weapon. "Clear. They're with me."

Paul acknowledged him and the tension eased from his face. Sam sighed.

The only vehicles in the weedy asphalt patch were a large champagne-colored Cadillac Escalade, a black Mercedes SUV, and Paul's silver Suburban. Mercedes had to belong to Burke.

The two rough-looking men approached them: Banana, a huge dude with long blond hair and a massive jaw, and David, a burly, round-faced, dark-haired giant. Two of Cherlenko's men she'd partied with that night at Emma's birthday party in the City. The bodyguards' exteriors were scary, but inside, they were kittens. She'd shared a few kisses and gropes with David in the back seat of Burke's limo. Not a bad kisser, actually. Her body loosened.

"Hi Banana. Hi David," Sam said.

Banana approached the group. "Hey Sam, good to see you. No one's been here, boss. Just heard from Ty that they spotted the bad guys, high-tailing it out of the other parking lot. He took pictures of the car and Bobby's running the plates. Cops arrived right as they left and Ty sent them after the bad guys."

"Good." Burke tucked his weapon into the holster on his hip.

"This area's clear and secure, all the way to the main road," David reported. "We got more security waiting for us there." He turned and gave Sam a good up and down examination, his dark eyes lingering on her breasts. "Lookin' good, Sam. Hey, I finally figured out who you remind me of. Remember at the club, I kept trying to remember? A young Ann Margaret."

She grinned. "I should have helped you with that one. I get that a lot. I just wish I had her money and boobs."

All the men's collective attention went to her breasts. Her face warmed. She felt like she'd just chummed the piranhas. *Note to self: never mention your tits in a crowd of men again.* She moved her attention to the parking lot, hoping to direct the men's focus elsewhere.

"Keep an eye on the entrance," Burke said to his men, pointing off in the distance, "just in case. We'll be heading to Zane's shortly."

"You got it, Boss. Glad you're okay, Sam," Banana said.

David grinned at her. "Me, too, girl."

She smiled. "Hey, we gotta party again sometime. You guys were fun."

"Us?" Banana said.

He and David exchanged glances and laughed.

David said, "You're a pistol, girl. A real pistol."

Chuckling, they turned away and headed to the entrance of the parking lot.

While she appreciated the compliments, she wished they'd used different language. Associating her with a pistol at this point, while ironic, wasn't exactly helpful.

As if her worst fears had come true, Paul approached her. "Hey, I am worried about you and that gun, Sam."

Burke gave an icy nod.

"Don't. I've taken a bunch of classes, I go to the range at least once a week, and I spent all last summer training with that military nut...job." *Fuck!* When would she shut up? She busied herself with picking bits of forest duff off her shirt.

Paul and Burke's focus on her intensified.

"You took military training? Why?" Paul asked.

She had to get better at deception and warfare. A few gunshots and her entire brain had blown apart. This sniper crap was kid stuff compared to her ultimate mission. Those live-fire exercises should have helped. Disappointing! "Uh...felt like it," she said in the most unconvincing tone. Her belly gnarled. "Just for fun," she tossed off.

Both men raised their left eyebrows at the same time.

She decided to ignore them rather than dig her grave deeper and turned her attention to a small tear in the leg of her shorts.

Burke shook his head.

Paul heaved a large sigh and took her in his arms. "I'm worried about you, Sam. Guys after you, all this gun stuff. Do me a favor? Listen to Burke's advice about protecting yourself. And listen to me if I suggest something, okay? Don't fight us. We're on your side. I'm on your side."

Even though his words inflamed her, his manner was so sweet and gentle, she couldn't help but nod. And maybe Burke and his friends would teach her tactics she could use later. "Okay."

Paul grinned, his blue eyes shining with affection. He leaned in and kissed her.

He tasted good and the kiss was nice, but all she could think about was running from him. And from Burke. With their military backgrounds and the questions she'd aroused in them, if they caught wind of her preparations, she'd be screwed.

"Should we meet you at Sam's?" Paul asked.

"No. I need her to come with me in my Mercedes." Burke pointed to the black SUV. "I and my colleagues at Rampart need to debrief her. Could be things she's forgotten that would greatly help her chances of survival. Who she saw and exactly what she did in the apartment in Seattle when she was there."

Fight-or-flight juices swamped her. Every muscle tensed to rigidity and her stomach went into revolt. *Run!* No way could she withstand an interrogation at the hands of the Patriots. Not now. Not ever. She had a quick thought of grabbing Paul's keys and stealing his Suburban. "What if I don't want to be questioned? I'm super tired."

Burke stood taller. "It's important we talk to you now while the memory is fresh in your mind."

"I'll be fresher after I sleep."

"We need to keep you safe and to do that, we need information," he said forcefully.

"I don't think I can handle it right now." *And I have to get to Seattle tonight!*

His firm expression didn't change. "We won't keep you long."

Breaking out in a full body sweat, she shook her head. "Burke, nothing happened up there. I'm not part of this whole conspiracy thing, anyway. This is your deal, not mine."

"Need I remind you that *you* made the decision to steal those keys and break into that apartment?" Burke took a step closer. "Emma knew nothing about your plan. We're offering you protection, the least you can do is tell us what you did and what you saw."

Sam winced. Now Paul knew she'd A) lied and B) committed a crime. Great. But no way was she going with Burke. "I really want to go home, shower and go to bed."

Burke held her gaze, unflinching. He turned away before she could respond. "Paul, she'll be available later tonight."

How did this bastard steal her power so fast? So what if she'd broken into that apartment? She had rights. She opened her mouth to speak, but Paul talked over her.

"Can't it wait until tomorrow? She just got shot at, I think she's had enough for one day."

Staring up at Paul, she was stunned. Someone coming to her defense other than Emma? Wow. Give him huge points for that.

"I wouldn't ask if it weren't absolutely necessary," Burke replied evenly, his irritation clear.

Paul held up his hand. "Wait a minute, okay? Let me get my head around this. These attackers think that Sam is Linda Anderson and that she works for Rampart Security and she has some information they want, right?"

Burke's dark eyes glittered with anger, but he kept a tight rein on his expression. "Right."

"And you asked her if she picked up a package addressed to Linda Anderson, so that's the information, right? That's what they think she has, is this package."

Paul was right. All she had to do was keep to her story that she didn't have the package and the Patriots might go away. At least long enough for her to make the copies and send them to Linda's apartment.

Burke's frown deepened and he made a dismissive wave. "Yes, but she—"

"You don't have the package, right, Sam?"

"No," Sam stated with absolute confidence.

"So why do you guys need to question her? She doesn't have the information and said she was only there for a few minutes. What could she know?"

"Who might have spotted her," Burke said like it was all so obvious. He clearly thought Paul was an idiot for questioning him. "We need to know exactly what she did from the moment she arrived at Anderson's apartment until she got back to her hotel. This is about her safety. The sooner after the experience we question her, the better we can protect her. You know this if you spent anytime in the military."

"True, but she's been attacked and chased today, I think her memory's gonna be pretty hosed, don't you?"

Burke heated gaze rested on Sam. "Do you want Rollin to explain it to you?"

Sam's throat constricted like Burke had thrown a noose around her neck and pulled it tight. She swallowed hard. "Rollin's in on this?"

"He's the one calling the shots on this operation. He feels responsible. He's the one who's insisting you come."

Trump! "Oh." A straightjacket of guilt and obligation trussed tight around her and she kicked the ground. "Shit."

"You don't have to go unless you want to, Sam," Paul said in a firm voice.

"I can't say no to Rollin. Burke, yes. Rollin, no. He totally came through for me a few months ago. Ah, pickles, I'm exhausted." She tried to sound a little pathetic. Not actually pathetic, but with enough pain in her voice to tweak Burke's protective side.

Didn't work. His stone-like expression remained unchanged.

Burke motioned that she should get in his Mercedes SUV. "She can call you after we take her home."

Paul kept his attention on her. "Want me to go with you? Moral support?"

While his inner Neanderthal had infuriated her on the trail, she certainly appreciated the attribute now.

Burke's eyes turned fiery and his body tensed. Didn't like that idea at all. Why not?

No matter. Didn't behoove her to have Paul listen to how she'd broken into someone's apartment. Nor did she want him to have that much power over her. Couldn't afford to rely on anyone now. Just herself. And if he was this protective now, imagine how crazy he'd get if he found out she was plotting to bring down and/or kill a US Senator.

Sam blew out a stream of air through her lips and rubbed her forehead. "No worries. I'll go alone. I know these guys, they're my friends. I'll be fine. I'm just tired. Thanks, though. You're a really good man." She hugged him and gave him a big kiss.

Paul wrapped his muscled arms around her and took control of the kiss. Very nice. She was too freaked out to respond completely, but the man was winning her heart. Finally, a guy who wanted to be on her team. Amazing.

And totally disappointing. Figures she'd find a guy right when she was about to disappear for good. Or die.

He ended the kiss and smiled down at her. "See you back in San Mateo." He shot Burke a wary glance, then looked her right in the eye. "Call me if you need me." He offered his hand to Burke. "Good to meet you. Thanks for taking care of Sam."

"You're welcome," Burke said, but it was clear he didn't mean the platitude. He didn't like Paul. Sam got the feeling Burke saw him as the enemy. But why?

Paul winked at her. "Sure know how to show a guy a good time, Sam. Very stimulating date."

"I'm sorry."

"Teasing. I'll see you later. Glad you're okay." With a caring and kind look in his blue eyes, he kissed two of his fingers and pressed them to her lips.

A warm rush went through her entire body. What a doll.

Paul turned to Burke. "Go easy on her."

Burke gave a brief nod.

She wished she'd met the guy another time. But who knew? Once Larry was dead or in jail, she'd have nothing to fear. Maybe he'd still be around when she got back.

If not—as she'd learned time and time again—there were other fish in the sea. She checked out Burke's finely muscled forearms and broad shoulders. Unfortunately, plenty of hot barracudas in that same ocean.

Dragging her feet, she reluctantly got into Burke's car. Which was sleek, black, gorgeous, and smelled like him. Top of the line Mercedes. Leather bucket seats and a dashboard that looked like the control panel in the space shuttle. Maintained perfectly. No dirt, no dust, no possessions scattered about. Like he'd driven it off the showroom floor.

"Nice Mercedes," she said with a sarcastic edge.

He raised an eyebrow. "Don't like it?"

"Couldn't afford it, so I hate it."

He laughed, which changed his entire expression, making him even more handsome. She gave an inadvertent gasp. What was it about him? This was a man she should hate, not ogle.

"You'd really hate me if you knew how much extra money I poured into customizing this," he said, clearly proud of his upgrades.

"Let me guess, you James Bonded it."

"Complete with rotating license plates."

"No."

He gave a smug shrug, then chuckled. "No ejector seat, however. Although, with someone like you riding in my car, it might have come in handy."

"Now who's the brat?"

His dark eyes sparkled.

Her heart beat faster, and a thrill went through her nether regions.

The Patriots collectively glared at her from her mind, extinguishing the fires of her hormones. *Burke was the enemy. Remember that.*

They wound their way down the forest mountain on the twisting one-lane road, followed by Banana and David.

"So how long will this stupid interrogation last?" she grumbled.

He shook his head and sighed. "We're not interrogating you, we just want to talk."

"Okay, fine. How long with *the talk* last?"

The look in his eye sharpened and a slight smile curved his full lips. "You are sassy."

"How fucking long, Burke?"

"I don't know. Depends on how long it takes you to tell the story. But probably no more than an hour or so."

Her shoulders relaxed. An hour wouldn't be too bad. "Good."

As they approached the entrance to Butano State Park, a dark SUV pulled in front of them.

Burke touched his earpiece. "Good. We're taking Highway 1 to 84 to Zane's in Woodside. No, Stage Road takes too long. Ty's handled the cops and we're covered. Those boys won't try anything else, one's on the way to the hospital by now. Excellent. See you there." He clicked off.

Her stomach dropped. Who was on their way to the hospital? "Did you shoot someone back there?"

He kept his attention on the road. "A little."

Her pulse jumping, Sam stared at him. "*A little*? How do you shoot someone 'a little'?"

"He'll recover," Burke said, clearly unworried.

Christ, he was flippant about shooting someone. While she planned on blowing away Larry if it came to that, she was anything but flippant about it. Emma was right, Burke was dangerous.

He followed the SUV onto Cloverdale Road and they headed for Pescadero and the highway.

Sam checked out the small farms and horse properties along the two-lane country road, trying to avoid looking at or thinking about Burke. Or what was about to happen to her.

After a few minutes, Burke glanced at her with a million questions on his face. There was no way she was asking what he was thinking because she knew. She'd blown it. Not only had he found out that she carried a concealed gun, she hadn't shown any initial surprise at being shot at. For a man like Burke, his curiosity over her unusual reaction must be overwhelming. But that was his problem.

Her problem was recreating the scene in her head at Linda Anderson's apartment, memorizing it, and sticking to it. No matter how many times they asked, nor in how many ways. Which sucked. Right now, she had the brain power of a flea.

What a crappy end to a crappy day. She'd been so looking forward to getting closer to Paul. And now she had assassins trying to kill her and she was stuck in some evil bastard's car on the way to be grilled by some of her best friends. How much more shit would she have to take to bring down that asshole Senator?

Easy. Whatever amount of shit it took to make that jerk pay for his crimes. She needed to stop whining and adapt. She was a survivor. Facing the Patriots was nothing compared to what she'd already been through. No one knew how strong she was. Not Emma, nor Rollin, nor Burke or the hired killers.

She'd win this game.

She had to.

If not for herself, for Dad.

Her throat closed.

And Mom.

THREE

When Sam hit the doorway to Zane's expansive beech-paneled office, the grave expressions on the Patriots' faces made her gut clench and her legs want to run. Whatever she'd done, the fallout was worse than she'd thought. Not only was her life in danger, the packet she'd snagged meant a great deal to the men. Past that. Vital.

And why should that surprise her? Larry was running for President. And the other guys in the incriminating pictures were all high-level government officials.

She took a step inside the office, but couldn't make herself go any further. Her heart was trying to pound its way out of her ribcage. If she didn't know him, Zane would have made her pee her pants with fright. His long hair looked darker, his chiseled face appeared carved out of granite, his large green eyes were icy, and his wide mouth, a grim line. Captain looked like he had the weight of the world on his broad shoulders. His pale blue eyes were hard, and his tanned, weathered face seemed drawn. Even Mr. Jovial, Rollin, looked like she'd just run over his cat. His dark eyes guarded, his muscled arms crossed over his chest, he leaned on Zane's desk, his mouth tight.

A wave of guilt made her stomach do a break-dance, emphasis on break. She loved these guys. Normally, she'd give them her left tit if they asked for it.

Burke gave her a little shove.

"I'm going, I'm going." Sam shuffled into the room, reviewing her strategy. To do this right, she had to take control of the conversation as soon as she could without drawing attention.

"Sorry Emma put you in this spot, Sam," Rollin said, a hint of warmth coming through his eyes.

Her shoulders relaxed a bit. She loved Rollin, the big jerk. "I hope you're not mad at her."

"Of course, I'm mad. How could she think something like that?"

"Duh. Every man in her life has cheated on her. And I read those letters. I was convinced. And you're damn lucky they turned out to be fakes, I was gonna kick your ass."

Finally, the men's grave expressions broke and they all chuckled.

"You guys wouldn't think it was funny if you were on the receiving end of one of my ass kickings," she said with a large gesture.

Zane raised his brows. "I'll bet."

Sam stood tall and faced Rollin. "The only reason this happened was because she loves you so much."

No reaction. "I know. She told me. She's still in the doghouse."

"What bullshit! You set her up! What the hell were you thinking hiding those fucking things where she could find them? Why didn't you hide them at your place?" Sam pointed at him.

Arms still crossed, Rollin didn't react. "I did. She found them in the back of my closet. That woman is way too tenacious with her cleaning frenzies."

"Don't blame her for your sloppiness. You put her and me at risk."

His dark eyes sparking with anger, he swept the hair out of his face, pushed away from the desk and stood. "Did I send you to Seattle to break into some woman's apartment? No."

Sam didn't flinch. It was imperative she stuck to the story she and Emma had concocted. "I didn't have to break in, you had the keys. And what man has love letters from a woman and the keys to her apartment but isn't fucking her?"

"You took the keys, Sam," he said, testier. "Emma said she didn't ask you to check on Linda Anderson. She didn't even know you'd broken inside the apartment until you called to tell her."

A total lie, but he'd never find out. Sam jabbed her thumb toward her chest. "I'm her best friend. You were cheating on her. I was going to find out who your bimbo was and if I should beat you up and help Emma get a divorce attorney. Oh, wait. You still haven't married her. That couldn't be the reason for her insecurity, could it?" she said, her voice dripping with sarcasm.

Rollin's face flushed red and he jabbed his forefinger at her. "Hey! I'm going to marry her, I'm waiting for things to calm down."

She thrust out her chin. "In your line of work nothing ever calms down."

Captain got up and stood between them. "We're completely off point here. No one could have foreseen this. Not Sam, not Emma, nor you, Rollin. Forget the reasons why it happened go and deal with the fallout, okay?"

Sam backed down. Rollin gave a sharp nod, but his eyes were still churning with fury. Good. Maybe he'd finally marry the girl.

Sam's legs and back ached from the hike and from Burke tackling her. The comfy leather couch underneath the window opposite her beckoned to her, but no way was she giving the impression that she wanted to stay. Rubbing her lower back, she asked, "Can't you just tell these people that I'm not Linda Anderson? I mean, they must know by now that I'm Samantha Murdock."

"Everyone in our business has aliases," Zane said.

Rollin motioned toward himself. "Okay, first we need to know exactly what you did in Seattle. Retrace all your steps from when you got there until you left. Why did you go up there, anyway? Emma said to pick up some merchandise and see an old school chum."

Heart thumping, Sam stifled a gasp. Holy shit. If they talked to Ursula, she was screwed. They'd find out her true identity and know for sure she had the information. "I don't see how what I did in Seattle is relevant. I stopped by Linda Anderson's on the way out of town."

The men's attention on her intensified. She fought a cringe. Swallowing, she kept her face neutral. Pickles! That was a completely normal question and she'd blown the answer. Why hadn't she lied?

Rollin's brow wrinkled. "So you didn't hook up with an old buddy?"

Sam tried to hold his gaze, but ended up pretending to look at Zane while focusing on the wall near the giant's head. "I picked up that shipment of jewelry for Emma's store. I didn't have much time."

Rollin frowned. "But you went up on Thursday morning and didn't get back until Friday late. You had a lot of time."

She gave a small shrug. "The trouble started when I got into Linda Anderson's apartment. And only then. Has nothing to do with what else I did."

"So why don't you just tell me who you saw?" he asked, looking at her like she'd lost her mind.

She had to stay mysterious and make them think it had something to do with a personal matter. Which it did. "Because it's none of your business. I like to keep my private life private."

Rollin gave a harsh laugh. "Since when? Aren't you the woman who described in detail the last six guys you fucked over dinner last week?"

Her face went hot and her insides boiled. Irrefutable logic and an insult all in one shot. He was good. "I didn't discuss it on the Late Show with David Letterman. That was in the privacy of your home with you and Emma only, as I recall."

"Wish I'd been there," Zane added.

"And only after I'd had two bottles of wine."

"Want a drink?" Captain asked.

She pursed her lips. "Cheeky bastards." Sighing, she gestured sharply. "Listen, I went to Linda Anderson's apartment. I looked around. Nothing was there. It was weird. You guys needed to do a better job of setting up a fake apartment. None of the cosmetics matched and there was no toilet paper. Nor any tampons or anything under the sink."

"Catherine set that up," Rollin said. "I trusted her to put in the women stuff."

She glanced at Burke who'd been remarkably silent since they arrived. His burning dark gaze seared her. Her gut wrenched. Okay, clearly his silence didn't mean he wasn't tuned in. Shit. She had to get out of there. "Look, this is all beside the point. I went in there, found nothing, saw nothing and no one, and left. Now can I go?"

"What about the ambulance, police, and firefighters?" Burke asked. "You were in the middle of quite a scene in the lobby."

Her heart rate leapt higher. How did these guys know so much? "Mrs. Branch—who lives on the first floor—came out on her walker while I was in the entry hall and fell. The postman and I picked her up and carried her into her apartment. He called 911. When the emergency personnel showed up, I split."

Rollin narrowed his gaze. "So why were you in disguise as a housekeeper with that black wig?"

"How did—" Her stomach scrunched painfully tight. "You had cameras in the apartment."

Rollin gave a slight nod. "And the lobby. So?"

Holy bejeebus! How would she combat these guys? They were so out of her league! "I didn't want you recognizing me if I ran into you. I was trying to be stealth."

Rollin returned to the desk and leaned against it. "So what happened after you left the old lady's apartment?"

"Went back to my hotel, called Emma, and crashed."

"What about the package?" he asked, the look in his eye sharp. "The postman gave you the package right as you left."

Her gut caved in, but she held her expression steady. Rollin was fishing. They didn't have proof or he would have already demanded she produce the box.

"What package? What the hell is this package thing you keep asking about? Burke won't drop it and neither will you. What's in it?"

No way had they seen her with it. The postman had given her the Priority Mail box when she was out on the street. The postal truck had been parked under a giant tree when he had handed it to her—providing amazing cover—and no one had been in the direct vicinity. Sam had kept a wary eye out, paranoid that the real Linda Anderson would show up and expose her lie.

"You really don't know?" Rollin asked, seeming like he was trying to look inside her mind.

"No."

He didn't believe her. Fuck! Sam kept her face hard and didn't react. Didn't matter if they bought her story or not, she wasn't giving up the evidence.

"What about the next morning?" Captain asked. "What did you do then?"

She gave a slight shrug. "Slept in, had a nice breakfast in my hotel room, checked out around noon, did some window shopping and went to the airport. Caught the plane at six. End of story."

Captain walked to Zane's desk and picked up a small stack of papers. "Says here you checked out of your hotel at nine in the morning."

Four pairs of x-ray eyes trained on her.

Her stomach tightened so hard it burned. Dudes were formidable. Made her feel naked.

What was she thinking? She was Sam Murdock. She pulled herself up to her full height, put her hands on her hips, and scowled at them. "Why the fuck are you guys grilling me? What the hell did I do? All I did was walk into her apartment and now suddenly, I'm on trial here?"

Zane motioned downward with his hands. "Sam, calm down. We're only trying to help you. We need to know everything you did from the time you landed until the time your plane left so we can get footage from surveillance cameras and figure out who spotted you, when they spotted you, and when they followed you. We need to know what they know."

"How could you guys get surveillance footage from the streets of Seattle? I was all over the place."

None answered, they just continued to stare at her.

Her entire body went cold, the blood left her head, and she got dizzy.

The men did not miss her reaction.

This was bad. Very bad. Eventually, they'd catch her in a photo or video, holding that box. Or worse, catch her on camera with Ursula.

Rollin took another step toward her. "Sam, this is me, Rollin. I know you pretty damned well. You're playing with us right now and I want to know why."

"None of your fucking business," came out of her mouth before she could stop herself. And much more forcibly than she'd have liked. Damn it! There was her confession to lying. She had to repair the damage and quickly. "Look, this is no big deal. I just don't want you bothering my friend or approaching her or getting surveillance pictures. I have my reasons. So does my friend. I don't owe you an explanation."

Rollin clearly had not expected this response. He'd never seen this side to her, either. She could tell he'd lost his bearings.

"We're trying to keep you alive, Sam," Burke said.

"I appreciate that, but my business had nothing to do with Linda Anderson. I went to that apartment on Thursday at what? About three?"

Carter referred to his stack of papers and said, "Two-forty-five and you left at three. Then you were in the lobby or the elderly woman's apartment for the next half hour. You left the building at three-thirty-five."

"Well, then if you know, why are you asking me? I wasn't thinking, gee, I should note everything I do and everywhere I go so when I get interrogated later, I'll have a straight answer."

"You're making our job harder, Sam," Rollin said, his mouth tight. "We're on the same side here. Whatever you tell us won't leave this room."

"I already told you. And you seem to have all the information you need, in that stack of spy papers," she said indignantly, gesturing toward Captain.

Rollin made an exasperated noise. "Sam. This isn't like you. Just tell me."

Sam crossed her arms, hardened her face, and said nothing.

Rollin threw up his hands.

"You retrieved that package from the postman, didn't you?" Burke said.

Thankfully, Sam was still angry. She narrowed her eyes, let her mouth twist and faced him. "For the fiftieth time, no I didn't. I visited the apartment for fifteen minutes. I left. I helped an old lady. The end."

All the men glared at her, then one by one, turned away, disgusted. All except for Burke.

He kept his focus tuned in on her face completely. "And I think you're lying."

"And I think you're an asshole."

His jaw twitched and his gaze went darker and colder.

Goosebumps raised on her arms, her stomach fluttered and she held herself tighter. Damn, the man was foreboding. And hot. If her sex could have waved at him and invited him inside, it would have. Why was she always so attracted to guys when they were mad at her? Rotten hormones.

"We will find out everything and everywhere you went," Burke continued. "There was a GPS in your rental car. We already have all your credit card statements."

Her stomach dropped to the floor. Had she paid for lunch? She couldn't remember. Hopefully, she'd used cash.

The bank! Holy bejeebus, if they found out she'd rented new safe deposit boxes, they'd know where she hid the package.

But how the hell was she supposed to get back to Seattle with the Patriots following her every move? Damn it! She didn't want to use her last few fake IDs, she needed them for when she carried out her final plan.

"Sam?" Rollin asked.

He'd been talking to her and she'd missed it all. Her face throbbing with heat, she couldn't look at him. She rubbed the aching muscles of her forehead.

"I've got a question for you, Sam," Carter said, looking up from a laptop computer. She hadn't noticed but he'd been sitting at Zane's desk for the previous few minutes.

"What?"

"Where'd you live before 1994? There's no record of your existence before then. And the Samantha Ann Murdock that was born on April 10, 1978 in Sacramento died on September 20th, 1978 in Sacramento. Who are you, really?"

A 10.0 earthquake shook her world. The room flew around her and her knees buckled. The contents of her stomach surged up her throat, she had to swallow hard to stop it. Then a wallop of adrenaline sent a fifty thousand watt blast through her. Bolting upright, she prepared to run.

You are blowing it! Save your ass, woman!

All at once, her sanity and self-preservation took hold. She fought hard to rein in her wild stampeding emotions and forced the fear from her face. "What the hell is wrong with you people? What do you mean, Samantha Ann Murdock died? Obviously not, I'm standing right here. If you're gonna spy on people, at least hire competent investigators."

She'd practically sent up a hundred-foot-wide lighted banner that said, "I'm LYING!" with her previous unconscious reaction. No way out, but she'd keep repeating the same story and stick to it, no matter what.

Carter tilted his head slightly to one side, his pale blue eyes suspicious and cold. "So you're saying that you're Samantha Ann Murdock?"

"Yes. Have been for all my life."

He glanced down at his laptop and shrugged. "No school records, no nothing."

"We moved around a lot."

"You've told us before that your parents are dead, but it says here that the Murdocks are alive and well in Sacramento, had five more kids and they all still live in the area. They never moved. They were apparently very upset when questioned about you."

Her stomach hollowed and all the blood drained from her head. The room grayed out. She caught herself on the credenza with a hand. "A-are they coming after me?" she stammered.

Then she realized that she'd just admitted to her biggest lie. Her body contracted and a deafening sound like a jet engine roared in her ears. She blinked back the tears. *Run!* Now not only did she have to hide from Larry and his evil friends, she had to hide from a whole new group of people. Unreal.

"No. Not yet," Carter replied. "We were careful not to give them too much information but it won't take long for them to figure out that someone stole their child's identity. They'll come after you, you know."

The information hit her so hard, she left like someone had punched her in the gut with a wrecking ball. Her vision shifting, she couldn't breathe. No way did she have time to liquidate her assets now, she had to disappear. Without the money. All those years of carefully building up her stockpile. All that hard work. All those homes. Gone. Just like that. She stumbled and fell into a chair. "You fucking bastards," she said in a horrified whisper.

Her brain went blank with overwhelm for a second, then a blast of rage hit her system like the switch being thrown on an electric chair. Leaping to her feet, she let out a yell that shook the windows. The men all jumped. "You thoughtless assholes. You went and talked to the Murdocks? How dare you meddle in my life? How dare you do this to me? Why don't you just take out a gun and shoot me, you motherfuckers? Stay away from me, all of you! And stay the fuck out of my life!"

She stormed toward the door. Burke moved to block her. She shoved him so hard, he reeled back and fell against a bookcase.

"Sam! I lied about the Murdocks. They don't know about you," Carter called out.

Mid step, she stopped and her body froze. Molten lava coursed through her veins, dumped into her belly and exploded. She had to press both palms to the sides of her head to keep it from blowing off her shoulders. Turning to him, with the most loathing she could muster, she tried to kill Carter with her blazing glower. "You sick bastard. You've destroyed me. I've never hated anyone like I hate you right now." Glaring at the roomful of men, she threw as much anger at them as she could. "Stay away from me, all of you," she growled. "I'm leaving and none of you better come near me again. If I see any of you bastards, *I will fucking kill you*."

Blinded by tears of rage, she blasted out of the room and headed for the front door.

Now she had no money to fight Larry and she was left with only one choice: killing the bastard. With no resources to survive afterwards.

The Patriots had just sentenced her to death.

Burke felt like a tractor-trailer had slammed him against the wall. His gut seared with guilt. He'd rarely seen anyone that terrified. The pain on her face. Devastating. His instinct was to run after her, sweep her into his arms, and reassure her. Take care of her. Find out who was after her and kill them.

The last time he'd seen someone that upset was Emma right after he'd tried to take her store from her. That volcanic passion and fury. Her life had been on the line, too. He hated that he'd caused this kind of pain to yet another woman he cared about.

He had to fix this. Had to make things right. He had to save Sam. He'd give her a few minutes to calm down, then go after her. Thankfully, Zane's driveway was two miles long and a good forty-five minutes by foot to reach Highway 84.

"Wow," Zane finally said.

Rollin rubbed his brow. "Damn, I thought that information had been wrong, Captain. Sam with a secret past. I can't believe it. Emma doesn't know."

Carter gestured toward the laptop. "Well, it's been secret for a long time. Since 1994. And she's built a great life for herself. Good job, five houses. And we just put all that in jeopardy."

Burke pushed away from the wall and held himself tall. "We have to convince her that we'll protect her identity. But I'm afraid she'll disappear. She looked almost feral. Like a wild, cornered animal."

"Fuck," Rollin said. "I feel bad. Who's after her?"

"I don't know, but when she came under fire today, she wasn't surprised," Burke said.

Rollin's focus on him sharpened. "What?"

"She was surprised the attack had to do with Linda Anderson. And relieved."

Rollin's brow went into a V. "Really? Damn."

Burke nodded. "Someone's clearly trying to kill her. Or has tried."

"Or she's running from the law," Carter said.

"Not Sam," Rollin said. "She's never done a bad thing in her life."

Carter shrugged. "We have no idea who she is, Rollin. Or how old she really is. She could have a record. Took this second chance sixteen years ago to start her life over and went the straight and narrow. All her hard efforts could be guilt over something she did in her past. We've both been fooled before. You saw the look in her eye when she threatened to kill us."

Rollin waved his hand dismissively. "No, she didn't. Like Burke said, it was a feral self-protection mechanism. She's probably calmed down by now. Let me go after her."

Zane held up his oversized hand. "Let her cool off a bit. We have time. It'll take her a half an hour to reach Highway 84 even if she runs the whole way. And it's dark as hell out there."

Burke's heart beat faster. He wanted to bolt out of the room to catch Sam. But he didn't want the Patriots to know his plans for her.

They didn't trust him with women. They didn't trust him, period. With good reason, but this was different. Sam was different.

Captain said, "Well, whatever's going on with Sam, we need that package. Are we sure she has it?"

Burke nodded. "Yes. The surveillance will prove it, but I'm positive. The only thing I can think is that she recognized someone in the photos and that it must be the person who's tried to kill her."

Captain whistled. "That would be very, very bad."

"The highest levels of government, super powers, all of them," Zane said with a frown.

Rollin ran his hand through his long hair and scratched his head, making some strands stick up. "So who's in the packet that we know of? Dawn Bridwell, CEO of NineCom. Congressman Thom Pintello. Senator—soon to be presidential candidate— Lawrence Tyrell."

Burke's mind went dark at the mention of Tyrell. What a peach. Sadistic murdering pedophile freak. He hated Captain's plan to control Tyrell. But he was in no position to offer his opinion. Besides, the decision had been made while he wasn't part of the group, while he'd been tying up the loose ends of his criminal persona.

And his return to the Patriots had not been an easy transition. Without Rollin's impassioned advocacy, Captain would have never let him back in. And no one but Rollin, Catherine and Bobby had welcomed him. It was a tenuous truce. Stefan hated him, Zane was still frosty, and Captain rarely said anything to him. But he had to convince them to let him protect Sam.

Zane broke out coughing. "I can't believe a guy that sick is so close to the Presidency. I can't believe we're actually gonna be doing business with him if we get that evidence back. Sure we want to do this?"

"We all hate it, but we decided," Captain said, his face hardening. "Right now, this is the way to go. Besides, if Tyrell wasn't rotten we wouldn't be able to control him."

"I thought the Patriots would play things differently," Zane said with pure disgust on his face.

Burke's interior burned and he wished he could join in the criticism. Thank God for Zane.

"While I agreed with the strategy—hell, okay, I came up with the plan—I'm not sold on it," Captain replied, edging on a defensive tone. "Nothing makes me sicker than allowing that creep to breathe the same free air as the good people of this country. But he's more valuable to us out of jail. Greater good, Zane. We can get a lot done with him in office."

"Greater good would be stringing that bastard up by his nuts," Zane bit out. "He sleeps with little girls. He runs a criminal organization that put him in power. You can't get creepier than Tyrell. And how many murders has he ordered? I still think we should blow the whistle."

Burke kept his jaw tight so he wouldn't shout his agreement.

Rollin shook his head. "That would be a very ugly war. We agreed. Gotta play this one behind the scenes."

"I hate this job sometimes." Zane shook his head and sat on his desk, stretching out his mile-long legs.

"Will someone please go after her?" Captain said.

"I'll go," Rollin took a step toward the door.

Burke made a stop motion with his hand. "Let me try. Your earlier exchange could cloud the matter. Sam needs to trust someone. Let's see if I can win her over."

"No way, Burke." Rollin said. "Because of the Emma thing. I'll go after her. She used to like me."

Rollin went to move past him, but Burke blocked him. "I'm more neutral. She isn't worried about losing me as a friend, Rollin. And I just saved her life."

"True. Still…"

"I'll convince her," he said in a tone that left no room for argument. Without waiting for Rollin's reply, he turned to the Captain. "Did you alert the Murdocks?"

Carter shook his head. "But we did look into it. Hopefully, that won't get back to them. Sam's only on record for owning property. Her name isn't on any other papers. She doesn't even vote."

Burke walked to the doorway. "Keep an eye on the Murdocks. If they make a move to investigate, we'll help her create another identity. We have to get her to trust us. When are we getting the surveillance files? When will we have the proof Sam took the packet?"

"Bobby had problems retrieving the data." Carter stretched, bending his lanky frame to one side. His back made a popping sound and he winced. "Hopefully, we'll have it by tomorrow morning."

"Let me know as soon as you can," Burke said with one foot out the door. "And get Bobby to find out Sam's true identity."

"Emma said something bad happened to her as a kid," Rollin said. "Something she never talks about. Only thing Emma's got out of her was that she has no family, that her parents died when she was a teenager, before she came to California from the east coast. But Sam's told everyone else she came from Sacramento."

Burke pointed at the group. "Before I forget, out in the forest, Sam's new boyfriend, Paul Strong. I think he's Cabal. Nearly a hundred percent sure he set up that sniper attack. Not because he knew Sam was Linda Anderson, I think he's trying to infiltrate us."

"What?" Rollin demanded.

All the Patriots focused on him.

Burke quickly relayed the story, his mind half on Sam.

Captain shook his head. "Go take care of Sam, leave Strong to us. We'll reconnoiter later."

"Good," Burke said. "I'll assess Sam's property and assign a detail. Banana and David are available. I'll take care of her protection. And I'll find out why she has the package. And who she's hiding from."

"Good luck. She bites, my friend," Rollin said.

Burke grinned. "I bite back."

Burke drove his Mercedes SUV down Zane's winding, private road, thrilled he'd pulled off this coup. They hadn't even questioned him. Maybe he had more power with the group than he'd thought. Excellent.

Now all he had to do was turn Sam around. She'd better listen to him. She'd better trust him. He wouldn't let up until she did. There was something about this woman. She'd already dug past a wall of his defenses. He wished he just wanted to fuck her.

Every cell in his body felt more alive when she was near him. His need to protect her overwhelmed him. His emotions were nearly out of control. He couldn't remember the last time he couldn't get detachment. But he'd been off kilter for weeks. Between what happened with Joseph and ending his six-month relationship with Valerie, he hadn't felt like himself in a month. Hell, even before that. Ever since Emma had opened him up to love again, everything had gone crazy.

He'd started to crave a real relationship with a real woman. He wanted more than a beautiful ornament. He wanted to fall in love with someone who wasn't damaged and who had similar goals. Make love and have a good time and build a life together.

He'd tried with Valerie, but she'd been a poor choice. Full of abandonment issues, she'd pushed him away one too many times. This time he didn't want a fixer-upper, he wanted a solid woman.

So why was he falling for a Class A-1 drama queen? What was it about Sam? He didn't know, but he was going to find out.

Much further along than he expected, he came upon her storming down the road holding a flashlight. He pulled the Mercedes beside her and rolled down his window. "Would you like a ride?"

"Fuck off!"

"You won't lose your property, or your safety net. And you won't lose your life, I promise. No way do we want to put you in danger or cause you to lose your livelihood. We'll protect you and your identity."

Her expression didn't change, she didn't look at him, but she did slow her pace. Took a long time for her to come to a stop. She finally turned to him, her gaze wounded, tweaking his heart. He wanted to gather her in his arms and cradle her. Kiss all her worries away.

"And what do I have to do in return?"

"Help us if we ask for it. But even if you don't, we'll still protect you."

"Why?"

"Because you're part of the family, Sam."

Her lower lip quivering, she searched his face. A tear rolled down her cheek. Looked about six years old. "Do you mean that?"

The urge to hold her grew stronger. "Yes. We're sorry we scared you. We had no idea."

The adult returned and her face went hard. "I'm not a spy."

"Didn't think you were."

"And I'm not a fugitive." Her hazel eyes flashed with defiance, giving his cock a rush.

"I believe you."

"I won't lose my property?"

"No. I promise."

Sighing, she crossed her arms and rubbed her forehead.

"Let me take you home, Sam. I want to set up a detail to protect you."

"I don't trust you."

"For now."

"Arrogant bastard." She chewed on her lower lip and her gaze darted around. Grumbled and muttered to herself. "Well, I can't exactly walk home from here. And those guys did try to kill me. And I don't want to die. I've worked too hard to give up now. I'm gonna retire on a beach in Mexico if it's the last thing I do and no one is going to stand in my way. Not you, not any of those fuckers back there."

"We wouldn't dream of it."

"Jesus." She sighed and rolled her eyes, then resumed glaring at the ground. She finally nodded, then walked around to the passenger side of the car, and climbed inside.

The pressure on his stomach eased. Amazing how well the truth worked. He'd have to use it more often in the future with her.

Sam couldn't stop trembling. She hadn't been this scared since the night Larry tried to kill her. Buckling herself into the seat felt completely counterintuitive. She wanted to run and keep running. But the Patriots could find her wherever she went.

No matter what Burke said, her identity had been exposed and there was no way back.

She'd planned on disappearing after taking care of Larry, but it had always been in the future. Contacting Ursula had just been the first step of many. How could she have known what that one visit would set in motion? That trip to Seattle had lit the fuse on a keg of dynamite and she was almost out of time before her whole life exploded.

But how could she have missed the emotional impact? She'd built a home for herself over the past sixteen years. A real home. Now she had to give up everything and everyone she loved. If she'd known how much her new life meant to her, she would have never contacted Ursula.

But how could she live knowing that Larry had gotten away with his crimes?

Moot point. Now that her cover had been blown, she had no choice. The news would get out. Larry would find her. There was no way to stop him.

Her insides hurt like a lion was using them for a scratching post. Tears dripped onto her lap and she wiped her eyes.

"Sam, you're safe."

With a dismissive noise, she rummaged through her backpack for tissue.

"You don't have to run."

The absolute stupidity of the statement made her chuckle.

"We all lead double lives, Sam. You know secrets about us. We won't break your trust again. How can I reassure you?"

"You can't." She kept her eyes forward and tried to rub the pain out of her gut.

"You're going to run, aren't you?"

Glancing out the window at the lights of Redwood City and the Bay beyond, a sob caught in her throat. She'd miss the Bay Area so much. She swallowed a huge lump.

"I hope you decide to stay and fight for what you've built. We can provide you with all the documentation you need. I can help you. I want to help you."

"And why would you want to do that?" she bit out harshly.

"Because I like you. And you need help."

"Disappeared once when I was much younger, I can do it again."

"Do you want to leave?"

"Hell no."

"Then don't."

"I'd rather live, thank you."

"No one will kill you on my watch."

"You're overestimating your abilities."

"No, I'm not. But now is not the time to make this kind of decision. Besides, how could you walk away from Emma?"

Emma's sweet face popped into her mind and an eruption of sorrow blew out of her core. Tears streamed down her cheeks. Holding herself, she wracked with sobs. Emma was her only family. The only one in her corner. For sixteen years, the woman had been by her side. More than anyone else in her life.

Images flashed through her brain. Dolly and Emma throwing her a birthday party. Celebrating the purchase of her first house.

Her life in San Mateo had been wonderful. And now it was all gone.

A part of her noticed that the car had stopped. In one smooth action, Burke unbuckled her and gathered her into his thick arms. She jerked away with a violent motion.

He grabbed her tightly and pulled her close. "It's okay. Let me hold you. You need to know people are here for you. You need to know you're not alone."

The sudden comfort of his strong warm body and his words sent her further over the edge. Her interior seared with pain like all her ulcers had started bleeding at once. She made a half-hearted attempt at pushing him away, but he stayed with her.

"I won't let anything happen to you."

"You can't save me."

"I can sure as hell try." He held her even tighter.

A torrent of emotion poured from the gaping wound in her center. Her whole body shook. She sobbed so hard, she could barely breathe.

Burke petted her head, stroked her, and murmured, "You're strong. I'm here for you. Emma's here for you."

After a long time—could have been five minutes or a half an hour —she calmed.

How odd that Burke was capable of this level of tenderness. While she didn't believe his act for a minute, she needed someone. Weird that it was Burke.

She wiped her eyes and retrieved the tissues from the pack in her lap and blew her nose. Burke was right about one thing. This was not the time to plan the future. Or try to get to Seattle. After being shot at, interrogated, and exposed, it was all she could do to stay upright and conscious. She couldn't afford to take a misstep. Everything would have to wait until morning. Goddamnit.

"Are you all right?" he asked.

"Getting there."

"Good."

She gave him a squeeze. "Thanks."

"My pleasure."

She let go and met his gaze. Strength and self-assurance emanated from the depths of his dark brown eyes. And compassion. And emotional availability. But she must be misinterpreting that. Compelled, she couldn't stop staring at him. He was so beautiful. A part of her wanted to burrow back into his arms.

Alarms sounded from the back of her brain. *Don't trust him!* This man was her enemy. He wanted what she had.

His attention dropped to her mouth.

Her libido screamed from the deep reaches of her sex. *Kiss him! Fuck him!*

An uppercut of fear bashed her on the chin and her body stiffened. What the hell was she thinking?

He smiled and didn't move closer. "I should get you back home. You need to rest."

"I'll say."

He moved away and she had to stop herself from reaching for him.

Proof positive she wasn't in her right mind.

Burke started the car and pulled back onto the freeway. "Tonight you'll be protected by two bodyguards. I'm going to brief them and then I'll return in the morning to oversee the installation of the surveillance system and set up your protective detail for the next week. I want to stay tonight, but I have business to attend to at home."

"It's cool, Burke. I don't expect you to stay. And thanks. I need sleep, too. I'm getting the five-minute warning that my brain is about to shut off."

He sent her a sweet smile. "We're almost there."

By the time Burke pulled into the driveway of her bungalow, exhaustion had claimed her mind and body. She barely heard what he said. All she could think about was crashing.

Two big hulking bodyguards arrived just as she was closing her bedroom door.

After brushing her teeth and taking her ulcer medicine, she grabbed her Spongebob pajamas and threw them on. With her last brain cell, she stuffed her double bed to make it appear as if she slept there. Then she stumbled into her walk-in closet, shut the door, and crawled into her safe sleeping spot. Curled up with a fully-loaded rifle, she instantly fell asleep.

FOUR

A monster from Hell chased her down a long ornate hallway with white walls and maroon carpeting. She recognized this place. The Governor's Mansion in Concord. Heat from the evil creature's breath seared her back. Sam looked over her shoulder into giant red glowing eyes. The monster morphed into a hideous caricature of Larry. His mouth opened revealing rows upon rows of razor sharp teeth. Roaring, his mouth engulfed her. Darkness consumed her.

Sam woke up shaking, covered in sweat, her heart pounding, clutching the rifle in a death grip. Her body buzzed like it was hooked up to a generator. Every cell screamed at her to run. Her stomach convulsed and she swallowed. Panting, she tried to control the nausea.

As she shook the nightmare from her conscious mind, her true nightmare bombed her. The shooting. Her cover blown. Linda Anderson. The Senator. She set the gun aside and wrapped her arms around her knees. Rocking back and forth, she concentrated on centering herself. Being strong. Being like Dad before he turned on her.

Tears dripped off her cheeks and onto her pajama bottoms.

Emma's mom, Dolly, had made her promise never to tell anyone the truth. *You let that secret out to anyone and it goes out to the world. No stopping it. The only way to protect yourself is to forget about your past. Don't ever call home. This is your home. Repeat after me: I'm Samantha Murdock. Lie all the way to your grave.*

Dolly had been so smart. Look what happened the one time Sam had broken the rules.

She lightly slapped her face. "Snap out of it," she whispered. "You have to be strong. Now is not the time to fall apart."

Wiping the tears from her eyes, she focused on her goal. Get to Seattle ASAP.

Right. Easy. With the Patriots and hired killers stalking her. Her stomach wrenched with pain.

"What the fuck?" came a loud deep voice from her bedroom.

Gasping, she nearly had a heart attack. She leapt to her feet, grabbed her gun and aimed it at the closet door.

"Banana! Get in here! The bed's been stuffed! Sam's gone!"

Burke. Frantic.

She heaved a sigh of relief and let the rifle's barrel drop. But what was wrong with Burke? He sounded tortured. "No, I'm not gone!"

Oh, shit. Now he was going to find out she slept in her closet. No one knew that but Emma. Burke would think she was certifiable.

The door to the closet opened and Burke appeared, his handsome face grooved deep with worry lines. "Sam?"

"Yes," she replied in a sheepish tone.

He looked at her stuffed bed, then at her, then at the tangle of bedding behind her in the corner of her closet. His brow went into a deep V and he frowned. "You sleep in the closet?" His attention went to her rifle. "With a rifle? Let me guess, it's loaded."

"Probably."

Concern flashed in his dark eyes. "Why do you sleep with a loaded rifle?"

"Because teddy bears don't provide much protection."

He didn't even crack a smile. "How long have you been doing this?"

"Ever since I woke up with a guy on top of me." Her practiced lie came out smoothly.

His focus on her sharpened and his shoulders and mouth went hard. Like he wanted to kill the guy. She knew it was his job to protect her, but she couldn't help but love his guard dog routine. With a man like this on her side, she almost felt safe. Almost.

"When did that happen?" he demanded.

"When I was nineteen. So when I get scared, I sleep in my closet."

He eyed the rifle and then her in a way that told her he was about to order her to surrender it.

She held her head high. "You got a problem with that?"

His ears moved back slightly and his gaze went harder. "No." Not the best liar.

"Stop looking at me like that. I'm not crazy."

"Just keep telling yourself that." He sent her a teasing smile.

She chuckled, and the pain in her gut eased. Thank God, he'd turned it into a joke. "Good morning to you, too."

He backed up and she followed him out into her bedroom.

His smile widened and his gaze warmed. "Are you okay?" he asked softly.

That weird caring Burke was back. She much preferred the adversary. Even though her stomach needed his kindness.

Her attention went to her rifle. "Yes, even if the evidence is shouting the contrary."

He stepped closer and took the gun from her. After inspecting it, he sent her a daring glance and popped out the shells. "I'm unloading this for me, not you."

"I had on the safety."

"Which could easily come off in your sleep."

"Hasn't happened so far."

He briefly raised a brow, then handed her the rifle, and poured the shells into her upturned palm.

"I'm just gonna reload it."

"Could you wait until I'm gone?"

"From the room or the house?"

He pursed his lips. "The house. Brat."

She grinned.

"Really, Sam. Let us protect you. It's our job. Haven't lost one yet."

"I'm still sleepin' with this thing when I need to."

"I recommend a man." He sent her a predatory half-smile, his eyes shining with amusement.

She blew out some air between her lips, but gave half a thought to stripping him naked and throwing him on her bed.

A flash of fear made her gut tighten. No fucking Burke. Ever. God, that's all she'd need. To fall in love with a player. No more reruns.

Besides, she had no time for love games. Not even with that hunk Paul.

"Why don't you make coffee so I can take a shower and get out of my pjs?"

He focused on her sleepwear. "Speaking of which, what the hell do —Spongebob? You have Spongebob Squarepants pajamas? What are you? Ten?"

"Yes. I'm ten. I like Spongebob and I won't apologize for it. Now go make yourself useful and put on the coffee. You'll find everything you need in the cupboard to the left of the fridge."

He appraised her body and gave an appreciative nod. "You do look rather cute in those."

Scowling, she pointed at the door. "Get out."

He chuckled, then turned and left, closing the door behind him.

Gorgeous asshole.

The smell of coffee met her when she walked out of her bedroom. She found Burke closely inspecting the knickknacks on her fireplace mantle. Her body tightened and a brush of irritation scraped her nerves. He was sizing her up, doing a profile on her. But the way he held his shoulders pissed her off. Something about the way he carried himself said he owned the place. He was so sure of himself. While most men put on an act of bravado and self-assurance, Burke wasn't acting, nor was he covering up for low self-esteem. He actually believed in himself. Solid as a rock. Annoying.

And invasive. She was still in shock that her secret was out. She'd never felt more naked. "Good morning, Mr. Cherlenko."

He didn't turn to her, but continued examining her house. "Interesting décor. Snow globes and small replicas of buildings." He cast a sideways glance at her and returned to her collection of famous architectural icons.

"I love the little buildings. You can thank Emma for the snow globes. I hate them."

He turned to her, incredulous. "Then why do you have a shelf covered in them?"

"Because of the memories they're associated with."

His face relaxed with understanding. "Emma gave them all to you?"

"No. To get even with me for short-sheeting her bed in college when she'd finally managed to seduce this hot guy—God, she was pissed, it was so funny—she spread this rumor that I loved snow globes. So half are from people who honestly think I like them and half are from friends who love giving me a bad time."

"They are...unusual." He pointed to a French fries and hamburger snow globe, raised his left eyebrow high, and sent her a *get real* look.

Sam shrugged. "This guy Jose and I worked at a horrible bank and always said we'd rather be working at McDonald's. He got that for me when we both quit. I have a story for each one. Emma's greatest triumph. She said if she could assign enough positive value to the horrid things, that I'd grow to love them."

"Has her plan worked?"

"No." She laughed and he joined her.

"So why the interest in buildings?" He tuned into her face completely.

Guy was so intense.

Unable to take his stare, she focused on her collection. "I've wanted to be an architect since I was a kid." She picked up the Sears Tower and blew off a layer of dust.

"So why haven't you?"

"Hard to start out in that field. Dad always said, anyway. He told me to be practical. So I went into finance in college."

"Didn't like it?"

"No. I worked at that bank, but it sucked. I made more as a cocktail waitress working less hours. But I wanted money, so I lived on nothing and invested in real estate. Did sweat equity during the day on rentals and worked high-end clubs at night." Her miniature Taj Mahal had a resident dust bunny.

"Impressive. But you like running Emma's store now?"

She put the Sears Tower in its place and picked up the fuzzy Taj Mahal. "Much more than navigating drunk grabby men. Three years ago, when my rentals started to cash flow and I didn't have to work that hard, I became a club manager. But I hated working nights. Emma offered me the job of running her place and I jumped on it."

"How's that going?"

"Oh, perfect." Sam took in a large breath and blew the dustball out and onto the floor. "I need to clean more. Jesus. Anyway, Emma and I work well together, always have. And I love that store. Being right on Union Square is so exciting."

"What if you had all the money in the world? What if you didn't have to work?"

She studied him. Nothing out of the ordinary. He just seemed interested. "That's easy. And part of my plan. As soon as I get enough rental income, I'm going back to school and becoming an architect."

"Why not make that happen now?"

"I have a few things to take care of first." She wanted to suck the words back into her mouth the moment they left.

His focus sharpened. "Like what? Something to do with your past?"

She returned the Taj Mahal to its space and adjusted the positions of other knickknacks on the mantle, but didn't turn to him. No way was she going there.

After a long moment spent staring at her, Burke turned away. He finished examining her living room and walked into her guest room/library. She followed. Floor to ceiling, the walls were covered with her precious book collection.

His head jerked back. "Damn and I thought I had a lot of books." He sent her a penetrating stare. "Why didn't I take you for a reader?"

"Because I'm a cocktail waitress. Or was. Almost everyone thinks that I don't use my head, just my mouth."

A corner of his mouth twitched and his brown eyes sparkled.

His sensual aura slapped her libido awake. Burke's personal power went beyond animal magnetism, he had more like animal electro-magnetism. His field of energy buzzed the whole area.

Sam knew men. She knew how to handle men. But he defied categorization. She wasn't sure how to control him. Needed to observe and test him.

On all of two brain cells.

Pickles, this was too much.

After touring her bungalow, Burke said, "I'm having a surveillance system installed this morning. Like last night, I'll have two men stationed here 24/7, one inside, one outside. You know both David and Banana, I assume you feel comfortable enough with them to have them around during the day?"

David and Banana, perfect. She could work them.

"I made out with David, so yeah." Why did she mention that? "And Banana, he's just a sweetheart."

"He's in the front of the house right now, David is covering the back from 24th." He arched a brow in disapproval. "I wish you didn't have such easy access to your backyard."

"Me, neither, but this was what I could afford in the neighborhood. Short sale, made a killing on this place."

"Good for you. So along with the two men outside, I'll also be here during the day to supervise and provide protection."

The floor shook. "*You'll be here?*" Her heart did a drum solo. Her sex tingled. Then a punch of fear to the gut. How the hell would she escape to Seattle with Burke hovering nearby? Shit. She might just have to sleep with him. How else could she get control over him?

He sent her a sinister smile. "Do I disturb you, Sam?"

"Yes."

"Good."

"Not in that way," she added quickly. But her tone betrayed her.

"Now that was a clear lie," he stated with a slight smile on his lips and a victorious spark in his dark eyes.

Before she could react, he turned away to examine some photos on her mantle. "Who is this standing with you and Emma? Is that her mother?"

Annoyed, titillated, but relieved for the distraction, Sam nodded. "Yeah. Dolly was a hoot. Took me in when I was nineteen, when I moved to San Mateo. Got so close, I called her Mom. Damn, I miss her." And that wasn't the half of it. Dolly had saved her life. Took a terrified sixteen-year-old and made her strong again.

"So you have no family left?"

"Nope."

"No cousins, no aunts, no uncles?"

Aunt Belinda smiled at her from her memory. Her distinctive high-pitched laugh rang in her ears. A burning pain made her throat close. "Nope," she said with a straight face. "Parents died when I was a teenager."

Shut up!

"And somewhere along the line, you changed your name. So who's after you? Who's trying to kill you?" he asked in a deceptively casual tone.

His sneaky question hit her like he'd whacked her on the forehead with an iron pan. Her thoughts scrambled, she fought for clarity, then turned to him and sent him a nasty glare. "What the hell are you talking about?"

He looked at her with pity. "Sam. Can we please cut the bullshit? You're afraid of someone. You changed your name to hide from them. You believe your life is in danger. No sense in arguing any of those points."

She pinched the bridge of her nose. "Burke, I really don't want to talk about it."

"You know we'll keep digging."

Crossing her arms, she stood taller and leveled her guarded gaze at him. "Whatever I told you now, you'd have to verify. You'll keep digging no matter what."

"Rollin said you came from back east."

"Did he now?"

He jerked his head in a quick upward move. "So what do you tell people when they ask where you went to high school?"

"I normally turn it on them and ask them where they went. So where did you go to high school?"

"San Francisco. Graduated in 1986 when I was fifteen."

Her brow furrowed hard over her eyes. "You graduated high school at fifteen?"

"I could have graduated at eleven, but I didn't want to go to college that young. I was a freak as it was."

She stepped back and her mind took a twist that hurt. "You? A freak? No way." She couldn't picture him as anything but cool and chic Burke Cherlenko.

A small nod. "Chess nerd."

"Whoa. So...were you in clubs and stuff?"

"Competition. A prodigy if you can believe it."

She took another step back. "Like written up in magazines and on TV and junk?"

"Yes. International Grandmaster at fourteen."

Her belly went cold and her mouth dropped open. "At fourteen? Holy bejeebus." She'd known he was smart, but not this smart. How the hell could she defeat a Grandmaster?

With a slight shrug, he said, "My mother kept copies of all the articles and videotapes of the interviews. Along with a small moving van's worth of trophies. Have them in storage somewhere. Need to get rid of them."

"Why? You should be proud."

His brow wrinkled, a hint of pain grew in his dark eyes, and he looked away. "Yes," he said like he'd said "no".

A story there, for sure. One he didn't want to talk about. But if she could get him to open up, maybe he'd reveal a weakness. Something she could use against him other than sex. "So how did you end up a Marine, then a Navy SEAL?"

"Wanted to challenge myself physically."

"Did you get beat up as a kid?"

A brief raise of his thick dark brows. "Routinely until I convinced my father to let me take judo."

She still couldn't imagine him as anything but the rock solid man standing in front of her. "Damn. A chess nerd."

"What group were you in?"

"Sports, but I liked to read and most jocks don't. So sometimes, I'd hang out with the smart nerds. The computer and science guys. But most of the time I hung out with a little group of girls." Mainly because Larry wouldn't allow her to befriend guys.

One corner of his mouth turned up. "Were you the ringleader?"

"No." They were just a group of girls she hung out with when she couldn't be with Larry. He'd been her whole world.

Burke did a quick tour of her body and hunger grew in his eyes. "You must have had the boys' interest."

"Yeah." The first time she'd met Larry, he couldn't take his eyes off her. She'd never had anyone look at her like she was a goddess descended from the heavens. She'd felt so adult. So sophisticated. So privileged. Larry was so smoking hot, all the girls in the Sheriff's teen outreach program had flirted with him. And he'd chosen her. She'd leapt to cloud nine and stayed there for an entire year. Then Larry got weird. Or weirder. But that first year had been the best of her life.

"That looks like a good memory."

She swung her attention to him and he appeared to be reading her like a magazine. She turned away and walked into the kitchen.

Good. Ha.

"You loved him," Burke called out behind her.

"Yes, I did." She reached for a coffee mug and absently filled it from the pot.

Eleven o'clock at night. The bitter chill of New Hampshire in fall. Hiding in the bushes three doors down, waiting for Larry to pull up in his patrol car.

All those nights behind the billboard on the interstate. Larry's hands all over her. *"Let's try somethin' new, darlin'."* What that man did to her. She'd thought all men made love like that. She'd had no idea she'd started off her sexual life with the King of Kink.

Her face warmed.

"And that's a very interesting memory, isn't it?" Burke purred next to her.

She turned to face him. Almost crowding her, he wore his patented smirk.

Her fist closed into a ball and she imagined punching him. "No, and we're done with the interrogation."

His cocky and playful expression didn't change. "I'm not interrogating you, Sam, I'm just talking. I want to know more about you. I find you fascinating."

She'd finally had enough and got into his face. "Bullshit. Do me a favor? Don't work me. I can see through your little games. And here's where I'm at: no, I'm not telling you about my past and no, I'm not fucking you."

His brows went high, his eyes widened, and his mouth opened a bit. Recovering quickly, he sent her an amused smile. "Funny, I don't remember offering."

Curling her lip, she made a noise in the back of her throat. "Oh, please. I see the way you look at my ass. And my tits. I was a cocktail waitress. I know what men think and when they're thinking it."

He broke out into a lascivious grin, blinked rapidly a bit, and leaned in. "So what am I thinking now?"

Insufferable bastard. She stepped back and put some distance between them. "That you're charming enough to get me into bed whether I want to or not. Because you've had so few women say no. But I've known too many men like you. It's all a game. And I'm not into games anymore. I'm looking for long-term and honey, you scream one-night-stand."

He tilted his head and the confident look in his eye intensified. "I can assure you, you've never met anyone like me. And don't presume to know what I think."

"Your motives are like any other man's and I only judge people by their actions. And I've seen plenty of your actions, boyfriend."

"You saw what I wanted you to see," he countered smoothly.

She laughed at his audacity. "You're a player, Burke. I don't want a player."

"You're the one playing games and I'm only trying to help."

"Perhaps. And I don't want to seem ungrateful. I just think you have ideas about me and I don't want you to."

"Because you're afraid of what might happen between us." His attention dropped to her mouth. Then he sent her a smoldering smile.

A thrill went through her, lighting her sex on fire.

Damn, he was evil.

"You're wrong." Which was the worst lie she'd ever told anyone ever on record.

A knowing grin on his arrogant face, he shrugged. "Lie to me, fine, just don't lie to yourself."

She met his eyes and opened her mouth to argue, but got lost in him and forgot what she was about to say. The heat between them ignited her whole body. She stopped breathing, turned away, and grabbed the half-and-half.

He let out a quick breath through his nostrils, clearly amused by her reaction.

Okay, at this point, Burke was too much to handle. And given her attraction, sleeping with him was too dangerous. She'd have to come up with another plan. Fast.

After Seattle, Sam Murdock had to die. Once underground, she could resurface as one of her aliases. But she needed money to complete her plan. Damn it, she wished she had time to sell the rentals. Her stomach and back tightened. She only had the cash on hand to assassinate Larry, not enough pursue the long, drawn-out legal fight to bring him to justice. Shit.

But first she had to get to Seattle. All under the watchful eye of Burke and his pals.

Crap. How the hell would she—Emma's shop! All she had to do was go to work, slip out, and disappear into busy downtown San Francisco. Easy!

Her body relaxed. No worries! She grabbed the sugar bowl and scooped a heaping teaspoon into her mug.

Burke leaned against the counter too near her. "Oh, I meant to tell you. Emma called twice and so did Paul."

The way he said "Paul" told her exactly what he thought of the man. He hated him and wanted him out of the picture.

Giving her a great idea. If her current plan failed, she'd use Paul. Perfect.

"Thanks," Sam said, and really meant it.

Paul calling twice was a great sign, he'd be easy to manipulate. If for some reason, she couldn't escape in the City that day, all she had to do was have Paul take her on a date to a place of her choosing, set up an escape route, and get the hell out of there.

Damn. Poor Paul. He didn't deserve this.

Either he would understand that or he wouldn't. If she survived. And if she ever returned to California.

Burke continued to stare at her. "Are you going to call them?"

"Not now."

He studied her carefully. "I thought you were all hot for him."

"I am." She stirred her coffee.

"You sound delirious," he drawled in a sardonic tone.

When would he stop playing? She turned to him and shot him a glare. "Burke, for God's sake. I got shot at yesterday and had my life taken away from me. Do you really believe I'm thinking about a dude at a time like this?"

His eyes went blank. "I…uh…"

"I don't need a man. I like men in my life, but I don't need one. I'm not gonna rush to the phone every time he calls. Doesn't mean I'm not interested, it means I care more about myself. And since yesterday, my priorities have changed. So while I will more than likely call Paul back today, first I need to get my head together." She returned the half-and-half to the fridge. "And now I have to go to work. I'm due at ten." She checked the clock above the door. Nine-thirty. "Oh, pickles, I'm gonna be late."

"You're not going to work."

She snapped her attention to him. "What do you mean, I'm not? I'm on the schedule."

"Emma removed you. You're on an extended leave of absence."

Her interior heated white-hot and her body went rigid. "What?"

Burke didn't react. "It's too dangerous and we don't have the manpower to protect you there. Too many vantage points for snipers in Union Square."

"Oh, come on. I'll stay back from the windows."

"No."

"What do you mean, no? This is my life."

His face hardened. "And if you'd like to keep living it, you'll listen to me."

Her house suddenly seemed much smaller. She could feel the walls press in all around her. "Holy shit. I'm in prison."

"Only until we can determine the threat assessment. If you provided us with the information we requested, perhaps you could return to work sooner."

She narrowed her eyes. "So what? Now you're blackmailing me?"

"No. It's the truth. We discussed your situation and won't press you for details about whom you visited before you went to Linda Anderson's apartment—and we won't ask about your true identity—but we would like you to tell us what you did after you left the apartment until you got home here to San Mateo."

Focusing on her cup, she sipped her coffee. "I told you guys."

"No, you didn't. We're getting footage now that will tell us most of what we want to know."

She almost spit out her mouthful. "All I did was go to the apartment then back to my hotel and I didn't go out again until morning, until I checked out." She cleared her throat.

"You checked out at nine. Where did you go from nine to four when you arrived at the airport and called Emma again?"

Anger scorched her interior. "Shit, this is fucking invasive! I don't have to—"

He pulled himself up taller and his eyes bored into hers. "Do you want to live?"

"—take this shit from you people! You're invading my privacy!"

"If I leave, those men will find you, torture you for the information, and then kill you like they murdered Joseph O'Reilly."

"Joe? What does this have to do with—wait, Joe's dead?" She stopped and checked his expression. "Not Joe O'Reilly."

"I thought you'd heard. Died four days ago."

Her mouth dropping open, she backed into the red Formica kitchen counter. She pictured Joe's winning smile, square jaw, and those heavenly blue eyes. They'd flirted heavily at Emma's party the month before and shared a lingering kiss by the beer fridge in the garage. When he got back from up North, he'd promised to look her up. Joe. Gone. Just like that. Unbelievable. A flash of grief made her stomach convulse. "Shit, Joe. But he was the nicest guy in the universe, he—"

"They don't care about how *nice* someone is, they only want that information. And they'll do worse to you if they get their hands on you, Sam. Men like that love to make pretty girls scream."

Shuddering, she wrapped her arms around herself. "Shit." All the blood chilled in her veins. This was real. These people would kill her. Why was it so hard to grasp?

"Now tell me what you did after you left that apartment. They probably had you followed. They might know where you went and what you did with the package."

God, he was good. And smooth. And crafty. Thankfully, she was still lost in thought about Joe, and managed to keep her face free of reaction. "What package? Oh, the phantom package I lost somewhere."

Forcing her body to continue its morning routine, she opened her breadbox and withdrew a loaf of whole wheat sourdough. So unreal that Joe was dead. Just unreal.

Was she the Black Widow? Did everyone who ever loved her or liked her die?

Back to the plan, kid. No time. Grieve later. For all of them. Getting to Seattle is all that matters.

Since escaping from San Francisco was out, it was time for Plan B. Paul. Until then, she had to make sure that Burke got no more information out of her.

"I know the package is not here." He moved into her line of sight with a dare on his face.

"What?" She searched his expression.

"Where did you put it in Seattle? Rent a mailbox? Give it to your friend? Hide it in a vent in your hotel room?"

"Whoa, whoa, whoa, wait a minute. What do you mean—you searched this place?"

No apology on his face. "While we were still out on the trail."

Her stomach went into a giant knot and she almost screamed. Closing her eyes, she took a deep breath. Bastards! Thank God, she kept her plans in a safe deposit box, and did all her research on library computers. Her paranoia had paid off. But this made her blood boil.

"That doesn't make me happy at all," she bit out. "But then you know I don't have it." She slipped the piece of toast into the toaster oven, then withdrew a small cast iron pan from the cupboard next to the stove, and set it on a burner. She resisted the urge to pound him across the face with it.

His gaze lasered into her. "You stashed it somewhere in Seattle. Why? All you were supposed to do was to verify that Linda Anderson was having an affair with Rollin. Why would you care about a packet of information that doesn't pertain to you? What's at stake here?"

She tsked and faced him again. "Burke, I don't have the package."

His expression remained fixed and hard. "I know you have it. I just can't figure out how that packet of information relates to your past. All your secrets somehow connect. You recognized someone. Perhaps the same person who you think is trying to kill you."

Her stomach spun and convulsed and spasmed like she was trying to digest a live alligator. She had no idea how to handle this man. A chess grandmaster. Just her luck!

"Maybe you crossed someone in the packet. Maybe you need that evidence to get your life back. Has to be a mistake you made in your past."

Scowling, she turned away, and took a ceramic bowl out of the cupboard above the stove. "My mistake was trusting you guys. Doing a favor for a friend."

"If you told me what I want to know about Seattle, then I'd have no reason to probe into your life."

"Burke, I haven't even had my breakfast. Could you please back off and let me wake up?"

His brow wrinkled and he looked away. "Of course. If you'll excuse me, I need to talk to Banana." He walked out of the room.

The tightness eased from her gut. God, the guy was overbearing. And before food no less. She took a long draw from her coffee mug and glanced at Burke's broad shoulders as he walked out the front door. Damn it. There was only one sure-fire way to control him. Burke may be tricky, but he was still a man.

But sleeping with him would be crazy and might backfire on her. Still, she'd do whatever she had to. Today, she'd rest and plot. Figure her way out and then execute the plan.

Just as Sam slid the cheese omelet onto her plate, Burke sauntered back into the house. "That's some Crown Victoria you have there," he said with a teasing smile.

Happy for the change of subject, Sam took her plate and moved it to the table. "Doesn't look as cool as it really is. Got a buddy who works at a place where they outfit police cars. He modified mine so the guts are the same as a cop's. Reinforced everything. That baby can withstand a hell of a head-on collision." She sat down and realized that she'd forgotten her coffee.

A small frown. "You frighten me. An obsession with guns and big cars."

Don't think about my guns! She chuckled to cover her reaction, stood and retrieved her coffee. Needed to keep his mind on the car, not her weaponry. Hopefully, he hadn't found her gun safe in the basement. "Yep. Emma thinks I'm a pig for driving Miss Vicky— that's what I call her—"

One side of his mouth turned up. "Tiny Tim's wife?"

As she sat back down at the table, Sam grinned. "Dolly thought Tiny Tim was hysterical. The way I figure it, if have to be in a car, I'm gonna be in a big one, goddamn it. Not Emma's little green, save-the-Earth, Coke can Prius. I'm not driving a vehicle that's pretentious. And says *I'm better than you.* Mine says: I'm a pimp or a cop. Or get the hell out of my way or I'll run you down because I'm old, rich and blind."

Burke laughed. "See? Frightening."

Sam chuckled and ate a bite of breakfast.

"Speaking of guns, I need to assess your weapons in the basement. Will you show them to me?"

Her stomach convulsed and she spit the eggs onto the plate.

Burke laughed.

Idiot! Cover your reaction! "Too hot." She turned red, and fanned her mouth. Her heart pumped hard. No fucking way! "What weapons?"

"The ones in your gun safe. I could get into it fairly easily, but I'd rather have you show me."

Her muscles went hard and she fisted her hands under the table. It had taken her a lot of time, energy and money to secure those weapons. And once he saw them, he'd be onto her.

"I only have a couple old ones down there. Not much to look at."

"For security purposes, I still need to see them. I need to know if any of them can be used against us in case the Cabal attacks. Or if we can use them to protect you if it comes to that."

"Oh." How was she supposed to explain the sniper gear? She'd pretend she didn't know much about the rifles. Tell him that she got the guns from an old boyfriend. "Okay, after I eat." She tried to enjoy her eggs, but her stomach was too tight.

While Burke read the paper, she stalled as long as she could. She washed the dishes and swept the kitchen floor and tried to think of any reason she could to keep from showing him her arsenal. But she came up with nothing. So she wiped down the front of the fridge and the cupboards, something she never did.

When he began to eyeball her again, she knew she'd taken too long. Her stomach jittery, she led him down to the basement.

As she walked down the narrow wooden stairwell, she ducked the big overhead crossbeam. "Watch your head."

"I see that."

The damp, musty and dark room with low ceilings was half-filled with boxes of books. She flicked on two rows of overhead fluorescent lights, illuminating the wall of boxes.

"More books?" Burke asked in an incredulous tone.

"Uh-huh. Need to cull my collection, but I really have a hard time parting with books. They're my only weakness." *Other than men like you.*

Her heart rate increasing with each step, she went to the far corner of the basement where the large gun safe stood, covered by a canvas tarp. She lifted off the fabric, rolled it up, and tossed it on the cement floor.

Felt like she was taking off all her clothes at gunpoint. Damn this man! Why did he have to notice her gun locker? Jerk better not take her precious weapons. She'd kill him before she let that happen.

Putting her hand on the combination lock, she sent a furtive glance over her shoulder at Burke.

He chuckled. "I could probably get into that as fast as you can."

She frowned, spun the dial, and opened the large cabinet. Swinging the door outward, she stepped back.

Burke went slack-jawed and his eyes grew large. "A couple old ones? Try a full arsenal." He looked at her like he didn't know her and then moved forward to inspect the weapons.

Damn it! Exactly the reaction she feared.

Of course, it was fairly obvious that her interest in guns went far beyond sporting.

He stared in disbelief at her astounding array of sniper weapons and semi-automatic rifles. "Uh, starting a war soon, Sam?"

This was so *bad*. "No. They just make me feel safe."

"They don't make me feel safe." He withdrew her prized Barrett M107 high-powered sniper rifle—which was almost as long as she was tall—and she held her breath.

Worst fear realized, he went right for the identification. Which had been professionally removed. Stupid rotten luck!

His expression went dark and he turned to her and raised a brow. "Sam? Do you realize how illegal it is to own this?"

"No. Why?" She tried to feign innocence.

"You know full well what I'm talking about. Who are you planning on killing?"

The room did a spin and she fought for a neutral expression. She whipped up some anger to cover her fear. "What are you talking about?"

"Don't lie to me, Sam. This is the weapon of an assassin. Why else would you own one?"

"Because I love guns," she said as casually as she could. "And I love to blow the shit outta stuff. We take these suckers out to the desert at a buddy's house and we shoot the hell out of all this junk he's collected. Refrigerators, logs, dishwashers. Then we blast melons and pumpkins. Culminating in a propane tank. Exciting."

Burke didn't buy a word. Even though it was partially the truth. "Sam, this is a professional sniper's rifle. Where did you get it?"

"Old boyfriend. I've had all those guns for years."

He pointed to a rifle in front of the large stash. "The Tac-Ops Green Hornet sniper rifle is new," he stated with a glare. "And not easy to come by. You worked very hard to assemble this weaponry."

"*Some* of the guns I've had for years."

As he perused the rest of the contents of the safe, his jaw tightened. "Kevlar vests, flash-bangs and Tasers." He turned to her. "Explain those," he demanded.

"Jimmy, my cop ex," Sam said as the lie came to her. "Presents."

Burke's eyes and nostrils flared, and his face flushed red. "Fine. Don't tell me. But you're keeping a load of information from me, Sam. I'm only trying to save your sorry hide and all you do is fight me. Why do you have this arsenal? Who are you afraid of?"

"No one and everyone."

"I have no idea why I'm bothering. Look, don't use these while we're protecting you. You let us do the job. Do you understand me?"

"Yeah."

"Good." His attention went back to her guns. "Very dangerous," he muttered. He examined her face like he could find the truth there.

She hated his mind. Almost no way to combat it. He'd guessed everything about her so far. Getting away from him fast was her only defense. She shut the gun locker and spun the dial.

When she turned back to him, his expression had softened. "Sam, honestly, I'm not trying to pull something over on you. I'm worried about you. Someone hurt you badly. And you want revenge. But revenge doesn't make anyone happy. Least of all, you. You're not a killer. Why won't you let me help?"

She looked him dead in the eye. "Because you're untrustworthy."

He winced nearly imperceptibly. "All right. I'll stop pushing. I just want you to know that you can come to me. And I'll do my best to help you figure your way out of your problems."

"And what's in it for you?" she snapped.

A flash of anger sparked in his eyes, then sympathy. His pain lines deepened. "I wouldn't do anything to harm you, Sam."

Her stomach tightened and she distanced herself from his reaction. Damn it, he was actually getting to her. She almost felt bad for being mean to the overbearing jerk. Irritated, she said, "Yes, you would. If you had to or thought you had to. You'd hurt me plenty. You might even convince yourself it was for my own good, but you'd hurt me to get your objectives accomplished."

"And you'd hurt me."

She snorted. "You? You're impervious to pain."

A brief raise of his brows and a chuckle. He glanced away. "Talk to my last girlfriend about that."

"Girlfriend? You? Let me guess. Lasted a week."

"Six months. We split two weeks ago."

Her mind did a jog. No way had she taken him for the long-term type. Burke? With feelings? Say it ain't so. "You miss her?"

"Yes. But she was too self-destructive and I couldn't save her. And finally after this last drama, I was done. And so was she. She ended it." His gaze hollow, his attention on her boxes of books, he absently ran his forefinger down the scar on the left side of his face.

His gaze was unguarded; he clearly spoke the truth. He wasn't saying it for effect, he was talking about a matter that had meant a great deal to him. And he had been hurt in the relationship.

Her heart cracked open. Maybe he wasn't a completely soulless bastard. "I'm sorry. I hate the endings of relationships."

"Me, too. But we were pretty detached of late. The last month was…unpleasant."

"Did she give you that scar?"

The look in his eye sharpened and his attention snapped to her.

"You were rubbing it." She pointed at the thin pink line near his eye.

His brows went high, then he gave a barely perceptible nod.

"Did she slice you?"

He rubbed the marred skin. "No. This happened while I was defending her dishonor."

"Huh?"

He smiled, but it wasn't a happy one. "Valerie had, uh, issues. She wasn't a very good person as it turned out. Thought I could save her."

"So she fucked someone over and you protected her?"

"Yes. Which quickly became a full-time job. Exhausting. I believe relationships should add to your life, not subtract."

Sam gave a knowing nod. "Agreed. I just ended a one-year relationship about three months ago for that very reason." Bending down, she snatched a book from the floor that had fallen, and placed it back on top of the stack of boxes.

"So what happened?"

Her jaw hardened with anger and she growled. "Tried to get me to sign him onto my deed here. Damn, he seemed so together. Good job, good history, fun, smart, well-educated, then we get together and suddenly, he's all dependent and wants me to take care of him. So sick of that. I should have known better than to date a Masshole."

The edges of his full mouth quirked. "A Masshole?"

Sam grinned. "Snob from Massachusetts. Gotta stay away from Massholes, Vermonsters and Maine-iacs. Never met anyone from those states that I liked. I wasn't even going to date for a while, but I got on Match.com and found Paul and, well, here I go again. Even though, I'll bet you two bucks Paul will be running the other way soon."

"Not sure about that."

"I am. Unless this thing gets resolved. And I hope it does soon, because I can't take being home for very long without losing my mind."

"And we wouldn't want that to happen," he said with a little sparkle in his eye.

A tingle went through her. Damn, the man was hot. And so horribly fucking charming.

Burke climbed the stairs and she got an excellent look at his magnificent ass.

If only she'd met him at another time and another place…

In the early afternoon, Burke listened at Sam's door. Snoring. Good. She needed the nap and he needed the privacy. He walked into her library and called Bobby.

"What the hell you want, old man?" came Bobby's cheerful reply.

Burke snorted. "I thought Rollin talked to you about that moniker."

"Who's Monica?"

"Not Monica, *moniker*. I'll send you the link to the description."

"Don't want it. Know enough English. What do you want?" Sounds of crunching came over the phone.

"Don't tell me what food crime you're eating." Burke ran his finger over a set of world history books. A series he owned as well.

"Pork rinds." Exaggerated munching and lip smacking came over the receiver.

"For God's sake. Where are we on the surveillance footage on Sam?"

Heavy sigh. "We've recovered some footage, none with the package. Mailman who delivered that day went on vacation that night, he's camping and can't be reached for another three days. I broke into USPS computer, but since Joe didn't send the package using a tracking number, all I could find was that six packages were delivered that day to the apartment building in Seattle. Got two guys working on recovering more video, but this could take another day or so."

"But since no package has been delivered to Linda Anderson by any other service, we know Sam has it."

"Unless it got lost."

"Unlikely. Okay, I need information on some slang terms Sam used. I think it might lead us to her home or home state. Which East Coast state or city calls their neighbors Massholes, Vermonsters and Maine-iacs? Has to be New York or New Hampshire or Connecticut. New Hampshire would make the most sense since those three states surround it. We want teenage girls who went missing during the years of 1992, 1993 or 1994. Or a suspected homicide victim, but with the body missing. Pull up any pictures you can find."

"Okie-dokie." Crunching sounds, followed by a long slurp.

Burke lingered on a small framed picture of Sam and Emma dressed to the nines in Vegas, holding cocktails and laughing. Charming. "Also find out who's doing military training of civilians around the Bay Area. Find out if Sam's name comes up on a student list. I also want to know what guns she has registered."

"You got it," Bobby replied.

"What did you find on her hard drive?" He removed a few books and felt behind them for hidden objects. Nothing but dust.

"Not much." Bobby burped. "If she is planning something or keeping track of some guy, she isn't doing it on her computer."

Burke put the books back. "Covering her tracks…damn." He paced to the other side of the tiny room. "What did you find out about Paul Strong?"

"He checked out. A little too perfectly. I think you're right. While he's listed as an employee of DAE, his cubicle is empty and he's not on any of the meeting schedules. He may be CIA. Maybe Cabal. I've got some friends inside the CIA working on getting that information now."

"Good."

"He's got money, too. Sitting on a hundred and twenty million in assets. Has a big place at Lake Tahoe and a mansion in Washington D.C. That house in San Mateo is his cheapest house. Only one and a half mil."

Burke's face twisted in confusion. "If he has that much money, why does he drive a *Suburban*?"

"Maybe he's not like you, old man. Maybe he doesn't like all the bling."

"Everyone likes bling."

"I don't."

Burke thought of Bobby's two-carat diamond stud earrings and his thick gold chain and laughed. "Oh, right. What about those rocks in your ears and the anchor of gold around your neck?"

"They're so big, people think they're fake. Little skinny Asian dude like me? What could I have?"

"A new Porsche, three houses, four motorcycles, and ten classic cars."

Banana walked outside the window below him, patrolling the area, his long blond hair blowing around his shoulders in the ever present San Mateo wind.

"I got a big family." Another burp.

"A wife and two toddlers."

"Big to me," Bobby replied cheerfully. "When you gonna settle down, old man? Have some kids. Buy a house in the 'burbs. Mow the lawn." He burst into his infamous donkey laugh. "Oh, that picture's so funny. Beer belly and a folding chair in the backyard while the kids play in the sprinklers. Start drinking Bud Light."

Burke sighed loudly. "Are you done?"

Exaggerated, delighted, hee-haws. "Honey? You want me to put the hotdogs on the barbecue?" he called out, doing an imitation of Domesticated Burke.

Burke finally started laughing. "If that happens, you have permission to kill me."

"Nah. You need a nice girl, like Rollin."

"Rollin's already taken."

Bobby gave one hee-haw. "You know what I mean. You need a wife. Rollin 'n me been talking."

"Now you're frightening me."

"We like Sam."

"Back to Paul Strong."

"You like her," Bobby teased in a long drawl.

"*Back to Paul Strong*. Dig as deep as you can."

"Will do. Sam Cherlenko has a nice ring to it, don't you think?" Bobby released a series of high-pitched hee-haws.

More than you could ever know. "I'm hanging up now." Guy was as relentless as Rollin when it came to teasing. Damn them both. They'd better keep their mouths shut. He didn't want to scare off Sam this early.

Marriage. To Sam.

Exciting. Terrifying. Challenging.

Damn, it might just work.

Was she the one?

He sighed.

She'd kill him.

FIVE

Sam woke up and checked the clock. Seven. She wanted to sleep in, but Burke would be there by eight. No way would she let him see her with morning face.

She kicked herself. What the hell did it matter what she looked like? What did it matter what he thought of her?

Still, she needed to be awake to handle him. At least this is what she told herself. After she spent ten minutes instead of her usual five applying her make-up, she grew even more disgusted.

Burke arrived at eight sharp looking horribly cute. Black distressed jeans, a long-sleeved blue collared shirt, and some expensive looking shoes. Not one thread was out of place. No one could be this perfect.

He sent her a little smirk, which morphed into a smile. Already playing a game and he'd just arrived. "You look nice this morning," he said, giving her an up and down examination.

"Thanks. You, too, Snidely Whiplash."

He pursed his lips. "Insults so soon?"

"Teasing."

A wicked grin came over his handsome face. "Teasing. I like the sound of that."

"Too early for flirting, Burke."

"It's never too early for flirting."

"And the games start."

"Tell me what I want to know and I won't have to play any games."

"You are annoying and I've only had one cup of coffee so far."

"Coffee sounds good." He walked past her and into the kitchen like he'd lived there for years. "I brought some beans. Your coffee was great, but I wanted you to try this kind." He reached into the cupboard and pulled out her coffee grinder.

He already knew where everything was.

She followed him as far as the doorway and leaned against it. "Okie-dokie. Oh, Rollin said it was cool that I see Paul tonight. Did he talk to you?"

Burke's expression went cold. Turning his back to her, he used the coffee grinder, filling the air with noise. Ground the beans for a long few seconds. After setting the grinder on the counter, he withdrew coffee filters from the cupboard.

His response was like a giant flashing billboard that read: *I'M JEALOUS!*

"So he talked to you about it?"

He didn't turn around. "He did."

"And it's cool."

"Yes, of course," he replied in a flippant tone, but his underlying fury seeped in. "We have the security detail all set up."

She couldn't resist torturing him. This was so fun! "Great. Paul called last night after you left. He wants to cook for me. Homemade ravioli. Sounds heavenly, doesn't it?"

Burke angled a glare at her.

She had to hold back laughter.

The phone rang.

Burke watched Sam answer her phone. She looked past good this morning, she looked dynamite. Pink, orange and white flowered Capri pants that made her ass look good enough to eat, paired with a cute orange tank top that showed off her luscious curves and tanned, toned arms. When could he get her into bed? Even a second was too long to

wait. He had her all to himself that day. By the end of it, he'd make
sure she forgot she had a date.

She didn't care about Paul. Burke had seen the way she'd looked at
him when he'd walked in that morning. She'd been happy to see him
and had spent quality time inspecting his clothes and body. Loved
everything she saw. She wanted him, all right. Paul was a smoke
screen because he frightened her. Why else would she tease him so
mercilessly?

But, goddamn, he wanted to beat the shit out of that Paul fucker.
Scare him away. Claim his territory by sticking his dick in her like a
country's flag on a newly captured mountain.

But the Patriots had decided to let Sam see Strong with the hopes
that he'd show his hand. They'd wired the house and would have a
team ready in case Strong tried to hurt her. God help the bastard if he
laid a hand on her.

Sam's expression went to stone and she held the receiver tighter to
her ear. "What? Just calm down, Lisa. Where are you? No, I'm on my
way. Just stay locked in there. Don't come out for anything." She hung
up, her face pale. "Shit." She quickly punched in a number.

"What?"

Her face etched with concern, she held up her hand to quiet him.
"Emma? Jimmy's got Lisa trapped in the bathroom and he's lost it.
Can you meet me there in ten? Yeah, bring some bags, we're moving
her out. I don't care if she fights us, this has gone too far. I have Burke
and Banana with me and we're gonna need 'em. Okay, ten."

No way were they leaving the house. Burke opened his mouth to
speak.

Sam pointed at him, her face hard. "Shut it. I'm going to go rescue
my friend and there is no way you can stop me. I need you to get
Banana and we're going in my car. I'm driving. There's no way I'm
letting a 280 pound man beat up my friend."

He sighed with exasperation. "Why don't you call the police?"

"Because Jimmy's a cop."

"Well, they should know one of their—"

"He has sole custody of his daughter and he'll lose her and that can't happen. His ex-wife is a meth addict living on the streets of San Jose. Now get Banana and wait in the car, I need my purse." She hustled away from him.

Grabbing her by the arm, he stopped her. "Sam—"

She ripped out of his grip and sent him a look that made his stomach wrench. "Don't try it," she growled.

Holy God, what a force of nature. Thankfully, he had the whole neighborhood under tight surveillance and nothing was out of the ordinary that morning. He let out a groan of frustration and went to find Banana.

Soon they were in Sam's gigantic Crown Victoria, barreling through an older and established San Mateo neighborhood. She drove like a maniac: cutting corners and blowing through stop signs. He'd considered taking over, but so far, they hadn't had any near misses or even close calls.

Sam's brow sat hard over her beautiful hazel eyes. "Those idiots! I told them this would happen. I told her to stay away from him. They had such high chemistry, I knew it would end badly. I mean, didn't she learn anything from me? Dude is a needy, controlling bastard. Loves his daughter, but he's a train wreck."

Burke stared at her. "You went out with him? Did he ever hurt you?"

"Me? Are you nuts? No. I had that boy cowed in a day."

Burke inwardly chuckled. She'd met her match in him. He'd rein her in like a wild pony. "Let me guess, that's about the time you lost interest."

"Pretty much. I loved his kid, so I hung in there longer than I should have. Lisa's way too nice for the guy. He's someone you have to keep on a short leash or he'll control your whole life."

Burke eyed Sam. Was she jumping into this chaotic scene to distract herself from her own issues? Or really trying to help a friend? "I'm concerned. Domestic disturbances can escalate fast. Sure you want to get in the middle of this?"

"No. But no one can handle him like I can. I'm just pissed I'm being put in this position," she spat. "If I didn't care about his kid so much, I'd call the cops, and let his coworkers handle him. I bonded with that girl. Kara. She's fourteen now. Was eleven when I got involved with her father. I still take her out once a month to keep up with her. Nice kid. Terrible living situation. I'm trying to keep her sane. Despite all this horrible drama. I'm so sick of Jimmy. Narcissistic jerk."

She sounded reasonable. Whether she was or not remained to be seen.

As it turned out, Sam was extremely reasonable. With one word, she had the large, screaming, red-faced police officer under control. Twenty minutes later, they were back on the road. Emma had left a few minutes before they did with a crying Lisa and her belongings, apparently headed to a relative of Lisa's.

"Well, that was a load of bullshit," Sam bit out as she left the street and turned onto a four-lane thoroughfare.

Examining her sweet face, he grinned. She had much more depth, reason and people skills than he realized. This woman wasn't a trifle, she was solid, and worth her weight in platinum. "You handled that very well."

"Thanks. I hope that's the end of it. I mean, come on, screaming and pounding on doors and all that whining? Why can't adults act like adults?"

Burke thought about his relationship with Valerie and inwardly cringed. Yes, far too much drama and screaming and pounding on doors. He was glad it was over. But he certainly missed having a woman in his bed.

Sam stopped at a stop sign and he gazed at her face. That small nose with the slight bump in the middle, her full lips, and electric hazel eyes. Gorgeous. He wondered what it would be like to grow old with her. His entire body warmed and a charge went through his dick. She'd never be boring and would never lose her fire.

Beyond her, through the window, a truck bore down on them fast, clearly intent on ramming their car.

Adrenaline flooded his system. "Sam! Watch out!"

Screaming, her eyes large, she slammed on the gas. Burke was thrust back against his seat.

The truck barely missed the back of her car.

"Assholes!" Sam exclaimed, her face red and twisted with fury.

The truck spun a u-turn and pursued them.

His body buzzing and his heart racing, Burke opened his mouth to take control of the situation.

Sam cut him off. "Men! Guns out! We're under attack!"

More or less what he'd planned to say. "Good plan, Sam, but let me give the orders, okay?" Burke whipped out his Lugar and Banana withdrew his Kimber 1911.

Sam focused on the street in front of her. "I'll lose 'em. I know every street in this town!"

Banana hung out the window and shot at the large black SUV.

The passenger, a man in dark glasses, returned fire.

The back window shattered. Burke ducked, his heart thumping against his sternum.

Sam screamed and hit the gas. "Hold on, boys!" She hung a sharp right. The Crown Victoria's tires screamed in protest, but she managed to keep the large boat of a car upright.

He'd prepared to take over the driving, but she was doing fine.

A half a block later, she veered left, toward an oncoming school bus.

Gasping, his heart stopped and his limbs froze. Spoke too soon! "Sam!" he yelled, stomping the floorboards as if the brake pedal were there.

The school bus driver's mouth opened wide in a scream and she laid on the horn.

"Don't worry!" Sam shouted.

She missed the school bus by inches and suddenly they were bombing down a skinny alley. Wooden fences, overhanging flowering shrubs and garage doors flew by in a blur. Slamming the throttle, she pressed him back against the seat.

He could barely breathe.

He checked her expression and posture to make sure she was in control and wasn't overwhelmed with emotion. Sam reminded him of a race car driver: fierce, focused, determined. With a decided lack of fear. Scary as hell. But she was handling the situation fine. For now.

Another half block later, she pulled the wheel to the right and aimed for a solid wall of ivy.

Every instinct told him to jump out of the car.

"Sam!" Banana yelled in his ear.

"No worries!"

Burke gasped and braced his hands on the dash and pushed back against the floor with his feet.

They blasted through the plant matter and ended up in another tiny alley.

His pounding heart couldn't take much more.

Sam checked her rear view. "I think I lost 'em."

Burke let out a sigh of relief and forced a composed exterior. "Good job."

"Fuck me," Banana mumbled.

Sam shot him a confident grin and gestured. "Now, do I hide or try to get back home?"

"Back home." He scanned the surroundings, but couldn't get oriented. "Wait, where are we?"

"We're about to come out on Maple. We're only about fifteen blocks from the house."

Burke withdrew his cell from his pocket and pressed Rollin's number on his cell. "You there?"

"Present and accounted for, sir," Rollin said in his "nerd" voice.

Burke caught him up on the situation. "We're headed to Sam's now."

"Sam's kickin' some ass today, isn't she?" Rollin replied in his natural voice. "Emma told me how she handled Jimmy. Guy's a nut job. I almost killed the idiot once."

Burke enjoyed a long, lingering examination of Sam's sweet features. Her razor sharp hazel eyes, the confident tilt to her chin, and the strong set to her slim shoulders. Her intoxicating scent filled the car. "She was pretty amazing."

Sam did a double-take and her face pinched. "Stop trying to butter me up!"

"Shut up, wench," he countered.

She shot him a surprised look, her brows raised. Turning back to the road, she fought a chuckle, forced a straight face, and huffed. "Boris Badenov."

His dick went hard. "And she's exceedingly trying," he drawled into the receiver.

Rollin laughed. "See you at her place."

Sam's mouth quirked to one side and she pointed at him. "I'm gonna take Alameda. El Camino's too exposed."

He shrugged. She knew the town better than he did.

They drove up a residential street and hit a green light at Alameda de las Pulgas. Sam took a left and drove down the four-lane thoroughfare toward her house.

They passed 20th Avenue, went up over a rise, and down again.

A half a block in front of them, a black SUV jumped the median and aimed straight at them.

His pulse skyrocketed, and his body hyped up and readied for action.

"Those fuckers!" Sam's eyes narrowed, her teeth bared, she barked, "Hold on, Banana! These bastards are going down!" Slamming on the gas, she headed for the SUV.

Burke's heart beat so hard he could barely breathe. "Sam! Stop!" He reached for the steering wheel and she punched his hand away.

His knuckles burning, he yelled, "Goddamn it, Sam!" He lunged for the wheel and grabbed it.

She smashed down on his wrist, but he hung on. "Fuck them! Die motherfuckers!"

"Sam, let go!"

The two men in the oncoming SUV screamed, their mouths open wide.

Banana roared in his ear. Burke said a brief good-bye to the world, his last regret was not fucking Sam.

At the very last millisecond, the oncoming SUV veered to its right, popped up on the median, caught air, and spun. Landing in the path of several cars in the middle of the opposite lanes, the sport vehicle rolled over and over.

Horns honked and cars skidded, but missed the rolling truck.

"Whew! Shit! I should have thought about the other cars!" Sam exclaimed, slamming on the brakes. "Duh! Thank God, those assholes missed 'em!"

The SUV finally came to a stop on its roof on the sidewalk.

His entire body pumping with adrenaline, every muscle solid as granite, his heart drilling a hole through his ribs, Burke worked hard to breathe. Letting go of the wheel, he clutched his chest.

Sam flipped a U-turn and headed back to the overturned SUV. "Let's get 'em!"

He contemplated strangling her. "Jesus Christ, Sam, will you warn us before you play chicken with hired killers?"

"Who was playing chicken?"

He stammered for a second, staring at her with his mouth open. "Are you crazy? You almost killed us!"

"I got air bags," she said like he was the one with mental problems. "This car is super reinforced."

He could only gape at her audacity.

Banana burst into raucous laughter. "I love this girl! Who was playing chicken!" He roared and slapped his thighs. "I got air bags!"

"We wouldn't have died. But those guys might." She sped toward the overturned enemy vehicle.

A new dump of fight-or-flight juices swamped Burke's system. "Sam! Don't! We need to know who they are!"

"Oh." Sam slammed on the brakes, the Crown Vic skidded sideways and came to a stop five feet from the front end of the truck.

Holding his stomach, Burke almost puked. "I'm never letting you drive again."

"Don't be silly, I wasn't going to kill them. Just teach 'em a lesson. Oh, look," she said, pointing out the windshield, "Rollin's here. And Ty."

Rollin raced up to the enemy driver's window with his gun drawn. Ty covered the passenger.

"Don't go anywhere," Burke snapped. Drenched with sweat, he got out and found his legs shaky. A wind whipped up and chilled his body. Damn that woman!

He rubbed the moisture from his forehead and approached the two Patriots.

Rollin hit the driver with the butt of his pistol and the guy cried out. "Who hired you?"

"I don't know!"

"That's not the right answer."

There was a thump and the passenger yelled.

Ty had punched him. "Who hired you?" the brawny Aussie demanded.

Sirens wailed from blocks away.

"Who?" Rollin yelled.

"A guy named Eric McDonald," the driver groaned. "But that's not his real name."

Ty grabbed the other man's ID and two weapons.

Rollin reached into the car and withdrew the man's wallet and gun. He checked the street and turned to Burke, flashing a lop-sided grin. "Let's get out of here. I'll meet you at Sam's. And tell her not to play chicken on the way home, okay?"

The image of that truck coming at them was burned in Burke's mind forever. "Did you see that?"

Rollin laughed. "How could I miss it? You all right?"

His jaw twitched. "No. I'm going to kill her. Or she's going to kill me."

Rollin shook his head, turned away, and jogged to his car.

Burke walked back and stood at Sam's door. "Get out."

"No, I'm driving."

"Hell you are, lady. Get out or I'll drag you out."

"Cops are almost here, get in the car!" Sam yelled.

He scowled at her. "If the police weren't about to arrive, I'd throw you in the trunk." He reluctantly went around and slid inside. After securing his seat belt, he jabbed a finger in her face. "If you pull one more stunt like that, I will personally tear up your license."

Sam rolled her eyes and eased out into traffic. "You are overreacting."

"If my head had blown clean off my shoulders, the reaction would not be too severe," he bit out at her. "Insane lunatic! When I grab the fucking steering wheel, you let go!"

She shrugged, unaffected. "Whatever."

"No, not 'whatever', you listen to me!"

Unmoved, sent him a bored look. "We're fine."

His pulse pounding in his ears, he treated himself to a nice fantasy of turning her over his knee.

Banana chuckled all the way back to the house. Burke concentrated on regaining his equilibrium. The woman was a human atomic weapon.

Rollin and Ty arrived right when they pulled up. As soon as the group walked into the house, Sam headed for her refrigerator.

She shook her head and rubbed her forehead. "What did I say about drama? I need a beer. Anyone else want one?"

"Yes," Burke answered quickly. He followed her into the kitchen.

Banana nodded vigorously as he joined them. "Shit, yeah."

"Got any tequila?" Rollin said as he sauntered in. "Watchin' you almost killed me."

Burke leaned back against the counter and crossed his arms. "You should have been in the car. I can't believe I survived," he said dryly.

Sam handed out beers to everyone, him last. She sent him a grin. "I thought you guys were Navy SEALs. Both you and Banana screamed like little girls."

Rollin and Ty broke out in belly laughs.

Her words stung his ego, but tweaked his dick. He'd make the little brat pay for that line. Squaring his shoulders, he faced his tormentor. "Your driving would make a corpse come back to life and scream like a little girl."

Banana nodded. "I almost crapped my pants."

Sam made a face. "I had everything under control. I've gotten out of worse scrapes than that."

"Please don't tell me," Burke said, holding up his hand. "Not now. After the beer." He took a long, exaggerated draw off the Heineken.

The group cracked up.

The woman was certifiable. And the hottest lady he'd ever met. He thought he'd wanted her before. All he could think about was pinning her to her bed with his dick so she couldn't get into any more trouble.

Every resource in his brain tuned to the challenge.

This would be the most fun conquest ever.

Late that afternoon, Burke worked on his computer in the living room while Sam read on the opposite couch.

Gasping, she stared at her watch. "Holy shit, it's after six already? I have to get ready. I'm supposed to be at Paul's in forty-five minutes." She put down her book and stood.

"Are you sure you want to go out?"

"Why not? I'm still alive." She yawned and stretched. "When you're alive you gotta live. If I stop livin' they might as well kill me."

A wave of lust and admiration made his body go hot. Nothing would ever stop this woman. He smiled, utterly charmed. "Will you tell him about your day?"

"Hell no. I don't want to scare him off anymore than I already have."

"Will you be spending the night?"

Pursing her lips, she crossed her arms. "Subtle, Burke."

He sent her a look like he thought she'd lost her mind. "Hello? I'm protecting you?"

"Oh," she replied, startled. Her brow wrinkled a bit. Then her shoulders relaxed.

She believed him, good. He had to be careful with her. Had to make it her idea to come to him.

She gave a quick shake of her head. "No. Love to stay the night, but no. I don't want Paul to think I'm easy. And it's such bullshit," she said with disgust. "I am easy if I like the guy. But if I bag the man too soon, I take the train straight to Slutville."

He laughed at her candor. "The right man wouldn't judge you."

"Bullshit. I've met plenty of the right men and they do judge me. It's a societal thing."

"You haven't met the right man yet."

"No, I'm looking for love. You can't find love if you do the guy too soon," she said matter-of-factly. "After five dates at the earliest."

"I disagree. Valerie and I met and it was a rather swift trip to the bed. I didn't disrespect her. I hate games. I'd rather have honesty from the beginning."

"Yeah, and you and Valerie worked out so well."

He made a face. "Same with Toni, my girlfriend in college. And we lasted five years."

"Well, okay, maybe there's one man on the planet who's like that, but I ain't datin' you."

He had to fight a smug grin. *Not yet, you aren't. But you will.*

"I'm dating Paul and goddamn it," she said with a sharp gesture. "I'm gonna make him think I'm more of a lady than I really am."

He tilted his head to one side. "Subterfuge and so early?"

"Shit yeah." She thrust out her chin.

"Do you swear as much around him?"

She kept a straight face. "Shit no." She laughed. "Must keep up pretenses for awhile. Although, he has seen some of my, uh, outbursts. Like when I punched you. Oh, well, that will only serve as a warning not to screw with me. He can screw me, fine, but he'd better not screw *with* me." Bursting into laughter, she turned away. "Okay, I gotta get going." She stopped and swung back. "How long you hangin' around?"

"Another hour. I'll be escorting you to Paul's. Banana and David will take over at that point and drive you home at the end of the evening."

"Okay," she said and left.

Twenty minutes later, Burke was perusing the meager information Bobby had recovered on Miss Samantha Murdock when she walked into the room, holding a black leather jacket.

His jaw dropped and his cock raged to action.

Absolutely stunning. Her lined, yet sheer black top—with its see-through sleeves and tight stretchy solid tank—clung to her magnificent breasts leaving little to the imagination. Something about the sheer material over her gorgeous curves conjured images of her naked under a negligee. Lovely. Her black pants fit like a second skin; featuring and highlighting the line of her long legs and the rise of her luscious ass. Strappy three-inch black sandals completed the outfit. Casual yet dressy, boyish yet feminine, she'd struck the perfect balance between sex and style. Even with the subtle gold trim on both the pants and the top, the outfit was understated and tasteful. While all he could think of was how she'd look out of it, she looked like a million dollars. He couldn't have picked a better outfit. The woman knew how to show off her assets.

His tongue was probably hanging out of his mouth, so he casually allowed his face to go to neutral. But he didn't dare stand. "You look nice."

"Thanks. Think Paul will like it?"

"He'd have to be blind and stupid not to."

She grinned, making him want to jump up, sweep her off her feet, and kiss her.

And then drill her straight through the mattress and fuck her all the way to China.

"Oh, yeah, my purse," she said, turning and walking back to her room.

Thank you. He adjusted his raging hard-on and stood.

When she walked out, every hormone in his system demanded he take her.

Had to watch himself. The woman already had too much power over him. He needed to take things slow. To catch and keep a woman like Sam, he had to have all his wits about him.

But he wasn't worried about Paul. Clearly, she was using the man to distance herself from him. She wanted him. And badly. Half the reason she'd worn that outfit was for his benefit.

As he escorted her to the car, her necklace caught his attention. An oval gold pendant with a clear glass center filled with loose diamonds hung on a sparkling gold chain. Looked damned familiar. But it couldn't be.

After they got settled in his Mercedes, he gestured toward her. "Where did you get that necklace?"

"Emma, why? Do you like it?" Sam asked, fingering the gold chain.

A punch to his gut made him skip a breath. "Uh…yes. Very nice."

Sam leaned in and checked his expression carefully. "Why do you look so weird? It's just some cheap costume jewelry."

He went into a coughing fit. Fifteen thousand dollars wasn't chump change.

"What's the matter with you? Some old boyfriend gave it to her. She said he got it at Walmart or something—"

A plume of steam shot from his gut and nearly made his head explode. "Walmart!"

Sam's brow wrinkled. Then her eyes shone and the corners of her mouth slowly rose into a sly smile. "You got it for her."

He tried to close off his expression, but he'd clearly blown it.

Sam laughed delightedly. "You did!" She pushed him on the shoulder. Then all the color left her face and her jaw dropped. "Holy shit, this isn't fake."

"No."

She gasped and clutched the necklace. "Holy bejeebus, do you know how many places I've tossed this thing? Christ all mighty—wait. How much is this worth? How much did it cost?"

"I'd rather not say."

"Where'd you get it?"

"Steiners."

"Steiners?" Sam shouted. "Oh, my God, I love that place. I've always wanted jewelry from there. Steiners, wow." She gazed down at the pendant. "I thought this looked pretty sophisticated for Walmart."

His blood pressure skyrocketed. "Walmart. I can't believe her."

Sam eyed him suspiciously. "She referred to you as her old boyfriend. I think she liked you a lot more than she let on. No wonder you fell for her, she fell for you."

His foundation shifted slightly. He quickly regained control. "That's what I thought, but she denied it."

"Yeah, no wonder Emma had that strange expression on her face when she handed it to me. Like she didn't really want to let go of it. She mumbled something about having to move on and let go of the past."

New information. While he'd known that Emma had been attracted to him, he hadn't believed she'd returned his deeper feelings. "She didn't give it to you as a wrapped gift?"

"No. About two months ago, we were going out and I forgot my jewelry at home. So we went through her jewelry box so I could borrow a necklace. I saw this and whooped it was so pretty. She picked it up, looked at it for a long few seconds, then handed it to me and said, 'Here, keep it.' Of course, I argued, but then she gave me the story. I mean, she didn't mention the dude's name, but it was clear she'd been hung up on him. You know? I think she actually loved you," she said like it had been the last thing on her mind.

He arched a brow. "Is that so hard to imagine?"

"No. But you and Emma?" She shuddered. "You guys would have been terrible for each other."

"How so?"

"You'd have owned her," she said and snapped her fingers, "like that. I love the girl, but she's no match for you. And once you conquered her, you would have gotten bored, she would have gotten rebellious, and you'd have killed each other."

Dead on. He nodded slightly. "Agreed."

"You want this back?" She reached for the back of the necklace to unclasp it.

He held up his hand. "No, please, keep it."

"You sure?"

"Positive. It suits you. Better than Emma, I think." He allowed himself a satisfied smile.

"Really? I feel weird now." She touched the pendant.

"Don't."

"So how much was it?"

"I'm not saying." He started the car.

"You know I'm going straight to Steiners to find out, don't you?"

So saucy! He laughed. "You are so bad." He pulled away from the curb and headed down the street.

Giggling, she shook the pendant, her eyes shining at the diamonds. "Real," she whispered.

A rush of pleasure went through him. His mark on her and so soon. Now she had a reminder of him around her neck on her date with that asshole. He couldn't have planned this better.

"Wicked cool. Do I need to have it insured?"

"I would."

"So when I call my insurance guy, how much should I tell him to insure it for?" She couldn't keep a straight face and laughed.

Enchanted, he could only shake his head. "When you call your insurance agent, I'll get on the phone."

"Oh, come on."

"No."

As he drove her to Strong's, some part of him realized he was giving her over to the competition. He'd show her a much better time. Limo, expensive restaurant, club and an after dinner drink on his deck. Followed by a fuck-a-thon the likes of which she'd never experienced.

But for the time being he'd play it cool, like he wasn't that interested. And he'd be right there when it didn't work out with Paul. After the bastard revealed himself to be a spy. Hopefully, soon.

He walked her up to Paul's door. Strong didn't even try to hide his reaction when he saw Sam. His tongue lolled, his eyeballs bugged out of his head, and he looked like a male dog surrounded by forty female dogs in heat. So smooth. Burke almost punched the moron.

Sam stepped forward and kissed Paul on the cheek. "Hi, Paul."

"Wow. Sam. You look *amazing*," the dickhead gushed.

She burst into a radiant smile.

It took all of Burke's inner strength to give a casual nod, wish them well and walk away. All he could think about was picking her up, throwing her into the Mercedes and whisking her to Las Vegas to get married.

A powerful wave of fear flattened him and he almost bumped into his car.

Did the thought of *marriage* just cross his mind?

Dear God, he was falling for her. Like really falling for her.

Hard.

No. He wanted to make love to her, not be in love. He wanted her to love him first. He wanted to enslave her. Once he was sure he had her, then maybe he'd open up. But not before.

Marriage.

Waking up next to her. Every day. Fucking her crazy. Every day. Feeling those curves against his naked flesh. Every day.

His cock hurt as it strained against his pants.

His stomach roiling, his heart cracking open, he headed to Rollin and Emma's house. He and Rollin had to discuss some details of the overall plan regarding Sam. The one involving business, not plundering her.

His mind was so full of her, he missed his turn.

SIX

Sam's hot new outfit worked. A little too well. Paul could barely talk for the first half hour. She should have worn the blue dress. Her "Lewinsky" as Emma called it. Not as sexy, but flattering. Damn it, she needed him to be interested, but not this interested. She had to keep him hooked, but not frustrate him. Striking the balance here would be tricky.

If only he were taking her out. She'd suggested it the night before, but he'd insisted on cooking for her. Maybe she could con him into another date the following day. She had to get to Seattle!

Paul gave her a glass of white wine and they made small talk while he cooked a red sauce in a copper-bottomed fry pan. Tomatoes, garlic and Italian herbs filled the air, making her hungry. Homemade ravioli sat ready and floured on a wooden cutting board near the ravioli maker. A large pot of water boiled next to the skillet he worked. He'd set out a platter of crackers, Cheddar and Brie cheeses, and sliced apples on the polished wood bar dividing the kitchen from the dining room. Below the bar on the kitchen counter was a vibrant green salad in a blue earthenware bowl.

Wandering into the living room, she sipped her wine and examined his Eichler. Furnished with period modern furniture, he'd maintained the original flavor of the house, yet had updated the electrical and computerized the temperature controls. But with the round white globe overhead lights and the wood-paneled walls, Sam felt like she was in a movie from the 60s. Very retro. The Hawaiian music playing on the living room stereo added to the vintage feel.

She searched for personal touches. He was neat and not into possessions, nor into bling. Pictures of him wakeboarding and performing tricks were grouped over modern wood couches with orange cushions. Family photos hung neatly on one wall. She examined them closely for pictures of him with women, but she couldn't tell who were sisters or who might be girlfriends or wives. Seemed like he'd been living alone for quite a while. Other the photos, there weren't many personal items.

She didn't feel comfortable exploring more than the living room, so she headed back to the kitchen. When she walked in, he sent her a sexy grin.

A wave of electric energy pulsed her erogenous zones. Paul's heavy jaw, strong nose and brow, plus the evenness of his features made him so manly. His ropy neck, broad shoulders and buff pecs, along with his solid forearms and bulging biceps, reeked health and vitality. Come to think of it, he was probably one of the most physically perfect men she'd ever dated. And so nice.

Much nicer than Burke.

Burke would snap out orders and expect to be obeyed instantly. He'd fuss over her appearance and try to quiet her. He'd continually challenge her. Get in her way and bother her.

And probably fuck like no other guy could.

In two months, she'd have Paul trained. In forty-seven years, she wouldn't have a thing over Burke.

Stop all thinking NOW! She gave herself a good inward shake. Neither man was in her future. More than likely death and/or jail would be her fate. Probably end up being some fat tattooed lifer's bitch.

"So did something bad happen today?" Paul asked. "That frown and fear in your eyes couldn't mean anything else."

She wanted to laugh, but kept a straight face. No way was she revealing her thoughts to him. "Uh, no. I just remembered something I had to do."

He angled a glance at her and his thick brows came together. "I drove by your house today. Ton of guys there. Something happen?"

She could hear the gunfire and feel her back window shatter. She involuntarily hunched her shoulders and shivered. A picture of the truck bearing down and Burke screaming flashed through her mind. Her tense stomach burned. She wrapped her arms around herself, sighed, and looked at his maple dining table.

"Something happened? What?"

She ran her hand over the back of one of the curved, modern dining chairs. "I really don't want to talk about it."

"Did someone try to kill you again?"

She nodded. Without warning, a storm of emotions swept through her, she blinked back the tears, and swallowed hard. Grabbing a mental shield, she closed it around herself. She'd be fine. It was over.

Paul put down his knife and came over to her. Wrapping his arms around her, he squeezed hard. "I'm so sorry."

His kindness and caring—along with his warmth and musky scent —made her want to snuggle against his iron pecs and stay there for a week. She craved his comfort, but didn't want to impose. She made a half-hearted attempt at escape. "I'm okay."

He moved back, but kept his large hands on her shoulders and met her gaze. His expression sweet and sympathetic, he said in a soft voice, "How could you be, Sam?"

Her heart opened a bit and she slammed it shut. She stared at her shoes and wanted to run. Shame burned her. She planned to use the man and he didn't deserve it. "I have to be."

"No, you don't." He tucked his finger under her chin, his attention went to her mouth, and he kissed her.

His taste filled her, his tongue commanded her mouth yet he didn't push, he led. A tingle began at her feet and raced through her, setting her skin on fire. Her sex zinged with lust. She ran her hands over his defined upper arms and he pulled her closer.

Her mind hit a bump. What was wrong? She couldn't put her finger on it. He kissed great, he was hotter than hell, strong, muscular and kind, but...

Dear God, she was thinking of Burke.

How was that possible? Kissing a total hunk and thinking about a rat?

Delusional and sick. She needed hospitalization or half a bottle of tequila.

Both.

Thank the Lord, she could kiss really well on auto-pilot.

He pulled away, his dark gaze clouded with lust, and sent her a hungry smile. "Wow, lady. You just get hotter and hotter."

She smiled with what she hoped was a sexy edge. "You're the hot one."

Paul brought her to him and hugged her tight to him for a long moment. Felt good.

All at once, his body tensed, and he sighed.

Pushing him back a bit, she checked his expression.

Very troubled.

Her stomach dropped. "What?"

He shook his head and appeared to be fighting with himself. Looking around the room, he frowned and finally focused on her. "Can I be honest with you?"

"Please."

"I think you're in over your head."

His truth bomb blew her out of his arms and back a couple steps. She averted her eyes, but couldn't help herself and nodded. "Yeah, well..." *I've been in over my head since I was sixteen.*

He lowered his voice. "I did some digging on your friends."

She snapped her gaze to his.

His expression turned grave.

Her stomach clenched and her back tightened. A dark foreboding aura permeated the room. Like someone had changed the channel on the ambiance from light and airy to prison-like and treacherous.

"Dangerous people," Paul continued. "Especially Burke."

The tension in her body ratcheted higher. Biting her lip, she focused her attention on her wine glass. "I know that." But she couldn't get her head around it. He was a handful and a master game player, but dangerous? Emma had said so. But the story seemed so unbelievable. She couldn't picture him kidnapping Emma and tormenting her. It didn't seem real.

But she knew Emma wasn't lying. Burke had even admitted to what he'd done.

All too much to comprehend.

She realized she'd been absently playing with his pendant. She let go and resisted the urge to take off the necklace and hide it in her purse.

Paul stared at her with intensity. "I'm not sure you do understand or you wouldn't be hanging around with them. Nor would you let Burke within a mile of you. I know you and Emma go way back, but she just met these guys seven months ago. She has no idea who she's living with. Neither of you can comprehend what they're capable of."

"I have a good idea." Which was a lie.

Paul sent her a look that said he saw through her. "The government fears them. The military can't control them. They're responsible for the murders of dozens of American citizens."

She checked Paul's expression carefully. Read his eyes. Watched his lips. From what she could tell, he wasn't lying.

The wine churned in her stomach and she gave him a nod. "I guess I kinda suspected that." The ground underneath her feet got shakier and shakier. She thought of her closet and her rifle, and longed to have her precious weapon in her hands.

"And your friend Burke's the worst of the bunch. He was feared even when he was in the SEALs. You know I was in the service?"

"Yeah."

"He and I have mutual friends. One guy told me this story about how Burke and his team had snuck into an Al-Qaeda encampment to rescue a Marine. Turned out to be a trap. He was the only survivor. In a crazed frenzy, he single-handedly massacred thirty insurgents along with ten of their support people. A total bloodbath."

A powerful wave of nausea rocked her body and she rubbed her gut. "Wasn't that his job?"

"Yes, but not to wipe out the whole camp. He killed teenagers, cooks, unarmed men. He even murdered a twelve-year-old boy."

Her body went cold and her stomach soured like the wine had turned to vinegar. Could Paul be telling the truth?

"Scared the hell out of his commanders. That's when they suggested it might be time for him to retire. But he refused. So they sent him to Afghanistan and gave him an impossible mission, hoping he'd quit afterwards. Or get killed. Against all odds, he completed the task. Tracked down a high level Al-Qaeda officer and kidnapped him. Problem was, his support got killed on the way back. Burke kept his prisoner in a cave alone for a month while waiting for back up. When they finally found him, he was paranoid and raving mad. Almost killed his own rescuers. Right after that, he quit the SEALs and disappeared. Finally resurfaced with Rampart Security."

She couldn't reconcile the Burke she knew with this image of an unbalanced maniac. Yet something about the story rang true. "Huh."

"He'll do anything to accomplish his objectives, Sam. You are in grave danger."

Ugly information. But how did Paul know? And what was his stake in all this? This was only their fourth date, he shouldn't care about her this much. And given how long he appeared to be single, he didn't form bonds with women this fast. What was his game?

She checked his expression. He wanted something.

A weird feeling overtook her body, like snakes slithering over her skin. Her instinct was to run out that door and never look back. Was Paul working for Larry?

No, she'd be dead.

But Paul being the enemy didn't make sense. She'd met him far before the scene on the trail. Before she'd stolen the packet.

But come to think of it, Paul had reacted to the sniper a little too well. Like he'd expected the attack.

Fear and panic welled in her belly, but she made sure none of her feelings showed. If Paul was a bad guy, she couldn't let on that she suspected him.

Of course, he could be telling her the truth. She was super tired from her day so she could be misreading him. And Paul's military background might account for his poise under fire.

Still, her gut told her not to trust him. He knew too much and she could feel his sense of urgency. Why would he need her believe him? Was it simple jealousy?

She examined his face again. He held her gaze easily. Strong and steady. His shoulders straight, he seemed confident to his core.

Damn, she wanted him to be lying. Her stomach hurt like she'd drunk a cup of battery acid. "I need to sit down." She walked quickly to the couch in the living room and sat.

He followed her into the room, but thankfully didn't crowd her. He stopped a good seven feet away. "I'm sorry, Sam."

"Don't be."

"I have friends who can help you. If you want. I don't expect you to trust me, but I have no stake here, except your welfare."

"I appreciate that, but for right now, I have the situation under control."

His expression darkened. "You're playing with these guys. And there's only one way the game can end. With you as the loser. They could get you killed. They've already taken your freedom."

"Clearly."

"Look, there's no expiration on my offer. If you want help, if you want out, let me know. I can get you out of there. Tonight if you want."

She spun her pinky ring around her finger. "I have to think."

"As you should. Meanwhile, let me get you another glass of white."

"How about a vat?"

He shot her a nice, reassuring grin. When he returned with the wine, he wanted to say more, it was all over his face.

After taking the glass from him, she let out a long breath. She didn't want to hear it, whatever it was. "What?"

He looked down, then met her gaze. "I don't want to overload you."

"I'm already overloaded. What?"

"You realize all your phones are tapped, everything you say inside your house is being recorded."

A spike of anger jolted her. She took another deep breath. "I knew. I mean, no, but yes, I suspected. But I'm always careful about what I say and especially what I do on my computer. Burke just put a surveillance system in the house and I assume he installed spyware on my computer."

"To watch you as much as protect you from their enemies."

"Probably."

"Not probably. Don't get lulled. They need what you have."

"But I don't have anything," she said and then sipped her wine.

He sent her a small smile. "You aren't the best liar, you know."

She gazed up at him sharply, but said nothing.

"You have that package, don't you?" he asked in a quiet voice.

She held back a gasp. FUCK! He might as well have hit her. While all she wanted to do was bolt, she forced a calm expression. "No," she said, focusing on the golden liquid inside her glass.

"I don't care. But whatever the information is, it's putting you in danger. Is what's inside worth your life?"

She rubbed her eyes, half hiding behind her hand. She couldn't let this guy know anything. She couldn't let any of the people in her life know what she had. Bringing the Senator to his knees was paramount. Nothing and no one else mattered.

"What's in that packet, Sam?"

Finally, she shot him a glare. "I don't know, I don't fucking have it," she said, over enunciating her words.

His lips thinned, but his intense gaze didn't leave her face. "Something's going on with you and it has nothing to do with Rampart. Is someone from your past trying to hurt you?"

She wanted to get up and fly out the door. "No. Can you please back off?"

"I'm a straight shooter, Sam. Always have been. So are you in danger? Not just from Rampart? An ex-boyfriend or something?"

She attempted to look him in the eye, but her gaze slipped to his chest. "No. I'm fine," she tried to say evenly.

"I've seen people get shot at for the first time in their life…" He let his sentence hang in the air.

Sam made an exasperated noise in the back of her throat. "I know I reacted weirdly in the forest. But it was because of that live-fire training I told you about. I'd just gone through it not long ago."

He looked at her like he could see right through her. "And you went through live-fire training, why?"

"I wanted to. It was exciting. I like guns." She pulled the sheer sleeve of her top down toward her wrist.

Paul jaw hardened, he looked a little pissed. "You don't trust anyone, do you? You don't let anyone in." He turned, walked into the kitchen, and resumed cooking.

Sam's gut hurt like Burke and Paul were playing tug-of-war with it. This was all so screwed up! Was Paul telling the truth? Or was he manipulating her? She couldn't trust him. She couldn't trust anyone.

Especially not the Patriots. She'd been lulled.

All signs pointed to the obvious. No more bullshit. No more delays.

She looked at the entryway. Should she just leave?

Not yet. If Paul had ulterior motives, she needed to know. Hopefully, she wouldn't have to evade both him and the Patriots to complete her ultimate plan. But the cold feeling in the pit of her stomach told her something was wrong with her new boyfriend.

She stood and reluctantly wandered into the kitchen. "Thank you, Paul. You're a really nice guy, and I appreciate your caring and information. You've helped me a lot. And I won't forget it."

He glanced up at her with a razor-edged look, then returned to stirring the sauce. "You're leaving."

"I didn't say that."

He snorted. "Sam, you can't escape them on your own. You need help."

"I'm sure I do. But I'm not dragging anyone into my mess."

"Are you on the run from the law?"

"No."

"Someone's after you."

"For your protection and mine, I can't talk about it."

He frowned. "Are you in the Witness Protection Program?"

"No. Not nearly as dramatic. I had some troubles. I've figured out solutions and I have to go face—handle some old business."

"And Rampart's packet will help you?"

"I don't have it." She allowed her frustration to show. "I really don't." Her nerves were frayed. Why wouldn't this asshole leave the subject of the packet alone?

"Yes, you do. They have evidence that proves it. Footage of you in Seattle, carrying the package."

Adrenaline injected into her body. Her heart banged her ribs and her muscles went hard. "How the hell do you know this? Did you have the Patriots under surveillance?"

He didn't react. "Calm down, Sam. I'm not your enemy, I'm your friend. Rampart—the Patriots—and I have mutual friends. And the point here isn't me, it's you. Maybe that woman they have on camera with the package is someone who looks like you, but you'd better be prepared for a tougher interrogation, maybe even tonight. I'm surprised they haven't drugged you and questioned you already."

She stopped breathing, her legs went shaky, and the back of her knees and neck started to sweat. They knew. Burke knew. She was screwed. She slumped on a barstool.

"What's in the packet, Sam?"

Her thoughts sped in fifty different directions at once. Talk about a chess game! How much should she admit to? She needed to reveal just enough information to find out what Paul knew and whose side he was on. But she didn't want to give him anything he already didn't know. "I can't explain."

He glanced over at her and then continued to stir the sauce. "There's something inside that relates to your past somehow, huh? You don't have to answer that. I'll shut up. And I'm sorry. It's killing me watching someone as nice as you get caught up in all this mess." He turned to her and his gaze sliced into her. "Your life can't be worth what's in that package."

She rubbed her forehead and the bridge of her nose, but didn't make eye contact. The information certainly was worth her life. That information was going to save her life.

"If you want, I'll help you get rid of it. The sooner you do, the safer you'll be."

Paul was right. She was playing on a gameboard she'd never seen before with no rules, no boundaries, surrounded by lethal enemies. And she was the only pawn. Maybe she should ditch the idea of going to Seattle, and just go shoot the goddamned senator.

Her hand tightened on her glass. Damn it! No, because the Patriots wouldn't leave her alone until they had the evidence.

But how to handle Paul was the immediate concern. Eying him, she tried to figure out what to do. How did she get him to reveal his secrets without blurting out her own? Had to watch everything that came out of her mouth. Silence hung heavy between them.

Frowning, he appeared pained. He threw down the wooden spoon and shook his head. "I can't do this."

"Can't do what?"

"Keep up this charade any longer."

Her stomach hollowed and she broke out in a full body sweat. The wine began to travel up her throat. She swallowed hard. She'd wanted the truth, but could she handle it?

He focused in on her. "You need this information, I have to come clean with you."

"You're scaring me."

A different man stood before her. Darker, harder, stronger. Professional. He seemed taller. And older. "I haven't been completely honest with you."

RUN! "Now you're really scaring me." It would only take her a few seconds to get outside. She mentally ran through several escape scenarios.

"Don't be afraid of me, Sam. I work for the good guys."

"You aren't a salesman, are you?"

"No. I work for the government."

She clutched the bar for support and almost puked. Fuck. Well, her ploy worked. The man was indeed her enemy. She had to get out of there.

If he let her.

She tried to keep her expression passive and not reveal any fear. "That's how you know so much about the Patriots."

"Yes. And I also know about the men who are trying to kill you."

"Shit." She looked toward the door, then realized she was showing her hand and quickly shifted her attention back to him.

"Don't run yet. Hear me out. I know you're scared and you should be. You're involved in something far more dangerous than you realize. The four people who possessed that information packet before you are dead. You should not still be alive. You're lucky that Rampart didn't have the proof until a couple hours ago. Time's up, Sam."

She swallowed hard.

"Your only way out is through me. I have the back up. More than the Patriots. I can get you to Seattle tonight. One phone call and we are on a plane. Once that information leaves your hands, you are safe."

She believed him and she didn't believe him. She couldn't picture any of the Patriots hurting her.

But then again, the information she had could bring down some of the most powerful men in the country. She took a deep breath and stared at the polished wood surface of the bar.

"This may be my only chance to help you."

She finally looked at him. "I need that information."

"Why? I know you don't work for any spy organizations. But I also know your real name isn't Sam Murdock. And I know you appeared out of nowhere in summer of 1994 here in San Mateo."

Her throat went tight and she fought to breathe.

"We can leave right now."

There was no way in hell she was trusting this guy. He wanted the packet, he'd say anything and do anything to get it. And would probably kill her right after she gave it to him.

But she had to let him think that he'd convinced her. But he'd get suspicious if she relented too fast. She had to play him right.

She let her shoulders relax and twisted the wine glass in her fingers. "I can't leave right now."

"Why not?"

She had to use some truth or he wouldn't believe her. She set the wine glass down on the bar a bit too hard and faced him. "Okay, let's be real here. Why the fuck would I trust you? You know way too much. You say you work for the government, but you could work for the bad guys. You lied about yourself and have been dating me, why? To get close to the Patriots? To keep an eye on them? To infiltrate them?" she demanded, the ideas just occurring to her.

He snorted and smiled. "You're way too smart for your own good."

Blackness filled her mind and rage slammed her gut. She fought to keep her thoughts straight. But she had to let some anger show. "You don't even care about me," she spat.

His gaze flared and he pointed at her. "Now that's not true."

"Bullshit. You were probably behind my attempted kidnapping today."

"I was not. My group and Rampart aren't the only ones who want that packet."

"Why should I believe you? You've been using me from the start."

"Yes, initially I had a plan when I started dating you. But…" He rubbed his hand through his hair. "I've never met anyone like you." He chuckled. "Fiery, smart, savvy. I respect you and I know you're in trouble. You're afraid of someone. Don't bother denying it. People don't change their name and disappear for no reason. And once this whole thing blows over, I'd like to date you for real."

She held back harsh laughter. Now he wanted to be her buddy? After lying to her and betraying her? What a fuckwad!

Paul's expression earnest, he leaned in. "I want to help you straighten out your past. I like you, lady. And I like that you're seeing through me. I like that you're seeing through the Patriots' true-blue act."

Uncomfortable with his intensity, she stared down at the bar.

"And I don't expect you trust me," he said. "Not when I've lied to you. But I want you to look me in the eye now."

Sam reined in her fears and looked into his steel-blue eyes. "Yeah?"

"You give me that packet," he said in a strong, sure voice, "and I'll make sure Rampart and no one else hurts you."

"Give me a minute here to think." She had to get out of there gracefully. If the man was showing his hand this early, it meant he had very few alternatives. It meant he was desperate. And desperate men were dangerous. She wouldn't put it past this guy to kidnap her if she refused his help.

His life was probably on the line along with hers. The evidence packet was that dangerous.

Holy bejeebus. Sam felt like she'd stepped into a different dimension. A dark, terrifying dimension with endless maze-like corridors, and danger around each corner. She'd been so fixated on the Senator, she hadn't really fully understood the craziness of her actions. And the gravity of the situation or the true value of the information.

Even though it was pretty damned obvious. She'd been blinded by her need for revenge. Shit.

Paul put his hands on his hips. "And I'm really worried about Burke's interest in you. He didn't have to lead that security team at your house. He did that because he wants you and that makes him even more dangerous. He wants to own you, Sam."

She waved her hand. For some reason, Burke didn't frighten her. While she hated hearing about his exploits in the SEALs, that's what the military did. They killed people. Horrifying, but not surprising. "He just wants to fuck me."

"No. You don't know his pattern with women. He's not just a danger to his enemies, Sam, he's always been a danger to his women."

"And you are privy to all this information?"

"Yes. I've studied all the Rampart guys and especially Burke. I've interviewed some of his ex-girlfriends. He's a totalitarian dictator and can be very cruel. And his bedroom habits are disturbing."

"How so?" she said, feeling stupid she'd bitten his hook.

"Man is a sadist. One of his girlfriends, Giselle, told me stories that made my hair stand on end. Now I'm all for experimentation. I don't judge people based upon what they do in the sack, but this guy is a whack job."

Paul was making up stuff to scare her.

She hoped.

"Specifics?" She did not want the answer.

"Really into S and M, and B and D. Tying up the girls and whipping them and spanking them. He did all kinds of things to Giselle. Stuff she couldn't talk about."

Unfortunately, this all fit. Far too well. She could see Burke in leather with a whip in his hand and a gleam in his eye.

A cold shiver went through her. No one knew what dark secrets lurked in the minds of people. Just like serial killers. They have families. They have friends.

But Sam didn't want Paul to know he'd gotten to her. She gave an indifferent shrug and raised an eyebrow. "This isn't exactly the witty repartee I was expecting on this date."

He laughed. "I really like you, girl."

The pot behind him boiled furiously. Paul returned to the stove and threw the ravioli into the steaming water. "Three minutes and we'll be ready to eat. If I haven't destroyed your appetite yet. I'm sorry about this, Sam, and I apologize for deceiving you."

"So why come clean with me now?"

"Because you're smarter than I thought. You would have figured me out before I could have gotten any closer to them. But mostly because of that packet. Scary shit," he said, his eyes wide.

A chill froze her to the bone. He was probably right. The information on that packet would destroy Larry. And Larry had become more powerful than God. He was about to announce his candidacy. And too many people needed him to be president. Too much money rode on it. That packet would end his chances for election and would affect his whole rotten network.

And if they found out that she had access to a gun that linked him to a murder, she'd be wiped from the face of the Earth.

Her immediate problem was Paul. If he was telling her the truth about himself, she was in just as much danger from him as from Burke. Maybe even more.

So what was stopping him from kidnapping her and drugging her for the information? Nothing. Only two guards stood outside. From what he told her, Paul and his network could overpower them in a second.

So why was she still there and about to eat dinner with him?

Paul served the ravioli onto plates and spooned chunky sauce over them.

If the Patriots had this much at stake, wouldn't they have Paul's house under tight surveillance? "Have the Patriots rigged this place with surveillance equipment?"

"Yep." He brought the two plates over to his dining table.

"But…"

Paul sent her a smug grin as he passed her to return to the kitchen. "They're listening to loud Hawaiian music right now," he said, pointing at the stereo on a shelf in his living room. And their cameras are aimed at the side of the dining table where we won't be, and the couch in the living room. I've been guiding you away from the hot spots."

"Do they know you know they're watching you?"

"Probably. I tipped my hand when I went on a 'cleaning binge'," he said, using his fingers to make air quotes, "right after they rigged the place. I moved the stereo so it was right by their microphone."

"Holy shit."

Paul picked up the salad bowl, carried it to the dining table, and set it between the two plates. "They already suspect I'm not who I say I am. I know they've been doing extensive background searches on me. Those guards out there aren't just to protect me."

More unwelcome news. She hoped none more was forthcoming.

They sat down and began eating.

She picked at her food. She had to make him think she was considering his offer. "I'm not saying I'll go along with you, but what's your deal?"

"You take me to the information and hand it to me and I guarantee your personal safety. I'll relocate you to another town, another state, and make sure you're set for life," he said with no duplicity on his face.

She looked away and pretended to think about it. "I am so screwed."

"No, you're not. Not yet. You take me there tonight and you'll be saved."

"I can't tonight."

"Why not?"

She cleared her mind, turned to him, and allowed the lie to flow. "First, I need sleep. I'm ready to drop and am not thinking clearly. Then I need something I don't have with me. Something I have hidden. Then I can retrieve the packet."

"Where is it?"

She sent him a half-sneer, half-smile. "Come on, Paul. I'm not stupid. I tell you and I'm dead."

He seemed offended. "Sam, I'm not the enemy, I'm on your side."

"So you say."

He let out a breath through his nose, just shy of a snort, and took a sip of wine. "I know it's in Seattle somewhere. Probably a safe deposit box or a train station or an airport locker."

She held his gaze and didn't allow a muscle in her face to move.

He studied her for a moment and then returned to his food.

They ate in silence for a while.

Enough with being on the defense. She had to take control. Her gut said this man would not let her out of his house unless she outmaneuvered him. He probably already had the plane booked. And probably had a pocketful of Roofies, ready to deploy if she really fought him.

Taking a deep breath, she faced him. "Okay, here's my counter-offer. You get me to Seattle tomorrow."

"And?"

She summoned all the power from her reserves, allowed her gaze to go cold, and hardened her expression. "In exchange for the packet, I want a Kevlar vest, two Barrett M107s without serial numbers, a few hand grenades, a Glock, hollow-point ammo for all the guns, and five hundred thousand dollars in unmarked hundred dollar bills. Oh, and three Tasers. With chargers." As she said the words, she realized that this bluff might actually be the right way to go. This guy could get her all that and more.

His eyes dilated to the size of dinner plates. His mouth fell open. Then his gaze sharpened. "Are you nuts? Why would a nice girl like you need all that shit?"

She kept her features hard and fixed. "That's my business. Do you want the packet or not?"

"Are you serious?"

"Dead."

"Shit." He pushed away from the table and ran his hand over his forehead. "Lady, you just threw me for a loop."

"So? Do we have a deal or not?" she clipped out.

"Yes, of course. Easy. But Sam…"

She held up her hand. "No more."

"Fuck that," he said, his gaze fiery. He leaned in as far as he could and pointed at her. "If you're going after any of the people in that pack —it's suicide. It's a miracle that information was gathered in the first place and ended up out of their control. They have layers upon layers of protection. You can't understand their power, their reach. We'll be lucky if we can keep you alive long enough to retrieve the evidence."

She kept her affect and didn't react. "Who says I'm going after anyone? I stepped on a land mine here and I'm going do everything in my power to save my ass."

He snorted and sat back. "Nice lie. But you've got vengeance in your heart, girl, I can see it. That thirst. That hunger in your eyes. Someone did you wrong and you're gonna make sure they pay for it. I've known a lot of people like you. And they're all dead."

She stared at him with her gaze as frosty as she could make it. "Pick me up at seven o'clock in the morning at Beresford Park behind the baseball diamond."

Paul studied her, clearly displeased. He couldn't really care about her, could he? He gave a slight shrug and sighed, seeming defeated. "Okay." His gaze cleared and face went stony. "You'd better not be playing with me."

She curled her lip slightly. "And you'd better not be playing with me. You'd better have that fucking plane ready tomorrow morning and I want to see that money before I take you to the information. You got that?"

His brow wrinkled a bit. "Yeah." Wary, he did not look happy. He took a sip of his wine and his expression softened. He gazed at her thoughtfully. "Just don't allow your hate to control you. I wasted a bunch of time and energy and got screwed doing the same thing you are. Give up that revenge shit, it's poison."

He certainly seemed as if he was telling the truth. Seemed like he cared about her.

So what? He was the enemy. Burke and the Patriots were the enemy.

Time for Team Sam to take control.

Her team of one.

Tears rushed into her eyes and she fought them. Emma. Her life in San Mateo.

She gave herself a good mental slap and hardened her heart. No more fucking sentiment. Her love for Emma had weakened her. She'd known her life in San Mateo would be short. She'd known it from the beginning.

Now the end had come. Once she retrieved the packet, she'd make a secret copy, and stash it somewhere. Then she'd contact Rollin and Paul and sell the packet to the highest bidder. After figuring out a safe way to exchange the package for the weapons and money, she'd take care of Larry and start a new life.

Yeah. She liked this new plan.

And thank God Burke was off duty and she wouldn't ever have to see him again. That man twisted her mind. While she didn't believe everything that Paul said, much of his story rang too true.

But despite all the new information, she still liked Burke.

Which meant she had to avoid him.

Forever.

SEVEN

Burke left Rollin and Emma's house and headed home after an unexpected, yet overall pleasant evening. What had started out as a quick business meeting had turned into a cozy dinner. Once the ice was broken, Emma had treated him like an old friend. Nice. He'd always liked her even when he'd loved her.

As the evening wore on, and he'd gotten perspective on the situation, Sam's words had rung true. He and Emma would have killed each other. Emma *was* way too sweet for him. Way too nice. Way too accommodating. Perfect for Rollin, but he would have taken advantage of her. Ugly, but true.

Sam, on the other hand, would never let him pull anything over on her. They'd be fighting for Alpha position constantly. Which made his cock ache with longing. A match made in Heaven or, depending on how he looked at it, Hell.

At the end of the evening, the Patriots had had a video conference call in Rollin's office. Bobby had played a tape of a brief clip of Sam carrying the packet in downtown Seattle. But that was all they'd recovered. They knew she had it, but not where.

The decision had been made to restrict Sam's movements and force her to reveal where the packet was located. They'd let her sleep at home tonight, but the next day, if she didn't give up the information willingly, they'd move her out of her comfort zone to one of the

Patriots' hideouts until they could either find the information themselves or break her.

Burke looked up and slapped his palm against his forehead. How did he miss his turn-off onto 92? Damn it, had his subconscious really taken control? Was his burning need for Sam this out of control?

Answer: yes.

He made an exasperated noise. He had to see Sam. Aside from the new information, he couldn't help but be rabidly jealous of Strong. He had to find out what happened. How far they'd gone sexually. Banana had reported she'd gotten home an hour before. Burke would casually "check out the house" and see if she was still awake.

Aside from his concerns about their relationship, he also needed to know what Strong had revealed. Strong had found the Patriots' bugs; the Hawaiian music hadn't fooled anyone. But his ploy had masked his conversation with Sam. Even if he didn't reveal himself as a spy, he might have said something that would help the Patriots.

Sam's parted lips beckoned to him from his memory and a charge went through his dick. He ached to cup her firm, high breasts. Make that wicked spark in her eyes turn to lusty hunger.

He gave his head a shake and adjusted his hips on the seat. Time to stop fooling himself about the real reason why he wanted to see Sam.

Even if she'd fallen for the defense yahoo, he'd turn her around. He had to step up his game. He had to seduce her. Once he got her in bed, their bond would seal the deal.

Somehow he had to maneuver her to his house. The Patriots wanted to move her somewhere safer. He didn't want to show his cards too soon to his friends, but somehow, he'd trap Sam at his place. Then he'd get the packet and the girl.

And the respect of the group again.

He smiled. *Good one, Cherlenko.*

After turning onto 24th Avenue, he drove behind her house to check in with David. The bodyguard was nowhere to be seen. David's car was there, but it was empty.

He frowned and headed for the front of Sam's house on 25th to find out where his man went. As he turned the corner, he glanced in his rear view mirror. A dark figure hopped down from Emma's back fence and ran in the opposite direction.

A burst of adrenaline kicked his metabolism to high. A bomber? A kidnapper?

Burke whipped the car around and accelerated. The person sprinted away. He called Banana. "I'm behind the house on 24th and just spotted someone jumping down from Sam's back fence. I'm in pursuit. Check on Sam. Where's David?"

"Taking a leak." Banana's breathing increased and his footfalls thumped in the background. "No, she's here and she's asleep."

"Make sure she's breathing."

"Sam? Honey? Are you—shit! It's not her! I mean, she stuffed the bed with pillows and tucked a wig into the top of her sheets."

"Check the closet!" Burke ordered.

"That's right, she sleeps there." More huffing. A door squeaked. "Sam? Fuck! She stuffed this bed, too! Or someone did! Shit, she's gone!"

Burke's blood pumped hot through his veins and he clenched the steering wheel hard. "No she isn't, Sam's right here. I'll catch her."

Just then, Sam pushed through a back gate and disappeared behind a house.

Burke clicked off the phone, jammed on the brakes, and leapt out of the car. "Sam! Damn you, come back here! I know it's you!" He stalked to the fence. "And unless you want me to cause a scene in front of your neighbors, you'd better damned well show your face." He slammed through the gate.

"Will you keep your stupid voice down?" came her hushed reply from next to him, behind a hedge.

Hot fury radiated from his vibrating body. He kept his balled fists at his sides so he wouldn't hurt her. "Get out here," he commanded.

She came into the dim light, her gaze scorching, looking like she wanted to kill him.

Feeling was mutual. All he could think about was ringing her neck. Putting herself in danger like this? Was she crazy?

He grabbed her arm, dragged her to his car, and threw her inside. So mad he couldn't speak.

He checked her expression. Furious. Clenching her fists and her jaw, she was barely contained. And she wouldn't look at him.

There was something else in play here. Aside from the fury in her fiery gaze, there was also fear. Of him. Her entire demeanor toward him had changed.

Strong. He'd said something. Done something. Warned her.

His gut clenched. Or told her about his past.

Fuck.

Every muscle in Sam's body tensed to the point of shaking. She wanted to shoot Burke. Punch him and kick him and throw his body into the bay. She was absolutely one hundred percent screwed. Goddamned the man! Was he psychic?

Bristling with anger, he drove his car around the block toward the front of her place. His mouth twisted and his brow sat heavy over his flashing dark eyes. She could feel his heat from across the car.

But his emotions were his problem. Why would she care what this guy thought of her? He was an animal who killed twelve-year-olds. A crazy guy who liked to whip women.

Or was he?

Paul could have made that all up.

Burke had been nice to her. Saved her life. It was possible he actually cared about her.

No, he wanted the packet. Period. She was just another woman in a never-ending stream of girlfriends, flirtations and affairs. He'd been in love with Emma not six months before and had a girlfriend right after that.

After he pulled up and parked in her driveway, Burke opened her car door and hovered near her all the way into the house.

As soon as he shut the door, he spun on her. "What the hell was *that*?"

She rolled her eyes.

His face turned crimson and his flaming gaze roasted her. "Don't you fucking roll your eyes at me, lady. I am busting my ass trying to protect you and this is how you treat me? Where the hell were you going? Seattle?"

All the air left her lungs like he'd thrown a bowling ball at her gut. She sat down on her living room couch and stared at her hands, unable to make eye contact. Her mind was a mass of dark conflicting thoughts and emotions.

She had to focus. She needed the Patriots' protection. If she was stuck there, she needed them on her side. And she'd just blown it.

Burke paced in front of her. "Where were you going?"

"I can't."

"Drop the bullshit."

She flinched. "Could you please not yell at me?"

"No! You put yourself in danger!" he said gesturing wildly, his eyes nearly black with anger. "You would have cost us how many man-hours and resources trying to find you to protect you? This isn't a game! Your life is on the line and so are ours."

"Burke, really, I can't tell you."

"Stop. You won't. At least own your choices."

She averted her gaze and waved him off. "I can't deal with this right now."

He took a step closer, invading her space. "Too bad. I want answers."

"Burke..."

"You want us to leave you here alone?"

Her stomach convulsed. "No." She had to get him out of her face, calm him down, and still keep him interested in protecting her. She'd clearly breached his limits. And she didn't blame him. She'd probably be just as angry. "Look, I wasn't thinking straight."

"Something happened at Strong's. What?"

Unreal. How could he read her mind?

"Look, I'm too tired to deal with this." She got up and made a break for her room.

He caught her by the arm. "I understand you're terrified. That you believe a powerful man thinks you're dead and will kill you if he finds out you're still alive. But you don't have to face him alone. I'm here. I'm offering my help."

His gaze was so intense—and she could feel his need propelling his emotions—she pulled out of his bruising grip and looked away. "I can't trust you."

"You do or you wouldn't have allowed me into your home." He moved into her line of sight. "Sam, wake up. You're in my world now. And I won't let him hurt you. Even if he's powerful. Even if he's in that packet of information."

"You can't understand. No one could." She stared at the carpet.

He stormed away from her, then spun back. "So what am I supposed to do, huh? You aren't thinking clearly. You have no idea who you're up against. The people after Linda Anderson are sadistic sociopaths. You need protecting."

"Look, I appreciate this, Burke. But—"

"Don't give me any buts, woman. You're the one who whisks in and stops your friends from hurting themselves. Have you forgotten Lisa this morning at Jimmy's house?"

She picked at a thread on the back of the sofa. "No."

"What if you were Lisa and I was you? Huh? Or what if Emma was pulling this shit?"

She kept her attention on the couch. "I'd be in their faces," she muttered.

"Damned right, you would. Pack your bags."

She met his blistering gaze. "What?"

"Pack your bags, you're moving in with me. You're too distraught to make rational decisions. Like you did for Lisa, I'm temporarily taking away your choice."

Slack-jawed, she stared at him and tried to catch her breath. "You can't do that!"

He didn't budge, but the darkness in his gaze intensified. "Watch me."

This was preposterous. She'd never get away. She'd never be able to kill the Senator or blackmail him. Burke would imprison her.

His expression dared her to fight him. "Pack. It's late, we both need some sleep."

"Burke—"

"You almost got killed today, yet you decided to go to Seattle in the middle of the night, alone, without anything but a couple pistols. Pure suicide. You might as well go down to your basement, take out your Glock, and shoot yourself in the head. Think, Sam. Even if you managed to get away from us, you're too tired—not to mention completely unprepared—for the network of professional assassins who are trying to capture and kill you. You want your revenge? You really want to kill the man who hurt you? Then don't fuck yourself now. You die now and he will never be held accountable."

His irrefutable logic nailed the door shut. He was one hundred percent right.

You have to kill the senator!

Yes, she did. But when she launched her attack, she had to make sure her timing was perfect, that she was absolutely ready, and she was at the top of her game mentally and physically or she'd die and the Senator would stay free.

Besides, she had a lot of control over Burke. He liked her and wanted her. Anytime she wanted, she could fuck him, tase him, and escape.

Her fire dissipated and profound fatigue set in. Sighing, she met his gaze. "So if my judgment is off, how do I know moving in with you is the smart choice?"

His intensity diminished, his shoulders relaxed, and a slight smile crossed his full lips. "Good point." The smile faded and he crossed his arms over his broad chest. "Think of it this way. It's not a choice." He jerked his head toward her bedroom.

She narrowed her eyes. "Don't get bossy."

His hard expression didn't waver. "You gave me a heart attack. If you saw what those animals did to Joseph…" His mouth pressed into a firm line and his gaze burned into hers. "Christ. Stuffing both your beds like some fucking teenager. Go," he clipped out with a sharp flick of his wrist.

She stared at him and wondered if she should put up a fight just to piss him off.

Breathing hard, his forehead sweaty, the man was way too emotional. Almost crazy. His eyes glittered with fury and exasperation.

Why would he be this upset?

Because he liked her even more than she'd thought.

Good. "Do you think your place is the best option?"

His expression remained fixed like it was cast in iron. "Yes."

"But…"

"My penthouse is defensible, exclusive, and set up specifically to protect me. You never saw the protection mechanisms, but the condo is built like a bunker."

"It's made of glass."

"Don't let the openness of the place fool you. No one can get in or out without my permission. No one."

She wanted to laugh. *Oh, yeah?* But no way would she let him know what she was thinking. With a mask of misery on her face, she shuffled down the hallway to pack.

As much confidence as she had in herself, a part of her felt like she was picking out a prison outfit. Solid orange or white with black stripes? Burke was an awesome force of nature. Smooth, cunning and calculating. One of the greatest foes she'd ever faced.

She gave her head a good shake. She'd find all his weaknesses and exploit them. With the little extras she'd tucked into the false bottom of her suitcase—three disguises, her Smith and Wesson, and a few of her fake IDs—plus a cash stash—she'd have many options for escape.

Burke, honey. You are goin' down.
And not on me.
Hopefully.

EIGHT

Sam woke up completely disoriented in a luxurious bedroom suite. The previous night's memories raged back and she closed her eyes.

Shit. She was at Burke's. She'd been so tired by the time they got to the City, she'd barely been able to make conversation.

Now she had to face him.

How awkward, already. And she'd just arrived.

She didn't crack the door to her bedroom until she was fully made up. Doors had closed somewhere in the apartment and the smell of coffee wafted into her room. Her body craved caffeine, but she wasn't going to step foot out in that kitchen until she looked perfect.

Which was humiliating. Why the hell did she care so much? This man was only a steppingstone to her ultimate plan. No relationship possible.

Besides, if she really thought about it, she wasn't his type. She was loud, crazy, and outgoing, and he was sophisticated, controlled and quiet. She only had a BS degree, the man was a brainiac. A human computer. She managed an antique store. He managed a global network of spies. How could that work? Besides, she wasn't certain the man was capable of long-term liaisons. The only reason he still wanted her was because he hadn't had her. He'd be bored in a week and leave her and then she'd get pissed, cut his balls off, and end up in prison for the rest of her life.

And even if the circumstances were different, who said she wanted him? She needed a simple man. Guy who came home in the evenings, had a couple beers, screwed her, and then watched TV.

Of course, she'd had three guys like that and none of them had worked out. She'd gotten bored with them. And their beer. And their TV watching.

Maybe she was the problem.

No. She knew her problem. Senator Larry Asshole Fuckwad. She'd always known that she had to settle her past before she could deal with her future. A couple days of rest and planning and then she'd vanish.

She walked into the kitchen and tried not to gasp at the beautiful picture. Burke sat at the kitchen table next to floor-to-ceiling windows with the most magnificent view of San Francisco and the Bay behind him. While the fog was in, the room was airy and bright. His yummy cologne and the intoxicating aroma of fresh coffee filled the air, warming her belly.

Clean, showered and shaved, he wore a black polo shirt which showed a lovely bit of dark chest hair and part of his sinewy neck. She couldn't put her finger on it, but something about the simple way he sat drinking his coffee—comfortable in his own skin, relaxing at home, reading his paper—made him so attractive. She'd never seen him like this. Calm. In his own world. Who knew the guy had a normal side to him?

Paul's image of him intruded in on her dream. She pushed it away. She had to hear the story from Burke's own lips.

His very kissable lips.

"Are you going to stand there staring at me, or come over here and pour yourself a cup of coffee?" he asked in a sardonic tone without looking up.

Immediately shattering all her illusions of his normality.

"Morning to you, too, dickhead."

He finally looked over at her and smirked. Then he noticed her outfit, her make-up, her nails, her legs, her breasts, and everything else about her in about a quarter second. He lit up. "You look lovely this morning."

"You look…uh." She almost complimented him, but couldn't bring herself to stroke his ego this early in the morning. "Good, too."

He raised a brow.

"Okay, you look hot," she snapped. "You always look hot, okay? And you know it, so why are we having this pointless tête-à-tête before I've even had my first cup of coffee?"

He chuckled and grinned at her affectionately. "Would you like me to pour you one?"

"No," she said, turning away and walking over to the coffee pot. "But I hope you have half-and-half."

"Banana dropped some by last night. I knew you'd want it."

She turned to him. "You did?"

"Yes."

"Well, thanks." Was the polite thing to say. But what was his angle with all this nicey-nice stuff?

"I want you to be comfortable."

"Thanks." *I think.*

"Although, I'm still angry with you for that stunt you pulled last night."

"Can you berate me after I have coffee?"

"Yes, and I'm sorry. I had no intention of starting off our day like this."

"Neither did I." She looked down, gathered her thoughts, and held his gaze once more. "And before I fully wake up, I have to say this. I may be fighting you every step of the way, but thanks for protecting me. You're a…shit, I'm gonna choke on it. Good…" She exaggerated a huge coughing fit. "Man…" she croaked out and held her throat, gasping dramatically.

Smiling, Burke shook his head and snorted. "What have I done to deserve you?"

"Didn't you get the memo? I'm your Karma, Burke. I'm here to torture you."

"Brat. Watch it. I won't stand for impertinence."

She laughed. "Anyone who makes a statement like that deserves all the trouble they get. I swear, Burke, you're channeling Gengis Khan half the time. Lucky for me, I don't take you seriously."

"Didn't we discuss your lack of judgment last night?"

"Yes. Which is exactly how I ended up here."

He smiled. "Touché. And all without coffee. Boggles my mind to think what you'll be like with some of my French Roast inside you."

I can think of other things of yours I'd like inside me, came a saucy little voice from her sex drive.

Shut up, libido, we don't want him. Too dangerous.

Hell, we don't.

"I'll try to be nice. It'll take some big effort on my part, but I will try."

He shook his head and returned to his paper. "Enjoy tormenting me while you can, I just got a call from Rollin and we're headed to Seattle."

She almost poured the coffee on the floor.

"We saw the footage of you carrying the packet."

Her breathing stopped, and she froze, holding the coffee pot in mid-air. She wished she were in an action movie with her escape helicopter hovering outside. She wanted to run, break through the window, jump on the copter and fly away, never to be seen again. While Paul had told her that the Patriots had seen footage of her, she hadn't completely believed him, concerned he might be manipulating her.

"We're checking a few places we think you might have hidden it. But if we don't find it..." He leveled his gaze at her, then shrugged.

"Could you please fucking wait until I get the goddamned coffee in me?" she snarled.

"Sorry," he said, not sounding sorry at all.

She had half a mind to throw the pot of coffee at him. "I don't want to run."

"You can't."

"Don't be a dick. Don't take my power away from me. Help me make this my choice to be here."

"You took that choice away when you tried to escape last night. You'd be dead right now, don't you get that? Cut up into little chunks and fed to the sharks. After being raped and tortured."

"Burke, could you please stop antagonizing me? And terrifying me with horrible imagery? I'm vulnerable, I'm exhausted, I've been on the run a long time, I have everything to lose—including and especially my life—and I can only take so much shit. I may be strong, but I'm on the verge of losing my mind."

His gaze went wide and the lines on his forehead deepened. He came over to her, put her cup of coffee on the counter and took her in his arms. "I'm sorry." He gave her a squeeze.

She resisted for about a half second. Then she let him hug her.

And oh God, did he feel good.

His warmth, scent and proximity did a little voodoo spell on her brain. And her lower organs.

He released her, but didn't move back very far.

He had the longest dark brown eyelashes. And his eyes were so gorgeous. Dark brown with black flecks. But behind them, his brain sparked and worked at breakneck speed. So fascinating and compelling. She could stare at him all day.

Her focus briefly went to his mouth and her body urged her to kiss him.

Then she realized she hadn't answered him. "It's okay," she said quickly.

"No, it's not. I'm being a hardass and I don't want to be. Not with you," he said, running his hand down her arm. "All my anger is coming from my need to protect you. Trust me. Tell me what's going on and I'll help you."

Sorry.

He looked away and his features went dark. "And I'm under a lot of pressure to get this information. Shit, woman." He sighed and met her gaze. The player vanished and a very nice man stood there. "I want to help us both."

His kindness nailed her. A wall of her defenses came down and a wave of guilt made her stomach roil. He was helping her and all she did was fight him.

But she couldn't tell him. Her emotions welled until her throat closed. She fought the tears. "I can't tell you, Burke. I can't," she said, hating the weakness and pleading in her voice.

He put his arms around her. "Do me one favor?"

"What?"

"Think about trusting me. I know I haven't done much in your eyes to deserve it—what happened with Emma and all—but I want you to give it some thought today. Okay?"

She saw a totally different man in front of her. Real, honest, vulnerable, caring, sweet and strong. The urge to kiss him became a demand.

Wait. This could just be another one of his ploys. He was a killer and untrustworthy.

She searched his face, but still only saw honesty. He was being real with her. His shields were down and she could see inside him. So normal. Shocking. To see him as a man. That simple man she wanted. "Yeah. I'll do what I can."

He smiled and let go. "Good."

Her body wanted him back.

"How would you like your eggs? And would you like one or two?"

She blinked fast, trying to catch up to the switch of subject. "Uh. Two. Over easy."

"Two eggs over easy, coming right up. Why don't you sit and read the paper and I'll just whip this up. What kind of toast do you prefer? Sourdough, wheat, rye?"

"Uh, wheat."

"I've got some good wheat from a local bakery." And then the man transformed into yet another person. He actually hummed while he worked.

She tried to read the paper, but she mostly ended up staring at him in confusion. Happy Cook Boy and Burke Cherlenko didn't even seem like distant cousins. Who the hell was this guy? And how many people lived inside him?

Had he really massacred forty people including a kid?

She couldn't believe it. Paul would have said anything to drive a wedge between them. He had to be wrong. Burke didn't seem capable.

She just wished Burke wasn't so damned hot. He was really starting to turn her head. And all her other body parts. She had to keep her distance.

After a very surreal and nice breakfast, Burke got up and cleared the breakfast dishes.

"I'll do 'em," Sam said.

"Not a problem, I'll attend to them later."

"Burke, what else am I gonna do today? You don't know me. I don't sit. I don't lay around."

He sent her a half-smile. "I thought your big dream was to lie on a beach in Mexico for the rest of your life."

"That's different. That's after I get a bunch of work done."

"All right, do whatever makes you happy. I'll be back around seven tonight. I've left you a stack of menus from restaurants where I have accounts. Tell them the address and say you're my sister or something."

"Better than wife," leapt from her lips. She stared at him, astonished.

He seemed very amused. "You just terrified me," he said, not looking terrified at all. "Married to you."

They stared at each other briefly. Fear, then lust, then warmth flashed through his dark eyes.

She saw an image of him at eighty, with a smug grin, tossing out an arrogant comment about the best kind of wine. In her mind, his face softened, he reached for her. *"Have I told you how much I love you?"*

Her entire body tingled.

Then she saw a younger cold Burke with his hand out. *"Give me the keys to the car. No more driving for you."* A storm of reality doused her happy dream.

A relationship with Burke would be doomed from the start. Even if they'd met under different circumstances, they'd kill each other.

They both busted out laughing at the exact same moment.

"Don't need to go see a scary movie, one just played in my head," Sam said.

Burke pointed at her. "Me, too."

Their laughter died down, leaving an awkward pause. Then Burke sent her a covetous look that told her he'd claimed her.

Damn it, she'd sold him on the idea. Her mind grew dark and her belly ached with sadness. This was a man she planned to blackmail. He would hate her. He would become her true enemy.

And Burke was no man you wanted for an enemy. Especially if his anger was fueled by caring. She shivered.

He stepped forward and grabbed her arm. "Sam? What's wrong? You lost all the color in your face."

"Nothing. I think I'm more tired than I thought."

"Well, rest today then." He sent her a warm smile and gestured toward his kitchen. "Make yourself at home. You want to cook, you'll find plenty of food in the cupboards and fridge."

"Great."

He checked his Rolex. "If you'll excuse me, I need to get ready and get out of here. Rollin's waiting."

Emma called right when Burke was walking out the door, so it spared them any awkward good-byes. They waved at each other and he was gone.

While Sam loved talking to her buddy, she couldn't tell Emma anything of her future plans. She felt so awful for having to lie to her, she got off the phone fast with a fake coffee pot emergency.

As she washed the dishes, she formed and rejected several escape plans.

There was only one that would work. She just didn't like the option.

She headed to her room to retrieve her gun and fake IDs. Hopefully, Banana and David would believe her rabid act.

Maybe she should just drug them. She'd brought a bottle of Ambien. She could crush up the pills and put them in a batch of brownies. Then just walk out.

Might be a better plan. Still, she needed to check all her supplies and get them together.

She closed and locked the door to her bedroom and hustled to her suitcase. She lifted out her clothes and removed the false bottom. And stared.

Took her a long few seconds for the realization to hit her.

Her gun and fake IDs were gone.

A truckload of dynamite blew off in her belly, all her muscles turned to rock and she roared. Shaking her fists at an imaginary Burke, she screamed, "I'll kill you, you bastard!" She threw herself on the bed and punched the pillow until she didn't have anything left inside. "That fucker! That shithead!"

He must have come in the night before while she was asleep and taken them.

Holy bejeebus. She felt like a big ol' honkin' fly stuck to a billboard of flypaper. Like he'd velcroed her to a wall. Imprisoned! Really, horribly imprisoned!

He was so lucky he wasn't home or he'd be bloody.

It took her a full hour to get hold of her anger.

She had to find her stuff. Those fake IDs were integral to her plan. Vital. They had to be in the apartment somewhere.

His room. But what excuse did she need to dig through his closets and drawers?

Easy. The jerk stole her stuff.

She headed to his room and stopped midway there. The only way he'd have known about the false bottom in her suitcase was if he'd watched her unpack the night before. Which meant her room must be under surveillance. Which meant the whole place was wired with cameras.

If she started tearing apart his bedroom, Banana would come in and stop her.

First thing she needed was knowledge. She wandered the apartment, "marveling" at the view from the floor to ceiling windows and secretly searched for cameras. She found nine, pointed at various vantage points. There were probably many more she hadn't found.

What kind of surveillance set-up did he have? Was it like the one he'd installed at her house? Or the type Rollin had installed at Emma's store? She'd trained herself on both systems. But where was the control center? Burke had to have a bunch of monitors and a place he stored the data. Probably the same place he'd put her gun and IDs.

After a third turn around the apartment, she found no computer anywhere. Might be in his bedroom, but what excuse did she have to go in there?

A wonderful idea occurred to her. Cleaning would give her an excuse to poke around everywhere. Especially his room. While his house wasn't super dirty, there was a thick layer of dust on many of the surfaces. And the carpet hadn't been vacuumed in a long time. Odd for a neat freak like him, but he was a busy man.

She found the vacuum in the hall closet, along with a variety of cleaning supplies. She whipped out the machine, started with her room, and worked her way down the hallway. His bedroom door was slightly ajar, but not shut.

Sam inwardly giggled and vacuumed her way into the room.

She gasped. The room was gorgeous, offering a magnificent view of the Golden Gate Bridge through more floor-to-ceiling windows.

The man had taste. His king-size bed was perfectly made with a dark blue satin comforter. Beautiful modern cherry wood furnishings included the bed frame, matching bedside tables, and a long, chic dresser. Spacious, understated and masculine, his bedroom fit him.

The master suite had a small adjoining room with more floor-to-ceiling windows. A flatscreen TV hung on one of two interior walls with a couch set up in front. On the adjacent wall was a giant, inset bookshelf. His own mini-living room. Cool. Her bedroom must be next door, beyond the plasma screen.

Drawn to the books, she couldn't stop herself and took a quick second to inspect his offerings. The books were ordered meticulously by subject and alphabetized by author. Lots of history, mainly military. Then she spied *Pride and Prejudice* in between two sets of history books. An ex-girlfriend must have stuck it there.

She scanned the area for hiding places. Where would he stash her stuff? No where in this little hang out. His closet in the next room? She'd check that next after vacuuming the TV area.

The carpeting in his bedroom and this little den hadn't been cleaned in forever. She wondered if he'd had a maid who'd quit.

She plugged the vacuum into the wall and ran it over the mashed-down cream carpet of the TV area. The traffic patterns were weird in this room. They led right up to the bookcase.

What the hell?

Marks from shoe imprints went right up to the bookcase and half a footstep ended right *underneath*.

Her heart started beating wildly, hope burned bright inside her. She'd found Burke's secret hiding place! Her fake IDs and gun had to be inside. Sweet!

She studied the markings on the carpet. The hidden wall swung inward or slid aside because there were no door scrapings on the cream pile. Hmmm.

She inspected the bookcase closely and tested it by pushing on the center. Nothing. Pressed another upright. No go.

Couldn't be activated by pulling down a fake book, could it?

Pride and Prejudice. Couldn't be that simple. She reached for the book, pulled on it, and it came right off in her hand. Bummer.

She reached up to the top of the bookcase and felt along the back of the facing. She found a bump. And pressed it.

The bookcase started to slide open.

A surge of victory flooded her body. She'd be out of there within the hour! Whoo-hoo!

The bookcase opened all the way.

A black, solid steel door with a numerical keypad and a biometric handprint reading plate stood before her.

Her heart sank, her shoulders drooped, and her stomach tensed with frustration. Of course he'd have major security features guarding his precious stuff. But she'd never seen the sophistication of this locking device. The system was clearly designed to keep high-level trained security personnel out. Which meant she didn't have a prayer.

Tears burned her eyes. "Now I'll never get out of here!" She sighed heavily and pressed the button again. The bookcase slid shut. "Fuck!" She kicked the vacuum.

Her only hope would be to find the keycode. But opening the vault might require a numerical code *and* Burke's handprint.

She growled and punched a giant book on Chinese history. She didn't want to clean his place, she wanted to light it on fire. Chop off his fucking hand, press it against the locking device, and get her goddamned gun back. "God, I hate this guy! There has to be a way inside this thing." She took a deep breath. "Calm and focus."

When hadn't she gotten what she wanted? Well, except for that shooting crap when she was a kid, every other thing in her life she'd set out to do, she'd done. She gave a firm nod and straightened her shoulders. She'd break out of Burke's. Period. There had to be a code that unlocked the vault hidden somewhere in his apartment. All she had to do was find it.

She continued "cleaning".

Next place on the Snoop List was Burke's gigantic walk-in closet. She vacuumed her way over, pushed open the door, and was astonished by its organization and the clothes inside. Hermes. Gucci. Prada. Louis Vuitton. The entire value of her wardrobe was equal to one of his jackets.

"Holy bejeebus, you are a clothes whore, Burke. I've never seen anything like this." Everything was sorted by color and type of clothing. His jackets, shirts and pants hung at precise, measured intervals. Unreal. "And man, are you *anal*."

He would be a difficult man to please.

While she wouldn't be caught dead spending all that time organizing, she appreciated the effort.

Even if it was a little OCD.

In the very back of the closet, behind a line of suits, hung a military uniform. She pulled it out and took in a sharp breath. It was covered in multi-colored bars. Hardly any material of the jacket showed. She didn't know what any of the decorations meant, but they were incredibly impressive. She carefully hung the uniform back on the rack and made sure the spacing was right.

A highboy dresser stood against the back wall of the huge closet. All the drawers were labeled. Tie tacks. Cufflinks. Medals.

"Medals?" She slid open the drawer and found the actual medals that corresponded to the bars on the uniform. The biggest was a gold star on a blue ribbon. She picked it up and inspected it. "A Medal of Honor! Wow!"

She quickly checked out the rest. Two Silver Stars. Four Bronze Stars. And another ten or fifteen other assorted medals.

Paul's stories must have been at least partly right. Her admiration for Burke leapt off the scale.

Not that she trusted him. But she did admire him.

She checked all the drawers carefully for any sign of the code to the vault. None.

What about his clothes? Code could be in any pocket. But she didn't have time to search. Banana was bound to notice her disappearance.

And Burke was probably watching her remotely on a surveillance system. He wouldn't allow her to paw through all his belongings. Besides, if he'd seen her discover his vault, he'd know what she was looking for.

Pickles!

Leaving the closet, she dusted his room. As she ran the cloth along the top of his dresser, she gave a quick peek in his drawers. Everything was folded neatly, including his socks. But she found nothing odd, no weird sex toys, no whips, no chains.

And no numbers or letters written anywhere.

She found condoms in his bedside drawer, but nothing else incriminating. Not even any porn. He couldn't be this normal.

Wishing she could tear apart the entire room, she reluctantly finished vacuuming and left.

As she scrubbed down her bathroom, everything clicked into place and an awesome plan crystallized in her mind. She couldn't allow herself to get locked into her original plan. So what if she didn't have all her fake IDs and weapons? All that mattered was escape. She had an emergency kit stashed in a friend's attic. She'd get away from Burke, snag the kit, and worry about securing more guns later.

But she'd be playing this game far too close to the edge.

She looked at the clock and her stomach tightened. Bummer. Too late to make her plan happen today.

Which presented her with another problem. She had to go on the assumption that Burke had seen her searching his place for an escape route. Her actions had made her intentions clear. She had to reassure him that she had no plans to leave so he wouldn't double the guards or change them. Her plans hinged on manipulating Banana and David. She had to make Burke think she'd given up. She had to distract him.

A perfect idea came to her. A way to throw him off her scent without having sex with him. While Burke was the smartest man she'd ever met, he was still a man.

When Burke opened the door to his penthouse, he was met by a wave of delicious smells. Tomato-based sauce, onions, garlic and beef. Sam cooked? After he left her a stack of take-out menus? While he'd invited her to use his kitchen, he certainly hadn't expected it.

Last he'd seen she'd been vacuuming the living room. That was after he'd watched her discover his vault. And go through all his drawers. He laughed.

He'd immediately realized that Sam had used cleaning as an excuse to look for her gun and IDs. He was very impressed that she'd found his weapons vault. But why had she continued cleaning? And then cooked?

She must have been bored to tears.

And he had to admit, his place was in bad need of a cleaning. His maid had quit a month before to have a baby, and he hadn't had time to hire and train a new one. The place had been bothering him to the point where he'd planned on cleaning it himself later on in the week. But Sam had beaten him to the punch.

He chuckled and headed for the kitchen. As he passed the dining room, the table caught his attention. The smoky glass-topped dining table glistened. Sam had polished the chrome on the buffet. The entire room shined.

He gave a quick check of the rest of his house. The hallway carpet looked new. The living room sparkled. Sam had outdone herself.

Smiling, he went to see his lovely houseguest.

When he turned the corner to the kitchen, the sight that met him, entranced him. Sam stood at the stove, stirring a red sauce in a large fry pan. Wearing one of his large aprons, it appeared as if she were naked. Lovely white flesh covered in a dark green apron. She turned away, revealing a pair of white shorts and a teal tank top. Her shorts accentuated her high rounded ass and the tank top revealed her finely muscled back and arms.

His dick turned to rock. He had a quick thought of bending her over one of the bar stools.

She worked the stove like she'd lived there for years. She fit.

He flashed on the next forty years: Sam in various outfits and hairstyles cooking with him. Kissing under the mistletoe she'd hung by the fridge. Toasting with Cristal on New Years.

Fucking her from one end of the house and back again, day after day after day.

Happiness filled him. She comforted, aroused, and entertained him. Screw his fear of marriage. This woman would be wearing his ring ASAP.

"So are you going to stand there staring at me all day or you going to come in and pour yourself a glass of wine?" She sent him a saucy little grin that almost made him come in his pants.

How would he get through the evening without dropping to his knees and begging her to fuck him?

Control, man. Control.

He smirked. "Good evening to you, too, brat."

"Great timing, I almost have dinner ready."

"What have I done to deserve all this niceness on your part? Last I saw you, you were complaining to Emma on the phone about being imprisoned in Burkatraz."

She laughed delightedly, her hazel eyes dancing. His heart burned like a supernova and it took all his strength to maintain his smug expression.

"You heard that, huh?"

"Yes," he said, sending her a sly and knowing grin.

"Well, I'm going crazy. I must be to have cleaned your whole house."

"I'm forever in your debt for that. I've never seen the place shine like this." His attention went to the large All-Clad pan on the stove. "And you've cooked dinner?"

"Yeah, needed some comfort food."

His shoulders tensed. What if he didn't like her cooking? How would he lie? He was a total snob. Damn, he didn't want to hurt her feelings, but if it was terrible, there was no way he could keep that from her. "Huh. Comfort food."

She gave him a sideways glance and snorted. "Don't worry, you'll like it. Everyone likes this recipe. It was my Mom's. Well, as close as I could make it given the constrains of your ingredients." She turned to him and looked at him like he'd just been beamed in from a space ship. "Burke, you have the weirdest foods in your cupboards. No mayo, but you have bearnaise from France. No yellow mustard, only weird-ass mustards from all over the world. Everything is from another country, I can't read the writing, and I can't tell what most of the stuff is from the pictures on the label. Where the hell do you shop?"

He laughed. "Globally. Most of my supplies I pick up in the countries when I visit them."

"You're fucking crazy. I had a hell of time making something normal."

"So what did you make?"

"Sloppy Joes."

A fifty-ton wall of bad taste slammed him to the kitchen floor, forcing all the air from his lungs. Dear God, could it be any worse?

"All the color left your face."

"No…Sloppy Joe's sound—"

"Terrible to you. I know you'd love to cry out in horror, but you're only allowed to do that after you taste them. And let me make something clear, I don't care what you think of my cooking. I've been through enough picky boyfriends to last me a lifetime. I like this recipe, I needed to eat these to make myself feel better, and so that's what we're having."

"I'm sorry. I…"

"Burke, you can't help but be who you are. I don't fault you for your tastes. And I know mine frighten you. But give the Sloppy Joes a try before you run screaming to a restaurant."

"I wouldn't do that. And they smell great. But yes, they do frighten me. I don't want to hurt your feelings."

"You couldn't. Well, not with my cooking. I know it's good."

"So what's the recipe? What ingredients did you use?"

"Ground beef, onions, canned peeled tomatoes, garlic, mushrooms, zucchini and some other junk. Don't have hamburger buns, but the sliced sourdough will work fine. Oh, and I made a Greek salad."

"Wow."

"Sit."

Ground beef. His stomach dropped. She couldn't have. He casually walked over to the garbage and his worst fears were realized. She'd used his last pack of ground Kobe beef. Cost him over a hundred and fifty dollars a pound, plus the cost of the trip to Japan.

It was a trifle in the scheme of things, but he couldn't believe she'd just—wait. Mushrooms. Not the morels! He checked the cupboard. His shoulders slumped. Yes. The morels. Another two hundred dollars making these the most expensive Sloppy Joes on the planet. As he turned away from the cupboard, the empty bottle of Bordeaux sitting on his granite counter top stopped him. Holy shit. A five hundred dollar bottle of wine that had been half-full the night before. Add two hundred and fifty dollars to the travesty along with the criminal misuse of fine wine.

He couldn't decide whether to laugh or cry so he shrugged it off.

"What?"

"What, what?" He spun on her.

She studied his face, seeming concerned. "You went pale again. Did I use an ingredient I shouldn't have?"

"No, no. Not at all."

"I did, didn't I?"

"No. Let's eat." He ignored her searching stare and took his place at the table.

He dreaded the first bite, but had to get it over with. The sacrilege of sacrileges, Kobe beef Sloppy Joes. He'd never imagined such a culinary catastrophe.

As he bit into the sandwich, a delightful flavor met his palate. More vegetables than he expected, maybe a fourth chopped zucchini done perfectly with a nice finishing crisp. The Morels added a wonderful richness. Garlic. And he couldn't help but admit that the two hundred and fifty dollars worth of wine infused the dish with a sophisticated flair. The rainbow of flavors meshed perfectly. A gourmet Italian delight. Far exceeded his expectations.

"These are very good," he said in more of a shocked tone than he would have liked.

She burst out laughing. "You sound floored."

"I am. Sorry, but I am. These are delicious. I need the recipe."

"Okay."

"For what I know about Sloppy Joes and remember, they didn't have this quantity of vegetables."

"My mother was the sneakiest person on the planet. She snuck vegetables in everything. Oh, look, we're having Sloppy Joes. And I'm a stupid idiot and don't realize that I've just eaten a pile of vegetables."

He chuckled. "Your mother sounds charming."

"She was awesome." Sam's eyes clouded with pain, her sorrow lines etched deep.

He wanted to kiss all her pain away. "She's gone."

"Yes. They're all gone. Everyone." Her expression darkened, then lightened for a moment. She frowned and looked at the food on her plate.

"What?" he asked.

"Nothing."

"Say it."

She examined him carefully. "How much did these cost?"

Was she a mind reader? Were his thoughts this obvious? "It doesn't matter."

"Just answer me. How much did these cost?"

Should he tell her?

"Come on, Burke."

After a moment, he shrugged. "About five hundred and twenty-five dollars. Plus the cost of a trip to Japan on a private jet to purchase the Kobe beef."

Her eyes grew huge, her jaw dropped and she stared at him for a long few seconds. Then all at once, she burst into loud laughter. She held her sides and rocked back and forth. Her face grew redder and redder. Gasping for breath, she roared, "Kobe beef Sloppy Joes!" She thumped the table with her hand and howled. Tears streamed down her face. "Oh, I have to call Emma. This is hilarious!" She leapt up from her chair and dashed out of the room.

Burke stared after her, his mouth slightly agape, feeling like the luckiest man in the world to have such a vivacious, wild and outrageous woman in his home. Cooking him million dollar Sloppy Joes.

He'd never let her leave. Somehow, someway, he'd keep her there until she fell in love with him. He knew she liked him, he saw the way she stared at his body. She'd even made a slip earlier and referred to him as a boyfriend.

But he had to do this right. Sam was his future. He couldn't make a mistake this time.

An explosion of laughter came from her bedroom.

Damn, he loved her. Already.

His gut twisted.

Love. Again?

But this was worse. Much, much worse than anything he'd felt before. Obsession. She uprooted him, enticed him, and bewitched him.

He had to have her.

But this was terrible timing for what he'd planned to do to her tonight.

After he was through with her, Sam would hate him. And more than likely, their romantic future would be dead.

NINE

Burke's phone buzzed in his pocket. Rollin. "You rang?"

"Five hundred dollar Sloppy Joes?" Rollin hooted.

Burke speared a piece of zucchini with his fork. "My fucking Kobe beef, a five hundred dollar bottle of a perfectly balanced Bordeaux, and Morels I had flown in from Washington, yes."

"So do they taste good?"

"Not worth five hundred and twenty-five dollars, but yes. She's a remarkable cook."

"So what did she say?"

"Haven't got there."

"Have you fucked her?"

"Won't you know before me if it's going to happen?"

Rollin chuckled. "Oh, yeah. I keep forgetting about the pipeline. We were just talking about you guys. What an excellent couple you'd make. Either that or you'd kill each other."

"Agreed. What does Sam think?"

"She doesn't want to like you."

"But she does."

"A lot more than she's letting on."

Warmth spread through his body and blood flooded his cock. "Good."

"You won't hurt her, will you?" Genuine concern filled Rollin's voice.

"No. I think she might be the one."

"Seriously, dude? I don't think you know what you're getting into. You can't control her."

"I know."

"I think the little head is thinking for the big head."

"Trust me, they're both in accord."

"Oh, God. Dude…" Rollin laughed. "This is gonna be amusing. She's gonna torture you."

"I'm counting on it."

"And are you gonna torture her."

"More than likely."

"And you'll never leave the bedroom."

Burke smiled widely. "My thoughts exactly."

"Hey, I hate to drop this on you, but Sam has to tell us where the information is by tomorrow morning. If not, Captain and I have to come over there and drug her and make her. But I'd rather pull out all my teeth with wrench than do this to her, man. You have to work her. Pull the ol' Burke magic. And do it now. Strong disappeared. He's CIA, but we also think he's Cabal. We need to know what he told Sam."

Burke's stomach lurched. Sam would kill them all. "Shit. I'll do my best."

"Hey, I gotta go. Emma's off the phone. Good luck. With everything. Call me when she tells you."

"Okay," he replied in a resigned tone. He'd only planned on dropping one bomb on her tonight. Now it looked like poor Sam was in for a blitz attack.

His dick was not happy with him.

Sam bounced into the room. When she saw the food, she started laughing again. "Oh, God, I have to stop. My stomach hurts and I want to eat these suckers."

She plopped down and dug into her food. The woman could eat.

After polishing off a giant Sloppy Joe and a huge pile of salad, she pushed her plate away. "I'm about to bust. I must have worked up an appetite cleaning the place today."

Raising his glass, he said, "Thanks to my lovely companion for an amazing and very entertaining meal and for cleaning my house. Much appreciated."

She clinked her glass with his. "You bet." She screwed up her face like she was thinking.

"What?"

"Can I ask you a question?"

"Certainly. Doesn't mean I'll answer it, but fire away."

"So what do the Patriots do and who is the Cabal exactly?"

"The Cabal owns the country. Actually, the globe."

"I don't understand."

He sighed. "Do you really want to know the truth about how the world works? Why there's poverty, why we engage in wars? Why the infrastructure is crumbling, yet more and more money is being made by fewer and fewer people?"

"So it's true? There is a group of rich people controlling the world?"

"Yes."

"Kinda figured. So you guys fight them?"

"We try. We're no match for them. We fight them as best we can through back channels. While they control the world's resources and communication channels, there are still underground networks they haven't penetrated."

"But what about…we're alone, can I talk about this?"

"About what?"

"About what happened with Emma and you and that…that thing."

Dark, unresolved emotions twisted his gut. Not a shining moment of his life. "You aren't supposed to know the full details about that."

"I was sleeping in Emma's guest room one night while I was having my house fumigated and she and Rollin were talking right near the vent…"

His shoulders relaxed and he fought a smile. "You eavesdropped?"

"Uh-huh. So you were trying to take out al-Qaeda all by yourself?"

He rolled his eyes. "Not a great plan as it turned out."

"Rollin said it would have worked and he was bummed he screwed it up for you."

"My mistake was involving the Patriots. I actually thought I could outsmart them. And they were essential to my plan. The people I was dealing with wouldn't have believed me if my friends hadn't come after me."

"So your plan was to get the nuke—that came from God knows where—the one Adam stole, disable it, plant a homing device and another remote-control bomb—that wasn't a nuke— inside the case, follow the bomb to the al-Qaeda hideout and blow them all up?"

He gave a shrug. "Might have worked. Had I involved the Patriots directly. But I was worried my plan might go afoul. I had to protect them."

Her eyes big, she looked at him with wonder. "Wow. That's crazy, Burke. I can't believe the guy that's sitting across from me plays such dangerous games."

He loved the admiration on her face, but it wasn't deserved in this case. "Had no problem with that part. Betraying my friends, that was rough. Even though my loyalty is to this country and I fight everyday for our freedom and welfare, my first priority is to my friends. No matter what."

"I agree," she said and sent him a sweet smile.

Damn it, he had to get that information. Not only did the future of the Patriots rest on obtaining the evidence, his future with the Patriots depended on it.

He examined her carefully. Her expression was open and receptive. And she was so beautiful. His back and neck tensed hard. What he was about to do ran completely counterintuitive to the plans his dick and heart had for her.

Life could really suck sometimes.

Sam was impressed. Burke's had been doing a lot of thinking.

He opened his mouth to say something, then shut it. He looked down at his plate, his gaze darting about. He sighed and his attention refocused on her. "Sam. I have to ask this. And I really need the answer."

Sam's gut contracted around the Sloppy Joes. She wanted more wine. Unable to take his intense stare, she found a piece of black fuzz on her white shorts and concentrated on removing it. "Yeah?" she asked absently.

"Is the information safe?"

Staring at the fuzz, she carefully pulling it away from the cotton twill. No way was she biting that hook.

She picked up her plate and hustled it over to the sink.

"Is it safe?" he asked again, this time in a much firmer tone.

This guy would never give up. She turned on the hot water.

"I saw you holding it. Tell me. Can it be compromised?"

"For God's sake, I'm not stupid," she blurted. Then growled with exasperation. *Shut up!* Fuck!

"I'll take that as a yes."

Her jaw popped from clenching it so hard.

"What happened between you and Strong?"

She took a deep sigh to suppress a scream and busied herself with the dishes. Concentrating on her breathing, she tried to calm. "We ate. He made some wicked cool ravioli."

"Sam," he said in tone that told her he knew she was withholding vast amounts of information. "What did he tell you?"

"Nothing. Well, other than his wakeboarding and movies and junk, why?"

"You are a terrible liar. He disappeared today."

"Probably just went on a sales trip," she said with a shrug.

"He's not a salesman and you know it."

She finally turned to him. "What do you mean?"

Burke's gaze pierced hers. "Don't play dumb. What did he tell you about us? About me? You haven't looked at me the same since you got back from the date. And the timing of your escape was just too coincidental. Were you going to meet him? Did he offer to protect you from us?"

She snorted. "Why would he? He's a salesman."

Burke threw his napkin down on the table, his brows hard over his dark eyes. "Cut the bullshit. We need to know what he knows. He's a very dangerous man."

She returned to the dishes. "Heard that more than once lately."

"Sam? Come over here."

"I'm tired." She rinsed a bowl and set it on the dish drainer.

"I don't care. You know a lot more than you're letting on."

"I am not some criminal mastermind like you, Burke. I'm a simple woman."

He gave a harsh laugh. "Simple, my ass. Did you tell him where the information was hidden?"

"No."

"So he did ask."

She sighed, but still wouldn't look at him. "Okay. Fine. Why don't you tell me what you know and I'll confirm or deny it."

"Sam, goddamn, it, don't play with me," he bit out, angry. "Paul Strong is fucking CIA. Do you know what that means? Did you know he was trying to infiltrate the Patriots? Were you helping him?"

Her body turned to fire and she faced him, her jaw tight. "How dare you accuse me of that, you prick! Do you know what Rollin has done for me? Like I would stab my best friend's boyfriend in the back?"

Burke's expression remained fixed. Cold and hard. "You don't seem surprised by the information. What did he tell you?"

She turned her back and leaned on the counter, working her mouth. A drop of sweat trickled between her shoulder blades. What should she tell him? What should she reveal? He would pick up on any slight nuance of her duplicity. "Fuck. You aren't going to leave me alone, are you?"

"No."

She stared at the bottle of dish soap for a long moment. As long as she didn't reveal her plans, she could tell him what Paul told her. She just had to be very, very careful and measure each word. But damn, she wanted to punch Burke. Hard. She gritted her teeth and threw the sponge in the sink, splashing water everywhere.

Pushing away from the counter, she reluctantly walked over and sat down. After a large swig of wine, she crossed her arms and legs, then leveled her gaze at him. "He said all kinds of shit."

"Did he admit he was CIA?"

"Not specifically."

"Who did he say he worked for?"

"The government."

"Did he admit he was using you to get to us?"

"Yes."

"You must not have been too happy to hear that."

"I wasn't."

"What else did he say?"

Okay. He wanted to play? Fine. She uncrossed her legs and arms and glared at him. "He said you massacred forty people including a twelve-year-old boy."

Burke looked like she'd punched him full force in the jaw. He jerked back in his chair, his mouth open, his eyes wide. Took him a full few seconds to recover. His gaze went volcanic, and he looked away. Pain, hurt and fury crossed his handsome features. She'd hit a nerve all right.

Even though her heart told her to back off, her mouth took on a life of its own. "Did you really kill a twelve-year-old?"

His brown gaze went cold, he pulled himself up taller and he looked her dead in the eye. "When you're looking down the barrel of a grenade launcher with a twelve-year-old on the other end of it, you don't think. You kill him. I was lucky he was inexperienced and took an extra moment to release the safety or I wouldn't be here."

Her cheeks flushed warm. She felt like an asshole for questioning him.

He dared her with his dark, hostile gaze. His muscles hard, white-hot energy radiated from his core. "What else? Out with it. All of it. What other shit did he say about me?" He practically spat the words at her. She'd never seen him this mad, this fired up. There was an almost feral quality behind his eyes. Kill or be killed. Deep wounds. He'd witnessed terrible things.

She took a deep breath and a long draw of wine.

He leaned in, all squared shoulders and electric fury. He assaulted her with his gaze. "What? At least have the decency to allow me to defend myself. What else did he tell you?"

She sighed and then related the story Paul had told her about the massacre.

Burke's ears went back, he snorted and scowled at his plate. His intensity filled the room. "That fucking story is going to follow me my whole life. Doesn't matter what I tell you. That will always be between us. When you look at me, all you'll think about is how I murdered forty people. That I went crazy," he said, making an insane face.

She'd never seen this much pain in anyone's eyes before. Part of his soul had been crushed. Part of his world had collapsed. And he'd never fully healed.

But he was still Burke. Sure of himself, strong and centered. Just deeply, deeply wounded.

She hated the government for doing this to him and she hated hearing what had happened to him. But she needed to hear his side of the story. Paul *had* shaken her belief in Burke. He *had* turned her against him.

Burke calmed almost imperceptibly. He sat back an inch or two and the temperature of his gaze fell a couple degrees. But he still had a kiln of rage burning inside him. He locked gazes with her. "I'm only going to tell this story once. Believe it or not. I don't care."

She held up her hand. "Burke, you don't—"

He jabbed his forefinger at her. "No, you're going to hear it." He took a short pause, then looked like he aged ten years. "Yes, I massacred forty people. The story is true. But there wasn't one innocent person in that camp. For the record, I have never killed anyone who didn't deserve it. Who didn't try to kill me first. And those bastards murdered my whole team. Our mission was to rescue a captured Marine." His face ashen, he took a deep breath and shook his head. "If anyone had seen what those animals did to that poor Marine and my team, they wouldn't have questioned my actions."

He let out a long, scorching breath through his nostrils and gripped his napkin so hard she half expected it to scream. "For fuck's sake, I was only trying to survive. I was outnumbered thirty to one at that point. So, yes, I went nuts. I went crazy. I sliced and stabbed and shot and blew up every single one of those bloodthirsty fuckers." His gaze went even more haunted. "And I will never get those images out of my head. I will never forget the smell of the blood and the dead. The stench of sliced intestines and gunpowder. The piles of bloodied bodies. My dead friends. The lives I took. That vacant soulless look in the eyes of that twelve-year-old kid."

She had no reference for his suffering. Unimaginable. Her horror was like a skinned knee compared to his. "I'm sorry, Burke.

"Did Strong tell you I got the Medal of Honor for that so-called massacre?"

"No."

"Of course not." Steaming fury poured from him. "The brass gave me a medal. And covered up the fact that after I killed all those people, I found more gold bullion in that camp than I've ever seen before. And, boy, was the brass grateful. Then they gave me direct orders to forget I saw it. They gave me that medal as hush money. When I wouldn't shut up, they sent a high-level CIA guy to talk to me. He offered me a special black ops mission—outside the SEALs—to assassinate the Al-Qaeda leader who set up the camp, killed my team, and ordered the torture and death of the Marine. And I jumped on it."

"I'll bet you did."

"But as it turned out, it was all a ruse. They sent me to Afghanistan to die. The man I captured and held had nothing to do with the camp or the killing of my friends. That's when I found out how the Cabal controls the world. How we're all puppets in their sorry game. They didn't send us to that camp to rescue the Marine, they sent us there to recover the gold. Then the Cabal stole it and ordered the brass to send me on a suicide mission."

Her stomach twisted with empathy. "I'm sorry, Burke."

Sitting back, he shifted his focus to his glass, twisting the stem with his long fingers. He shuddered. "I was so fucked up at that point, I wasn't sleeping, I wasn't eating, I wasn't even in my body. Then I faced the hardest challenge of my life. A month alone in an icebox of a cave with one of the most criminally insane motherfuckers I've ever met. Fucked my head up more than the massacre had. I had PTSD, was paranoid already—completely unbalanced—and then I played the hardest game of chess I ever had. For a solid month."

"Damn, Burke. Too much."

"Thankfully, Rollin found out what happened and that's when he and Captain and Zane started the Patriots. When they finally tracked me down, I was stark raving mad. I hadn't eaten in seven days. Every last brain cell of mine was spent trying to control that fucking murderer. When they came into that cave, I thought I was hallucinating them and almost killed Rollin. I didn't recognize him. Thankfully, Zane tackled me before I could kill either of them. Took the guys a long time to talk me down and convince me who they were."

Her heart went out to him. She wanted to hold him, comfort him and make all his pain go away. "Jesus, Burke."

"After that, I quit the military, and disappeared because for one, I was out of my mind, and secondly, because the CIA put out a contract on me."

Sam felt punched. She gasped and her mouth dropped open. *"What?"*

Burke gave a small fire-filled smile. "Yes. I worried them. And the CIA doesn't like being worried. Thankfully, Captain has amazing connections—and is ruthless—and got the contract cancelled. But when Captain told me about the hit, I had no ability to distinguish fact from fantasy. I thought he'd been brainwashed or was in with the CIA.

I freaked out and ran. Went to Colorado, rented a place out in the middle of nowhere in the mountains, and sat with a loaded gun in my hand and stared at the door, waiting for my enemies to come kill me. Thankfully, after a month or two, Rollin tracked me down. Of course, I almost shot him. Again. He dragged me out of there and forced me into counseling," he said, easing down in his seat.

Her shoulders relaxed. "God bless that man."

Burke nodded and sighed. "Saved my life. Yes, thank God for him, and thank God for that therapist. I'm very grateful that I had the ability to think my way out from that horrible abyss. But I doubt I'll ever get rid of the nightmares. I still only sleep about four to six hours a night. Nighttime isn't my favorite."

She'd never felt more rotten. "I apologize."

"Don't. You couldn't have known."

"Thanks so much for your service, Burke. I mean that."

His expression softened a tad. "You're welcome."

"You're one of the strongest, most brave and courageous men I've ever met in my life." The words felt paltry compared to the sentiment she wanted to express.

His sat back in his seat gave a slight nod. After draining his wine glass, he refilled it to the brim, his hand shaking.

They were quiet a long time as Burke drank his wine and calmed.

But his hostility remained. His eyes didn't lose their hard quality. And his anger boiled just below the surface. His dark gaze flickered to hers. "Anything else? Let me guess, Strong told you I'm into sadomasochism. That I do unspeakable things to my lovers."

Her throat went so tight, she couldn't speak.

He snorted and gave a small smile. "Figures. People love that rumor."

"I didn't believe him."

"Sure you did," he said with a slight curl of his lip. "I saw it in your eyes when I found you in the alley. The fear. The judgment."

Her body went hot and hard, and she pointed at him. "I'm not going to feel bad for that. I won't apologize for believing anything right now. You could still be lying to me. I'm being used as a ping-pong ball."

"Which is why you took off."

"I'd always planned on disappearing." She sat back and crossed her arms. "But Paul pushed up the timetable. I knew I was in deep shit when he revealed who he was. You're not going to blow your cover unless you're desperate. I had the feeling he wasn't going to let me go if I didn't play things right."

He nodded. "You're probably correct. Not that we would have allowed him to kidnap you. We had two teams on standby."

She took a sip of her wine.

"Did you tell him where you'd hidden the packet?"

She laughed. "Oh, yeah. First thing."

He narrowed his eyes.

"Burke, if I was going to tell anyone it would be you guys."

His expression darkened and he focused on his glass, then her.

A shiver went through her. "What?"

"If you don't tell me by tomorrow morning, Rollin, Zane and the Captain will come here, tie you up, and inject you with sodium pentathol and extract the information."

She almost threw up the Sloppy Joes. Pushing away from the table, she returned to the dishes.

"Save yourself the trauma and tell me now."

"No."

"Sam, goddamn it, you must understand the gravity of the situation. If you had made it to Seattle, you'd be dead right now. The CIA won't let that information out. Not when Strong is being controlled by the Cabal."

"I thought he was CIA."

"And Cabal. Time's up. Tell me. Now."

She stared at the dishes. She had to fight for that info. She'd never forgive herself if she just handed it over to the Patriots. "Paul was surprised you guys hadn't already drugged me."

"Do you miss New Hampshire?"

Her stomach contracted like he'd slammed her in the gut with an iron glove. The sink fuzzed out and her mind went gray. She had to swallow to keep from puking. Her knuckles whitened from gripping the counter so hard.

"Bobby looked up missing teenagers from 1992 to 1994 in the state of New Hampshire. You look remarkably like a young woman named Amanda Hutchins."

Her mind froze with horror. She couldn't breathe. She couldn't move. She hadn't heard or spoken the name Amanda Hutchins in sixteen years.

"Her father was killed by a transient. Amanda, or Mandy, disappeared at the same time, leaving behind a pool of blood by a riverbank. The transient was convicted of both murders even though Amanda's body was never found."

She had to hold herself up to keep from falling.

"Since there are only a few people in that packet and one is from New Hampshire, it doesn't take a rocket scientist to put two and two together. So you knew Lawrence Tyrell? He must be twenty-four years older than you. He couldn't be the boyfriend you're afraid of. So why do you need the information on him?"

Sam knees liquefied and she caught herself before she crumpled to the floor. Memories of Mom and Dad came flying back to her. Her mother's long auburn hair, her beautiful hazel eyes. *Mandy? Time for dinner, honey.* Her dad's crooked smile. *Hey, Salamander.* The way he'd tousle her hair. *How's my best girl today?*

She teetered on a precipice. If she allowed herself to confess, her whole life was over.

Focus! Stay strong! Taking a deep breath, she stood taller. "Well, thank God, you've figured everything out, Burke. Now I don't have to worry about holding back any secrets from you," she bit out in a surprisingly strong tone. But she still wouldn't turn around.

"I will find out everything."

"I'm sure you will."

"Tomorrow morning, actually. If you think our questions will only be limited to the packet, you are mistaken. Tomorrow we'll know every one of your secrets."

Tears blinded her, her gut convulsed, and every fiber of her being screamed at her to run. Stumbling out of the kitchen, she headed to her bedroom. Her room—ha—Burke's room. Surrounded by strangers and they were all going to hurt her.

She reached her bedroom door and she realized that the Sloppy Joes were about to make a comeback. Turning, she rushed into the bathroom and slammed the door behind her. She barely made it to the toilet.

She alternated between crying and puking, agony ripping her like Burke had taken his chef's knives to her gut.

Finally, she slumped down next to the toilet, tears running down her face, sweat pouring off her brow. She concentrated on breathing and trying to stop the pain in her belly.

Burke knocked on the door. "Sam?"

"Fuck off!"

"Talk to me."

"No!"

"I won't hurt you."

"Ha!" Sam's gut and head stabilized enough for her to stand. She wiped down the toilet and flushed, then went to the sink and washed her face.

"Let me in."

She let the water flow into her hands, then rinsed her mouth and spat.

"No matter what Tyrell did to you, this is not the way to get even with him. Not with this information. They'll kill you. Don't you understand?"

She swished more water around in her mouth and spat it out.

"Goddamnit, Sam, open this door!" He knocked again.

"No!" Then she realized that the door was unlocked. She leapt forward and spun the lock. "You guys are gonna get your stupid information in the morning, so I don't have to talk to you now. You've taken everything from me! Everything!"

"No, I haven't. I've protected you and taken care of you."

"You've imprisoned me and invaded my life."

"Listen, you naïve idiot, this isn't just about you. You took our information. Now open this fucking door. Please."

"No!"

"Come on, Sam. You know I could get in there if I wanted to."

"Damn you." Wiping the tears away, she yanked the door open and brushed by him.

He caught her by the arm. "Sam, I have to talk to you."

She scowled up at him, but his expression was so sweet, so caring and so pained, he derailed her anger. "I can't handle much more, Burke. I'm ready to crack."

"Understandable. I've taken away your foundation of lies."

She tugged and he let go of her arm.

"Your protective layer of lies," he continued. "And now you're feeling vulnerable and terrified."

"That pretty much sums it up."

"I'm not going to apologize either, Sam. You're a grown up. You took that packet. And you have to be accountable for that. I'm sorry for whatever happened to you when you were a teenager. But it doesn't give you the right to steal valuable information from others. Joseph and three other good people died for that packet. You can't use that evidence against Tyrell."

She waved her hand in a dismissive gesture and walked into her bedroom. "Why do you keep harping on Tyrell?"

He followed her, his hard expression unwavering. "I saw your reaction. Your name is Amanda Hutchins. And you are thirty-two, not thirty-five."

Reality went blurry and distorted. Black shadows engulfed her. Adrenaline slammed her body, but there was nowhere to run.

Snap!

Wracking with sobs, Sam wailed and collapsed on the bed. The pain was so intense, the release so great, she couldn't lie. She had no control. Which made her freak out even more. Her body shook and her sobs were so violent, she could barely breathe.

From the glimpses she caught of Burke, he looked like he'd just broken something precious. Slightly horrified and very remorseful.

He moved in and tried to put his arms around her, but she pushed him away with a hard shove. "No! Don't touch me!"

He stepped back and gave her space, but didn't leave. Worry lines etched deep in his forehead and around his eyes.

When she started to calm, rage took the place of her fear. Chilled to the bone, her body trembled and her teeth chattered. She hated Burke right then. Hated him. "Who else knows?" she snapped.

"Your real name?"

"Yes."

"Bobby and I."

"Anyone else?"

"No."

"Keep it that way," she bit out in a growl.

"I will."

There was a long silence. She slowly began to numb. She'd blown it. She had one slight chance to delay them for a few hours and she'd have to take it. Shit. Playing this one far too close the edge.

She put her head in her hands.

"Sam. Please tell me where the information is. I don't want to drug you and force you to tell us."

She needed him to believe she'd broken completely. After a good, long, loud crying jag, she spoke. "The information is in a safe deposit box in Wells Fargo Bank in Seattle. Downtown. You'll need my fake ID under the name of Sheryl Blanc. And I have to give you the safe deposit key. Whoever goes and picks it up needs to be in a long dark wig and have my build."

She couldn't afford to look at him or he might see the duplicity in her eyes.

"Thank you, Sam."

Shit. This ploy had given her a bit more time, but it wouldn't be long before they figured out she'd duped them. They'd find a gun and nothing else in that box.

She kept her face buried in her knees. "You're welcome. Now get out of here."

"Do you want to talk?"

"No."

"Should I call Emma?"

"No, I don't want her to know anything." She lifted her gaze to his, her anger centering her and shielding her heart. "Don't ever speak that name again. Destroy any traces of your search."

"I will. And I'll tell Bobby."

She gave a nod.

Burke studied her. "Were you really going to try to assassinate a presidential candidate?"

She snorted and rolled her eyes. "No." *Yes.*

He saw right through her. "Don't let him win, Sam."

"He won't."

"What did he do to you?"

Her attention dropped to her lap and she shook her head.

"I'm sorry, Sam. I agree Tyrell is a bastard. But going after him right now is suicide. In a few years things will be different. You've waited sixteen years. If you can hang on a bit longer, the situation could change."

"Could," she spat at him with a glare. "Did you see the contents of that package? Do you know what he's capable of? And this is a man you want in the President's office?"

His face clouded. "No. I don't. But if he does get in there, I'd like a shot at controlling him."

She sneered. "You guys are playing his game."

"It's the only way to win."

"I don't like your world, Burke. Mine is simpler."

"No, it's not. Not if you go after Tyrell."

"Everything changed tonight, Burke. Everything."

"So you won't go after him?"

She looked away. "I don't know anything anymore."

"I'm here for you, Sam."

She couldn't look at him or she might break. "I appreciate that, Burke. But now I need some sleep."

"Certainly. If you need me, I'm right down the hall. Like I said, I don't sleep much."

"Night, Burke."

He closed the door and she sat up and shook her head to clear it. Burke was a plague. He'd completely infected her brain and heart. She needed to eradicate him from her system. Distance should help with that. But, holy bejeebus, what a mess.

Sam forced herself to focus. She had a lot to plan that night if she was to get to Seattle before the Patriots discovered she'd lied.

TEN

By the time morning came, Sam was ready. Her plan was insane. Absolutely one hundred percent foolish, reckless and dangerous.

Her only chance was to appear totally defeated. She had to make Burke think she'd been demoralized, that she was too exhausted to do anything but sleep.

She decided not to put on make-up or get out of her pajamas. Even though a part of her rebelled, she left her hair a mess.

Sam shuffled out to the kitchen and tried not to notice how amazing he looked.

Damn, she wished she'd met him another time.

Thankfully, Burke seemed properly alarmed at her appearance. "Are you all right?"

"No." She poured herself a cup of coffee.

"Is there anything I can do for you?"

"No." After retrieving the half-and-half, she returned to her cup.

"Do you want some breakfast?"

"No." She dumped sugar and half-and-half into her coffee, put them both away and headed back to her room.

"Sam…"

She stopped, but didn't turn around. "You going to be here today? Or are you going to Seattle?"

"I'm leaving in a half an hour to meet the rest of the guys. I don't know what the plan is yet, but I won't be home until late."

The tension in her stomach eased one notch. Plenty of time to escape. "Come by my room and I'll give you the safe deposit box key."

"Sam…" His voice was full of longing.

She couldn't let him affect her. Her emotions for him were screwing with her head. Without a glance behind her, she walked out.

Step one complete.

Step two would suck. She needed to hand him the key without looking at him or talking to him.

She'd just settled into bed with the cup of coffee and a magazine when he knocked. "Come in."

He opened the door and she hid behind her *Rolling Stone*. Part of her wanted to blurt her plan out to him. Have him talk her out of doing something so stupid. Hold her.

Then fuck her brains out.

Wake the hell up, Sam. Burke is the enemy.

"Key is on the dresser," she said without moving the magazine.

The key scraped across the wooden surface of the tallboy.

Sam looked at the words on the page, but paid no attention to them.

She felt the weight on the bed at the same time his cologne hit her.

Damn it!

He pushed down her magazine. "Sam, look at me."

No way.

He gently tucked his finger under her chin and turned her face to his.

His dark gaze was intense, powerful and extremely affectionate. He looked good enough to eat. She shifted her focus back to the article. The man was extremely unhelpful.

"Sam. I know you think I'm your enemy, but I'm not. And I want to be more than your friend. I think you know how I feel about you. I'm falling for you."

An avalanche of emotion flattened her and she gasped for breath. Her chest hurt like he'd punched her heart. She bit back a sob and hid in her hands.

Could her life get any harder?

Snap out of it! You can use this against him!

The plan. Keep to the plan.

Sam summoned every bit of her inner strength. She had to take control of the situation and fast.

Before she could move, Burke pulled her into his arms. He felt warm and glorious. His rock-like body fit hers like two halves of a whole coming together. His inner energy cast an evil spell over her. She flashed on a series of images: walking down the aisle while he waited at the altar. Their baby in his arms. Holding his hand while walking around a lake when they were old. She looked up at his weathered face, his dark eyes loving her from under gray brows.

She wanted to stay in the man's arms forever.

Hello? She had a job to do. What the hell was she doing, getting all caught up in the guy? He was a freakin' psycho-terrorist, dismantling her mind and destroying her focus.

She wanted to pull away, but her body stayed put. "I can't, Burke. My head is too fucked up."

He held her tighter. "I don't expect anything from you. I wanted you to know how I feel. How much I respect and admire you. How much you enchant me."

He wouldn't find her very enchanting when she screwed him over. He'd hate her. "You don't know me, Burke."

He pushed away to face her. Love and confidence shone clear in his brown eyes. "The hell I don't. I know everything that's important. I know your heart."

"No, you don't." Unable to take the adoration on his handsome face, she tried to hide in his chest, but he held her firmly by the shoulders and forced her to look at him.

"You're overwhelmed and exhausted. When I get back, I want to talk to you more about this. I—I want you, Sam."

"Burke…"

He silenced her with a kiss. Her instinct to push him away was obliterated by his off-the-scale sexual energy. Her whole body thrummed and vibrated. His intense energy enveloped her, encompassed her, ripping away her foundation.

He tasted so good. The way he manipulated her tongue was perfect. Her center ignited with white-hot love for him, and she kissed him back with her whole being.

It was like she'd been dead and he'd reanimated her.

Fuck her plans and her future. All she could think about was Burke. And how badly she wanted him inside her. She felt an overwhelming hunger for him, like she'd never been fed until now.

He ended the kiss and stared at her, his gaze wide, seeming as surprised as she. "Did you feel that?" he whispered.

She grabbed him and kissed him hard. She needed him. Wanted him. Had to have him. Damn the consequences.

They tore at each other's clothes and mauled each other until he stopped and pushed away, his expression tortured.

"Wait, Sam. I can't believe I'm stopping this, but I can't right now. I was supposed to leave twenty minutes ago. And I'm not going to ruin our first time. You deserve the best night of your life and I'm going to give it to you." He grabbed both her hands in his and kissed them. His expression went even more pained. "It kills me to leave you. You're all I think about, you're all I want."

She started to respond, but he pushed his fingers to her lips. "Don't. I know I'm overloading you and I'm sorry. I want you to think about us today. I can't predict the future and I know your head is swimming, but I need you, Sam."

The vulnerability in his eyes pierced her heart. She clung to him.

He would definitely hate her.

And she'd be saying good-bye to probably the most perfect match she'd ever have. As crazy and picky and stubborn and controlling as he was, he was right for her. Their chemistry was off the charts. If they'd met any other time, she'd propose.

Sorrow and longing for him turned her gut inside out. She took a mental cement mixer and poured fresh concrete over her heart and sealed all the cracks.

"I don't want to go," he said softly, nuzzling the side of her face.

His warmth and scent made her sex go soft and wet. "I don't want you to go," her libido and heart replied.

He pulled away and sent her a dazzling smile. "I'll be back tonight. We'll talk more then, okay?" he said with a sweet look.

Yet another Burke sat before her. Open, kind and loving with sparkling, fire-hot energy blazing from every pore of his body. She'd never seen a sight more beautiful.

And her heart hurt like he'd crushed it in his powerful fists.

He kissed her on the cheek, ran his hand down her face and stood. "I'll be back as soon as I can. Rest, darling. I'll see you later."

"Okay. Bye Burke."

"Bye Sam."

He left with a wink, a gorgeous smile and a bounce in his step.

And she'd never felt more horrible in her life.

She could stop him. Tell him the truth. Give him the right name and box number and key and bank.

Fuck. That.

She lightly slapped her face. Damn, she was fragile. She had to get stronger. She had to keep her head together.

Love meant nothing.

If she didn't kill Larry, he'd kill her. And if Larry found out she was in love, Burke was a dead man.

She wouldn't be surprised if Larry knew by now that she'd survived his attack. Once Bobby and Burke had found out that Amanda Hutchins was alive, the timer had started. They couldn't be the only ones who'd figured it out. Paul Strong probably knew, too. Which meant she only had a few days or hours before she'd be hunted down and erased. Everyone thought Amanda Hutchins was dead. How convenient for Larry.

No one would know what happened to her. Her friends in San Mateo might worry, but eventually they'd forget. Burke would move on.

Her whole family would be forgotten.

And Larry Tyrell would become President.

Sam got up and headed for the shower.

Time for action.

Around noon, Burke and Rollin sat in their rental car, stuck in traffic in downtown Seattle. Burke fidgeted and tapped the steering wheel. An accident up ahead had jammed up three square blocks and was finally being cleared. They inched forward, headed to Wells Fargo Bank. Zane and Catherine were already there. Catherine was accessing the safe deposit box in a long black wig with Sam's fake ID.

Burke's phone rang. Zane. "Yes?"

"It was a misdirection, we only found a gun in the safe deposit box."

His heart stopped, then his body kicked into overdrive. All his muscles went hard and he broke out in a full body sweat. That *bitch*! "Fuck!"

"What?" Rollin demanded.

"Sam screwed us. Only a gun in the box." Sam had pulled something back at home. "I have to call Banana—she's fucked us and I'll bet she's gone. Fuck!" He hung up on Zane and punched in Banana's number. No response. "Banana's not answering! She did something to him! Goddamn her!"

"Damn. Sam's lost it. Absolutely fucking lost it," Rollin said, his eyes large, wonder in his voice.

Burke's vision twisted and went red. A war raged inside his gut. He'd never seen a better actress. He wanted to ring her neck.

What a fool, he'd been! He'd bought her whole act that morning. The way she'd looked at him, like she loved him. Her promise. The way she kissed him.

Goddamnit! She'd used him!

He gripped the phone so hard, his hand shook. He punched in David's number. Went to voice mail. He threw the phone onto the floor and almost careened into a bus.

Rollin barely reacted to his crazy driving. "She took out Banana *and* David?"

Burke nodded and focused on the road. If he didn't stay alive, he'd never be able to track her down and take revenge for what she'd done to him. "I'm going to kill her."

"Sounds reasonable. So other than killing her, what's our plan? Where do you think she's headed?"

"Up here somewhere. Could you hand me my phone?"

Rollin chuckled, retrieved it from the floor and handed it to him. "Doesn't mean she doesn't love you, bub. Means she's bent. I know that girl. And this ain't like her. Any way you look at it, Sam has lost her mind."

"I'm still going to kill her. Bobby?"

Choking sounds. Prolonged coughing. Slurping. More coughing. "Here, old man. Heard about Sam." Coughing. Bobby cleared his throat. "She wasn't on any flights from the Bay Area, no one who looked like her. Got facial recognition on everyone who flies into SEA-TAC. I think she's driving. Take her seventeen hours if she drives straight through. Ran some probabilities about what other bank she might have used, matching up new accounts with the date she was there and the areas she visited. I'll send you the list, we'll get them all covered."

"What about Banana and David?"

"Fine. Well, they got bad headaches. Sam loaded a batch of brownies with Ambien."

"That witch!"

"But apparently, they woke up as she was leaving and she shot them with your tranquilizer darts."

The information was too much to get his head around. *"What?"*

"She raided the hell out of your weapons vault."

The taxi in front of him blurred, heat melted his brain, every muscle burned. He wanted to rip the steering wheel from the car. *"How?"*

"She found the combination to the vault in Banana's wallet."

"Fuck!"

"And she took the Mercedes."

Burke screeched to a halt on the side of the road, threw the car into park, and leapt out with a roaring bellow. He pitched the phone into his seat, slammed the door shut, and punched the side of the rental until it was completely dented and his fists were bloody. "Fucking *bitch*! I fucking armed her!"

He was the single stupidest person on the planet. "Outplayed by a cocktail waitress!"

Outrageous. Unbelievable. Unreal.

He paced around the car. "How dare she play me like this! No one does this to me! She is pestilence! An infection! I need antibiotics!" He punched the car again, only this time it hurt.

His head in his hands, he slumped against the car. He couldn't love her this much. But it was clear she didn't love him.

Emma all over again.

Would he ever find a woman of substance who loved him back?

Sam was perfect. When they'd kissed, he'd been thunderstruck. Heard the damned heavenly choir. He'd never wanted a woman more.

He blew out a stream of air. Of course, he couldn't have her. Because of all the bad things he'd done. Karmic payback.

"Buddy?" came Rollin's voice from behind him. He wrapped an arm around Burke and gave him a squeeze, then pulled away and smacked him on the back. "You'll be okay, pal. Don't give up on her yet."

"She used me and led me on." He hated the pathetic note in his tone. He felt like a teenager experiencing his first heartbreak.

"No, she's in love with you, man. She slipped it to Emma. Don't take this personally, she's trying to protect herself or someone else. I know people. And I know Sam. And there isn't a better person on this planet. If you love her, cut her some slack."

Rollin was right. Why was he so crazy? He hadn't been this nuts in years. Emma made him a little whacked out, but Sam had pushed him over the edge.

"Why didn't I just hand her the fucking weapons? Have I suddenly gotten stupid?"

His buddy sent him an affectionate smile. "Hormone goggles are notoriously opaque."

"And I'm so—fuck! I'd only tell you. I'm so fucking judgmental. And narrow-minded. Cocktail waitress, that's all I think. Even after she showed me her bloody library! She has a degree in business and is the furthest thing away from stupid I'd ever met, but I completely underestimated her."

Rollin's expression turned sympathetic. "Dude, when are you going to realize that you're human?"

His best friend always cut to the quick. Burke sighed. The pain in his tight stomach lessened. "Maybe never, but thanks."

"You'll be fine. My prediction is after a long and drawn out battle, and lots of yelling and fighting and fucking, you two will end up married." He smiled widely. "And I've never seen a more perfect fit."

"Truthfully, I don't think I could take it," he admitted in a weary tone.

Rollin chuckled. "Which is why she's perfect for you."

"God help me." He finally cracked a smile.

An image of Sam loading his precious sniper weapons into his custom Mercedes wiped the grin from his face and made his neck twinge.

Forget going easy on her. He couldn't hold back any longer. She fought dirty, so he would. He'd do whatever it took to get her under control. Not only did he need to save her from herself, Sam needed to understand his boundaries. No matter the reasons for her deception and betrayal, the woman would learn never to cross him again.

ELEVEN

Sam circled the downtown Seattle block in her rental car, searching for one of her target parking places. She'd run the escape scenario countless times. Thank the Lord for Google maps and the two shortcuts she'd found the day she'd rented the safe deposit boxes.

As if the gods had planned it, her Number Two choice of parking places was open on a side street not very far from the freeway entrance.

She hoped this worked. Lack of sleep—along with heavy doses of caffeine—were affecting her ability to concentrate. Her thoughts raced, then skipped. She'd stopped at a few rest areas on the way up, but was too paranoid to stay for long. When she'd almost driven off the road and into a river, she'd downed an energy drink. Over the following ten hours, she'd downed five more. Her body buzzed wildly and her stomach hurt from the noxious brew.

After she parked, her heart beat so fast, she could barely breathe. Hopefully her elderly lady disguise would account for her shaking hands.

She checked herself out in the mirror and couldn't help but chuckle: big square-rimmed glasses, a short gray wig, a beige polyester pantsuit and orthopedic shoes. She attached large fit-over-shades that covered her glasses, got out of the car, grabbed her powder blue raincoat, an embroidered old lady purse, an aluminum cane, and became invisible.

Emma had given her the idea for the costume. Housekeepers and women of a certain age went practically unseen in society.

Problem was, under her old lady disguise, she wore a skin-tight yoga outfit for a quick change, and Burke's Kevlar vest. Even though it was a typical June Gloom morning with temperatures in the fifties— and the famous Seattle fog was thick—Sam was sweating.

Forcing all the fear from her head, she focused on her goal. She allowed herself to get into character. She ambled along with a slight limp, using the cane, imagining her right heel to be giving her problems. She concentrated on her physicalities, on her surroundings and on her plan. If she saw a Patriot, she couldn't react.

She'd better not see Burke. Her stomach convulsed. Horrible thought.

As she walked, her legs got shakier and shakier. Thank God for the cane. She took a deep breath, wishing her brain wasn't so scrambled. She'd need to make sure she slept before confronting Larry. And above all, avoid energy drinks.

She checked every person she passed with sideways glances and her peripheral vision, while keeping her head pointed forward. No one looked suspicious

Her heart rate flying high, she reached the bank, walked inside and expected to be attacked. She stopped for a second and pretended to be confused while checking out each person in the financial institution. No one gave her a second glance.

After a deep breath, she approached the safe deposit box area. "My name is Mabel Brown and I'd like to get into my safe deposit box if I may," she said in a strained and cracking old lady voice she'd practiced.

The plump fifty-something bank woman with short dark hair sent her a brilliant smile. "Certainly, Mrs. Brown. Welcome back. Just sign here." She slid the logbook over to her. With a shaking hand, Sam signed her fake name.

A few seconds later, she was in a small locked room facing her long, metal safe deposit box. She opened the lid. The pressure on her gut eased and she sighed. Everything was still there. She withdrew the evidence packet, a can of mace, and her Beretta Tomcat 380 semi-automatic. After checking the safety, she slipped the loaded gun into her shoulder bag. Then she tucked the can of mace in her pocket next to her Smith and Wesson 317 revolver.

Just in case she got caught, she removed one of Larry's most incriminating photos and a thumb-drive with information on his offshore holdings, and hid them in the secret compartments in her Battle Bra: one of many bras she'd modified with special hidden pockets. The rest of the intelligence went into her purse. If the Patriots captured her, she could give them the packet and still have evidence on that bastard.

After taking a deep breath and getting into character, she walked out of the small locked room and handed the box to the bank lady with smile. "Thank you, honey."

"You're welcome, Mrs. Brown."

She wanted to run out of the bank at full tilt. But she kept her gait slow, her movements creaky, and slowly made her way to the door. No one paid the slightest bit of attention to her.

Maybe this would be easy. Maybe there was no one watching her. Maybe she'd suffered over the past twenty-four hours for nothing.

Typical.

She pushed through the glass doors of the bank and hung a left onto the crowded downtown sidewalk. As planned, the noontime lunch rush was in full swing and provided perfect cover.

While measuring her steps, she scanned the myriad people on the sidewalk. *Keep the gait. Stay in character. You're just an old lady, walking down the street.*

With each step she gained confidence. Piece of cake.

This was good. If she could pull off covert stuff like this, stalking and kidnapping Larry—and/or killing him—should be a snap. A pulse of victory surged through her.

Halfway down the block, not one person had so much as looked at her. All she had to do was get to the stoplight, cross the road and duck into the restaurant. After that, her escape was guaranteed.

Her shoulders relaxed, her insane heartbeat slowed a bit. She was going to make it.

About twenty feet in front of her, a man in a dark suit wearing sunglasses stepped out from a doorway. He looked straight at her, touched his earpiece and spoke quietly.

Paul Strong.

A bomb of hyper-charged fight-or-flight-juices blasted her body.

But she'd planned for this moment.

She pointed at Strong with her cane and screeched at the top of her lungs, "He's got a gun!" Aiming for a nearby garbage can, she discharged her Smith and Wesson in her pocket, blowing a small hole through the bottom of her coat.

Chaos. People dove for the ground and ran in all directions, screaming.

Two burly Hispanic maintenance workers in blue overalls rushed a very surprised-looking Strong.

Sam ducked down and ran into traffic with a group of terrified business people, careful to limp in character. She hit the opposite sidewalk and kept going, her focus on the target restaurant. Jostled by the fleeing crowd, she didn't dare look around.

Sirens echoed through the street, bouncing off the tall buildings.

Not very far now.

In her peripheral vision, a dark car pulled up alongside her and matched her speed.

She couldn't help but glance over.

A man with blond hair wearing sunglasses pointed a gun at her.

Her heart rate skyrocketing, she dropped and dove behind a taxi. Gun blasts filled the air, pinging loudly into the sides of the cab. The taxi driver inside screamed in fright. The throng of people on the sidewalk scattered, yelling about guns and terrorist attacks.

Great, now she was putting others in danger! While tempted to fire back, Sam couldn't take the risk of hurting a bystander.

She made a break for the restaurant, thankful for the Kevlar vest.

"Sam!" shouted a loud deep voice from several yards away.

Gunfire rocked the area, shattering glass and blowing apart stucco on the storefronts. Sam ducked down, but kept running.

More gun shots.

"Sam!" the man screamed again. She recognized the voice. Zane.

She didn't even turn to look.

Loud gunfire came from behind her.

As soon as she put weight on her right leg, the pain nearly dropped her.

Fuck! She'd been shot! She hadn't even felt the bullet!

She limped for real now, straight into the restaurant, yelling in character. "That man is trying to kill me! Somebody stop him!" Without looking behind her, she hobbled through the kitchen, past several cooks who stopped their work to stare. Hot grease, onions, celery and grilled beef permeated the thick steamy air. A huge commotion broke out behind her.

Her leg hurt like a mofo. She glanced down and gasped. A red stain had bloomed on the beige material of her upper thigh and was spreading rapidly. She had to get to her car.

She stopped at the back door and peered out into the dark, narrow alley, half-filled with Dumpsters. Tall brick buildings lined the small weedy road. Two doors down on her right, a delivery truck nearly blocked the whole alley. To her left—her planned escape route—the coast was clear. But surely not for long.

She tore off down the alley, her leg killing her, her limp becoming more pronounced. Warm blood ran down her thigh and she fought the panic welling inside her.

Screw her leg. Escape first. Nothing else mattered.

At the end of the alley, she slipped through the break in the chain-link fence, went through some shrubberies and dropped down onto a cement stairwell.

Shooting pain blazed through her thigh and she cried out. She hopped/limped down the stairs, turned the corner and spotted her car. Thank God!

Sam gave a quick check up and down the block, but saw no one in pursuit.

Hurry! Before we bleed to death!

With shaking hands, she fished out her keys from her pocket. She reached her car, opened the door and leapt inside. A blast of horrid pain from her thigh jolted her. Crying out, she grabbed a t-shirt lying on the passenger seat and tied it above her wound. Felt like an alligator chomped down on her thigh. Bile rose in her throat. She panted, trying to control the nausea and pain.

She stuck the key in the ignition and took another quick look around.

A dark vehicle with tinted windows turned the corner behind her and headed her way. In front of her, about a half a block away, a man with short brown hair ran toward her. She gasped. *Burke.*

Her heart rate went out of control, her stomach twisted and tears stung her eyes.

Fuck! Hurry!

She started the car, sending horrifying pain up her leg. She jerked her injured limb out of the way with a yell and slammed on the gas with her left foot. Hurtling out of the parking spot, she ended up directly in front of the dark vehicle.

Crash!

Sam's head slammed back against the seat and her car jetted forward from a rear impact. She thought she heard Burke screaming.

"You fuckers!" She jammed down on the gas pedal and forced herself to look away as she raced by Burke.

Popping noises came from behind her. In her rear view, Burke fired on the vehicle pursuing her. Her stomach wrenched harder. He'd better not get killed!

At the next street, she hung a left on a yellow.

Smash! She jerked back in her seat and her car went into a spin from the rear impact. "Holy shit!" Her heart rate went crazy.

Apparently, Burke's attack had not been successful. She blocked horrible images of his bullet-ridden body from her mind.

As the front of her car swung by the dark attack vehicle, she came face-to-face with her assailants: two square-headed men with dark glasses and cold expressions. Her car kept spinning until she faced forward again. She slammed the gas and accelerated down the street.

The assailants slammed the rear end of her rental, this time harder.

Her head snapped backwards, the steering wheel jerked out of her grasp, and her car jumped the curb and careened onto the sidewalk. "Whoa!"

Her body shaking like hell, Sam fought the wheel. She sideswiped a brick wall, bounced off, flattened a flowerbox and sent a newsstand tumbling. Thankfully, there were no people in the immediate area.

Screaming, she finally regained control over the car and veered back onto the street.

A loud crash came from behind her. She checked her rear view mirror.

The attackers had hit a light pole! Sweet!

Her back window exploded and a bullet impacted her dashboard, blowing little bits of vinyl and foam into the air. Sam ducked, yelling at the top of her lungs. Sweat poured from her forehead and dripped down her neck.

More bullets pounded into the frame of her car. Her body jerked with every hit. "Stop shooting, you assholes!"

Speeding forward, she glanced in her rear view.

The sedan was pulling back from the light pole.

Crap!

Sam tore down the road and turned the nearest corner, her tires squealing.

Flying down the street, she hung a left into a small alley. Glancing in her rear view mirror, she saw no one following her. A little blaze of hope rushed through her. She zoomed through the tiny dark alleyway, and made a right onto a two-lane road in an industrial area.

A black SUV pulled out directly in front of her.

Screaming, she locked the brakes, skidded sideways and stopped a few feet from the vehicle blocking her.

Zane sat in the passenger seat.

"No way! No way!" Sam yelled.

She slammed down on the gas pedal and yanked the steering wheel to her left. Her tires squealed loudly, then finally caught. The car jetted forward and she zipped down the street, back the way she'd come.

An oncoming dark SUV pulled right in front of her.

"Fuck!" Sam jammed on her brakes and stopped just a few feet from its hood.

Burke sat in the drivers' seat.

Zane's vehicle blocked her from behind.

"Trapped!" She threw open the door, grabbed her bag, and jumped out onto her left leg. Hopefully, those gunmen weren't close by. Talk about vulnerable! Fucking Patriots!

When she landed on her right leg, excruciating pain tore through her thigh. Bellowing, Sam hopped and limped across the street, heading toward the nearest building.

Long, iron-like arms wrapped around her and picked her up off the ground, immobilizing her. Her wig and glasses were knocked to the ground.

"Gotcha!" came Zane's deep voice in her ear.

"No!" Her mind rioting with fury and frustration, she tried in vain to twist out of his grip. "Not now! Not when I'm so close!"

"Burke, cover us!" Zane yelled as he carried her toward his car.

"I'm on it!" came a horribly familiar voice.

Zane threw her into the back seat of the SUV. She landed next to Rollin who grabbed her and got her into a hold, smashing her wound against the seat. She cried out in agony. Felt like someone jabbed her leg with a dagger and twisted the blade inside.

"Ow! My leg! You sons-a-bitches!" Fueled by the pain and overwhelmed with disappointment and loss, she couldn't get a handle on her anger. She wanted to throttle them all.

Sam was pressed against the backseat as the SUV took off. Ty drove like a focused maniac.

Crying, spitting and practically foaming at the mouth, she fought Rollin for all she was worth, causing her leg to hurt even more. Which just infuriated her further.

Rollin yelled at her to calm down, but she could barely hear him over her own screams. She couldn't accept it. She couldn't believe she'd been caught. She couldn't believe she'd been shot. Again!

Part of her felt like she could scream reality away.

Through her blurred vision, she got images of the SUV careening through the Seattle streets.

Finally, Rollin clamped his hand over her mouth. "Sam! You have to stop! It's me, Rollin!"

Without thinking, she bit down on his hand, hard. He yelled loudly in her ear.

Something about his cry of pain shook her. She'd just bitten one of her best friends. Fuck. She'd lost it.

She stopped fighting and collapsed into him. "I'm sorry!" she cried, dissolving into frustrated tears. "I'm sorry, Rollin! I've lost everything!"

Gun blasts strafed the back of the SUV, making a hideous amount of noise. Terror replaced her fear and her tears stopped instantly. Why wasn't Rollin shoving her to the floorboards? She turned around to check the source of the gunfire.

A guy holding an assault rifle hung out of the large black sedan following them and fired. The bullets spiderwebbed the back window, but none penetrated the car. Bulletproof glass.

Still way too much. She ducked her head into Rollin's chest.

He held her close. "It's okay, Sam, we'll get you out of here."

An explosion from behind them nearly deafened her and a flash of fire came around the back of their SUV. Little chunks of stuff hit the sides and windows.

"Bulls-eye!" Ty exclaimed with a big grin. "Burke got 'em!"

She turned around. Where there had been a pursuing vehicle was now a ball of fire.

Another SUV drove around the burning vehicle and sped to catch up with them.

"There's another SUV after us!" Sam exclaimed.

"That's Burke," Rollin said.

She blew out a relieved sigh and faced forward again. Rollin still had a good hold on her.

Oh, God. She stiffened. Seeing Burke. After what she did to him? *Shit.*

Rollin slowly let go of her, then turned her face to look at him. "Sam?" he asked in a tender voice. His carved features were drawn with worry and his dark gaze looked haunted.

His expression took her by surprise. Shouldn't he be furious with her?

Her stomach hollowed. Shit, she wasn't that far gone, was she? She wasn't that crazy, was she?

No. She was in danger and fighting for her life. While she hadn't meant to bite him, this whole situation was intolerable. She closed her eyes to block out the horror.

She shouldn't be worried by Rollin's concern. He had no idea who she was. He was operating under the assumption that this was out-of-character behavior for her. But he couldn't comprehend the depths of her depravity. If he found out what she'd done to her parents, he wouldn't be surprised by her display.

He brought her close and held her gently. "It's okay, Sam. Everything's gonna be okay."

"No, it's not," she said in a shaky voice.

"Yes, it will." Rollin's attention shifted to her leg. He gasped. "Shit, Sam. You got shot?"

"Yeah." The pain in her thigh returned with a vengeance and she sucked in a breath.

Rollin's eyes went wide. "Fuck! Zane, call the doc and have him meet us at the house."

Zane turned around and checked out her leg. "How bad is it?"

"I don't know." She glanced down at the large red stain on her polyester pants and tried not to freak out. "Could be bad." Her voice cracked.

Rollin leaned across her to get a better look. "You've lost a lot of blood. But the tourniquet's working. How long ago did you put it on?"

"When I got into the car."

"That was well over ten minutes ago. We'd better untie it to see if the bleeding's stopped. Leave it on too long and you can lose the leg."

"O-okay." Hesitantly, she untied the t-shirt and watched the stain.

"Is it bleeding more?" he asked.

"I don't think so."

Zane flipped his long dark hair off his ear and touched his Bluetooth. "Brian? We need you, bud. Can you be at Safe House Delta, like now?" He chuckled, which rumbled in his wide chest. "Of course, it's an emergency. Isn't it always? See you there." The man was so tall he had to hunch in the seat, practically eating his knees. His shoulders exceeded the width of his bucket seat by a couple inches on both sides.

Her vision wobbled and she had difficulty staying upright. A wave of nausea overtook her. "I feel like I'm about to pass out."

Rollin threw his arm around her. He smelled of leather, cologne and his own unique scent. "Sam, hang on."

Suddenly, it felt like she'd taken an ice bath. Even though the sun had broken through the fog and streamed into the backseat—and Rollin provided warmth—she began shaking and couldn't stop. "I'm s-so c-c-cold. So cold."

Rollin brought her closer to him and rubbed her arms. "It's okay, honey."

Zane said, "Doc's on his way. We'll get you fixed up, Sam."

"Thanks."

"Sam?" Rollin asked.

Her stomach knotted. She didn't like his tone. "Yeah?"

"Is the packet in your bag there?" He nodded toward her embroidered shoulder bag sitting on the seat next to her.

"Yeah."

Zane reached for it. Breathing hard to control the pain, she picked up the bag and handed it to the behemoth.

Hopefully, Zane didn't know the full contents of the packet. Hopefully, he wouldn't notice anything missing. She'd better not have gotten shot and gone through all this hell for nothing.

After a few moments, Zane turned around and said, "Looks like the packet is intact. Captain's the one who packed the thing back in DC. He's flying in late tonight."

Sam focused on pain management and tried to pretend she wasn't worried about the package. She had until the Captain arrived to escape.

If she could escape. Hopefully, the doctor could fix her enough so she could use the leg. If not, she'd just have to convince the Patriots that she'd found the packet without the thumb-drive and the icky picture of Larry and the little girl. She could do it. She just had to keep her head together.

A sharp, stinging pain made her body jolt. Damn this fucking wound.

"I'm sure everything's cool," Rollin said with confidence, making her feel like a rat. "Glad it's back in our hands."

"Finally," Ty said.

"Where are we going?" Sam asked.

"To a safe house in the hills of Seattle," Rollin said. "A doctor will be there to take care of you. You'll be fine, Sam."

Burke's face popped into her mind and her body went tense, sending another blast of pain through her thigh. "Ow. Highly doubtful. Burke's gonna kill me, isn't he?"

"Not after he gets a look at you," Rollin said with a squeeze of her shoulders. "No, wait. Strike that. Yes, he will kill you. Especially because you got shot."

"Pickles," she said to herself. Her face flushed and she stared at the blood on her thigh. "He must know I stole all kinds of stuff from him."

Ty took an exit. She tried to brace herself from the g-forces on the cloverleaf, but her wound throbbed horribly from the movement. She clamped her lips, but a grunt of pain escaped.

Rollin's expression went sympathetic. "Hold on, kid."

Sam took a few deep breaths.

Ty drove through an old residential neighborhood full of Victorians restored to their original glory with nicely manicured lawns.

Damn, she didn't want to see Burke again. Wait. Why did she have to? If the Patriots finally had what they were after, there was no longer any reason for them to hold her. "You guys have the packet. That's all you wanted from me. So I can go, right?"

Rollin looked at her like she grown a third eye in the middle of her forehead. "What do you mean, that's all we wanted? You're one of my best friends, I—and we all—want to keep you alive, Sam. Despite your obvious death wish."

"I would have made it out of there alive," she responded before she could shut herself up.

"Did you miss that whole scene?" he demanded, gesturing toward the back of the car. He pointed at her wound. "That was *the CIA* and *the Cabal*," he over enunciated. "You're on their hit list, girl. You have no idea the astronomical odds that you're still alive."

"Wait. This makes no sense. Once the evidence is out of my hands, I'm safe. That's what you guys told me. Even Paul said that. And they must know you guys have taken possession of the packet."

Rollin's mouth agape, he made an exasperated noise. "Don't you get it? They're gonna kill anyone who's seen that material. But first, they'll torture you. They'll want to know why you wanted it, what you saw, and what spy organization you work for."

"But I don't work for a spy organization."

"And guess how they'll finally figure that out?"

Her gut convulsed and she wrapped her arms around herself tighter. "Oh."

"That's what they did to the first four guys that had that material."

Sam didn't know if he was making up stories to scare her into submission or if he was telling her the truth. Probably the latter, but since she would be hunted down by Larry soon and erased, she had no other choice but to continue on her plan. "So what do we do?"

Rollin said, "We put you in a safe house and protect you."

"For how long?"

"As long as it takes. These guys have a long memory."

Her ribcage contracted and she had trouble breathing. She felt smothered. "I can't live like that."

"Then you'll die, my dear," Rollin said without a shred of humor.

She slumped in her seat and burning pain seared her wound. She hissed and moaned. "Great." What he didn't know was that she had a hell of an arsenal hidden in Portland. All she had to do was get there.

She started shaking even harder and her teeth chattered from the blood loss. Even though the car was warm, it felt like the air conditioner was on full blast.

By the time Ty parked in the garage of a large, two-story woodsy lodge in the hills, reality had become distorted. Her vision was wonky, her sense of time and place was off, she couldn't get her bearings.

And she was in more pain than she ever had been. Her other gunshot wound hadn't hurt this bad.

Rollin helped her out of the SUV, then picked her up and carried her into the huge house.

Sam forced her brain to focus and checked out the place for escape routes.

He brought her through an entryway and into an enormous pine-walled living room with a thirty-foot-tall open beam ceiling. The centerpiece of the living area was a magnificent river rock fireplace flanked by giant windows that afforded views of a lush, rhododendron-filled yard. The room was furnished with over-sized distressed leather couches and chairs. Several closed pine doors led off the main room. To her right, there was a long hallway that went to the back of the house and next to it, a wide staircase with polished log railings that led upstairs. Many avenues of escape. She'd heal up and slip out in the middle of the night.

A horrid stab of pain made her grimace. First priority, fix her leg.

Rollin brought her past the stairs, down the long corridor, and into a large and airy room. A man with a big gray beard and kind blue eyes smiled at her from behind a padded examining table. Glass-fronted shelves lined one wall and were filled with pill bottles, bandages and other medical supplies.

"Hi Sam, I'm Brian," the stocky man said. He wore a blue work shirt and jeans. Tanned with thick forearms, he clearly spent a lot of time outdoors. "We'll get you all taken care of."

Rollin carefully laid her on the table, but the movement was excruciating and Sam cried out. Covered in sweat, yet freezing cold, her body shook.

Brian patted her on the shoulder. "I'll help you with that pain in just a second, darlin', but first I need to see what we're dealing with. Perhaps we should start by getting you out of those...er...lovely clothes."

Rollin chuckled. "Gotta say, Sam, I've seen you in some hot outfits, but..."

"Shut up," she said through gritted teeth as tears leaked from her eyes. "It worked. Almost."

"Did work." Rollin nodded. "Took us a long time to identify you. Strong made you first."

"The jerk." Sam shed her beige polyester shirt and worked on the pants. Her thigh screamed in agony, but with Brian's help, she removed the blood-stained trousers. Rollin helped her take off Burke's armored vest. Some part of her had bonded with the vest and she felt vulnerable without it. Probably because it smelled like Burke.

But the movement was killing her leg. It took all her strength to keep from puking and to stay conscious. "Should I take off the yoga outfit?"

The doctor examined her tight-covered leg. "Afraid I'm going to have to cut your pants off. Can't risk hurting that wound any further."

Rollin patted her on the back. "Don't worry, Sam, we have clothes here. I think you're just about Catherine's size."

"Cool." Pain jolted her once more. She groaned loudly.

Using a pair of sharp scissors, the doctor carefully removed her pants. Felt like he'd dumped kerosene into her bullet wound. The contents of her stomach burned her throat and she swallowed hard. Tears streamed down her face.

Brian examined her thigh.

Sam glanced at the bloody mess and a wave of dizziness and nausea washed through her. "Ohh, I feel like I might puke."

"Rollin, help her lie down," Brian ordered gently. "And get her a cool cloth for her forehead."

Rollin grabbed a pillow from somewhere, put it on the exam table and eased her onto her back. He handed her a big fluffy blanket and covered her to her waist. He left for a second and returned with a wet, cold cloth and draped it over her forehead.

"T-t-thanks."

Rollin gave her some Kleenex. "You bet. Here."

She took the tissue and wiped her nose and eyes.

"Hang on, kid," Rollin said. "You'll be fine. Take my hand and squeeze it." He took her hand in his large one.

Her emotions partially seated. "Thanks, Rollin. You're the tops." She tried not to think about what the doctor was about to do to her. From what she'd seen of the bloody mess, the wounded area was about three inches in diameter and located a foot above her knee on the outside of the thigh. Right below the gunshot Larry had given her.

Did she have some magnetic force in her right leg that attracted all the bullets to that one area? Freaky coincidence.

The doctor prepared a syringe and gave her a shot in the left arm.

Almost immediately, her body went fuzzy, the pain lessened and she melted to the exam table. "I feel better," she slurred.

Rollin and the doctor chuckled.

Brian gave her a local anesthetic—which stung, but at that point she didn't care—and cleaned out the injury. Then he stitched her up and dressed the wound. "Good job on stopping the bleeding. And it looks like the bullet missed all the major arteries. And more good news, shot went clean through. You lucked out. Should heal up nicely and you shouldn't have a permanent limp. I'll leave aftercare instructions. And in two weeks, we'll take out the stitches. But you need to be careful. The muscle is damaged and will take time to heal. You'll need a lot of rest. Stay off it for at least the next week or so."

Not gonna happen. "Sure." Besides, she'd made it through the last time she'd gotten shot without proper rest. "I don't remember the other gunshot hurting this bad."

"It wasn't as deep, more of a grazing," he said, touching her old wound. "Seems like you have a target on your right leg here. Better than your heart, I suppose."

Rollin came closer to see. "Hell, Sam, no wonder you wear shorts to go swimming. When did that happen?"

"Long time ago." Even with the drugs addling her mind, there was no way she was talking about Larry.

Rollin gave her a small frown, then rubbed her shoulder to soothe her. She was so glad he was there. As much as she wished she'd gotten away from the Patriots, she loved Rollin like a brother. Ever since she'd met him, she'd felt like she'd known him forever.

After Brian wrote out the care instructions, Rollin carried her upstairs to a beautiful bedroom suite with tall ceilings and set her down on a four-poster bed covered by a lovely floral quilt. She sank into the softness, grateful for the comfort. The drug swirled in her mind and made her extremities tingle with warmth. Sleep would come fast.

"Got food coming, some light stuff," he said. "Zane's cooking. Your ulcer meds are on the nightstand there. Burke's bringing your suitcase and the rest of your stuff."

Her heart gave a thump and a tiny jolt of adrenaline cut through the fog. "He is?" Shit, Burke in possession of her stuff. Not good.

Rollin sent her a *you're-in-trouble* look. "Yeah. He went back and got your car so he could get his weapons back. And to figure out how you escaped."

She made a move to sit up, but her body refused to obey her. "What?"

"You have to know you've become a giant puzzle to him. He's going over your car and through your stuff with a fine-toothed comb. Cracking your psyche is his new hobby."

Her stomach wrenched and her mind went gray with doom. "Didn't think my life could get any better."

Rollin grinned. "He really likes you." He rubbed his chin and examined her face. "So how do you feel about him, Sam? Really? Do you love him or were you just using him?" His shoulders squared and the look in his eye sharpened. Protective. He was worried she'd hurt Burke. After all Burke had done to him, he still stood by him. Loyal to the end.

"If I weren't in the middle of all this hell, I would have married him by now," she said, slightly slurring her words.

Rollin chuckled and his body relaxed.

"Hated hurting him. Whole thing sucks."

Rollin studied her carefully for a long moment and his expression turned tender. "What happened to you, Sam?" he asked in a soft voice.

The tears came so fast, she had no time to block them. She stared at her lap and stopped them quickly. "I can't."

He patted her on the shoulder. "Okay, kid. Don't worry about it. Just concentrate on healing and resting. I'm worried about you. And so is Emma."

"Sorry."

"Uh, if you need your Ambien, you'll have to ask Burke for it. And you'll probably have to take it in front of him."

How many ways had she just screwed herself? That Ambien plan had been one of her best. "Shit."

"He should be here any minute. I just got off the phone with him. He's very anxious to speak to you," he said in a way that spoke volumes. In other words, prepare for a very angry diatribe.

Her gut tightened and burned. But Sam pretended to be fighting sleep. "I haven't slept much in two days, I can't stay awake much longer."

"I'm sure he'll be here, waiting for you to wake up. You can't avoid him, Sam. And I think you owe him an explanation if you really care about him."

"I know. He didn't deserve what I did to him."

"I sure as hell didn't," came his voice from behind Rollin.

She gasped, jumped and her heart rate leapt high. Her mind almost cleared.

Burke moved into view.

If her leg hadn't been so sore, she'd have jumped out the window.

His face appeared carved out of marble, immovable and cold, but his eyes belied his atomic emotions and blazed like molten steel. His heat and inner rage raised the cool temperature of the room to stifling.

Rollin shot a knowing look between the two. "That's my cue," he said and headed for the door.

She reached for Rollin. "Don't leave me here alone with him."

He sent her a lopsided grin. "You got yourself into this mess, you can get yourself out." He stopped next to Burke—whose fiery gaze didn't move from hers—and put his hand on his buddy's shoulder. "Go easy on her. Her wound was pretty significant."

Burke's jaw twitched. "That only makes me want to kill her more."

"I'm about to pass out," Sam said and fluttered her eyelids in an attempt to look sickly and wan.

Burke didn't buy one flutter. He stalked up to the side of her bed, pointed at her and growled, "Not before you talk to me, woman."

His cologne hit her and warm wonderful memories of their kiss played through her mind. Her stomach gnarled.

"I'll leave you two kids to play alone, then," Rollin said in a chipper tone. He left and shut the door behind him. She pulled the blanket up around her and concentrated on getting the edges neat.

"Sam. Look at me."

"I can't," she said matter-of-factly.

"Sam," he said, his voice an octave lower. "Look. At. Me."

She winced, hid behind her hand, and finally peered at him. Worse than she thought, his blistering glare physically hurt. Cringing, she said, "Burke, I'm sorry, okay? You know I am."

His expression didn't budge. "I do not."

She rubbed her face, partially covering her mouth. "I apologize. For stealing all your stuff and lying to you."

He examined her for a long moment, blinking fast a few times. "I don't think you are sorry."

She sat straighter and let her guard down. "Well, I am."

The lines on his forehead and around his eyes creased with pain. His mouth drew down. Deep longing radiated from his haunted gaze.

His vulnerability crushed her heart and she clutched her chest. The final nail in the coffin of her misery. She'd hurt everyone. Burke, Rollin, and herself.

Such a familiar pattern. And unfortunately, her only pattern.

Burying her face in her hands, she broke into sobs. She hated herself. So far she'd hurt every single person who'd ever loved her. Typhoid Sam. All she wanted was to love people and take care of them, and boy, what great job she'd done. Two in the ground and all the living wounded.

All because of her depravity. All because she couldn't say no. All because she slept with the wrong man.

Planet would have been a much better place if she'd hadn't been born. Or her parents had been lucky enough to have that boy Dad always wanted. Boys didn't have to worry about resisting their sexual urges. Boys couldn't be sluts.

Burke's warm arms came around her. She jerked and pulled away, but his embrace was gentle and she found herself snuggling close to him.

He held her until she stopped crying. Then he kissed her on the forehead.

"I thought you hated me," she said.

"I do."

She stopped crying, chuckled, and moved away to face him. His expression had become more guarded, but her heart melted at the caring in his eyes. "Then why are you comforting me?"

He raised a brow. "I decided to call a short truce. Seeing as how you got shot. And lost something very precious to you."

Tears streamed from her eyes, but she held his gaze. "He'll kill me, Burke. He'll kill you. He'll kill everyone I care about."

Sympathy softened his hard features. He took her in his arms and held her tight. "No, he won't. And if you stop running from me, I can protect you from him."

His scent and warmth comforted her, but she couldn't get Larry's sneering face out of her mind. "I can't talk about it now."

"It's all right, Sam. I don't think I've ever been this angry in my life, but…" He nuzzled her and said nothing else.

She clung to him even though she didn't deserve his kindness.

He held her for a while longer, then released her and stood. "We'll talk more tomorrow. We both need sleep." Various emotions flitted across his oval face; love, pain, then deep sorrow.

Made her want to take out her heart and shoot it with a sniper rifle.

After one last long hurt look, he turned and left.

Sam fought the tears and distanced herself from her wild emotions. She had to keep her head clear. She had to get some rest and escape from her friends that night. It wouldn't take long for the Patriots to figure out that she'd held back evidence.

But this time, the guys wouldn't catch her. No way was she putting them in any more danger. The further she got away from them, the better.

After she ate the meal Zane brought her, she fell into fitful sleep, her last thoughts of Burke. How much she loved him. And how rotten she felt about having to fuck him over yet again. Even if it was for his own good, he wouldn't see it that way. He'd despise her.

She thought she'd hated her life before. Nothing compared to this hell.

TWELVE

Sam awoke in a cold sweat, sitting straight up in bed, her heart pounding, her leg screaming in agony. Where the hell was she? What happened to her thigh?

The previous days' events spilled into her mind and her gut twisted hard. She fell back against the pillows and tried to get a hold on her emotions. She concentrated on breathing and centered herself.

Thankfully, the sleep had helped her brain. She felt clearer than she had in two days. Her watch read 3:00 A.M. Only seven hours of sleep, but she had to get going, no matter how tired nor what kind of pain she was in.

She swung her legs out of bed and tested the injured leg. Terrible burning and weakness. She limped over to the adjoining bathroom—an unpleasant journey at best.

Feeling around for the light switch, she flipped it on and yipped. A horrifying image met her in the mirror. Along with the flattened-on-one-side bed hair, her mascara and eyeliner had turned her face into a Picasso painting. But that was fixable. What lay underneath was not. Beyond the streaky make-up and horrendous hairdo, she looked like an extra from a zombie movie. Her cheeks were sunken, her complexion gray. Huge dark circles featured prominently under her bloodshot eyes. The picture of beauty.

She washed the make up off her face—which only marginally improved her appearance—and attempted to brush out her hair, but it fought back. A rat's nest at the base of her neck refused to unknot and strange, gravity-defying curls remained where she didn't want them. The hours on the road plus the wig hadn't exactly done good things. Even her normal coppery highlights seemed faded and dingy. Swearing to herself, she tied her hair in a ponytail. Exposing even more of her ravaged features.

But she had no time to mourn her looks. The men in the household would wake up soon. She limped out of the bathroom and dressed—nasty pain. No matter how she moved, her leg screamed. She needed more Vicodin, but had to keep her head clear.

Not only did her wound hurt, her stomach flamed. Her ulcers were more than acting up, they were acting out. Felt like she'd eaten a jalapeno and pepperoni pizza with a gasoline chaser.

A voice in the back of her head told her to hang back and heal up for a day or two before she left for Portland. But she couldn't let the Patriots get her evidence against Larry.

Burke had thoughtfully delivered her luggage the night before. Sam chose an all-black outfit from her suitcase—a pair of sweats, a t-shirt and a hoodie—and grunted and groaned as she dressed. She slipped on a pair of running shoes and grabbed her ulcer meds. It was time for Samantha Murdock to die. She didn't know who she'd be afterwards—if there would be an afterwards—but the identity had become too much of a liability.

Next stop: Ursula's. Her old best friend lived less than three miles away in a residential district. Getting there on a bum leg would be the trick.

She moved to the door, put her hand on the doorknob and turned it. Stuck. She used more pressure. Wouldn't budge.

Took her a long second for the realization to dawn on her: the door wasn't stuck, it was locked.

Her stomach knotted and her blood steamed. She held back a scream. Of course, they'd lock her in. What did she expect?

Sam walked over to the twelve-foot-wide window and tried to slide it open, but it wouldn't move. A blast of fire hardened her body. She had to stop herself from breaking the window with her fists. Goddamn these sons-a-bitches!

Breathing hard, she stared at the obstacle. She could bust it. Quietly.

It was then she noticed the small silver catch on the side. Duh! She flipped it up and the waist-high window slid open, giving her a nice, six-foot-wide egress. After removing the screen and setting it aside, she poked her head outside and looked down. She gasped. The darkened ground appeared to be miles away. Maybe fifteen, twenty feet, but it still looked scary. Shit. No wonder the Patriots hadn't put a better lock on the window. This was crazy, even for her.

But not impossible. She'd had lots of practice escaping from second story windows. Granted, her old bedroom had a handy porch roof halfway down, but she was confident she could pull this off.

Sam quietly slid a chair over to the door and pressed the back under the doorknob to block the entrance. Then she stripped the bed and tied the sheets together, making sure there were plenty of knots to hang onto for her descent. After tying one end around a sturdy bedpost, she flung the rest out the window. But the rope wasn't as long as she'd hoped, there seemed to be a good gap between the end of it and the ground. Still, if she held onto the sheets until she reached the end, the drop shouldn't be too far.

Now for the tricky part. Her right leg was nearly useless.

Balancing on her left leg, Sam tucked her hand under her injured leg and lifted it up to the sill. A searing stab blazed through her thigh. She clenched her teeth and winced, but kept moving and carefully inched her right leg outside. With a hop up, she straddled the windowsill. Excruciating pain made her stomach convulse. Sweat pouring off her, her limbs trembling from the agony, she took the bedsheet in both hands and gripped it with all her might. Then she pressed up against the sill, lifted her unhurt leg and swung it outside.

Dropping onto the windowsill on her lower belly and hips, she gripped the sheets harder and pressed her feet against the house. Daggers of hell speared her wound. She clamped her lips shut and screamed quietly in the back of her throat. Shifting most of her weight to her left leg, she was thrilled to find the house faced with brick. Perfect toeholds. She hissed and panted and waited for a few seconds for the fire in her leg to diminish.

Fuck, this was nasty!

After a deep breath, she slowly lowered herself down the twisted sheets, hand-under-hand, using her left leg for support against the house and only her right occasionally for balance.

The sheet-rope vibrated. A hideous scraping sound filled the air, she dropped two feet, then stopped abruptly, the rope almost jerking out of her hands. She smashed against the house and bounced off. Unreal pain tore through her thigh. A sixty-gallon drum of adrenaline dumped into her system and she almost had heart failure. She'd pulled the bed across the floor!

Petrified, she swung back and forth and tried to get a toehold on the wall. How could anyone have missed the goddamned racket?

Go, Sam, go!

She stopped trying to get leverage from the wall and made her way down the sheet using just her arms. Her muscles burned like hell, but the fear juices dulled the sensation. Thank God for that little torturer of a personal trainer, Pedro. Evil man, but his relentless pushing was the reason she could handle this stunt.

Breathing hard, her lungs and limbs searing, she quickly reached the end of the rope. But the ground still looked far away, about a ten-foot drop. She examined the brick wall next to her. Maybe she could climb the rest of the way down.

Lights flooded the area.

Sam squinted from the sudden onslaught, her heart stopped, and then blasted into a crazy rhythm. "Shit!"

Seeing no other options, she let go of the sheet and jumped to the garden below, preparing to absorb most of the impact with her left leg.

Sam hit the ground, hard. A sickening ripping sound came from her left ankle and it felt like twigs had snapped inside her foot. Sharp shooting pain tore through her. She crumpled to the ground and landed on her gunshot wound.

Crying out, she willed herself to keep moving or the Patriots would find her within seconds. With her ankle pounding and her thigh throbbing, she crawled across the asphalt driveway, heading for a tall hedge in front of the large redwood fence that lined the property.

As she reached a small grassy strip in front of the tall shrubberies, she examined the hedge for a good place to push through, but the hedge was much thicker than it had looked from across the driveway. She quickly scanned the area for alternate hiding places. The garage was too far away and the other way led down the driveway to the front of the house and the street.

"Sam must be out by the garage!" came Zane's deep booming voice from the front porch.

She threw herself into the thicket. As she reached a tiny clearing by the fence, she scraped her wound on the thick end of a stick. Felt like someone had dumped acid directly into the injury. She clamped her hand over her mouth to hold back a shriek and shook so hard from the pain, she saw double. Sweat ran down her temples and between her breasts.

Footfalls on pavement stomped near her. She froze and stopped breathing.

"Shit!" Zane exclaimed. "She tied her sheets into a rope. Jesus Christ, this woman is tenacious. We should hire her."

"She couldn't have gone far. Search the grounds!" Burke called out.

"I'm on it," came Rollin's sleepy reply. He yawned loudly.

"She landed here," Burke said slowly. "Then headed…"

Footfalls clapped across the pavement, the sound dampening as he stepped onto the grass.

"Sam? Are you inside that hedge?" Burke asked, far too close to her.

She didn't make a sound.

"Sam, please don't make me ruin this Versace sweater. Are you in there or not?"

"Hey, Mr. Fashion, I'm only wearing Sears flannel," Rollin said. "You think the Birdwoman from Alcatraz is back there?"

"See the marks in the dirt? The gap in the hedge?"

"Let's have a little look-see then, shall we?"

Sam pressed her body against the damp ground and prayed Rollin wouldn't find her.

Branches snapped. Leaves crunched.

"Why hello Miss Murdock, out for an early morning stroll?"

She didn't move.

Rollin poked her shoulder. "Sam?"

"Fuck!"

"She's here!" Burke called out.

"Didn't like your bedroom, huh?" Rollin asked. "You could have just asked for another one."

Sam closed her eyes and wished so hard to transport to her bedroom closet, when she opened them, she was shocked she wasn't home.

Rollin tapped her shoulder. "Sam? Are you coming out of there or do I have to drag you?"

Her vision blurred and her head pounded with fury. "Fuck! I'm coming, I'm coming. Owww!"

She crawled out to the grass where Burke and Rollin stood and sat at their feet, careful to avoid eye contact with either. She held her ankle—which hurt more than her goddamned gunshot wound—and tried to assess the damage. Pretty bad. She gently set her foot on the ground, and her ankle and lower leg flamed. Her mood took an even deeper nosedive. She checked her gunshot wound. Blood seeped through her pants. "Goddamn it!" She pounded the soft earth of the ground with her fist.

"Sam, get up," Burke ordered curtly.

"I can't," she replied, her voice cracking.

He snorted. "What do you mean, you can't?"

Tears burned her eyes and she wiped them away with a violent sweep of her arm. "I sprained my fucking ankle and landed on my fucking gunshot wound and I'm about to pass out from pain or I would have escaped."

"Doubtful," Burke said.

Rollin gestured down at her while turned to Burke. "She's covered in leaves and sticks. You want me to carry her? Don't want to ruin your Versace," he teased with a grin.

"Please." Burke shot her a cold, narrow-eyed glare, then turned and walked away.

"Burke seems a little angry with you," Rollin said in a mock-surprised tone.

Sam glowered at the ground. "No one could be as angry with me as I am."

He smiled and put his hands on his hips. "You'll be fine, kid. But you have lost your mind. You do realize that, don't you?"

"I'm just determined, that's all," she grumbled.

"Determined to injure yourself as much as possible? Congratulations, you've succeeded." Rollin moved close to her, bent down, put an arm under her knees and the other around her back. "Okay, here we go. Upsie daisy." He picked her up and his arm slipped, hitting her wound.

Sam cried out and shuddered.

"Sorry, girl." He adjusted his hold. "That better?"

"Yeah," she grunted. Her wound throbbed so hard it felt like someone was tapping her leg with a torch.

"Hey, look on the bright side," he said as he carried her down the driveway toward the front of the house. "You haven't broken your arms or dislocated your shoulder. You still have lots of body parts left to injure."

She pursed her lips. "You really are a butt sometimes."

He sent her a silly grin and batted his eyelashes.

Rollin carried her into the living room, past Zane and Burke, and over to a large leather couch. Burke's freezing mood made her skin prickle.

Rollin set her down gently. Her ankle and leg blazed. Bile shot up her throat and she swallowed hard. Panting, she tried to control the pain.

Burke came near and towered above her, skewering her with his dark, disapproving glare. "I had an easier time keeping Mohammed Al-Adhami under control," he spat.

Sam winced and eased into the couch. Unable to take his icy fury, she stared at the tall river rock chimney. Exhaustion and disappointment washed through her and tears ran down her face.

She tried not to look at Burke directly, but couldn't help but hone in on him through her peripheral vision.

His mouth twisted. "So? Going off to kill Lawrence Tyrell with a fresh gunshot wound? What was your plan? *Bleed on him to death?*" he bit out in a caustic tone.

Her stomach contracted and her jaw clenched tight. Jerk. How dare he mention Tyrell?

Rollin stared at her with his mouth open. "Tyrell?" His face went red, his eyes became moons and he exploded in a series of large gestures. "Holy shit! Are you insane?"

Rollin, yelling?

She checked him out, unable to get her mind around his emotions. She'd never heard him yell before. Or seen him this animated.

He waved his arms and paced, and then turned to Burke. "You knew she was going after Lawrence Tyrell? One of the most powerful men on the planet?"

Burke's shoulders twitched. "I promised her I wouldn't say anything."

"Yeah, some promise," she muttered.

Burke's dark eyes went wild and he pointed at her violently. "You ran away from me! You lied to me! And you ripped me off! All bets are off, lady!" He gestured like he was a referee calling a baseball player out.

While a part of her wanted to cower, the rest of her itched to wrap her hands around his thick neck and squeeze. She narrowed her eyes. "You tell them my real name, and I will never speak to you again," she said in a low growl.

Burke's hard expression didn't change.

"You know her real name?" Rollin demanded. "Where the fuck have I been? When did you promise her not to tell?"

"The night before she took off."

"I feel so out of the loop," Rollin said to himself. "But Sam, really? Could you have picked a more dangerous person?"

Burke pulled his phone out of his pocket. "Yes, Captain? No, you're not waking me. Yes, she's still here. Yes, I'm sure, I'm looking at her. Imagine that. She did try to escape, as a matter of fact. We just caught her."

Sam's stomach felt like an entire cloud of butterflies had taken flight. Her pulse pounded in her ears. She pictured erecting thick steel walls around herself and concentrated on brushing dirt from her shirt. She could feel Burke's gaze settle on her.

"Really," he said in a deadly cool tone. "I'll call you right back."

She'd never wanted the power of invisibility more.

"Sam," he said in a very unfriendly voice. "Hand. It. Over."

"Hand what over?" Rollin demanded.

Burke's mouth went ugly. "Seems like there were a couple things missing from the packet. Surprise, surprise, most of the information on Senator Lawrence Tyrell. Nothing was taken on the other ten targets, just a picture of him with a young woman and a thumb-drive of financial information. And what a shocker, Sam just happened to try to escape tonight. Give them to me now, woman." He thrust out his hand, palm up.

Sam summoned all her reserves and forced herself to face him. "Give you what? I already gave you guys everything that was in the box."

He assaulted her with his dark gaze. His demeanor turned menacing. "Don't."

She worked hard at keeping her face free of any emotion but anger. "Don't what? I don't have anything."

Burke's eyes dilated and he took a step toward her. "Give me that information or I swear, I'll strip search you right here and now!"

She flinched, but managed keep her expression hard. "Go ahead. You won't find anything." She'd kill him if he tried.

His teeth gritted, he lunged for her.

She recoiled and held up her hands to protect herself.

Rollin grabbed Burke and pushed him back. "Ease up, cowboy. We know she has it. She isn't going anywhere. We'll get it."

Burke's frosty gaze went slightly unfocussed. "Yes, and right now. Sam, do you really want to be stripped naked in front of all of us? Don't think I'm not capable. Don't think I won't do it. No one has ever pushed me as far as you have, and I'm about to push back." He reached for her.

Rollin blocked him with two hands to his broad chest and walked him backwards. "Burke, why don't you get some bandages so we can redress her wound? I'll make sure she doesn't sprint away."

Burke's nostrils flaring, cold rage poured from his center. He finally looked at Rollin. "What?"

"Bandages? For her wound?"

"Oh." Burke frowned and after a beat, nodded. He stared at her for a long moment, breathing hard. "Okay, but don't think you're getting away with this, *Murdock*." He abruptly turned and left the room, muttering to himself.

Rollin sighed. "Sam. Game's up, girl. Please give it to me." He outstretched his hand and wiggled his fingers.

"I swear, Rollin, I don't—"

Rollin's expression was calm, but determined. "No more lies. Hand it over. Please. Or I'll help Burke strip search you."

Sam shook her head and fell down a long dark, deep hole. She crossed her arms over her face. Tears flowed down her cheeks. She'd never felt more defeated. More alone. More angry.

She'd almost gotten away. Almost.

Fuck!

"Now, Sam," Rollin said in a firm tone.

Took all her strength to force her arm to move. She felt like she was locked in a vacuum chamber and was giving away her last tank of air. Now the super tricky part. She had to retrieve the evidence on Tyrell while protecting the rest of the contents of her Battle Bra. Time for a sleight of hand. Wait. Or an attack of modesty.

She frowned at Rollin. "Don't look."

He rolled his eyes, sighed, and finally turned away.

She reached down through the neck of her loose and stretchy t-shirt, pulled apart the Velcroed right side compartment of her Battle Bra, moved past a thin packet of cards—her debit card and two fake IDs—and removed the folded photo. After closing the hidden pocket, she moved to the front of the bra, dipped her hand inside and ripped off the tiny thumbdrive, taped to the interior of a cup. She readjusted her t-shirt and cleared her throat.

Rollin turned to her and she handed the evidence to him with a scowl.

"I know how hard this was for you, Sammy, and I'm sorry. But I have to protect you."

"No, you have to protect your buddy Tyrell."

His face went stony and his gaze sharpened. "He's not my buddy. But I would like to know what he did to you."

She looked away. "Nothing."

"You could at least come up with a better lie than that."

Burke walked into the room. "Is she lying again? Didn't she give you the information?"

She'd never faced a harder test. Saying no to Burke was becoming second nature, but she'd never turned down any of Rollin's requests. Together, the two were even more difficult to handle.

Rollin eyed her and blinked fast as if rethinking his strategy. "No, she gave me the information, but she won't tell me what Tyrell did to her."

"Too fucking bad!" she snarled.

Rollin's brow furrowed hard over his dark eyes, and his mouth drew down. He rubbed his chin and fingered his soul patch. His wary expression softening, he sat on the coffee table beside her and took her hand. "Sam," he said in a gentle voice. "I'm really worried. You're the straightest shooter I know. The most dependable person I've ever met and the most loyal. But you are fucking out of your mind."

She stared at her swollen ankle.

"Sam, please. Look at me."

She finally did.

"Emma would never forgive me, and I'd never forgive myself if I let you go off half-cocked to kill Lawrence Tyrell. I don't know what he did to you, but I'm sure he deserves killing for it. I don't doubt he's capable of the most horrific shit possible. But he's got the power of God right now. His reach is everywhere. He's the one who's been trying to get his hands on that packet. He had the first four carriers killed. He oversees all his executions. He had you shot, girl. He knows everything about you. Samantha Murdock is at the top of his hit list."

Sam's jaw fell and terror took hold of every muscle in her body. Time stopped. The room and everyone in it faded out. Rollin kept talking but she couldn't hear him. Her worst nightmare had come to life. She was back on Larry's radar. She'd totally, utterly, completely fucked herself.

Holy shit, he must have already seen a picture of her. She looked just like her mother! A gut punch forced all the air from her lungs and she sat straight up. "Oh, God, no! He must have recognized me! I'm dead! *Dead*." She broke into wrenching sobs and collapsed back onto the sofa, tears running into her ears.

"Sam?" Rollin asked. "Tell me what did he do to you. How do you know him?"

She shook her head and buried her face in her hands. She felt so naked and vulnerable, like she was duct-taped to a billboard outside Larry's office. Her element of surprise had vanished. The main cornerstone of her plan was gone.

How had she missed that incredibly important connection? Paul worked for Larry. Once Paul knew she had the packet, of course Larry knew. He must have been shocked to find out that she was still alive.

"Sam?" Rollin jostled her. "You hear me?"

"Fuck," she whispered. Her body shook. Larry sneered in her mind, his handsome face twisted with hatred and lust. The hair stood up on the back of her neck. Her blood chilled. She felt like he could see her all the way from Concord. The end of his 38 had looked like a, giant bottomless pit. The cold murderous soulless look in his eye. The darkness within him. How would she defeat him now? How could she get close to him?

As she sobbed, she grew disgusted with her emotions. Because it would be her weakness that killed her, not Larry. Her own stupidity and naiveté. She should have never taken on the Patriots. After talking to Ursula, she should have gone straight to Concord and retrieved the murder weapon. Then built the case against Tyrell. If the gun had been gone, she could have killed him. But Larry wouldn't have found out she was alive until it was too late.

Paul's words kept ringing in her ears. *Revenge is poison. Let it go.*

But there was no way back. If she didn't kill Larry, he'd murder her and everyone she loved. She'd reached the point of no return. She had to fight the Patriots. She had to keep going.

She fought hard for equilibrium. She wasn't sixteen any longer. She had experience now. This time she could take it. This time it was different. This time, she would win. Or die trying.

Her mind focused. She let out a huge lungful of air, wiped her eyes and glanced around the room.

Rollin, Zane, and especially Burke, stared at her, their eyes wide like they expected an alien to pop out of her chest.

She couldn't help but chuckle and shake her head.

The guys took a collective step back.

Which made her laugh harder. "Don't worry, I was just a little freaked out. I won't barf up any pea soup. My head will not start spinning around on my shoulders."

Three sets of shoulders relaxed, but the men were still wary of her.

After a long awkward silence, Burke finally came forward with a box of tissues.

"Thanks." She blew her nose and wiped her eyes.

Concern etched his face and his penetrating gaze fixed on her. He clearly wanted to demand answers, but held himself back. "Can I check your leg wound?"

She took a deep breath and looked down at the wet stain on her black sweats. "Probably be a good idea."

Great. Now she had to take her pants off in front of all the guys. Her face heated. She laughed and rolled her eyes. "Here I am, facing certain death and I'm worried about you guys seeing me in my underwear." She pushed down the elastic waistband and it caught on her wound. Pain jarred her body. She groaned loudly. After much grunting and hideous torment from her ankle, she finally removed her pants. Her skin slick with sweat, she collapsed on the couch and concentrated on breathing to control the pain and nausea. She did not want to hurl.

Burke inspected her wound and his brow went into a deep V. Then he gently examined her ankle. "Rollin, can you get some ice for her ankle? And an ace bandage? And some ibuprofen for the swelling?"

"Can't take ibuprofen," she said. "Ulcers."

Burke sent her a disapproving stare, but there was warmth deep behind his gaze. "Haven't been taking very good care of yourself, have you?"

Zane said, "Doc gave her Vicodin. When was the last time you took some?"

"Before I went to sleep," Sam said.

"I'll get the bottle," Zane said and headed upstairs.

Stabbing pain came from her gunshot wound. She groaned, winced and wiped away a tear.

Burke carefully removed the bloodied bandage and inspected her wound. "Stitches haven't popped, good. Just bleeding. Looks very raw."

"Hurts like a mofo."

His anger softened into sadness.

His pain went right to her core. Her emotional shields had as many holes as Swiss cheese and she couldn't take his need. She couldn't help but want to fix him. Make him like her again. Tell him whatever he wanted. Give up her plans and love him.

Warning! Stupid Attack Imminent!

She pictured putting her hands on her shoulders and giving herself a good shake. Christ, she was fragile. And a sap. Burke was a plague on her reason and emotions.

Larry. He was all that mattered. *Get it together, Murdock!*

Zane came into the room and handed her a bottle of painkillers. "Here we go."

"Thanks, doll. I'll need some food with it. Just a piece of bread or some milk if you've got it. I hate to put you out."

The giant smiled at her, revealing his straight white teeth. "No problemo, Yosemite." His pet name for her.

For her fake name, anyway. She gave him as much of a smile as she could manage.

He winked at her and headed to the kitchen. When he reached the doorway, he ducked his head and bent over to get through.

Rollin returned from the back of the house with an icepack and an ace bandage. He carefully laid the ice on her ankle, making it flare. She sucked in a breath through her teeth. "Thanks, Rollin."

"You bet."

"Sam?" Burke's focus was on her leg, but not her wound. Below it. What now? "Yeah?"

"There's another gunshot scar." His focus on her sharpened. "Who shot you? Larry?"

Just when she had it together, the dude torpedoed her defenses. Asshole! She shifted her attention to the back of the brown leather couch. With the exhaustion, pain and defeat clouding her mind and emotions, she had trouble masking her reactions. Her shields weren't functioning. She felt like he could see every one of her thoughts. "No. It was an accident," she said in a very unconvincing tone. She wouldn't look at him.

Burke opened his mouth to say something and then shut it. He muttered under his breath. Then he leveled his powerful stare at her. "Did Larry try to kill you? Or was it really a transient?"

She rubbed her brow with her hand and hid behind it.

Burke looked at her for an extra long moment, then cleaned up her wound—which hurt like hell—and redressed it. After he finished with the gunshot, he carefully lifted her leg and began gently wrapping her ankle with the ace bandage.

Her foot and lower leg complained loudly and she cried out.

"Sorry," he said. But she wasn't sure he was.

Burke finished his torment and set her foot down on the pillow without causing too much agony. Zane brought her a tray with a bowl of steaming hot oatmeal, a small dish of brown sugar and a carton of milk.

A twinge of guilt tweaked her gut. "You didn't have to do that."

"My pleasure. Worried about you, Sam." Zane's formidable black brows knitted together, but his green eyes radiated fondness.

Heaving a sigh, she tried to smile at her big buddy. Why did she always end up fucking over those she loved the most? Seemed like ever since she'd turned twelve, all she'd done is hurt and disappoint her family and friends. "Thanks, Zane. Thanks to all of you. I'm sorry I'm such a pain in the ass."

"That you are, girl," Zane replied.

"An understatement," Burke bit out, displaying none of Zane's warmth.

Zane looked at her oatmeal. "Think there's some strawberries in the fridge." He disappeared into the kitchen.

Rollin said, "Be back, gotta check my email." He walked over to the staircase and went upstairs.

Leaving her alone with Burke.

He pulled up a chair and faced her. "You had me worried half to death," he said in a soft voice.

She finally looked him in the eye, which wasn't easy. While his expression had lost much of the anger, his disapproval remained.

"I wish I'd met you another time. I like you a lot. And I don't want to hurt you. I…"

Burke's attention kept wandering to her bare legs. And crotch. Frowning, he grabbed a blanket and covered her. Then his features went pained. "All I want to do is help you."

"I know. I'm sorry."

He studied her tight mouth, her knotted fists, then he looked directly into her eyes. "You aren't giving up, are you? You probably already have another plan in place."

She should have expected it, but she couldn't stop herself from looking down at her lap.

"I won't let you hurt yourself again," he said, his tone quiet. "I had no idea of your capabilities."

She checked his face and her stomach dropped. Dude was solid and strong as a granite mountain. She'd thought he was a handful before. "Well, I'm too tired and too injured to fight you today."

One side of his mouth turned up and he said nothing, but smug disbelief was all over his handsome face. He thought he had complete control over her. Wrong. His expression turned searching. "Where are the rest of my weapons?"

Forcing herself to appear contrite, she held his gaze and let her shoulders slump. "Sorry." While she felt bad about stealing his stuff, he had forced her into it. If he'd let her keep her own weapons, she wouldn't have had to take his.

He raised a brow, and his eyes and mouth hardened. He leaned in. "What happened to them?"

She winced and grimaced. "Uh, stolen."

He jerked back in his chair. "Stolen?" he shouted.

She jumped and a fresh wave of pain went through her thigh and ankle. "Owww."

"How? Where?" he demanded, his eyes fiery.

She pinched the bridge of her nose and stared at the green plaid fleece blanket covering her. "Uh, that motel I was staying at here in Seattle."

"The one on Montgomery?"

"Yep. I had two cars. I split the haul into two loads so in case I lost one, I'd still have the other."

"Worked," he said, his voice freezing and hot at the same time.

"I apologize." She sent him her most vulnerable look.

His eyes widened and his anger lines turned sympathetic. Bingo.

A split second later, his features went stony and cold. Then softened again. Dude was having a hell of an inner fight. Finally, Mad Burke won. His dark brows angled hard toward his nose, his mouth became a grim line and he crossed his arms. "Not ready to forgive you. Not by a long shot."

The amount of emotion pouring out of him made her heart happier than hell, but also made her feel like a total piece of shit. She had no choice but to use his feelings against him. Which would hurt her as much as him.

She imagined a force field around her heart. Keeping her distance was imperative. While she loved Burke, this was war. And unfortunately, he and the Patriots were the enemy. She had to keep her priorities straight. No more emotions.

Rollin walked into the room carrying a pair of crutches. "Come on, Sam, we got a new room for ya."

"A new prison," she muttered.

Burke narrowed his eyes and opened his mouth to yell at her, but Rollin just laughed and clapped his buddy on the back. "She'll get it soon enough, Burke, don't worry."

"No, she won't," Burke said with a curled lip.

Rollin ignored Burke's anger and said in a chipper voice, "Since the crutches won't help on stairs, you want to carry her up there or shall I?"

"Screw that, I'll make it up there myself." Sam heaved herself off the couch and her leg felt like she'd jabbed a sharp stick in the wound. Gasping and groaning, she set her left foot on the ground and pain burned through her ankle. She yelped. This sucked. How was she supposed to escape when both legs were completely useless?

Burke did an eye roll, stepped forward and swept her into his arms.

Her gaze met his and everything stopped: her physical suffering, her breathing, and all thoughts except for the singular desire to kiss him.

Raw hunger filled his eyes.

His scent, energy and heat intoxicated her. She remembered their amazing kiss and her attention dropped to his full, inviting lips. She wished to God he were carrying her away to fuck her. Every hormone in her body cried out for him.

His pain lines returned and he looked away, holding his chin straight.

The spell broken, she finally breathed. What the hell was wrong with her? She mentally threw a cup of water in her lap. The man held far too much sexual power over her.

Burke carried her to a room across the hall from her old one. Larger, this room had the same pine walls as the rest of the house, but its windows overlooked the lush gardens and brick patio of the backyard. The airy room had high ceilings, two queen beds and a much larger adjoining bathroom. He carefully set her on one of the beds, then grabbed a pillow and gently placed her left foot on top.

The contents of her Battle Bra popped into mind. The men might search her belongings. Couldn't take any chances. "Oh, hell, I need to use the restroom," she said, sitting up. "This should suck."

"Do you need help?" Burke asked.

"No, I'll suffer, it's okay."

After an excruciating trip to the bathroom on the crutches, she shut the door behind her and quickly sat on the closed toilet. Ripping off her shirt, she removed her bra and slipped the t-shirt back over her head. She unzipped the secret compartments and withdrew her last two fake IDs, a debit card linked to a bank account under one of the false names, plus a special toy of Burke's: a three-inch-long pen with a tranquilizer dart hidden inside.

As she scanned the bathroom for hiding places, she spotted her overnight case sitting near her. Killer! She put the IDs and debit card inside a feminine hygiene pad and slipped Burke's tranquilizer pen into a tampon tube. As long as Catherine didn't show up, she had it made. All men were totally squeamish around anything to do with a woman's period. She tossed her sweaty, nasty bra in a side compartment of the case, making a mental note to wash it as soon as she could. After flushing the toilet for effect, she hobbled out and Burke helped her to the bed.

Rollin brought her a bottle of water and excused himself to work on his computer.

Not only her toiletries, but all her belongings had been moved to the new room. *The Girl with the Dragon Tattoo*, half-read, lay on the nightstand between the two beds. She grabbed it for an excuse to ignore Burke.

Burke lay down on the other bed and opened his own book.

She frowned, annoyed. "I can't get away, you don't have to watch me."

His flinty gaze flickered over to her and then returned to his book. "Rather than test that theory and risk wasting any more time chasing you, we've decided to keep you under constant surveillance. Will probably save us untold amounts of money in bandages and the like."

Sam let out a humph. "Funny." She made a big show of turning away from him and buried herself in her book.

While she loathed the idea of having a babysitter, these would be the last moments she spent with him. Moments she would treasure when she was alone in her prison cell.

If by some miracle she survived her mission and managed to complete it without detection, she'd track him down and apologize.

But she knew the cold hard truth. She didn't deserve happiness. And she certainly didn't deserve a good man like Burke. God wasn't done punishing her. Doubtful she could ever make up for the crimes she had committed. How the hell could she atone for the deaths of her parents?

Fifteen minutes after Sam allowed herself to be distracted by her book, she fell asleep. The rest of the day, she only woke up long enough to eat. She couldn't remember being more exhausted, nor more depressed.

During the short periods of time she was awake, she did her best to be sweet to Burke, but as day turned to night, it became increasingly clear that his feelings for her had changed. He was polite, but distant. None of his normal warmth showed through. He seemed like a completely different guy. Locked up tighter than a safe. He only spoke to her to inquire about her pain level or to ask if she was hungry. The rest of the time, he hid behind his book.

Thankfully, she kept falling asleep because it sucked to be around him when he was this cold. She couldn't stop thinking about their kiss. The way his body had felt next to hers. The way he'd looked at her.

But his rejection would make leaving much easier.

Even if it hurt like hell.

Burke read and waited for Captain to arrive at the safe house to take over guard duty. He had to get to New Hampshire as quickly as possible. Since Sam wouldn't tell him anything about her relationship with Tyrell, he'd find out for himself.

He'd studied every single piece of information on Tyrell he could since he'd discovered the connection between the Senator and Sam, but nothing in the Patriots' information or from his hacker network revealed anything about the years Tyrell had served as Sheriff, except for the accumulation of awards.

The only interesting lead had been on the Sheriff's department website for Merrimack County, on a memorial page dedicated to Amanda Hutchins. The webpage outlined all of Sam's accomplishments in the teen sheriff outreach program, and related the story of her unfortunate death at the hands of a transient. In the picture, Sam stood next to Larry Tyrell.

A link to a related story had made his heart wrench. A story about Sam's mother's suicide. Six months after the murders, her mother, consumed with grief, had taken her own life. Burke couldn't imagine Sam's pain. Accounted for a lot of her violent, conflicting emotions.

But it didn't answer the Tyrell question. He must have been the one that shot her and killed her father, but why wouldn't Sam just say that? There was no shame in almost being killed by a madman.

Unless Sam had been abused by Tyrell. Knowing how much Larry loved little girls, the theory wasn't much of a reach. And it would account for her silence. And her father's murder. When her father found out, he must have threatened to kill Larry. A huge fight ensued leaving Sam shot and her father dead. Resulting in her mother's suicide.

Was it the guilt over her mother's suicide that drove Sam? Suicides always left devastation in their wake and guilt for the survivors. That plus the shame of molestation would account for her behavior and it would certainly account for why she wanted to kill Tyrell.

But the hypothesis left many other questions unanswered. Like if Tyrell had killed the father and wounded the daughter, wouldn't he have had to kill the mother? Wouldn't Sam's mother have known about the molestation before Sam's father? Did Larry threaten to kill her mother if she told? Did Larry kill her mother and disguise the crime as a suicide? If so, why wait six months after Sam and her father were gone?

And why did Larry think he'd killed Sam when there was no body found? How did she get away? Didn't anyone see her alive after the shooting? How did a naïve sixteen-year-old girl get out of Concord unseen?

Burke didn't want to, but he also had to consider the worst-case scenario. That Sam had accidentally killed her father during the confrontation. That would account for the soul-wrenching pain behind her eyes. The humiliation and shame in her expression. He'd rarely seen that kind of anguish on anyone's face but his own.

His muscles tensed, his stomach churned with frustration, and he almost threw the book at her. Why wouldn't she just tell him and save him the long plane ride? Didn't she understand who he was yet? Woman was damned lucky he'd gotten a bit more civilized over the past six months or she'd have already found herself drugged and interrogated. The old Burke wouldn't have put up with this crap.

Of course, the old Burke never would have landed her either.

Turning the page on his war novel, Burke shifted on the bed and Sam caught his attention. Again. He could barely get a paragraph read before she distracted him. She was so beautiful when she slept. Her auburn hair feathered on the pillow; her sweet red full mouth, slightly open; her long lashes on her high cheekbones; the tempting bit of milky white bare thigh peeking out from the covers. It took all his inner strength to keep from diving on top of her. To have her this close —laid out on a bed no less—and not be able to have her killed him. He wanted to fall between her long, gorgeous legs. Kiss every square inch of her. Love her. Never let her go.

And shake her until she spilled all her secrets. Knock some sense into that thick skull of hers. But she was unreachable.

He'd never been more exasperated in his life. Nor in more pain. No woman had tunneled past his defenses like this. He could handle evil Taliban leaders, no problem. Nuclear weapons? A snap. But this crazy beauty with fire in her soul? His greatest foe yet.

Hopefully, with the information he'd glean from the trip, he'd possess the weaponry he needed to penetrate her thick shields. He'd slam her with everything he had, break her, and then pick up the pieces.

If all went according to plan, she'd be in his bed shortly. And he'd make sure she stayed there. No more games. No more bullshit. She was his and it was time she realized that.

Captain appeared at the door. "Ready?"

Burke stood and sent a wistful glance at Sam's sleeping body. "Yes." No.

Damn woman. No one had ever made him this angry and stayed in his life.

God, he loved her.

THIRTEEN

Sam awoke the next morning to Zane reading on the bed next to her, his legs stretched out far past the end of the queen-sized mattress. At home, he slept on a huge custom mattress.

She stretched and bursts of fire flamed her leg and ankle. "Oww!"

"How ya feelin' Yosemite?"

"Pain. But it feels really good to sleep."

"I'll have Rollin bring up some food so you can eat and take your meds."

"Thanks. Where's Burke?" she asked before she could stop herself.

"Gone. Flew out last night somewhere. Said he'd be back before we move you."

"When are you moving me?"

"Next couple days."

Sam waited for Zane to give her more information, but he didn't. She got up—which was a horrid ordeal—used the toilet and checked her feminine hygiene products to make sure her secret stash was safe. Everything was exactly where she'd left it. Perfect.

The rest of the day was spent trying to stay awake, but the Vicodin —and her exhaustion—had wiped her out. She'd eat, try to read and zonk. Every time she woke up, there was a different man on the bed next to her. Either Rollin, Zane, Ty or the Captain.

But no Burke.

When she fell asleep that night, Ty was on guard.

Next day, still no Burke. After breakfast, she was perky enough to come up with several viable escape plans. But right before lunch, exhaustion overcame her and she crashed once more.

Late that afternoon, Sam awoke to Burke standing over her.

Her heart did a trip and she sent him a smile, but it was not returned. "Where'd you go? And why are you looking at me like that?" She yawned.

"I was just checking your color. You seem better."

"Sleep's helping."

He sat on the opposite bed. Then he leveled a penetrating stare at her.

"What?"

"Larry murdered your father and covered it up."

All the air rushed from her lungs, she lay back and closed her eyes. He might as well have smacked her forehead with a brick. "I need more painkillers."

"To answer your question, I was in New Hampshire. Boscawen, specifically. At the Merrimack County Sheriff's Department examining the report of your father's murder. And yours."

Her stomach convulsed and she turned away from him.

"Did you know that the transient, Anthony McCoy—the man who supposedly murdered you—is still alive? I talked to him at the state prison. He had some very interesting things to say about that night."

Curling into a tight ball, her muscles hardened to iron. "You can shut the fuck up now," she bit out in a growl.

"McCoy had fallen asleep in a drunken stupor behind a church when Tyrell grabbed him and threw him in the back of his patrol car. Tyrell took McCoy out to a deserted place by a river where your father lay dead next to his car."

She jerked and a sob caught in her throat. Like it happened yesterday, the image was fresh in her mind. Her father lying in a pool of blood, his body illuminated by the headlights of Larry's car. His sightless, staring eyes. That bloody hole in his chest. The shocked look on his face.

Her eyes filled with tears.

"Larry put a gun in McCoy's hand and forced him to shoot the corpse," Burke reported emotionlessly. "Then Tyrell beat the shit out him. Afterwards, at gunpoint, Larry made him sit in your father's car and leave his blood and fingerprints inside. Tyrell forced McCoy to take things from your purse—your wallet and jewelry—and put them in his pockets. Then Larry poured a pint of whiskey down his throat. McCoy awoke in jail, charged with two murders. Despite his claims of innocence, the jury deliberated a half an hour. He was sentenced to life without possibility of parole. And he's sat in that jail for the last sixteen years. An innocent man."

Sam had surmised the whole story, but each of Burke's words stabbed her gut. She wiped the tears from her cheeks and imagined being in her closet at home with her loaded rifle in her hands.

"When I questioned McCoy about the gun—since I guessed it must have been Larry's service revolver that ended your father's life—McCoy said it was an unmarked, unregistered gun he was found with. Larry must have carried a weapon just for the purpose of planting it on suspects and/or for his own agenda of murder and intimidation."

Sam would have given her liver and most of her internal organs to get away from Burke in that moment. How dare he dredge up all this shit when she was stuck there? She wanted to beat him with her crutches.

But wait a minute, she had the murder weapon. Larry must have planted a different gun on Old Tony. Sloppy ballistics. Larry probably paid someone off. Bastard.

"Clearly, Larry murdered your father." He paused. "Were you trying to protect your father when you got shot?"

Rocking, she scrunched her eyes shut.

"Or did something completely different happen? Something that would account for your shame. Did you grab the gun from Larry and try to shoot him but missed? Did you accidentally kill your father? Or maybe your father pissed you off and you meant to shoot him. Did you intend to kill your father?"

Her mind went black with rage and it took all her strength to keep from leaping across the room and strangling him. Trembling, she pictured herself far away. She pretended he hadn't said anything. She wrapped her arms around her knees and pulled so tight she couldn't breathe. It would be okay. All she had to do was ignore him.

"Fine," he snapped. "Don't fucking tell me. I will find out. Everything. You can count on it."

The bed squeaked, his footfalls stomped away and the door slammed shut.

Sobs wrenched from her. She had to leave, no matter how much she hurt. She had to get away from that bastard. Wiping the tears, she rolled off the bed and tested her legs. Sharp pain shot through her ankle and her thigh burned like hell. "Fuck!"

Slamming the metal crutches on the floor, she let out a bellow that shook the windows. A half second later, she realized her cries would send the Patriots running. She snatched up the crutches and raced for the door. After twisting the lock, she grabbed a chair and stuck it under the doorknob.

Did you intend to kill your father? reverberated through her mind. Losing touch with her surroundings, she was half aware of pounding the crutches on a dresser.

Burke scowled at Sam's door and shook his head. Crashing. More screaming came from the room. Every one of her cries and outbursts walloped him physically, like a lunge kick to the solar plexus. He'd broken her, all right. To the point where she'd lost her mind.

Good work, Cherlenko.

Rollin ran up to him, his eyes wide. "What the fuck happened?"

He hated admitting to what he'd done. "I told her what I had discovered and she didn't react. So I said some provocative things, trying to get a response from her."

"Bastard!" Sam bellowed, followed by a loud crash.

Rollin looked at the door, then turned to him. "Great job in provoking her," he said cheerfully. "What's next?"

Burke made a face at him and rolled his eyes. "I'm in the process of figuring that out."

"While you're at it, why don't you figure out how we're gonna get her out of there. I assume she locked the door and stuck a chair underneath the knob."

He shrugged. "She'll need to eat eventually."

Rollin chuckled and shook his head. "What did you say to her?"

Burke sighed and his face warmed. "Accused her of murdering her father."

Rollin's mouth dropped open slightly and then his expression turned incredulous. "You might want to rethink your strategy there, Burke."

"Clearly. I thought if I hit her hard enough, she'd open up. You can see how well that worked. But Jesus Christ, why won't she fucking tell me what happened? How hard is it to say: 'Larry shot me and my father and that's why I want to kill him.'?"

Rollin shrugged. "That transient wasn't around for the first part of the night, was he? Did he see Sam or any sign of her? Does he know what happened to her?"

"No. Nothing. The police report stated there was a trail of Sam's blood that led up to the banks of the Merrimack River. They assume she fell in or jumped in to get away from McCoy, but she was weakened and drowned, her body carried downriver."

Loud sobbing came through the door.

Burke's gut twisted and burned. He rubbed his aching brow. "She's killing me."

"Sounds like you're killing her, too."

"Rollin? How the hell do I get through to her? Drug her? Force her to tell me?"

"Sledgehammer Method clearly isn't working. Why don't you try honey?"

"I've tried to be nice and that doesn't work, either. Nothing works. She steals from me, lies to me, uses my feelings against me, she's a virulent disease. All I want to do is slap her into talking."

"You know, most women don't take to violence? They're funny that way."

Burke glared at the door, wanting to destroy it. He caught himself. Why was he letting her get the better of him? His neck hardened, he steeled himself and stood tall. His mind cleared. Sam would be fine. His only problem was his emotions. Provoking her had been the right course of action. He'd used the same tactic a hundred times. "We'll let her have her tantrum and wait her out. Did Zane secure the window?"

"Yep."

"Good. Can you take over here? I've been up for the last two days."

"That might have affected your decision-making process, huh?"

Burke leveled a Def Con Four glare at the man. "I made the correct choice. My techniques have always worked in the past."

Rollin smirked. "True. But were you in love with any of the other suspects?"

Smack! He felt that one, right across the frontal lobes. He hated the way Rollin could shake the logic out of his arguments. Burke's thoughts darkened and he sighed. He finally turned to Rollin and attempted a withering look. "Don't you ever get tired of being right?" Before Rollin could reply, he turned and stalked off.

Rollin chuckled behind him.

When Sam awoke, it was dark. *Did you intend to kill your father?* Her body went stiff and her fists balled. Jerk. He'd clearly been trying to provoke her into spilling her guts, but what a fucked way to go about it.

Her ankle throbbed and her wound hurt. She needed more pain meds and food.

Clock read 9:00 P.M. Damn it. She liked the door locked. She liked being alone in the room without a bodyguard hovering over her. But once she opened that door, she'd be surrounded.

"Fuck!" She punched the soft mattress of her prison.

"Sam?" Rollin asked from the other side of the door.

"No. It's Betty White."

"Betty? Do you want some food and Vicodin?"

All so intolerable. She let out a string of expletives under her breath.

"I can slip the pills under the door, but the only food I could get to you would be tortillas. Or fruit leather. Maybe a very flat hamburger."

Sam laughed. "Stop. I'll be right there."

She flipped on the light and grabbed her crutches. Inwardly kicking herself, she opened the door.

Rollin shot her a cute grin. "Hey, Miss Murdock. How's the leg?"

"Aren't you gonna ask if there's any furniture in here left unbroken?"

His smile turned sympathetic. "He's an idiot. Believe it or not, he was trying to help."

"I know. Makes it even more infuriating because I can't really get mad at him. Even though it's good he's not here right now. I still want to hit him."

"You guys seem to bring that out in each other. If I were you, I'd wear padding when you were around the other one. Either that or just get it over with and fuck."

Sam choked on her spit and coughed. "You're crazy."

"Sure I am," he replied cheerily. "Come on, Destruction Derby Girl, Zane made his famous lasagna. And I think there's a piece of chocolate cake left."

Still shaken by his casual reference to sex with Burke, she walked on her crutches, out of the room. Her leg and ankle complained, but the pain was manageable. Rollin fell into step beside her.

She glanced at him. "So where is the bastard?"

"Asleep back there."

"So how much money do I owe you guys now? How many man hours?"

Rollin threw his arm around her and gave her a squeeze. "You're worth it, Sam."

Emotions surged upwards through her, propelling her tears right to the surface. If he found out the truth about her, he'd kick himself for the time waste.

Damn it, Burke had almost uncovered her secrets. Almost. She hoped he didn't track down Ursula. Her old best friend was the only other one on the planet besides Larry who knew the sordid truth.

Her face warmed and she dropped her attention to the floor, pretending to watch her feet and the crutches. Her interior turned in on itself and shame seared her skin. She couldn't stand it if Emma found out. Or if the Patriots discovered what she'd done. Maybe she hadn't shot her father, but she'd been the cause. She'd killed her mother, too. She and her perverse drives.

She hoped she died after she took down Larry. Then the guilt would be gone and she could finally atone for her sins.

But first, Larry had to pay for what he'd done to her father. Then when she met Dad in heaven, she could look him right in the eye. And tell him how sorry she was. How she wished she'd been a daughter he could have been proud of. A daughter he could have loved instead of a whore that disgusted him. Hopefully, killing Larry would redeem her in Dad's eyes.

"Sam? Are you okay?"

Startled, she stared up into Rollin's concerned face.

"Yeah. I'm good," she said automatically, and shut down.

"You sure?"

"Absolutely," she said in a strong tone that reassured her. She'd be fine. She just had to keep it together a bit longer. Then all her suffering would end.

Next morning, Sam awoke to an empty room with the door ajar. Tempted to run, but knowing she wouldn't get far at this point, she opted to take a shower. Which wasn't easy, but at least she could stand for longer than a minute.

After dressing, she hobbled into the bedroom to find Burke sitting on the opposite bed, reading. He glanced at her and returned to his book. His expression flat, he'd retreated inward.

"Good morning," he said without looking at her.

Her muscles tightened and she wanted to throw something at him. How dare he treat her like this after what he said the night before? She snorted and headed for the door.

"Breakfast will be ready in about twenty minutes. Zane just got up."

"There's coffee, I would assume."

"Yes."

She opened the door to the hallway and walked through.

"Sam?"

She stopped but didn't turn around. "What?"

"I apologize."

Some part of her told her to accept his olive branch, but she was still too angry. "You're an asshole."

"I know," he said with no apology to his tone, merely an acknowledgement.

She chuckled, shocking herself. Then she shook her head, but still didn't look at him. "You drive me nuts."

"Feeling's mutual."

She continued on.

At breakfast, she and Zane joked and talked, but Burke stayed silent and reserved. He read his paper and didn't interact.

After breakfast, Burke sat in her room and read. And said nothing. Sam finally tried to engage him in conversation. He was polite, but distant. She tried turning on the charm, but nothing she said or did had any effect on him. He didn't leave her side, but didn't speak to her other than to inquire about her pain level. Cold as a freezer and talkative as a librarian.

He was either emotionally blackmailing her into talking or he was done with her.

By nightfall, it became clear. His emotions for her were gone. She'd finally pushed him away. Finally destroyed his love.

His rejection made her heart feel like he'd tossed it in a microwave and set the controls to Cook Until Dead. Hurt much worse than her gunshot wound or sprained ankle. She missed the old Burke more than she thought possible.

But at least she had nothing to lose anymore. And his hatred of her would protect him from Larry. As miserable as the situation made her, it was better for both of them.

Her only problem was that without a weakness to exploit, getting away from Burke wasn't going to be easy. Sam mentally ran through possible escape scenarios. She still had a few tricks in her bra. All she needed was to heal enough to walk and she was gone.

The next morning, Burke walked into the kitchen where she and Zane were having coffee.

"We'll be leaving within the hour," he announced.

"Where are we going?" Sam asked.

"That's what I wanted to talk to you about." His expression was neutral and remote. "You have a choice. Rollin and Emma's or my apartment." He seemed to have no investment in either option.

Her stomach twisted. "I don't want to put anyone out."

Zane made a face and flipped his long black hair over his shoulder. "We aren't letting you die. When are you going to get that?"

Sam frowned and looked at her coffee cup. "Emma has to run that store. Her sister just got better. She and Rollin just got settled. I can't do that to her. I don't want to be in the middle."

Burke waited with his arms crossed.

She turned to him and pursed her lips. "But you certainly don't want me moving in with you."

He raised an eyebrow and one shoulder. "As long as you lay off the five-hundred and twenty-five dollar Sloppy Joes, I don't have a problem." His face belied no preference either way. Still cold as an iceberg.

She'd rather shave her head bald than go with Burke, but she couldn't bring her drama to Emma. Her friend had been through hell and just found peace and love.

Besides, whomever she stayed with, she had to fuck over. And she couldn't do that to Emma. Burke already hated her. Nothing to lose there.

"All right. Burkatraz it is," she said, resigned and gloomy.

Zane laughed. "Burkatraz?"

"Charming, isn't she?" Burke replied in an acidic tone.

Damn. This would not be easy. But overall, she was glad he was being mean. Helped destroy her love for him. Helped wipe away any delusions she had about having a future with the guy.

But it still hurt like a son-of-a-bitch.

A few hours later, they flew to San Francisco via Burke's private ten-seater jet. In total silence. He worked on his computer and ignored her completely. She questioned her choice the whole way. The only slight positive was that she'd discovered she could put more weight on both her ankle and right leg. The injuries were still sore, but she was getting better. Two days of sleep had sharpened her brain, too. Shortly, she'd be on her way.

Banana and David glared at her when she met them at the base of the airplane stairs. She shuddered and winced, but she had to meet the problem head-on. She walked directly up to them on her crutches. Banana's thick blond brows furrowed over his deep-set blue eyes. He thrust out his lantern jaw. He actually looked kind of scary. David puffed up to his full six foot six inches and glared down at her. His dark brown eyes and swarthy complexion seemed even darker.

She looked into their stony eyes. "I'm so sorry for what I did to you guys. You've been nothing but wonderful to me. I don't deserve it, but I hope someday you guys can find it in your hearts to forgive me. The only reason I escaped was because I was trying to protect myself.

I never wanted to hurt either of you. I've felt like a rat ever since. I owe you both dozens of unspiked brownies."

After a moment, their expressions' softened. The tension left her shoulders and neck.

Banana worked his mouth, then said, "It's okay, Sam. I know you haven't been yourself lately."

David narrowed his eyes, but the hardness left his face. "I want my brownies with chocolate chips and walnuts. And no Ambien."

"Done. I'm so sorry."

David shook his head, reached over and tousled her hair. "Glad they didn't get 'cha, Sam. Sorry you got shot."

"Thanks, honey." She beamed at them. "Thanks you guys, you're the best."

They both gave her quick nods and smiled. They weren't thrilled with her, but they'd begun to forgive her. Sam breathed a large sigh of relief.

She and Burke climbed into the back of his limo. David drove and Banana sat next to him in the front. The window between the compartments was closed.

After they pulled onto the freeway, Burke shot her a nasty look and wrinkled his nose like he smelled something foul. "That was easy," he said in a sardonic tone.

"What?" she asked with a frown.

He scowled. "Getting the men's forgiveness. Bat your eyes, throw them one of your patented cute smiles, and they fall to pieces," he said, his voice dripping with revulsion.

Her interior flamed and her face flushed hot. She wanted to slap him. "What's up your ass? I'm not hanging out at your place if you're gonna pick on me."

"I'm not picking on you. I'm disgusted with how easy it is for you to con people."

"I'm not conning anyone. I don't like the fact that I had to drug Banana and David. Last thing I wanted to do."

Burke snorted, stared out the window and steamed. Worked his jaw. Jiggled his knee so hard, he moved the seat.

The man had been so cold, had barely spoken to her, what had set him off?

He finally turned to her, his gaze heated, his pain lines deep. "Why can't you tell me what happened to you? Why do you keep running from me? What have I done to make you distrust me?"

No wonder he'd shut down. He was hurt. Really hurt. He hadn't lost his love for her, he'd been so twisted up, he couldn't deal with his emotions. Shit. She should have gone to Emma's.

She looked him straight in the eye. "Burke, I know this is hard for you to get your head around, but my decisions were not about you."

"I thought you cared about me."

"I do."

"You used me."

"Yes. The two are not mutually exclusive."

He faced forward, his glare so fiery she was surprised the back of the front seat didn't melt.

"You can change your mind," she said.

He swung his tortured gaze onto her. "About what?" he snapped.

She kept a lid on her emotions. "About me living with you. I seem to be having a negative effect on you. I'll call Emma when we get to your place."

His attention darted around the car, his mouth drawn down. "I don't want you to go. I want you to stay with me. I just...I don't know how to get through to you," he finally said in a tormented tone. "I'm... I've never been more frustrated."

"You can't control me. And it's killing you."

He turned to her, his eyes hard, his mouth twisted. "No, it's not about control," he barked. His face reddened and the veins in his temples throbbed. "It's about logic, woman. Why can't you grasp how much danger you're in? Or how absolutely stupid your actions were?"

Her heart went out to him. She hated hurting him, but there was nothing she could do about it. Nothing would stop her from her mission. If she had to run over both their hearts with a steamroller to get the Senator, she'd do it. She reached over and grabbed his hand. "You're a good man to care about me like this, Mr. Cherlenko."

He softened, then his anger flared and he pulled his hand away and stared out the window. "Lot of good it's done me." He shot her a furious sideways glance. "Maybe I should have come down on your ass harder. Kept you locked up tighter." He shook his head and pursed his lips. "Jesus, all these weapons and escapes and car chases and disguises and *shooting off a gun in downtown fucking Seattle and almost getting killed*—I mean, you got shot!" he shouted with a wild gesture. "And you sit there and look at me like *I'm* crazy!"

She shrugged. "I know."

"You're bent on this path and you're going to die and there's nothing I can do!"

She couldn't argue with him. If the tables were turned, she'd be throwing all the same stuff in his face. She gave him a grim nod. "Doesn't really pay to be my friend these days."

"Tell me about it." He wiped the sweat from his brow and seemed alarmed by the amount of liquid on his palm. "I never sweat like this." He pulled his gray checked shirt away from his neck. "Christ, now you've got me ruining my new Burberry."

Sam erupted in giggles. The sincerity in his expression, the way he bit out his words was so funny.

His gaze narrowed, his fists balled, and his jaw clenched so hard his teeth squeaked.

Which made her laugh harder.

After a long second, his expression relaxed into a smirk. "Bitch. This cost me three hundred dollars."

"You are so damned cute."

He narrowed his eyes, but almost smiled.

When she walked into her room at Burke's, she found six suitcases full of her most-used clothing and accessories that Emma had packed for her. She put on her favorite black yoga pants and a white tank.

After unpacking to give the illusion that she planned on staying, she grabbed her checkbook and wrote a check to Burke to cover part of the cost of the weaponry she'd taken.

She found him working on his computer in the living room and handed him a check for ten thousand dollars. "Here."

He took the slip of paper, looked at it, and his dark brow furrowed. "What's this for?"

"For your weapons. And the Kevlar vests. And the Tasers. I know this doesn't nearly cover your losses, but it's all I have liquid."

He rolled his eyes, made an exasperated noise in the back of his throat, and shoved the check back at her. "Sam, I don't want your money."

She pushed his hand away with a crutch. "Keep it."

When she turned away, he said, "I won't cash it."

Her gut flaming, heat pouring from her nostrils, she spun on him and glared. "Do you want Emma to bring me the cash and have me stick each one of those hundred dollar bills up your ass?" She scorched him with her gaze.

He fought a smile. "No."

"Then cash the fucking check." She turned and stormed out of the room. "Stubborn bastard."

She thought she heard him chuckle behind her.

Burke had Thai sent in for dinner. When she came out of her bedroom to eat, all traces of his good humor were gone. He'd totally shut down. Barely made eye contact, read the paper through dinner and said maybe three words.

She flashed back on the ending of a particularly bad relationship. Jeremy had gotten cold like this. She shivered. Great. She hadn't even gotten together with Burke and they were already going through the throes of a bad break-up. As soon as the meal was over, she retired to her room. Thankfully, she was exhausted and fell asleep early.

The next day, when she got up, she found Banana waiting for her, but no Burke. He'd left coffee fixings for her and brief note about available food. But nothing personal. Just an information exchange.

She swallowed a large lump and pushed back the tears. Another day for her ankle to heal and then she was gone. She couldn't take Mr. Freeze's anger much longer.

But maybe she could get him to thaw out a bit. Worm her way back into his good graces through his stomach. Worked before.

Sam ordered groceries from Safeway on her computer for delivery that afternoon. When the food arrived, it created quite a ruckus with Burke's security team. The two bodyguards downstairs almost attacked the poor delivery driver. After a flurry of phone calls, the forty-something red-haired Safeway driver appeared at the door, white-faced and shaken.

Banana insisted on helping her prepare the meal, clearly making sure she didn't slip anything into the food that shouldn't be there.

At around seven that evening, as she was putting the finishing touches on the elaborate make-up dinner, she heard the front door open.

Banana left the kitchen and had a quick exchange with Burke. "Bye Sam," he called out.

"Bye Banana."

The front door closed.

She waited, but Burke did not come in the kitchen. After she set the table, she went to his room and found his door closed. Something was different about the bedroom door. It had two new deadbolts and the paint was a shade darker than the Navaho white walls of the hallway. She knocked. Metal.

She snorted. What? Did he think she'd dynamite the place to get at his guns? Besides, she'd already taken everything she'd needed. Idiot.

"Yes?" he said from the other side of the door.

"You want some dinner?"

Silence.

"Burke?"

"Yes," he replied in a glum tone. "I'll be right out." Like he'd agreed to clean the cat box.

Her mood plummeted, her jaw clenched and she turned away from the door. "Whatever." *Fuck this.* Tomorrow she was gone.

She served dinner, opened a beer, and sat down to eat. Screw waiting. He could eat leftovers the next day for all she cared. She scowled at her food. All this effort for nothing. Penis. He could go to hell.

A few minutes later, Burke walked in and his eyebrows raised when he spotted the offerings. Roast beef, scalloped potatoes, green beans with caramelized onions, Caesar salad and garlic bread. A little surge of pleasure flowed through her. The spread was luscious.

After perusing the meal, his brow furrowed and his gaze darkened. His mouth hard, he put his hands on his hips and glared at her. "Won't work." He didn't make a move toward his chair.

Her insides turned to fire. Her head throbbed. She gripped her fork so hard she flipped a piece of roast beef back onto her plate. "What the hell are you talking about? What won't work?"

"Lulling me with food. What's next? A carefully planned seduction?" he said with a sneer.

She closed her eyes and started counting to ten. She only made it to three before she jumped up. Her ankle and leg hurt, but she didn't care. She jabbed her forefinger into his chest. "That's it! You self-centered prick. You've shut every door in my face for the last two days. Fine. I get it. You're pissed. I hurt you. What? You think I enjoyed it? Like I'm some sadistic freak who likes to take advantage of people?"

He closed off even more and crossed his arms, his jaw twitching.

"I gave you no guarantees. No promises. Everything we shared was honest on my end. You just happened to ignore the fact that I'd lost my mind and decided to fall in love with me. Well, I think that speaks more to your self-destruction than to anything I did." She pointed at the table. "So why don't you shove that roast beef right up your ass? Because I'm done."

A human ice cube, he held up a hand to silence her, but she wasn't done yet.

Thrusting her chin out, she glared up into his dark eyes. "And don't you dare blame all this on me, buddy boy. You own fifty percent of this shit between us. And in the past four days, you've been a hundred percent of it. You're not the only one in the universe who's suffered loss or betrayal, you big asshole. So if you want to keep punishing me, you can go fuck yourself. I'm moving to Emma's."

She grabbed her crutches, and headed for the doorway.

"Sam, wait," he said in an exasperated tone that propelled her out the door faster.

She reached her bedroom and he took hold of her arm, stopping her at the threshold. "Sam, please. Can we talk?"

Her heart wrenched and she held her aching gut. "I can't take your shit on top of mine."

"I'm sorry." He closed his eyes and sighed. "I'm furious with you. And I have no idea where to go with it," he said in a super sad tone. With a haunted expression, he stared at the wall, then at her. Vulnerability and pain filled his dark eyes.

His raw emotions drew her in. Her instinct was to throw her arms around him and kiss him. She had to stay strong. She distanced herself from her reaction. "Can we talk without yelling?"

He shrugged. "I hope so."

The need on his face made her turn away. "Food's getting cold."

He put a gentle hand on the small of her back and she resisted the urge to fall into his arms. "Then let's go eat, shall we? I'll open a good bottle of red."

She turned to him and he tried to give her a smile. But he was hurting and couldn't hide it. She got the feeling he hadn't had many deep relationships. Nothing this intense.

Come to think of it, neither had she. Shit. And they hadn't even made love yet. So unbelievable that they shared this level of emotion for each other.

They ate dinner and made small talk.

Mid-way through the meal, he raised his glass to her. "You, my dear, are an amazing cook." He let a bit of charm show through. Sounded more himself. More centered.

She relaxed. Thank God.

But after they finished the meal, Burke sent her a naked, wounded stare. Like she'd slept with his best friend in front of him. Like they'd just ended a twenty-year-marriage.

So. Weird.

"Shall we talk in the living room?" he asked in a remarkably calm voice.

"Okay." Her legs felt rubbery and unstable. She had no idea how to handle this man. Or her own runaway feelings.

They sank into the plush leather couch and faced each other. Burke's intensity rose. Torn between wanting to run away and wanting to jump him, she'd never felt more conflicted.

"How do you feel about me?" His tone was neutral, but his gaze reflected deep pain.

His hurt ate away at her heart and resolve. She shifted her attention to her chipped nails. "What do you mean?"

"Relationship-wise. As a potential mate."

She took in a short breath and stared at him, startled by the truth bomb. "Wow, no beating around the bush."

"I've been beating around the bush for a week," he said in a tired tone. "You're done. I'm done. How do you feel about me? Do you love me?"

His words flailed her heart. She knew what kind of love he was talking about and she was too fucked up to feel much of anything but pain. This was the worst situation she'd ever been in with a guy. She'd finally found Mr. Right and she couldn't be with him. She shrugged and gestured vaguely, searching for the right words.

He paled and looked like she'd slapped him. His attention dropped to the floor.

"Burke…"

"No. I understand." He turned his body away from her.

Her chest hurt like he'd stabbed her heart with a letter opener. She wiped the tears from her eyes and tried to find her voice. "Listen. If I told you that I loved you, you'd map your emotions onto mine. Please, hear me out. I am going through the hardest time—second hardest time —I've ever been through. I am not myself. The last thing I'd ever want to do is hurt you."

He nodded and looked like she'd killed his puppy.

Gut punch. More tears forced their way to the surface. "Our timing is off, Burke. I feel the pull toward you. I feel the connection. Do I think we'd make it as a couple? If I wasn't in the current situation and I'd met you at a stable time of my life? You bet. I'd be all over you. But I can't love you the way you deserve to be loved right now. I can't love anyone like that. I'm sorry."

He stared at his feet.

The roast beef churned and lurched in her stomach. She'd led him on and stomped his heart to paste. No matter the circumstances or his fault in the situation, she felt rotten.

After a few moments, his brow still wrinkled with pain, he stroked his chin. Then he rubbed the back of his neck. He sighed and shifted his attention to the window opposite him. "Honest. Not what I want to hear, but completely understandable." He locked gazes with her, his expression tortured and starving. "God, I want you," he said, his voice laced with agonized longing.

He didn't say it to seduce her. He didn't say it to make her feel bad. He said it because it was his absolute truth.

He focused on the window again, flopped his head back against the couch, shut his eyes and let out a long breath.

So un-Burke-like. No shields, no defense, no games. Open, honest, vulnerable. She wanted to take him in her arms and comfort him. Love him.

Warning! Slippery slope!

She gave her head a shake and tried to shut down, but the pull toward him overwhelmed her. Not only did she want him, she needed him. Craved him. Had to have him. Almost like she couldn't breathe without him.

She took in his muscled abs. His hard pecs. His ropy neck. The slight cleft in his chin. The long dark lashes of his closed eyes. His full mouth. "It would be stupid to hop into bed right now."

He opened one eye and looked at her, but didn't move otherwise. "Really stupid."

"We would both more than likely get our hearts broken."

He opened both eyes wide, stared into space and nodded, his gaze hollowing. "More than likely."

After a beat, he angled a sharp glance at her.

Sam wasn't sure who moved first, but suddenly, she was kissing Burke with all her heart and he was right there with her.

FOURTEEN

Sam's body came alive, pulsing from top to toe, buzzing with heady power. Her skin tingled madly and moisture welled between her legs. She grabbed Burke's sweater, pulled it over his head and threw it behind the couch. With both hands, she took his pecs in her hands and kissed his chest, getting high on his cologne, scent, and the heat and feel of his firm skin and soft chest hair. He groaned deep in his throat, pushed her back, unbuttoned her shirt and removed it. Snapping off her bra, he tossed it over his shoulder.

When he laid eyes on her breasts, he gasped and his mouth dropped open. "Oh, my God, you're so beautiful," he whispered. He gently took her breasts in his hands, like he was handling fragile, precious objects, and began exploring them. Like he worshipped them. Like he was mesmerized.

She'd never had a guy look at her like this. Normally, they were inside her by now. But Burke admired her like she was a work of art. His face shone like he was the luckiest man in the world. Neither her ego nor her heart had ever been more inflated.

He slowly massaged her, running his thumbs around her areolas. Her clit pinged. She took in a long breath and delighted in the feel of his tender touch. A slow grin came over his face. He pushed her onto her back and took a breast in his mouth.

Running her hands over his ripped shoulders, she started breathing heavier. He spun his tongue around her nipple, and clamped onto her with his supple lips, sending a wave of lust to her sex. Suckling, he gently played with her other breast.

She wanted to attack him, but her body loved what he was doing so much, it wouldn't move.

Burke moved to her other breast, tasting and teasing her. Goosebumps popped all over her skin and pleasure pulsed her erogenous zones.

Leaving her breast, he kissed a trail upwards. Collarbone, neck, jaw and finally her mouth. He conquered her tongue with his. The weight of his body on top of her made her sex go even softer and wetter. She couldn't wait until he was inside.

Everything about him felt right. His taste, his feel, his scent and the perfection of his kiss. He parried with her tongue, toying, then dominating. He read exactly what would turn her on the most and executed the move precisely. Unreal.

Cupping her breast sweetly, he squeezed, tweaking the nipple between two supple fingers while driving deeper into her mouth.

She arched against him, moaning deep in her throat, feeling high on him. Reeling. Sailing.

She ran her hands down the smooth skin of his back to grab his taut, rounded, ass. Moaning into her mouth, he pressed his hard and impressive bulge against her thigh.

Sam couldn't take the teasing any longer and shoved him back. "This is bullshit. I need to be naked with you."

He laughed. "Far be it for me to stand in the way of clothes."

Easing her sweats over her wound, she kicked them off. He stripped her of her panties and unzipped his pants. Sitting up, she pushed down the waistband of his jeans. His fat cock popped out. Her mouth dropped open and her sex gave a cheer. The head was broad, the shaft bulky, with a nice slight curve, but thank God, not a cockzilla. Probably seven inches of gorgeous dick. Beautiful. A perfect fit for her. She smiled from the depths of her womb. "Oh my God, what a nice cock."

He shot her a satisfied grin and removed his pants. Then with a predatory, feral and dark look in his eye, he climbed on top and pushed apart her legs with his knees.

Her sex surged with tantalizing energy. "Oh, God, I almost came and you're not even inside me," she said in a husky whisper.

A short laugh, then his smile faded. His expression hardened to alpha dominator. Conqueror. All his competitiveness came to the surface. "Prepare for a ride, woman," he said in a growl, which would have sounded corny coming from anyone else's mouth, but he carried it off.

She rocketed right to the brink of climax. Touching herself, she said, "Let's go, I can't—"

Hello? You are about to have unprotected sex!

"—oh, shit!"

His eyes widened and his brow wrinkled. "What?"

"Birth control."

Mouth gaping, his face turned white. "Well, that's a first since I was a teenager."

In a flash, his expression returned to a king claiming his territory. With a lascivious grin, he picked her up, kissed her, and carried her toward his bedroom.

"Oh, God," she said into his mouth.

"Wait." He thrust his tongue further inside.

Kicking open his door, he strode to his bed, lay her on the comforter, moved on top and kissed her. His hand traveled down between her breasts and lightly touched her sex.

His fingers felt like heaven. She sucked in a breath through her teeth and arched her back, pressing her hips against his hand. She wanted more. Much more.

Burke slowly teased her lips apart with a forefinger and flicked her clit precisely and expertly. Electric hunger energy zapped through her bud, turning it to rock. She curled her toes and balled her fists.

Watching her every reaction, he adjusted his movements to bring the most out of her. Her orgasm built. What he was doing to her with just his finger was absolutely criminal. She'd never felt anything better.

All at once she was overcome. Screaming, she grabbed his hand and ground against him, but pushed him away right before she blew. Her sex hurt so badly from need, she cried out in a tortured moan of agony. Then she snarled up at him, "Get that fucking condom on before I kill you!"

He burst into a wide smile and chuckled. "Yes, ma'am." He gave her a quick, lusty kiss, then crawled past her, opened his bedside drawer and withdrew a condom.

After removing the protection from its foil casing, he rolled the latex over his steely dick and sent her a dark hungry stare. Her skin prickled and she shivered. Not only did the devilish look in his eye turn her on, his physique was beyond hot. From his six-pack abs to the dark chest hair dusting his well developed pecs to his thick thighs, Burke was a feast for the eyes. But his dick was the trophy. She wanted to suck him until he cried.

He crawled on top and angled his body above her. His gaze intensified. In that moment, he took ownership, she saw it deep behind his mahogany eyes. Holding his thick, hard cock in his hand, he slipped it inside her, all his attention focused on her face.

Burke slowly thrust into her until he hit the target zone. Sam's sex thundered with a violent orgasm, shocking her—she'd never climaxed on one stroke before! Screaming, she attacked him with her fists and squirmed to get away from the intense sensations.

He fought to control her, but didn't miss a beat with his fantastic hips. Catching her wrists, he increased the intensity of his thrusts. A succession of hard climaxes bombarded her womb. She roared and her walls clamped around his awesome tool.

Burke hit the money again. And again. Blinding energy blasted her and her body rocked with violent jerks. Widening her legs, she cried out in a feral growl, slipped out of his grip, grabbed his ass, and pulled him into her. She couldn't get him inside far enough or quick enough.

A loud moan verging on a battle cry tore from his throat, and he performed a devastating circular motion with his hips, blasting her g-spot with an assault that made her lose her mind. Her sex and clit quaked violently. The world took a spin, she gasped for air and he sent her over the edge once more. Roaring, she beat against his chest and pressed up against him to receive his powerful thrusts.

In a few quick moves, Burke took hold of her wrists and pinned her to the bed, his eyes dilated, his expression pure animal.

A scream started from her womb, gathered strength and blasted out of her body, shaking her ribs. He plowed into her g-spot and her center thundered with savage tremors.

She had no idea how much more she could take, but she never wanted him to stop. He hit his target again and again, torpedoing her barriers, sending her further into outer space until she heard a whining in her ears and she lost touch with where she was. All she could do was think of Burke and come.

His strokes got harder and faster, he shuddered and released into her, catapulting her to an even higher realm. She couldn't breathe, she couldn't hear, she couldn't see, all she could do was ride the tidal wave of ecstasy.

Slowly, her brain came back to her in bits and pieces. She came aware she was hyper-ventilating. Slowing her breathing, her body quivered with aftershocks. Burke kept thrusting into her, like he didn't want it to end.

Finally, he stopped, let go of her wrists, grabbed the top of the condom and moved off her. The sudden departure of his body heat, plus the breeze from his motion, chilled her sweaty body. Pulling the sheet over her, she sighed with pleasure. Her skin tingled and her sex sang. Her legs, her back, her neck, everything pulsed with absolute satisfaction and happiness. He'd given her orgasms on a scale she'd never experienced before. She'd never come so hard or so much in her life.

"Wow. I had no idea my body could do that."

He sent her a wide, appreciative grin. "Really?"

"Really. You got magic hips and a magic cock, Mr. Cherlenko. I knew it was going to be good between us, but I had no idea it was going to be *that* good. Look at all this time we wasted! I feel so cheated."

He laughed and lay down next to her. She kissed his chest and ran her hands though his soft, damp hair. Nipping along his tight belly, she licked the ridges of his lower abs and cupped his balls, rolling them gently through her fingers.

His muscles tensing, he pointed his toes and took in a quick breath of air.

She wrapped her hand around his half-shaft. His cock surged with blood and stiffened in her fist. Slowly, she moved her hand up and down, loving the feel of his hot, hard tool.

He pressed his hips upwards in time with her motions. She closed her mouth on his beefy head. Burke hissed and his body shuddered. Pulling her lips over her teeth, she bit down on his shaft as hard as she could without hurting herself.

"Oh, God…Sam," he groaned.

A charge went through her and her clit throbbed. Sliding her mouth over him, she took in his taste, the slight latex overtone, the saltiness of his cum and luxuriated in the sensations of him in her mouth. Slowly, she worked her way back up, then nibbled his stiffness.

With her tongue, she flicked all around his head, then found the seam at the top near the opening and assaulted it. He cried out.

She eased down on top of him, deep-throating him as far as she could. Locking her thumb and forefinger around the base of his cock, she jacked him slowly in time with her head bobs.

Burke made some unintelligible strangling/grunting noises and began panting.

Fast motion, she went for it.

He cried out, pushed her head off his cock, his face full of tortured agony. Throwing her back against the bed, he reached for the drawer. "I have to fuck you, lady, and keep fucking you," he said in a pained rasp.

Power and lust surged through her. So sweet having this much control over the great Burke Cherlenko.

He ripped off the foil top dramatically and rolled the condom onto his cock fast. His expression went from agony to pure evil.

A sharp pulse of energy jolted her clit, her juices flowed, and her legs went rubbery.

He sent her a dark, wicked smile and growled, "Up on your knees."

Her sex throbbed with want. Sam took in a huge breath and grabbed herself. "Oh, God, you're so hot."

"Do it," he commanded quietly, his face hard.

Another high voltage burst of desire revved her clit. "Sir, yes, sir!" she cried out with a giant happy grin.

Raising a brow, he sent her a predatory stare. She shivered with anticipation.

She stacked two pillows on top of another and settled on top, her knees underneath her, her back arched, her legs wide.

"God, Sam…" he said in a harsh whisper as he ran his hand over her butt.

Her skin came alive everywhere he touched.

He slipped his finger inside her and she contracted around him, her womb and lips swelling with hunger. Everything he did felt amazing.

"You're so beautiful." He slid his finger back out slowly.

She gritted her teeth to stave off the orgasm, but he wasn't making it easy on her, he traced her lips with the perfect pressure. Fisting the sheets, she panted. Around and around, he slid his finger over her opening, gently, patiently.

"Just fuck me!" Sam cried out.

"Not yet, my pet," he said in a menacing, low, yet horribly arousing tone.

He circled his finger around her sensitive folds once more, then lightly slid across her hard and hurting clit. Curling her feet, her shoulders tensed solid. Excruciating pleasure. She was about to blow.

"God, Burke!"

Increasing his pace, he spun his slippery finger around her head.

Ka-blam! Fireworks exploded in her mind and her womb contracted with a succession of hard reports. "Yeah!" she cried out, shuddering and exhilarated.

This was more fun than she'd ever had in her life.

As she came down, he slapped her a good one across both buns. A little jolt went through her. Lovely capper.

Without warning, Burke slid his cock into her in one smooth motion until he hit the prize.

An atomic orgasm annihilated Sam's mind and body. Barely conscious, she bellowed and shook, soaring straight through the Milky Way. One hand gripping the pillow, she pounded the mattress with the other, crying out loud and long until her throat went dry. She coughed and gasped for air.

"Are you okay?" he asked gently.

"Don't stop!" she croaked. "Fuck me, you son-of-a-bitch! Send me through the fucking headboard and out the goddamned window!"

Burke gave a rough chuckle. "As the lady desires." He grabbed her hips hard and plowed into her, impacting her at full force.

Sam roared with rapture.

Burke fucked her relentlessly, his thrusts precise, holding her hostage in the longest orgasm of her life. Her heart was in tachycardia, she couldn't breathe and sweat poured from her. And all she wanted was more.

Digging his fingers into her hips, his dick got even thicker and harder and he slammed into her, crying out in a deafening roar, sounding like he came from his soul.

Her vision blurred and her sex blasted into an even stronger reality-shattering orgasm. Head ringing, she ground against him, her body rocking with ecstasy.

After a last few grinds, he withdrew and stepped onto the floor. She collapsed to the mattress on her belly in a pool of useless muscles.

No breath in her lungs, she could barely see, and every part of her body burned with exertion, yet vibrated with pleasure. Her throat felt like a desert. Swallowing, she lay with her face squished into the pillow, her eyes closed in dreamy exhaustion. "You killed me," she said, slurring her words.

He laid a nice slap on her upturned buns. Her clit pulsed and she moved her hips against the bed. "Most. Fun. Ever."

After disposing of the condom, he snuggled next to her, his sweaty skin slick against hers. He kissed her cheek, then nibbled her ear while squeezing a bun in one hand. "Mmm, you smell nice."

She loved the feel of his skin against hers, his strong hand on her ass. "I smell like sex and roast beef."

He laughed. "No, you smell like tasty woman and Sam Murdock."

"I'm fairly partial to the Burke Cherlenko brand, myself." She wanted to hug him, but her tired limbs wouldn't obey her.

He nuzzled her face.

Her brain cleared a bit and she looked deep into his sexy dark brown eyes. "You are the best fuck in the universe."

He kissed her neck. "You inspire me."

She laughed when she heard her words. "Not that I've fucked the universe. But I know, just from the small sample I've had, you are the best in the entire world. You've ruined me for other men."

"Mission accomplished," he said to himself and hugged her tight.

"If you try to leave this room, I'll kill you. I have to rest a minute, but there is a whole buffet of things I've got stored up that I need to do to you."

His cock stirred against her leg. "My dick hasn't been this happy. Ever." He looked her in the eye. "Nor have I. At the risk of creating a social faux paz, Miss Samantha Murdock," he said, running his hand down her face, "I have never been more in love with any woman in my life."

Her heart ripped open and tears welled in her eyes. Before she could respond, he kissed her.

Her body humming, she rolled onto her side and pulled him tight to her body. Pressed as close as she could, she kissed him back with everything she had. She loved him so much it hurt. Her life would be a barren, desolated wasteland without him. She wanted to be next to him. In his arms. In his bed. Always.

She ended the kiss and gazed at him, entranced. "Now I know why my other men didn't work out."

One thick brow raised. "Why?"

"Because they weren't you."

His eyes dilated, his face went pained with love and lust and he kissed her hard. Running his hands down her back, he cupped her buns and pulled her tight to him. He pressed her onto her back, laid little kisses all over her face, down her neck and closed his mouth on her breast.

Massaging her, he teased the nipple. Then he kissed his way up to her mouth. He nibbled her lower lip, then darted his tongue in her mouth and played with her. She sucked on him and he slid his hand down between her legs. Teasing her folds apart, he lightly rubbed her clit with his forefinger. She launched right back to the edge of orgasm.

Jesus Christ, wasn't her body done yet? How could this guy have this much sexual power over her? Outrageous!

One side of his mouth curled at her reaction, and he moved down between her legs. Stroking her gently, he parted the hair and laid his tongue on her clit.

Intense pleasure overwhelmed her sensitive sex. Squealing, she backed away.

He laughed, grabbed her hips and pinned her to the bed. Lost in a haze of want, she cried out. Gently, patiently, he worked her head. She finally relaxed and he pushed her legs apart and settled between them.

While teasing and flicking her with the tip of his tongue, he lightly stroked the insides of her thighs, sending shivers racing through her.

Almost too much to handle. Wasn't there anything this guy couldn't do perfectly?

Around and around her pleasure center, he teased her with his tongue. Delicious sensations radiated through her clit and sex. Her orgasm built and her breathing increased. She worked her toes and gripped the comforter, barely holding back from coming.

All at once, he lay down a strafing run of licks on her pulsing clit. She rocketed into a head-pounding climax, screaming and bucking. But no matter how hard she flailed, he stayed with her like he could see with his tongue. Grabbing his ears, she ground against his mouth, crushing his head between her thighs. Her sex contracted with concussion after concussion. Delicious, mind-blowing joy.

As she slowly came down from her glorious orgasm, she made happy noises in the back of her throat.

Burke moved from her clit and chewed on her thigh. She squealed and pulled him on top of her and gave him a full body hug. Arching her hips against him, she loved the feel of his weight and heat. His warm hard shoulders under her touch. His soft, silky skin.

He sent her a dark and feral look, his brow raised. His cock throbbed against her thigh.

"Guess who's back." Giggling, she took hold of him and began stroking his hardness.

"I love it when you touch me. I love you." He kissed her passionately. Like he was savoring her, delighting and reveling in her.

No man had ever made her feel this special before.

She pushed back just enough to make eye contact. "I love you, too, Burke. So much it hurts."

His eyes widened, he groaned and kissed her hard. His hands were all over her. "God, I want to fuck you again," he said into her mouth.

She pushed him back. "Well, get the damned condom on and let's start the show."

He sent her a feral, yet happy grin, but shook his head. "The mind is willing but the body is weak and needs a bit of time. I won't be able to come for a while."

"And now, a brief intermission. Probably a better idea. I can only take so much. My brain is hosed. And I think I'm about to become part of this mattress."

He grinned, cupped her breast and sent her a heart-melting smile. "Why don't you rest and I'll get a bottle of wine and couple glasses?"

"Sounds divine."

She moved and her back twinged. "Holy bejeebus, I don't think my body's ever taken this much before."

"Wait," he promised with an animal-edged sideways glance.

"You are going to be the death of me."

He shot her a cute, but hungry smile. "But what a way to go, huh?"

Chuckling, she rubbed the sore muscles of her lower back. She'd never felt more blissful in her life. Wow. Talk about a turnaround.

What a great fucking night. Pun intended.

Larry's ugly face appeared in her mind and her stomach turned.

She forced all bad thoughts away. All you ever had was now. She had to remember that.

And now was pretty damned spectacular.

FIFTEEN

Sam grinned when Burke appeared at his bedroom door carrying two glasses of red wine. His beefy pecs, his steely dick, muscular thighs—and that broad smile—went straight to her sex. She rubbed herself and laughed. "You are so wickedly hot."

His smile widened and he offered her a glass. "No more than you, darling."

She took the glass and sipped, fully enjoying the sweet, fragrant liquid as it slid down her raw and dry throat. The flavor filled her senses. Mmm. Oaky and fruity and light. "Why does everything taste better after sex?"

He chuckled. "You sure do."

Sam made a face.

He set his wine glass on the bedside table and climbed in beside her. Rubbing her thigh, he gave it a squeeze. His attention went to her bandage. "How are you healing?"

"Still hurts."

His features went pained and he lightly kissed the band-aid. Then he sent her a sweet, sympathetic look and kissed her other gunshot wound.

Tears burned her eyes. The tenderness in his gaze nailed her. He wanted to heal her. He wanted to make her whole.

He took her wineglass and set it on the bedside table. Gathering her in his arms, he brought her close. "Sam, don't cry. They can't hurt you. He can't hurt you."

She clung to him. "I can't go there." Sorrow and grief wrenched her soul. Memories of her past flooded her mind. Larry's sneering face. Her body stiffened.

"I'm sorry," he said.

"Don't be."

"Let me help."

"Maybe." She nestled into his warm, inviting chest, wishing his strength could make her past and pain disappear. But nothing could wipe away the truth. And at some point, she had to deal with it.

He held her close and kissed the side of her head. "Tell me what happened, Sam. Tell me what he did to you."

Maybe he was right. Maybe he could help her. Maybe it was time to finally tell the story.

Even though she might lose him once he heard the whole thing. But she had to take the chance. He said he loved her, she'd see how far his feelings went. This story would make or break their relationship.

She pulled away, looked into his loving brown gaze and saw temporary safety there. Closing her eyes, she took a second to open her mental security gates. She hadn't talked about this in sixteen years. Pulling the story out of her would take some effort.

Sam shifted in his arms and lay on her back with her head on the pillow. Burke rolled up on an elbow, put an arm around her hips and a leg over one of hers.

After a long sigh, and a few more minor adjustments to mold her body to his, she stared out the window at a passing airplane. "I met Larry in the middle of my freshman year in high school. Dad..." Her chest tightened. She took a deep breath and moved out of her body. "Dad had really turned on me. I was his precious, wonderful Salamander. For twelve years. He taught me baseball and fishing, and how to tie a knot. How to change a tire. But when I hit twelve, I hit puberty hard. My tits grew in a month. My hips filled out and I had the body of a woman before I could comprehend what had happened. Dad was horrified."

Burke frowned, confusion marring his handsome features. "All you did was grow up."

"Yeah and it totally freaked me out. I tried to cover up my boobs by wearing big shirts. I tried to pretend I hadn't changed. But he became distant. Treated me like I'd suddenly become toxic. Diseased. I felt like I'd failed him. Utterly betrayed him." Her belly hollowed and a weight pressed on her chest. An ache from deep within her overwhelmed her. She fought to stay on track.

Burke ran his hand down her shoulder. "What an asshole. Like you had control over puberty."

Sam shrugged. "While he took a lot of anger out on me, I don't think he meant to hurt me. He just wigged out. But it did crush me. Mom said that a father/daughter relationship had to change. That I couldn't be that close with him anymore. That it was time I grew up and found my own way. At fucking twelve. Before I was emotionally ready for it. So I withdrew from the family and got into basketball." Intense loneliness choked her. She rubbed her throat.

His face hardened. "Your parents sound as stupid and short-sighted as mine. That's too young."

"I agree. What happened with yours?"

He shook his head. "You first. I'll tell my story after I hear yours. Go on, you got into sports."

"Yeah." She shifted her attention to her trembling hands, kneading them together to help release tension. "So two years later, Dad and I are still virtual strangers, and I'm a freshman in high school. I'm in math and Sheriff Larry Tyrell walks into class to pitch the Sheriff Department's teen outreach program. When he saw me, his jaw dropped and he stared at me like I was the most beautiful woman he'd ever seen. All my girlfriends noticed. Well, I wasn't sure about law enforcement, all I knew was that I wanted more of that attention." Her heart raced at the memory. The euphoria had been intoxicating.

"I'll bet."

Sam smiled. "I remember thinking he was the most handsome man I'd ever laid eyes on. I wanted to be a grown up so badly. I wanted to be sophisticated. I wanted him to like me. Which didn't take too much effort. Larry clearly liked me and enjoyed me worshipping him. He complimented every single thing I did. I was in heaven. The other girl I joined with dropped out because all of Larry's focus was on me. He took me on my first ride-along."

Burke's face went dark. "Bastard. A predator."

"No, I was the predator. I threw myself at him." Her face burned and she rubbed her forehead. "How could I know what I was setting in motion?"

Burke's intensity heightened. "Are you kidding? That wasn't your fault. You were how old?"

He'd clearly misunderstood the situation. Nice of him to take her side, but he had no idea what a bad person she was. What a depraved slut. Maybe now he'd see why they didn't have a future. "Fourteen and a half, but I was old enough to—"

Burke's expression remained unchanged. "And he was forty? Think about it, Sam. You're still not that old. I will be in six months and I have to tell you, fourteen-year-olds…" He shuddered. "Children. Why would a grown man want a child unless he's very sick?"

This situation was different. She'd been very mature for her age and had known better. "Okay, still, I threw myself at him. I'd never been more in love. On our third ride-along, he took me to a special place he wanted to show me. Behind a billboard on a highway. A place he'd hide to catch speeders. He parked and we were talking and he suddenly pulled me to him and kissed me. While he was kind of a weird kisser—only my second kiss and I wasn't sure about all this tongue stuff yet—I was out of my mind with rapture. He wanted me, a silly little nothing of a girl. The great Sheriff Larry Tyrell, the son of the governor, chose me. I'd never been happier."

"I'll bet."

"First time I tasted the power a woman has over a man. I really thought I was hot shit."

Burke grinned. "You were. Probably just as gorgeous as you are now."

Warmth spread through her. "I don't know, I always think I look dorky."

He chuckled and moved a wisp of hair off her brow. "I have many ways to describe you, but dorky is not one of them. How long did the affair last?"

"Two years."

His brows came down hard over his eyes. *"Two years?"*

"Yeah. A long time in retrospect. Of course, the second year got strange. He changed. Or maybe I did, I don't know. But he let more of his inner pervert show. Treated me more like a possession. His toy to use and abuse. Maybe he was trying to get rid of me because he pushed me really far that year. Did many unnatural things to me." She chuckled at the sheer craziness of their sex life. Larry's nasty smile. His obsession with foreign objects. Her skin and extremities got the creepy-crawlies. She shuddered. "I think he fucked me with every piece of equipment in that patrol car."

Burke gasped, a look of horror came over his even features, then his expression sharpened into disgust.

Sam took his hand and squeezed it. "Sorry, TMI. I shouldn't have told you that."

He brought her close to him. "No, Sam, please don't censor yourself. I need to hear it all. And moreover, you have to talk about this. His abuse was so severe."

Shrugging, she said, "Not really. I mean, I didn't know any better. I actually wasn't traumatized by the weird sex. I didn't find out until way afterwards that he was a pervert. I thought all men made love like that. And I didn't tell anyone what he did to me so I never found out. But he sure opened up a whole new world to me."

His face twisted with revulsion. "Jesus, Sam."

"I was so shocked after making love with Daniel for the first time," Sam said, laughing. "He was my first normal boyfriend. I was like, 'That's it? You're not gonna handcuff me to a tree and fuck me with a baton or hit me with it?' I thought sadomasochism was a normal part of sex. Just my luck my first lover would provide the most unusual, violent and extreme sex I would ever have."

Burke's body stiffened and he looked like he wanted to murder the man. "I'm so sorry."

"No more than I. Bastard sure took advantage of my naiveté. No matter how badly he treated me, I thought he loved me. I was in heaven. So dumb."

"No, so young."

"I thought I'd graduate from high school and we'd be married. He always talked about his political aspirations and I pictured myself as the governor's wife, living in the governor's mansion, entertaining all the dignitaries." She shook her head and angled a glance at Burke. "You know he even took me there once."

"Where?"

"Governor's mansion. Well, not the Bridges House, which is the official New Hampshire Governor's mansion, this was his family home. Bigger than the Bridges House. And since his dad was Governor at the time, this was his official residence. It was my fifteenth birthday. There's this secret tunnel that goes from an old abandoned mine shaft on the back of the property and leads inside the house—into the closet of the master suite. From when his grandfather was a bootlegger. Anyway, he snuck me in—down this dark, creepy, cobwebby, stone-lined tunnel—and into his parents' magnificent bedroom suite. Lots of gold gilding. Ostentatious. These long burgundy drapes. Actually, in retrospect, tacky as hell." She giggled, making Burke smile.

"Then Larry opened a bottle of champagne—my first taste of the bubbly—and made love to me on his parents' king-sized bed. Gave me an engraved gold heart locket in a red velvet box, and a dozen red roses." She rolled her eyes. "I think that night was the pinnacle of my life."

Burke briefly raised his brows. "I'll bet. Very impressive to a fifteen-year-old."

"Everything was going my way. I'd made captain of the basketball team, I was getting great grades and I had this secret illicit affair with Larry. All at fifteen. I remember thinking at the time that things would only get better." She snorted. "Never been more wrong."

He sat up, reached over her, and grabbed his wine glass from the bedside table. He took a long sip, then held the glass up to her lips. After she took a nice draw, he returned the goblet to its place on the table.

"So what happened?" he asked.

Sam stretched and he shifted onto his back. Nestling into him, she threw an arm and a leg over his warm, comforting body. "This one night, I snuck out as usual and met Larry at the corner and we drove to our secret spot by the Merrimack River, miles out of town behind a veteran's graveyard. So we're naked and just finished screwing when this car comes out of nowhere and pulls up next to us. We're at the end of a dead-end dirt service road. No one should be out there at that time of night. Larry and I scrambled for our clothes and put 'em on in like two seconds. Then Larry flipped on the headlights and got out of the car to confront the trespasser. Then I see it's my father's Jeep."

Burke's face darkened and his body tensed. "Shit."

"Yeah." She propped herself up on the pillow and faced him. Her lower lip trembling, her gut seared. Tears ran down her face as she stared into her past. "Dad must have seen me leave and followed me. He'd asked a lot of probing questions that night. Did I have a boyfriend? He'd hinted that I'd been spotted out past curfew. But I didn't bite. I deflected the questions, I thought, very cleverly. Typical deluded teenage move."

"What did your father do?"

Sam heaved a sigh to ease the tightness in her chest. "Lost his mind. Jumped out of the Jeep screaming and told Larry he was going to kill him. Then he turned to me and I'll never forget the way he looked at me. I'd never seen that much revulsion on anyone's face before. And then the words I'll never get out of my head. 'I didn't raise you to be a *whore*," she said in a deep growl, imitating her father's voice and inflection. "To spread your legs in the back seat like a slut for a man old enough to be your father. You disgust me!'"

Burke looked like she'd punched him. *"He said that?"*

Why was he so surprised? Pretty logical response. "Yeah."

His face went pained and he hugged her tight. "I'm so sorry."

She had no idea why Burke felt sorry for her—she completely deserved the comments—but she wanted to get the story out and pushed him back. "So after Dad wastes me, he got in Larry's face and said he was going to ruin him. He'd make sure that Larry never became Governor. That Larry would lose the respect of everyone in town and that he'd live in shame the rest of his natural born life. Then he punched him. Hard."

"Uh, oh."

"Yeah. That lit Larry's super short fuse, he pulled out his gun and shot Dad, point blank."

Burke's mouth dropped open. "Holy shit."

Sam felt strangely removed from the memory. The tears continued, but she didn't feel as much as she thought she should. It was like someone else was telling the story. "Fucking blood went everywhere, all over me, Larry and of course, Dad. Dad clutched his chest, looked down in shock at the bloody hole, then looked back up at Larry and said, 'You bastard, you've killed me.' Then he dropped dead at my feet."

"Jesus Christ, Sam. What did you do?"

"Screamed my fool head off. Dove down, grabbed Dad's lifeless body and shook him. You know, the whole Daddy-you-can't-be-dead tirade. Larry yanked me up by my hair and screamed in my face. 'You little whore, this is all your fault! You killed your father!" she said loudly, imitating Larry.

Burke paled. "Holy God."

His reaction startled her. She was so numb from the horror, she felt like a ventriloquist telling the story through a dummy. And something about speaking the words, while distasteful, was almost a relief. Like she no longer had to expel the energy to keep the story from falling out. "Yeah, so I lost it and screamed back and told him I was going to tell everyone what he'd done. The last thing on my mind was that he'd shoot me. But he got this weird look in his eye. Dead. But crazy, too. He lifted the gun and pointed it right into my face. Barrel was like fifteen feet wide. I pushed the gun out of the way, kicked him in the balls and ran for it. I only got about twenty feet away before I heard the first shot. He missed, but shot again and suddenly the side of my thigh felt like I'd burned it with a flaming stick."

Burke's eyes narrowed and his lips twisted. "Fucking bastard."

"Thankfully, I'd just seen a show on guns and learned that bullets were slowed by water, so I dove into the river. Fucking freezing, nasty, dark, creepy water. I swam down like six feet into the pitch blackness and felt around for a root and grabbed hold of this slimy thing, because the current was pretty strong at that part. He fired shots all around me. I can't believe he didn't hit me."

"Then what happened?"

She looked upwards as if she were peering through the murky surface of the water, remembering how cold she'd been and the loud bubbling and thundering sounds of the surging stream. "I saw his silhouette in the light coming from my father's headlights, searching for me. He emptied his gun into the river, then threw the freakin' 38 right at me. Landed on my foot, if you can believe it. I grabbed it, but God, I was so close to passing out at that point, I don't know how I stayed conscious. Lungs are burning, mind's goin' gray. Finally, Larry walked away. I swam to the edge and tucked myself up against the bank under some bushes, right beneath the two parked cars."

"And Larry didn't hear you."

"No."

Burke's body relaxed and he rubbed her arm.

"Larry took off in his car shortly afterwards and left my dad's car sitting there with the headlights on."

"So what did you do next?"

"Swam down the river a piece and climbed out at a bushy spot that wouldn't leave wet footprints so Larry would think I got swept down river. And then I limped my way to the graveyard and found a payphone and called my friend Ursula. Took her forever to come get me. I was shaking, hypothermic, bleeding and totally freaked out. Longest wait of my life." Her brow hurt from furrowing so hard. She ran her fingertips over the aching muscles.

He hugged her. "Poor baby."

"Thankfully, it was summer and a warm night. Ursula patched me up and calmed me down. I was so freaked out, I didn't even want to go home. I mean, what was I supposed to tell Mom? How could I face her? I'd just caused my father's death, you know? But then it hit me. If Larry killed Dad and thought he'd killed me, wouldn't Mom be next? So Ursula drove me to the block behind my house, I snuck home and the lights were all on. I peeked in a window and Larry was holding my mother on the sofa while she sobbed."

Burke looked at her like her head was spinning around on her shoulders. "Incredible."

"I was super worried. I almost burst in, but thought he might kill her. Or me in front of her. So I watched for a long time and that's when I saw the tenderness on his face. He was being really nice to her. While it was weird, he didn't look like he was going to kill her. Then I thought about how much better her life would be without me. While I wanted to kill Larry to protect Mom, I knew I couldn't face her again. Not after what I'd done. The only solution was to stay dead. So I ran back to Ursula's. She helped me hide the murder weapon, then I headed out of town. Broke into a few houses on the way and stole as much money as I could find, plus some clothes and a wig. Ended up with about four hundred bucks and a couple changes of clothes."

He ran his hand over her hip and kissed her shoulder. "Smart and resourceful. I didn't think I could admire you more. And you were only sixteen?"

"Yeah." Burke's reactions kept surprising her. Baffling her really. Couldn't he see she was not only a murderer, but a thief? Couldn't he see that she'd caused the whole catastrophe? Was he so much in love with her that his judgment was this far off?

"So then what did you do?" He brushed the hair out of her eyes and slid the back of his hand down her neck.

Tingles swept through her and she snuggled closer. While she didn't deserve his comfort, she loved his touch. "I made it to the next town on a stolen bike, got on a Greyhound bus and took it all the way to California. Ended up in San Jose. Thank God, Ursula and I had crashed a college party once because it gave me an idea. When I arrived in San Jose, I went straight to the university and pretended to be a student. Wandered around until I found a frat party, looking for somewhere to crash. And that's where I met Emma. We hit it off, she was too drunk to drive, so I drove her home. Carried her inside, met her mother, said my good-byes, then snuck out to her car and climbed in to sleep."

"And Dolly saw you get into the car?" He absently drew light little circles on her forearm.

She fought the urge to push his hand away. She didn't want to discourage his touch or reject him, but she couldn't help but flash on Larry's creepy wandering hands, so she gripped Burke's forearm. He gave her a slight smile.

Sighing, she continued. "Yeah. Five minutes later, a knock came on the window and Mrs. Holsten ordered me into the house. She sat me down at the kitchen table with a mug of hot chocolate, looked right through me and asked me who I was running from. I was so terrified, I cried and blurted out the whole story. She listened to the entire thing calmly like I'd just told her I'd gone shopping and bought the wrong bra size."

Burke nodded. "She'd been through exactly the same experience."

"Yes, as I found out later. So she said in her husky smoker's voice, 'Here's how it's gonna be,'" Sam said, imitating her, "'you're moving in here to Emma's sister's old room. But it ain't gonna be a free ride. You go to college, you get a job and you pay me rent. You keep up your grades and I'll throw in food for free. I'm getting you a new identity. I got contacts. From this day forward you forget Amanda Hutchins. You never speak the name. You never call back home. Your home is here now. How old are you?' When I told her I was sixteen, she rolled her eyes and said, 'Now you're nineteen.' A day later, she told me my new name."

"Did you ever call your mother or contact her?"

"Dolly said I shouldn't call because if Tyrell knew I was alive, he'd kill me. And if Mom knew I was alive, he'd kill her. She said I should count myself lucky, get strong, grow up, and then go after Larry when I was an adult. That there were no statutes of limitations on murder."

"How long did you stay with the Holstens?" He reached across her for his wine, took a sip and offered her the glass.

Sam drained it and set it next to her almost-full goblet on the nightstand. "I lived with them for two years, then Emma and I moved out together and the rest is history."

"You never went back to New Hampshire?"

Horrible images flooded her mind. She grimaced and her body tensed. "Uh, actually I did. Six months after I arrived in California. I couldn't stand it. I had to talk to Mom. I had to see her. I missed her more than I thought it was humanly possible. I've never hurt like that. And I had to warn her about Larry. So, unbeknownst to Emma or Dolly, I flew back home when they were visiting Dolly's sick sister. I just wanted to wake up in bed and have the whole thing be a horrible nightmare."

"You poor thing." He kissed her on the cheek.

His kindness made her stomach churn and she tried not to withdraw. His treatment was wholly undeserved and totally unfair to the memories of her parents.

"Sam?"

"Huh?"

"You went home?"

"Yeah. So, uh, right. Okay, so I snuck in through my window. And wow, that was weird. My room was exactly the way I left it: Backstreet Boys and Leonardo DiCaprio posters all over. My Algebra 2 homework sat on my desk. Stuffed animals on the bed. Felt like I'd been gone a lifetime. I totally started crying. Then I heard these weird noises coming from my parents' room. Mom cried out. I blasted out my door, hauled ass for her room and I don't know what stopped me, but I came to a screeching halt right before I burst into the room. I bent down and looked through the keyhole and…" She closed her eyes and put her hand on her throat to fight the nausea. After a deep sigh, she said, "Larry was fucking my mother." Her stomach tightened so hard, it burned. She'd never get that image out of her head.

Burke's eyes dilated. "Holy God."

"And that was the last time I saw her alive. The last picture I have of her in my mind."

The lines in his forehead grooved deep. "Terrible."

"Yeah, that's what I thought. I left and a month later, Mom killed herself," she said her voice cracking. She summoned her strength and continued. "The papers said she was despondent over the death of her daughter and her husband at the hands of a transient and took her own life." Tears rushed down her face.

He wrapped his long arms around her. "Sam, I'm so sorry."

She pushed away and grabbed a few tissues out of the box on the nightstand. After blowing her nose, she shook her head with disgust at her actions. "I was stupid. I should have ignored Dolly's advice and called Mom and let her know I was okay."

"No, you did the right thing. Dolly was right. Tyrell would have killed you both. You aren't responsible for your mother's actions. She made the decision to kill herself, not you."

The pain came deep from her womb, a sudden aching for her mother. Primal. Soul-ripping. She'd never dealt with Mom's death. Not properly. When she'd run, she'd set the grief aside. Some part of her had pretended it never happened. It just didn't seem real. Even though she watched her father die, she couldn't get her mind around it.

Since she'd moved to California, she'd skipped to the new reality. Which had felt like a long weird dream ever since she got off the bus. Nothing about her time in California seemed real. The only thing that seemed real was her past. But it was a fantasy of the past. Her parents still alive, her friends still in high school, and she was still sixteen. Like her real life had been kept inside a timeless bell jar.

It's why she never went back home after that last time. Not only was she afraid of Larry, she couldn't deal with the loss of her parents. Especially since she was the one who had caused their deaths.

She swallowed a lump in her throat and tears dripped onto the duvet.

He squeezed her. "I'm so sorry that happened to you, Sam. You didn't deserve any of that."

She wiped her eyes, pushed back and faced him. "Burke, look, I appreciate your sympathy, but I don't deserve it. Don't feel sorry for me, feel sorry for my parents. They're the ones who lost their lives because their daughter was a slut who couldn't keep her legs together."

His brow went into a V and he shook his head. "Sam, no. You have it all wrong."

He clearly didn't understand. "Yes, Burke. I deserve all the hell I've been through. If I hadn't seduced Larry, none of this would have happened."

"Sam, listen—"

Her belly twisting, she got more emphatic. "No, you don't get it. I had a way out and I didn't take it. After our first kiss, Larry stopped and said we couldn't continue and took me back to the office. I didn't let him end it. I stayed in the outreach program and stalked him. I did that. Me. Not him. I made that whole thing happen."

"No, you didn't. You were only fourteen, you weren't to blame."

"The hell I wasn't. You should have seen my father's face," she sobbed. "*I* killed him. *I* did it. Because I liked sex. He was right, I am a fucking slut."

"No, no, no," Burke said, taking her in his arms and holding her tight. "It wasn't your fault. In any way, shape or form. Get that out of your head." He moved back and caught her eye. "Is this why you couldn't tell me? Because you're ashamed? Because you blame yourself for your parents' deaths?"

She wiped her face on the sheet, her insides convulsing. "I blame myself because it *was* my fault. The whole thing. I killed my parents." She wept harder. "I took that knife and sliced my mother's wrists. I picked up that gun and shot my father in the chest. That was me."

Burke lightly shook her. "Bullshit. *Bullshit.* Look at me."

She couldn't.

"Sam, look at me," he said firmly.

Took all her strength, but she finally glanced at him.

"You were abused by Larry and your father," Burke said in a strong, sure tone. "Your father was an asshole. How dare he say that to you? When you were caught with a forty-two-year-old man? How could he possibly consider you at fault?"

She dropped her attention to the hollow at the base of his throat. "It was an honest reaction. I disgusted him. And Dad was right. What I was doing was disgusting."

"No, you weren't. Your father was wrong. Dead wrong. And mean. And abusive. Look at me, Sam. You need to understand this."

He seemed so vehement, so positive. She couldn't take his intensity, but forced herself to make eye contact.

"You were not at fault. You didn't kill your parents. You did nothing wrong. You were a healthy young woman who got taken advantage of."

"I seduced Larry, I wanted him."

Burke was adamant. "He was the adult. You were a child. He wanted you to think you were the seducer. He wanted you to blame yourself. It's how he gained control over you. You saw the pictures in that evidence packet. He's been sleeping with fourteen-year-olds forever. He's practiced at it. You were just one in a long line of abused girls."

She'd never considered it wasn't her fault. Never even crossed her mind before. Could it be true? No, Burke was just being nice. "I don't know." She ran her forefinger between her tight brows.

Burke moved into her line of sight. "Sam, think with your adult brain. Not your fourteen-year-old mind. Think about it rationally. Step back from the situation. If you saw a forty-year-old man kissing a fourteen-year-old, what would you think? Wait. Didn't your old boyfriend Jimmy have a daughter that age?"

Sam dropped her hand. "Kara? No, she's really young. She's…oh. Shit. She *is* fourteen and a half," she whispered to herself.

"What would you do if you saw someone my age kissing Kara?"

The picture disgusted her and she shivered. Then fire radiated from her belly, tightening her jaw and heating her face. "I'd kill him."

"Exactly. Would you blame Kara or the forty-year-old man?"

"I guess the man…" Wait a minute, *she* was the slut. She was at fault. "But I was mature for my age, I—"

"No, Sam, no buts. See Larry for who he is. A pedophile. You were a victim, not the abuser. Think of Kara."

She'd been more mature than Kara. So what if she'd still kept dolls in her bedside drawer at fourteen? She'd wanted Larry. She'd wanted to grow up.

Kara's sweet curls. Her innocent eyes. Sound asleep, cuddling with her pink bunny.

Sam had slept with a stuffed kitty named Mimi the whole time she'd had the relationship with Larry. She pictured her face in place of Kara's.

Something shifted inside her. Was this true? Had she been a child? Larry had made her feel older, so she'd considered herself an adult since she started seeing him. But Kara was not an adult. Not by a long shot.

Son-of-a-bitch. She *had been* a child. "Wow. This blows my mind."

"That's because you were never allowed to process the atrocities."

As she reexamined her past through adult eyes, she reeled. "Dolly was pretty mad at the guy and told me that it wasn't my fault. But I thought she was just being nice because I was so upset. I mean, I knew I didn't deserve being killed, but I believed I'd caused the deaths. I probably still do. It's gonna be awhile before I get this."

Burke took hold of her hand and squeezed it. "You will and I'll help. Larry is more of a creep than I imagined. I can't believe he killed your father. And caused the suicide of your mother. And he almost killed you. And you took full responsibility. No wonder you have ulcers. The guilt and fear has been eating at you all these years. Once this is all over, you should see a therapist to purge all the old pain."

"Probably wouldn't be a bad idea." She pulled her hand away and looked into his loving gaze. "But now you see why I latched onto that evidence. I really thought God had sent me a gift. A way to take Larry down without killing him. Because I don't know if the murder weapon is still where we hid it."

He brought her close and kissed her on the forehead. "Your actions make complete sense. I wouldn't have given up that packet for anything if our places were reversed. I wish we'd known. I wouldn't have been angry with you. How could I?" He paused and his attention darted away, then he sent her an intense stare with a wary edge. "Sam?"

Her gut tightened. "What?"

"You must allow me to tell Rollin and the others."

She wanted to jettison from the bed. She moved away from him, but he stayed with her. "I can't, Burke. I'd never be able to face them again. What they'll think of me! I can't take people knowing."

He took her in his arms. "Sam," he said gently. "Stop. They won't judge you. What happened was not your fault. You aren't a slut. And you didn't kill your parents. That was all Larry. Put the blame where it belongs."

She pushed on his chest, although half-heartedly. "Still, if they find out how easy I was—"

His manner smooth, his energy calm, he spoke over her. "My men are about to enter a very dangerous bargain with Tyrell. They need to know the depth of the depravity of the man. They know he likes fourteen-year-olds. They know he takes bribes from corporations. They know he controls vast offshore accounts. But they don't know he's this sick."

She tried to think of a good argument, but couldn't. She hated that the Patriots would know what she'd done. Horrifying. Burke might not judge her because her sluttiness had gotten her parents killed, but Captain sure would.

But if the Patriots knew the truth about Larry, would they still do business with him? She brightened and a tiny buzz of hope ignited inside her. "Do you think they'll use that information against him?" Her head swam with the possibilities. She'd never have to face Larry alone again? Too much to comprehend.

Burke shrugged. "I don't know what they'll decide collectively, but I'm not going along with their plan any longer. I can't. Not now."

Her heart beat faster. "Are you sure?"

"Sam, how couldn't I be? My whole life is about bringing criminals to justice. And protecting those that I love. And I love you the most. Even if we weren't together, I'd help you get that bastard. He's malevolent and evil and needs to be held accountable for his crimes. There's no way I'm letting him become President. I will do everything in my power to make sure he's brought to trial."

She stared at him for a long minute. He meant his words.

The world shifted. Joy filled her and her body pulsed with intense energy. Burke had lifted a fifteen-ton weight from her shoulders. Handed her back her sanity. She threw her arms around him and crushed him in a hug. "I can't believe it."

He chuckled and kissed her. "Of course, I'll be here for you, darling. I'd go to the ends of the earth for you."

She clung to him. Finally, a way out of the hell. Finally, someone she trusted on her team. Someone strong and dependable. She'd never considered this possibility. Not having to handle Larry all by herself? After all these years, she could barely grasp the idea. "Thanks, Burke. Thanks for all of this." She kissed him.

The room seemed brighter, more colorful. Not only did she have help to bring down Larry, she'd told her story and the world had not collapsed. And even more unimaginable, Burke had given her a whole new take on the situation. Was it possible her parents' deaths hadn't been all her fault?

The ideas were so rooted in her foundation, the new reality was hard to grasp. But Burke made sense.

She snuggled against him in bed and he drew her close. Was this real? Did she have a future? Did she get to stay with Burke instead of being killed or ending up in a windowless prison cell?

It was clearly too early to tell what would happen, but for the first time in a long time, her stomach didn't hurt.

SIXTEEN

Burke pushed her back on the bed and surveyed her gorgeous body, worshipping his new playground. "God, you're so beautiful." He noticed but wasn't surprised by the tortured longing in his voice. He wished he were nineteen so he could keep fucking her. Kissing her breasts, he lightly ran his hand over her stomach and down to the soft triangle between her legs. She sent him a sly, hungry grin and opened her legs. He closed his eyes in pure bliss. "How long I've imagined touching you like this. Couldn't compare to the reality." He looked deep into her hazel sparkling gaze. "You intoxicate me, woman." His attention dropped to her lips and he moved in to kiss her.

"Cool. Think how much money we'll save on booze." She giggled.

He stopped right before he reached her lips, and snorted. "You are terrible. And wonderful. And so sexy." He quickly kissed her before she could make another saucy comeback. She tasted of wine and flowers and sex. His dick went hard as a diamond. Hell, he almost felt nineteen again. Driving into her mouth, he got high off her. Her scent filled his nostrils and he breathed deep. The feel of her sweet breasts in his hands sent him further.

She moaned and looped her arms around his neck.

He couldn't believe he was touching her, kissing her. Seemed like a dream.

All except for the part about that monster Larry Tyrell.

There was no stopping her from killing him. Nothing he could do to dissuade her. The only way to protect her was to bring Larry Tyrell to justice himself. Or kill him. And Burke had to do it before she got the chance. He already had the blood of seventy-five men on his hands. He couldn't let her suffer like he did.

She pulled away and grinned at him, her eyes shining with love. He bestowed tiny kisses along her jaw and down her neck. Moving her hips against him, she made soft animal noises in the back of her throat.

His need to protect her overwhelmed him. He imagined whisking her away to a safe castle surrounded by a moat with a legion of armed guards. Anything to make her safe, keep her away from harm forever.

No way was he letting her near Tyrell. He'd handle this. With or without the Patriots' help. She was too fragile, too twisted up after being on the run for sixteen years to think straight. He hated that her sweet, amazing spirit had been dampened and scarred by the sick desires of a bloated, narcissistic madman.

He had to handle her just right. This would take all his finesse and cunning. She'd disappear without a thought. While it was clear she loved him, she still had a feral quality behind her eyes. She hadn't trusted anyone in years.

Sam's lips parted and she gazed at him like he was the most arousing man she'd ever seen. She ran her hand through his buzz cut, sending a delicious shiver down his back and a charge through his tool. He grinned down at her and kissed her supple, full red lips. Like drinking from the nectar of life. Her heavenly fresh-flowers and rain scent filled him.

He cupped her white breasts and enjoyed their weight, warmth and softness. Her nipples hardened, her breathing increased and she arched her back. His cock ached. Her sweet folds drew his hand between her legs like she'd pulled him there.

He gently explored her soft and moist flesh and settled his slippery forefinger on her hard clit.

She writhed against him and let out a heady groan. Took all his strength to keep from jumping her. He forced himself to focus on her pleasure and slowly moved his finger in a tight circle on her nub.

Her long eyelashes tight to her high cheeks, her lips got fuller and redder, her chest and face flushed. She fought to breathe. Opening her eyes wide, she cried out. Grabbing his hand, she mashed it to herself and rocked her hips against him. He almost came. God, she made him feel powerful. He pressed his cock against her leg while she imprisoned his hand in her wet softness and moaned and shuddered in the throes of orgasm.

He wanted to remember this picture forever. The way her auburn hair splayed out on the cream pillowcase. The rosy color of her chest, throat and face. Her half-lidded expression of pure bliss, the satisfied smile, the absolute relaxation of every muscle in her body.

She slowly opened her eyes as if coming out of a dream state. "Oh, that was lovely. Jesus. How are we ever going to get anything done? All I'm gonna wanna do is have sex. That's it. I'm giving up everything else."

He laughed, delighted from his soul. Taking her in his arms, he pressed his hips against her.

She put a hand to his chest. "Burke, I want to jump on you, but I need a snack. Coming always makes me hungry and I need some after-sex food. I know, real nice, you make me come and I'm gonna make you wait, but I have to eat something. Other than you. So I can do more stuff to you."

She kissed him and his body demanded he fuck her. His stomach growled. Maybe food wasn't such a bad idea. He hated to leave the bed, but eating would help his stamina.

"I think a short break would be a good idea. But you stay naked," he ordered.

Her face reddened and she laughed. "You are so bad. Okay," she said happily.

Chuckling, he kissed her on the forehead.

He followed her out to the kitchen so he could watch her bare ass move. Even with the crutches, she was enticing as hell. He couldn't wait to get her back in bed. Hustling up behind her, he took her globes in both hands and squeezed her taut warm buns.

She giggled. As they walked through the wide doorway to the kitchen, he put his arms around her and laid a quick kiss on her cheek. He pictured a lifetime of being with her like this.

Sam heated some garlic bread and he spooned fruit salad she'd made earlier onto plates. After retrieving the wine glasses from the bedroom, he refilled them and brought them over to the table where she had set out the hot bread. They downed their food fast, caught each other's eyes and laughed.

"Feel like I didn't have that giant dinner," Sam said.

"Me, too."

"So…" Her brow furrowed slightly and she gestured toward him.

His gut tightened. He hoped she didn't propose a plan to take revenge on Tyrell. His brain wasn't up to its normal capacity. All he could think about was her amazing pussy. "Yes?"

"I want to know what happened between you and your parents."

The tension in his gut spread to his neck and back. While relieved her mind was off the Senator, he hated talking about his folks. Hated thinking about them.

His face flushed. But she'd told him her secrets. She deserved to know his. He looked into her curious and caring hazel eyes and his heart opened. Not only would he take care of her, she'd take care of him. Stronger than any woman he'd ever dated, Sam could handle him. And his moods. And his past. "What would you like to know?"

"Are they still alive?"

His stomach contracted like he'd been kicked, but he kept his face free of expression. "No."

"Sorry."

"Don't be."

She leaned in and grabbed his arm. "I'd guess they screwed you over pretty good."

Was it written on his forehead? He checked her expression carefully, but only saw love and compassion there.

"Thought so," she said. "But you must have had a really good part of your childhood. That chess stuff."

Ha. Dark memories flooded back and his jaw clamped tight. His father was such an asshole. He pushed back from the table and sighed. "The reason I know what happened to you was not your fault is because I know what happened to me was not my fault. Nothing compares to the pain of your parents believing you betrayed them."

"What'd they do?"

He rolled his eyes. "Reader's Digest version. I'm sure you'll hear all the varied parts and chapters at some point, but I'll be brief now, mainly because I want to concentrate on you and your luscious body and stop torturing us both with our pasts."

She gestured toward him with her wine glass. "So, you were a chess prodigy."

"Yes. And Papa lived through me. I didn't see it. Not until I turned sixteen and announced I wanted to go to Annapolis and be an officer in the Marines. He went insane. Beat the holy shit out of me with his prized chessboard."

Gasping, she moved back in her seat, and her eyes widened. "No."

He nodded. "Busted it over my head. See this scar here?" He pointed to a two-inch-long scar near the top of his skull.

She stood, limped over to him, and pulled him into her warm and inviting arms. He buried his face in her breasts and forgot about everything but diving into her soft flesh.

"Poor kid, what a bastard."

Papa's ugly expression pulled him back from his bliss. He pushed away from her delicious body so he could concentrate and get the story out. "Yeah. Took fourteen stitches. I was so stunned. He'd been on my team until that very moment."

"Weird, isn't it, when they turn on you?"

"Painful. Not only physically."

"Wait, I want to hear this, but I'm freezing my ass off. Last one to make it back to bed is a rotten egg!" She turned, grabbed her crutches and headed out of the room, her lovely buns bouncing, her wavy hair flowing. He could only laugh and follow her.

He found her diving under the covers, her eyes shining with victory, her cheeks flushed. Enchanting. Joining her in bed, he took her in his arms. He wished he could forget his past and concentrate on her, but she needed the information.

She pressed her body close to his. "Okay, so the asshole beat you with his chessboard."

His mind warred between his tortured memories and the lovely fleshpot snuggled against him. Must. Finish. Story. "Yes. And forbade me to enter the military. Well, you know me. I made it my mission from then on to become a Marine. And moreover, get physically stronger than him. So I pretended to play his game and secretly took judo and every martial art I could. I applied to Annapolis and was accepted."

"I thought you had to be nominated."

"Yes, you do. Thankfully, during my chess tournaments, I made friends with a war hero Senator who nominated me. When Papa found out, he attempted to physically intimidate me again, but I had him immobilized on the ground a second after he threw the first punch. Not surprisingly, he wouldn't sign the paperwork, so I forged it."

"Why didn't he bust you for that?"

Burke shrugged. "He didn't trust the government. Was a Russian refugee and paranoid. Would never call the cops. After that, he wouldn't speak to me and wouldn't release my chess winnings. Mama took his side. Well, she was just weak. His supplicant and servant. Double betrayal. He reached out about six years after I left, but I was stubborn and hurt and pissed off and wouldn't talk to him. Just to show him how it felt. He died a week after that from lung cancer."

Sam's face etched with sympathetic pain. "Oh, no."

He nodded. "Yeah. I hadn't even known he'd been diagnosed with it. I rushed home and Mama lost her mind and blamed me for his death. Accused me of killing him. Absolutely irrational. She wouldn't even allow me to attend the funeral. So I said some choice words and blazed out of there, vowing never to return. Shortly after that, I found myself surrounded by forty hostiles alone. I think that's how I survived. Channeled all my rage and hate and fear and grief and…" His gut contorted in agony, his foundation slipped and a wave of severe disorientation overcame him. He fought hard to center himself. "God, I don't want to think about this." His throat felt like his father's hands were crushing his trachea.

He came aware Sam was holding him and stroking his arm. Warmth spread through his body, heating his heart and relaxing the stranglehold on his neck. She nuzzled him and he became overwhelmed again, only this time with gratitude. He'd never spoken about his past to anyone except his therapist. Not even Rollin got the whole story. It was such a privilege to be able to share his feelings. Sam understood him. Finally, someone he could trust with his heart.

"Amazing how similar our experiences are," she said, massaging his chest. "Prince and Princesses to hated. And we so didn't deserve it. Makes me question the good stuff. Had no idea love was conditional. But my mom…" Deep sorrow and pain marred her expression.

His heart wrenched. He held her close, wishing he could heal her.

"So what happened to your mom?" she asked.

Shame burned through him. The last picture of her in his mind was a disgusted scowl.

She rubbed his searing brow with her thumb. "I'm sorry."

He took her hand and kissed it. "Don't be. She died about two years ago. Which my aunt blamed me for even though I was in Pakistan with the Patriots at the time."

Studying him, her forehead wrinkled. "Why would someone as cerebral as you do such crazy, self-destructive shit like be a SEAL?"

Said the pot to the kettle. He raised an eyebrow.

It dawned on her what she'd said. "Oh. Well, I'm not as cerebral as you."

"Yes, you are. And that's why I understand you and your motivations."

"Yeah, well I get you, too."

They embraced and held each other tight.

After a long moment, she pulled away and looked deep into his eyes. "I love you more than I thought possible, Burke."

His heart ripped open wide. Taking her mouth in a passionate kiss, he rode high on the incredible feelings. After all these goddamned years, he'd finally found her.

Lost in a nice long, luxurious tongue-tangle with her, he never wanted to stop.

Sam ended the kiss and all pretense fell from her expression. All her guards were down. He saw right inside her, into her sweet, kind, precious soul. "I was wrong this evening when I said I couldn't feel love right now. I didn't want to feel love right now. But I'm so glad I dropped my shields and let you in. You're the man I've been looking for."

His dearest wish and dream, come alive.

Overcome, he clutched her in an embrace. His dick hardened and he tingled all over. Breathing in the scent of her hair, he worshipped the feeling of her soft, firm body against his. She felt so right, so natural. Fit like she'd always been there. He'd never felt more complete. Nor happier. He'd never let her go.

Nor let her near Tyrell.

That sadistic fucker faced a very dark and painful future.

Sam awoke in Burke's arms and sighed with happiness. Felt so good to be held all night. Best sleep she'd gotten in weeks. She felt so safe.

He stirred, his eyes opened and he sent her a radiant smile. "There's my girl," he said, kissing her.

After a nice, long arousing kiss, he pressed his hard cock against her leg.

She pushed him back. "Before we get up, I wanted to tell you that I got us both new jobs."

He frowned and blinked, still sleepy-eyed. "What?"

"Yeah. Condom testers."

Took a full second before he broke out in a beaming smile and reached for his bedside drawer. "Don't want to be late for our first day of work."

After a long and amazingly mind-blowing sex session, Burke finally pulled out of her embrace and got out of bed. "I'm going to be late to Zane's if I don't get a move on."

Sam eyed his gorgeous naked body and a pulse went through her sex. "Wish you didn't have to go."

He sent her a predatory grin. "I'll be back. And you'll never be the same."

"Too late. I'm already not the same. God, I love you, Burke."

His pupils dilated and he joined her on the bed to kiss her. He pushed away with an agonized moan. "I have to stop or I won't be able to. You bewitch me, woman." Standing, he headed for his bathroom.

She sat up and swung her legs off the bed. A pile of stuff on the floor caught her attention. A heap of condom wrappers. She burst out laughing.

Burke poked his head out of the bathroom with his razor buzzing in his hand. "What's so funny?"

She pointed below her. "Looks like a pile of Christmas wrapping."

A grin nearly split his face. "Felt like Christmas to me. And I can't wait to unwrap more presents later."

"Stop. I'm already horny and you just righteously boffed me."

"And I'll never stop. I'm going to make love to you from one end of this planet to the other. I can't wait to take you to Europe."

"Oooo!" She sat up and clapped her hands. "I've never been!"

He did a double-take. "*You've never been to Europe?*"

"Nope. I've only gone to Hawaii and a few places in America. I'm a saver, not a spender."

"We'll have to change that."

"I'm still gonna be a saver."

"Between what the two of us own and make, we'll be fine."

Bursting out in a huge grin, her heart—and whole body—warmed. A man who actually wanted to contribute money to the relationship? A first. Wonderful, heady emotions swept through her, setting her body on fire. Had her life changed this fast? Yes. Clearly. With Burke in her corner, she could handle anything. Especially Larry.

Giggling, her belly bubbling with joy, she dressed, grabbed her crutches, and headed to the kitchen to make coffee and breakfast.

After several lingering kisses, she said good-bye to Burke and watched him climb into the elevator. As the doors closed, he blew her a kiss and winked.

A little fireball of love erupted inside her. What a man!

Banana followed her back inside and waited outside her bedroom while she took a shower.

After bathing, she went through her suitcases, searching for a bra.

Emma hadn't known it, but she'd packed all of Sam's special bras —with secret compartments—and only one normal bra. Sam instinctively reached for a Battle Bra, then stopped and bit her lip. She was safe now, right? She didn't have to constantly wear her last fake IDs and that debit card, right?

Giving her head a shake, she reached for the sole regular bra, a red silk number. Burke would love the way it looked on her. At the thought of his expression, her sex warmed and her clit tingled. With a naughty laugh, she put on the bra and checked herself out in the mirror. Cute.

She reached for a flowered t-shirt, but suddenly froze. Her blood went cold and she began trembling. She felt too naked, too vulnerable.

"Damn!" She tore off the red bra and reached for one with secret pockets. Muttering to herself, she retrieved her fake IDs and the debit card from her feminine hygiene products, then hid them in the zippered compartment of the padded bra. She glanced at the tampon that held the small pen with the hidden tranquilizer dart. "Ridiculous. What? Like I'm gonna get attacked in his bunker?" Rolling her eyes, she left the bathroom. A second later, she found herself dashing back to retrieve the device.

She tucked it into the front of her bra, and her shoulders relaxed and she centered. "Crazy. Well, whatever it takes. When I finally feel safe enough not to wear an emergency kit, then I'll know I'm healed." Patting her bra, she shook her head and sighed. "My virtual Teddy Bear." Larry would probably have to be in jail a long time before she relaxed.

She flopped on the bed and moved around until she and her ankle were comfortable.

Pointing the remote at the TV, she hesitated. As her hormonal fog cleared, her doubts returned. Could she really give up her mission to get Larry? Could she trust someone else to do the job? Even Burke?

Her face fell and her mouth twisted. No. Damn it. She wanted to show Burke her loyalty, wanted to show him her love, but couldn't give up her quest. She'd promised herself at sixteen. Her whole life had been about this one mission. She had to bring down Larry alone. This was personal.

Besides, Burke had no idea of Larry's capabilities. Even after her story, he couldn't grasp the evil of the man. Larry would kill Burke. Especially if he knew how much she loved him. She had to protect him.

First, she needed to heal up. She'd make her move in a few days.

Oh, man, would Burke be pissed. No doubt about that. But she'd have to risk the collateral damage. He'd forgiven her a few times now, hopefully she could stretch that good will one more time. Now that he knew the whole story, he'd have to understand.

No, he wouldn't. He was an arrogant, immovable chunk of steel. He'd be furious.

She rubbed her aching brow. Screwing over Burke didn't sound fun at all. Horrible, actually. He'd been so honest with her. So upfront. So vulnerable. She couldn't stand the thought of hurting him.

Was getting revenge worth the possibility of losing Burke?

No.

Would that stop her?

No.

As much as she hated it, she had only one fate. So be it. But for the moment, she didn't have to think about her future. All she had to do was heal and love Burke. A nice respite before more hell.

She settled back in bed and flicked on the TV using the remote. A good movie was coming on TCM. *On Borrowed Time.* About a man who doesn't want to die and traps Death up a tree. With Lionel Barrymore. And some kid whose character's name was Pud. Cracked her up. *Pud.*

Banana poked his head in the room. "You okay?"

"Perfect."

"I'll be by the front door in case you need me."

"Okay, darlin'."

The lantern-jawed hulk grinned and disappeared, leaving her door open.

As she sat back to watch the movie, she caught a whiff of Burke's cologne coming from her t-shirt. Lovely images of his pecs and smile played through her mind. She grinned. He'd be home soon. All she had to do was watch the movie and at the end, she'd be back in his arms. She might be duplicitous, but she did love the man. And she was going to fully enjoy every moment she had with him.

Thump, thump, THUMP.

The bass response of the speakers of the home theater/HD-TV system was pretty impressive. Burke had outfitted the whole house with the latest high tech toys. Wicked cool.

Strange noises came through the audio. Like distant yelling that didn't match the action on the screen. Wait. Was Banana watching TV in the living room? She turned down the sound.

A low murmur of several voices came from the front room.

Her heart beat faster. Burke was home early? Yay! Sex! She couldn't wait to see his smiling face.

"Honey? I'm in here!" she called out.

Paul Strong appeared in the doorway. "Hello, Sam."

SEVENTEEN

Sam's body rocketed to full on fight-or-flight mode. Her heart slammed her ribs, every muscle poised for action, all thoughts tuned to escape.

Dressed in a dark suit with a steel-edged look in his blue eyes, Paul's posture was all business. He looked even bigger than she remembered. That menacing authoritarian was back. For the first time since she met him, she was afraid of him.

Five hundred horrible realizations hit her at once. Paul was CIA. He could be taking her to a black box in another country where she'd never see the light of day again. Burke could be dead. They would torture her to death. Either that or take her directly to Larry. Same dif.

She dove across the bed for her purse and pistol, landing on her stomach, arms outstretched, almost touching her bag.

The large barrel of a gun appeared inches from her face. "Don't, Sam. Hands up."

Her heart raced faster and her muscles tensed. She raised her arms and examined his face to access the danger level. Would he shoot her right there?

The planes of his handsome face were severe, but there was a twist of regret in the way he held his mouth. He had a job to do. If he had to, he'd kill her.

"Stand up slowly, Sam. Please don't do anything stupid. I don't want to hurt you. But I will. Have no doubt," he said in a quiet low tone that sent shivers through her. He'd killed before. Behind his eyes, she could see the raw, cold aggression of a predator.

No matter, she had to fight him. Her gut said if she went with him, it would be the last mistake she made. Could she push him through the wall of windows beside her? Could she engineer that? Worth a try. She slowly moved into a sitting position, then scooted to the end of the bed and gently put her feet on the floor.

He motioned upwards with the gun. "Stand up."

"I need my crutches." She pointed to aluminum aids, propped up against the dresser. If he handed them to her, she could jerk him off balance and throw her body at him. If he tripped over the pile of shoes at the end of the bed, he might go through the window.

Two large men in suits wearing deadly cold expressions walked into the room.

Fuck! Well, there went all her delusions of escape.

Paul put his gun in his jacket, retrieved her crutches and handed them to her. "You use those against us and I'll take 'em away and carry you out of here."

She shot him a look that told him she'd love nothing more than to kill him.

His gaze warmed and sparkled a bit. "Love that fire in you, girl, but don't get any ideas. No more games."

"Fucker."

His demeanor turned icy. "I'm not your enemy, Sam. And I'll prove it to you. Come on."

Burke! "Did you kill Burke?"

His mouth twisted and his eyes turned fiery. Jealousy? For real? "You won't care about him soon, Sam. Not after you see him for who he really is."

The pressure on her stomach and heart eased. Thank God, he was still alive. But what bullshit had Strong dreamed up? What evidence had he fabricated?

What did it matter? She'd never stop caring about Burke, no matter what crap Paul threw at her. "Right."

"He's not on your side, Sam. But you'll soon see that I am."

"Yeah, that's how you can tell who your friends are. They point guns at your head. And shoot you. Thanks for almost killing me and giving me a fucking hole in my leg."

A slight wince. "That was a mistake, they were aiming at Zane. Orders were not to hurt you. I apologize for that."

"He says while preparing to kidnap me," Sam said with a sneer. "Why am I not convinced?"

"I'll convince you," he said with confidence. A bit of his old self showed through and his expression softened. "Come on."

"Can I grab a coat?"

He chuckled, clearly assuming she was trying to pull something. "Why don't I get it for you?"

He walked past her and she caught his scent. She remembered his taste. The sensual way he kissed. His awesome hard body. Her spine stiffened and she balled her fists. She couldn't believe she'd made out with the guy!

Paul gestured to the rack of clothing. "Which one, Sam?"

"The black one, right there, with the hood." She pointed at her Volcom hoodie.

He checked the pockets carefully, then handed it to her.

After taking the sweatshirt, Sam looked right into his eyes. "How long are we going to be gone? Forever? When are you going to kill me?"

He smiled, snorted, and shook his head. "I'm not going to kill you, Sam. But you won't be coming back here."

Sure he wouldn't kill her. Dick. "Then let me get my ulcer meds, okay?" She stood, got into position on the crutches, and took a step toward her bedside.

Paul stopped her with a solid grip on her shoulder. "Where are they? I'll get 'em. You stay put."

She nodded with her head. "Right there on my nightstand."

He frowned and checked her face. "Ulcer meds, really?"

"Really."

He walked past her, grabbed the bottle and read the label. Unscrewing the top, he inspected the contents and gave a nod. Then he shot her a concerned look. "How long have you had ulcers?"

"I don't know. Few years."

He gave a sharp nod. "Running's killing you. That and your need for revenge. Told you it was poison." He tucked the bottle in his pocket. "I'll take care of these for you."

A bargaining chip. *Your gut hurts? Then do what I say.*

She scowled at him.

Ignoring her expression, he walked up to her and took her by the arm.

She ripped out of his grip.

His gaze flared and he grabbed her again, his expression darkening. "Don't," he said in a freezing tone. "You don't want me angry, Sam."

Her stomach hollowed. Dude could get scary fast. Probably not a good idea to antagonize him.

When she moved forward with the crutches, he slid his hold to her upper arm. They left the room and he kept his hand tight on her as they moved through the apartment.

The beefy guards followed.

When they reached the front door, a crowd of hulking dudes in suits and sunglasses awaited them, their faces hard and mean.

She fought a shudder and moved through the threshold.

A heap of bloody bodies lay in front of the elevators.

Sam froze, gasped, and cried out.

Banana, David, another bodyguard named Jose—plus two men she didn't recognize—lay in a motionless pile in front of the elevators, covered in blood, their limbs askew. Banana's long blonde hair, streaked with red, fanned out on the marble floor. Planter boxes were knocked over. Large holes had been knocked into the walls. Dirt and blood and shards of a broken mirror covered the area. Unreal. The boys had been laughing with her not twenty minutes before.

Paul's tightened his grip on her and dragged her into an elevator. "Burke thought adding a team of guards would protect you, but we took out the three guys down in the garage in thirty seconds, this bunch in two minutes. Except for the big blond guy. He could really take a beating."

The walls blurred and adrenaline powered her limbs. She let out a deafening battle roar, tossed her crutches aside, and threw herself at Strong. "You bastard!" Swinging both fists, she punched his jaw, the side of his neck, his chest and went for his face again.

He blocked the shot and locked his iron grip on her upper arms. Drilling his fingers painfully into her flesh, he slammed her back against the metal wall of the elevator. Pain blazed her skull and spine, and air got knocked out of her lungs.

"Stop," he said through gritted teeth. He assaulted her with his fiery steel-blue gaze.

Gasping for breath, her head, back and arms burned. Her instinct was to cower, but she managed to keep her reaction to a nod. "Owww, okay, okay." She tried to show fury and no fear.

Breathing heavy, his anger receded a bit and he slowly eased his grip. "None of 'em are dead. Just knocked out."

When he finally released her, she fought the tears, and rubbed the back of her head, then her sore arms. How dare this fucker come in and hurt her and her friends? She'd love nothing more than to take a baseball bat to the asshole. She didn't know when or how, but she'd get even with him for this.

He picked up her crutches and handed them to her with a wary look in his eye.

However unplanned it had been, attacking him hadn't been the best course of action. She had to calm down and take control. Keep her mind clear. Her only thoughts should be about the best way to defeat Paul, and hand-to-hand combat was clearly not the answer. Time to switch tactics. She'd pretend to go along with him. Be "convinced" by his evidence against Burke. Then fall into Paul's big strong arms and reenact the ending scene from a million melodramas. For her grand finale, she'd seduce him, then screw him—over.

Larry Tyrell, Strong, and the Patriots all underestimated her. She'd escape from Paul, all right. And take down Tyrell.

And afterwards, return to Burke's arms where she belonged.

Burke walked into Zane's office, his body pumped, anxious for the news. They'd received intelligence just an hour before that the Cabal planned to attack the Patriots. Supposedly because of the packet of evidence, but Burke suspected that the Patriots had grown too powerful and the Cabal wanted them permanently crippled.

Right after Rollin had called him, he'd ordered four more guards to protect Sam, bringing the total to eight. Overkill, but he wasn't about to take chances.

Rollin leaned against the beech-paneled wall near the custom, eight-foot-tall doorway. Ty and Catherine shared a leather couch in front of a window that overlooked the brown, rolling, oak-covered hills of Woodside. Zane sat in the corner with his mile-long legs stretched out, drinking a Dr. Pepper, and Captain sat backwards on a wooden chair next to the giant.

Rollin nodded at Burke. "We're waiting for word on when the offensive will begin."

Captain held up his cell. "If it will begin. Bob at the Pentagon is checking with his contacts right now. He's trying to get the order stopped and find out who initiated it. I mean, we know it's Tyrell, but we need a direct link. I tried Jenny at the Oval Office. She's got her people working on it. We should know any second. But the intel said it would be an offensive on all fronts at once. Total annihilation. Bob's pretty alarmed they're staging this level of attack on home ground. Tyrell's gone nuts."

Burke's gut tightened harder. Sam was in even graver danger than he'd thought. He should move her. The remote place in Colorado would work. They'd leave that night.

Rollin said, "I made Emma shut her shop and go home to the safe room. She wasn't very happy about it."

Burke nodded. "I'll bet. I ordered extra guards at my place, but I'm still worried."

"They'd better not try anything here or they're in for a very rude awakening," Zane growled.

Ty said, "What do Bobby and Greg say? Haven't they found out anything?"

Rollin crossed his arms and shifted his weight to one leg. "They both think this is the big deal that's been brewing for the past few weeks. But Greg just came on the case. He's on a flight now from Pakistan. Bobby's running point on this."

"The Cabal makes no sense," Catherine said. "They have to know the packet isn't with any of us at this point. Why come after us now?"

Zane snorted. "Since when does the Cabal make any sense?"

"This has to do with Tyrell," Burke said. "He must have found out we're protecting Sam. He wants her and the packet. And our heads mounted on his wall." He pictured strangling that bastard until his eyes bugged out and his corpulent face turned blue.

Rollin turned to Burke. "Speaking of Sam and Tyrell, what did she tell you?"

"Yeah, what's her history with him?" Captain asked.

Burke sighed, half sat on Zane's expansive maple desk, and related Sam's story.

Thankfully, they all had the same reaction as he did. Utter disbelief, disgust and revulsion. Catherine appeared horrified. A bit of weight came off his shoulders. He needed their help in protecting Sam, and he needed them on his side. Since he had credibility issues with the group, he'd been concerned about their reaction to Sam's past, and his recommendations for her continued safety. He hoped Captain agreed with his plan to dump the idea of helping Tyrell get elected and instead put him in jail for life. If Captain wasn't on board, it would be difficult to get the others' help. Which meant that Burke might be leaving the Patriots. This time for good.

Which would *suck*.

Rollin seemed the most affected by Sam's plight. His face white, he ran his hand through his hair and fell back against the wall. "Holy shit. No wonder."

Zane shook his head, making his long black hair move into his eyes. He swept it out of his face to behind him. "Okay, there goes all my anger at her. Her actions were completely justified."

"Unbelievable." Captain rubbed the deep creases between his pale blue eyes. "Dang, the rumors must be true. I mean, I knew it, but I didn't want to know. Not when we were so close." He stood, crossed his arms and faced the group. "Should have stopped this earlier, a few weeks ago when I found out about the disappearance of three members of his inner circle. The buzz said that Tyrell had them murdered. Another source stated he did the killing himself. I just couldn't believe it. A presidential candidate, a homicidal maniac? But it's clear the man is not only unbalanced, but a sociopath. We can't let him take the White House."

Thank God! Hope jazzed Burke's system. But how far did Captain's plan's go? Would he order the Patriots to go after Tyrell?

Captain's gaze pierced Burke. "Do you have any doubts about Sam's story?"

Burke gave a quick shake of his head. "None. I've corroborated most of it. She was in the Sheriff's teenage outreach program led by Larry. There's even a picture of them together on the Sheriff's department website with a link to her obituary."

Please decide to help me put Tyrell away. As much as he'd do anything for Sam, he really didn't want to lose his friends a second time.

Rollin held his head, then rubbed his mouth. "This makes me sick. Poor Sam. She was only sixteen when she came out here?"

"God Bless Dolly Holsten. And Emma." Burke shifted his weight further back on the desk and tried to read Captain's expression.

"Even if Emma knew, she didn't breathe a word to me," Rollin said.

"Good thing," Burke said, jiggling his leg. "Larry must know she's still alive. She said she looks just like her mother."

"Unreal," Captain shook his head. "And the cold bastard had the gall to sleep with her mother."

"Why didn't Sam tell us?" Rollin asked.

Burke's belly twisted at the memory of the pain on her face. "She believed, and still believes on some level, that her parents' deaths are her fault. Her father—"

"Was a fucking asshole," Rollin spat with a violent gesture. "Here this girl has been molested by a pedophile for two years and all Daddy does is blame her, tell her that she disgusts him, and call her a whore?"

"Got the same rap I did," Catherine said with disgust, vigorously rubbing her short pink buzz cut. "And people wonder why I'm gay."

Ty poked her in the ribs. "That's because you have good taste. Men, we're beasts."

She kicked him. "You're a beast."

Ty growled at her and then smiled.

Sitting fairly close together, Ty and Catherine made quite a pair. If Catherine wasn't gay and Burke didn't know better, he'd say they were in love. Of course, his hormone-colored glasses could be clouding his judgment.

His attention went back to the Captain. Burke willed him to officially and clearly change course on Tyrell.

"Sucks. Sam so doesn't deserve it," Rollin said.

"So you say she knows where the murder weapon is?" Captain asked.

Burke nodded. "Yes. If it hasn't already been discovered."

"Get the address, we'll recover it," Captain said. "That should be the final nail in Tyrell's coffin."

Excellent. Sounded better and better. However, getting the address where the murder weapon was located would not be easy. "I'm not sure Sam'll give it up or help us recover it," Burke said.

Captain swung on him with an incredulous expression on his weathered face. "She still wants to take him on herself?"

Burke snorted. "You don't know Sam. As soon as she's healed, the moment our security slips, she's gone. I saw the look in her eye. She's bound and determined. If we don't do something soon, she will."

"With the staff you added, we'll keep her contained," Rollin said with confidence.

Burke chuckled. "Don't delude yourself. She loves me, but she'd escape from me in a heartbeat if it meant she got to kill Tyrell. I'm feeding her tracking devices and doing all I can to keep her under control, but…"

"We saw what she's capable of," Zane said. "She's a force of nature."

"Past that," Ty said with a hungry look on his face. "Girl's a damned hurricane. Beautiful, but destructive."

Bristling, Burke fought the impulse to strangle his friend. Ty caught his expression and grinned widely. Catherine didn't look too happy with Ty, either.

Rollin studied him. "So, Burke. How did you get all this information out of her? Use a special *extraction tool*?"

Burke's face warmed. The room erupted in laughter.

Rollin pushed on his shoulder. "You devil, you."

"Well, that was inevitable," Zane observed with raised brows.

Captain shot Burke a penetrating stare. "Will this cloud your ability to protect her?"

"I'm not deluded if that's what you're asking. She'd use everything at her disposal to complete her mission. Including and especially my love for her."

Rollin asked, "Did you find out if she was carrying anything else in her bra? Emma said those bras of hers had multiple pockets."

"No. I checked every single bra she has and found nothing. I'll keep looking. And tonight I'll broach the subject of the weapons she took from me. I know she has them stashed somewhere. In Seattle, she gave me some cock-and-bull story about the sniper rifles and Tasers and everything else being stolen, but she was lying. She's got everything she needs to kill Larry."

"Can't say her motivation is flawed." Captain straightened his shoulders. "Well, that settles that. Let's bring Tyrell down. I hated the plan all along, and knew he was crooked, but not this sick. Are we agreed?"

Burke watched as one by one, each person nodded in turn. He heaved a sigh of relief and all his muscles relaxed. A warmth overtook him and the ground felt more solid under his feet. They were on his side. They were a team. He wouldn't lose them. Thank the Lord. And beyond that, now the Patriots would pool their resources to protect Sam and bring Tyrell down. His life was turning around beautifully. Finally.

Rollin shook his head. "I hated that plan."

"We all did," Zane said.

"Sure as shit did," Ty said. "Love to go a few rounds with that guy. Especially if he ordered the hit on us."

"We'll take care of him," Burke stated with a firm nod.

"Okay, Burke," Captain said. "Get the gun from her, anyway you can. Once we have the murder weapon, we'll have her protected and neutralized. And we'll own Larry's balls."

"I'd really rather not involve her yet. Wait a minute," Burke said, snapping his fingers. "I know who knows where the gun is, Sam told me. Her best friend from high school, Ursula. She lives in Seattle, not far from the safe house. I'll get Bobby to find her address. We'll need Dino's expertise. He can get any woman to tell him anything. Isn't he due back from Pakistan?"

"Yep, this afternoon. Both he and Greg are on their way as we speak," Catherine said.

"We go through the channels on this one," Captain said. "We build Sam's case and get this guy through the legal system. We'll hit him with everything at once. I want that creep behind bars."

"Tyrell will do everything in his power to silence Sam," Burke said.

Captain nodded, his expression grave. "We should get her out of California. Maybe we should hide her out of the country for a while. Why don't you take her to Paris, Burke?"

Burke smiled so widely, his cheeks hurt. Everything was falling into place. Such a turnaround from a week ago.

"Look at that grin," Rollin said, lightly punching him on the shoulder. "I knew you guys would be good together."

"Good is the understatement of the century when one is discussing Miss Sam Murdock."

Alarms sounded and red lights flashed over the doors.

Burke's heart ramped up to war mode. His body hardened for the fight. Spoke too soon, *fuck*! Everyone leapt to their feet and assumed battle postures.

Zane switched on the six-foot-wide plasma screen above his desk.

Four SUVs were barreling down the driveway. Burke planned their escape route in a split second. They'd need the helicopters.

"Fuck!" Zane yelled. "How the hell did they get past my gates?"

Sam! Burke's heart beat faster and sweat broke out all over him. He punched Banana's number on his cell. No answer. *Fuck!* Maybe the hulk's phone was turned off. There was no way the Cabal could take out nine guards in broad daylight in that building.

With even more urgency, Burke tried David's number. Nothing. A wave of adrenaline pumped into his system and his stomach twisted. He tried to reach Banana again and then each of the other bodyguards. None responded.

"Fuck! The Cabal just took out eight men to get Sam! They've overpowered David and Banana and six other guards!" Panic took hold of his gut. Sam had better be okay! "I have to get there now!" He rushed for the door. "Come on! We have to take the helicopter!"

Captain and Rollin followed, but Rollin stopped mid-stride to answer his phone.

"Rollin! No time!" Burke yelled.

Rollin's face went ashen. "It's Emma! Wait!"

"Shit, they're blitzing us," Burke said.

Zane stared at the screen, his green eyes wide. "We got five minutes before they get here." He punched a series of commands into his keyboard. "I only have one obstacle working, goddamn it. Hell of a time to rerig the mechanisms. The small drawbridge I just raised will only slow 'em down for a minute or so. Why the hell didn't I fix that fucking tire shredder?"

Sweat beaded on Rollin's forehead, he looked frantic. "Emma, good girl, stay there! You'll be safe, don't leave for anything. I'll call you right back!" Rollin hung up his phone and Burke pulled him toward the door. "Fuck! Some guys just swarmed the house. Thank God, Emma's hidden in the basement safe room."

Burke hoped Emma was safe, but could only think of Sam.

Catherine, standing next to the doorway, stared into space and stammered, "That was my neighbor, Billy. Three guys busted in my door and ransacked my place and some asshole shot my cat. They killed Fluffy." She burst into tears and Ty took her in his arms.

Lurid images of Sam being hurt tortured him. "Fuck! I never should have left Sam!" He wished he had a rocket to take to his place. He didn't want to shove Catherine out of the way, but he was close.

Ty guided a crying Catherine out the door in front of them. Burke, Rollin and Captain followed.

Behind him, Captain asked, "Zane?"

"You guys take the big helicopter. I'm staying here," the giant answered. "No way am I letting some assholes break into my place. If I have to, I'll take the four-seater copter. I'll catch up with you guys later. Go!"

Burke strode through the living room, his pulse pounding in his ears. He hit the hallway that led outside and quickened his pace. He pushed open the back door and headed for the helicopter pads, Rollin on his heels.

When he reached the copter, his phone rang. *Banana.* "Banana! What happened!"

"Boss! So fucked up!"

His heart stopped and he froze to the spot. "What happened?"

"A crowd of guys came out of nowhere," Banana yelled. "A ton of them. Led by Paul Strong. I fought them for as long as I could. Last thing I remember was Strong wailing a gun across my face while three dudes held me down. Jose and the five other new guards are okay—concussions and a few broken bones—but we couldn't wake up David. He and the other injured guys are headed to the hospital in ambulances."

Sam! Blackness claimed his mind. His gut turned to volcanic rock and every part of him wanted to kill Strong. "Strong took Sam, didn't he?"

"I'm sorry, boss." Banana sounded on the verge of tears.

"Any sign of struggle?"

"No blood or anything. They took her crutches."

The tension in his shoulders eased a notch. "That means they're not hurting her for the moment." He hadn't realized it, but Captain had lagged behind. The tall, silver-haired man pushed opened the back door and headed for them, waving the keys to the helicopter in his hand.

"Don't blame yourself, that was my fault," Burke said into the phone. "I should have hidden her elsewhere. I'm about to board a helicopter at Zane's. We're all under attack. Arm yourself with whatever you need."

"You got it."

"And if you're up for it, I could use your help finding Sam."

"More than up for it. I'm ready to kick some ass," Banana said.

"Good, I'll call you in a minute once I find out the plan." Burke hung up, feeling like someone had reached inside and taken all his vital organs hostage. He let out a roar of frustration.

"Sam's gone?" Rollin demanded.

"Paul Strong and a huge team came in and grabbed her. Fuck, I'll never forgive myself. I should have taken her to the Tahoe safehouse." Horrific images tormented him. Sam beaten. Stuffed in a trunk. Crying while Strong raped her. He fought to focus. He couldn't lose his mind now. "I'm not going to Seattle until I find Sam." He punched in the number for Bobby. "Bobby? Locate Sam for me and this is urgent."

"Burke!" Bobby shouted, frantic. "They hacked your cell, you have to call me from Rollin's phone."

"Shit!" He hung up. "Rollin, hand me your phone."

As soon as Rollin gave him his cell, the phone rang. Bobby.

"This is safe?" Burke asked.

"Move it!" Captain demanded from the pilot's seat of the copter. He slammed the cockpit door.

Burke climbed in and sat next to Rollin in the middle seats. Ty and Catherine got into the very back. All put on headphones so they could communicate.

"Bobby, I'm in a copter, switching to text," Burke said.

Captain made a check of the helicopter controls.

Have your phone fixed in a sec, Bobby texted. *Cabal hired Stillwater and Candler.*

Burke's gut burned. He'd forged an alliance with Stillwater when he'd been under deep cover as a criminal and had used them against the Patriots. Stefan—a fellow Patriot who'd been wounded in the attack— would never forgive him. The others still weren't happy. Even though he'd hired Stillwater because of their incompetence. But to hear that Candler had joined the Stillwater jerkoffs was not good news. The Patriots regularly partnered with Candler and his associates. No more.

"Fuck, the Cabal's reach is everywhere." *Find Sam*, Burke messaged. *Sending you information on all the tracking devices I planted on her and her clothing. Have no idea which ones will be on her.* He forwarded his surveillance file on Sam to Bobby.

Received. BRB.

Captain started the helicopter and the noise grew deafening. Burke repeated what Bobby had said over the com.

Loud expressions of disbelief came through his headphones.

Rollin sent him an incredulous stare. "Are you serious? Talk about a fucking breach. Does Candler have any idea what he's setting in motion?"

Captain's face turned to granite. "Loren's been itching to put us out of business since last year when we busted that weapons smuggling ring. But he crossed the line this time. Once we land, I'll take care of him. My contacts can beat up his contacts."

Gravity pressed Burke in his seat as the helicopter rose into the sky. Out of his peripheral vision, he saw a giant bird. He did a double-take. Another helicopter, closing fast.

His heart pounded. "Helicopter off our port side!" he called out.

"And our aft!" Captain shouted.

Suddenly, the helicopters banked and flew away.

"What the heck?" Captain demanded. "What scared 'em off?"

"Yeah, Zane!" Rollin was looking out the window to the ground below. His eyes were nearly popped out of his head. "Holy fuck, check it out!"

Burke followed his line of sight. A large tank sat below, Zane stood in the hatchway with the upper half of him exposed, pointing a shoulder-mounted Stinger missile at the fleeing copters.

"God bless that man's love of toys," Captain said.

Zane—and his missile—disappeared inside the tank and a few seconds later, the large armored vehicle turned and headed full tilt down the driveway with a huge plume of dust billowing behind it.

"Glad the copters chickened out, Zane would have dropped one right on his house," Catherine said.

Captain said, "Yeah, and if he'd missed, his rich neighbors would have gotten a wonderful surprise when a Stinger missile took out their Olympic swimming pool."

"Or the 280 freeway," Burke said.

"Looks like Zane has this well in hand," Captain said and turned the helicopter.

"Fuck, don't leave yet! Let's watch! Just for a second!" Rollin exclaimed.

Ty said, "Yeah, Captain!"

"You guys are like little kids." Captain rotated the copter and hovered over the action.

Rollin got a huge smile on his face. "Go Zane!"

Burke had little interest in the show—and was more than antsy about finding Sam—but a few seconds hopefully wouldn't matter. He shook his head. "Crazier and crazier. When did he get a tank?"

"About a year ago," Rollin said. "He already wants another one, he loves this sucker so much."

As Burke watched the tank descend upon the four SUVs, he couldn't help but grin.

"I love this guy!" Ty exclaimed.

"Dude is nuts," Catherine said and laughed.

The lead Cabal SUV slammed on its brakes, skidded off the narrow road, burst through the wooden fence, and went into the field to avoid the oncoming armored vehicle.

The driver of the second car hit the brakes, but the third car rear-ended him, propelling the second SUV on a sideways slide toward the fence. The driver tried to regain control, but Zane was on him and drove right over the front of the car—and part of the fence—flattening the hood. Smoke poured from the compressed wreckage.

The third vehicle smashed through the fence and followed the first while the last car backed down the long driveway at light speed.

Zane followed the two fleeing SUVs into the field and stopped. The turret swung around, and the tank's gun aimed for the disabled vehicle.

The back window popped out of the partially crushed and smoking SUV, and four men leapt out. They sprinted down the driveway after their friends.

When they were no more than fifteen feet away, Zane fired a missile at the disabled vehicle. An explosion rocked the area. Fireball. The four assailants were knocked to the ground from the concussion.

"Yeah! Zane!" Rollin yelled.

"Atta boy!" Catherine shouted.

Ty cheered, "Can't beat the bloke's style!"

The four bad guys scrambled to their feet and ran for the front gate.

Further down the driveway, the fourth SUV, which had been backing up, spun a u-turn in place and hustled for the exit. The remaining SUVs tore out of the field and onto the road, with the terrified mercenaries on foot running behind them, waving their arms.

Zane pursued the group.

Far off in the distance on Highway 84, a line of police cars with their lights flashing headed for the entrance to Zane's place. Between the cops and Zane, those mercenaries would not be having a good day.

Burke's Blackberry vibrated. *Sam's at SFO.*

"Sam's at San Francisco Airport!" he shouted to the group.

"We'll head there!" Captain replied.

Spoke too soon. Sam's signal just vanished.

Fuck! Black panic sucked his hope dry. Burke furiously typed: *Find out where they took her.*

Already on it.

"Sam's signal is gone! Bobby's trying to find her."

"Shit," Rollin said.

Captain spoke over his shoulder, even though he could only be heard through the headphones. "Don't want to upset you, Burke, but we should head directly to Seattle and find the location of the murder weapon. Strong could already have drugged Sam and found out. Best way to protect her is to get that weapon. Besides, Strong might be taking her to Seattle. He could know about Ursula. Could torture her for the info in front of Sam."

Burke broke out in a full body sweat. "Fuck."

Captain continued. "SFO's traffic is about to get bad and a take off time might be hard, let's head to our jet at San Carlos. After Seattle, we'll fly to New Hampshire. If they're not taking her to Seattle, then they're probably taking her to Tyrell."

Even worse! Burke fought to keep from puking. "I'll alert Bobby." He texted: *Let Zane and Banana know we're headed to Seattle in the*

Patriots' jet from the San Carlos Airport. Have Banana meet us there ASAP.

Done, came his reply.

FIND SAM.

You bet.

Captain banked the helicopter and headed east.

Burke worked his toes and kneaded his hands, ready to combust. Tyrell would kill her for sure. Hopefully, Strong still wanted to fuck her. That would keep her alive until he could rescue her.

"We'll save Sam." Rollin clapped him on the shoulder.

Burke gave a firm nod, but his stomach was in revolt and he could barely keep a lid on the tornado of emotions storming through him. He had to take control and use all his resources to save her, but his heart screamed so loudly, his thoughts kept jumbling.

Sam…

EIGHTEEN

Fuming, arms crossed, Sam tapped her foot and glared out the window of the private jet, ignoring Paul Strong, who sat on the other side of a large table. Even though Sam's chair was luxurious and plush, she was so uncomfortable, she might as well have been sitting on a cushion of nails. Twitchy, she kept crossing and uncrossing her legs. She wished she could jump out and get to that storage unit. Grab Burke's weapons and blow these dickheads away.

Thankfully, her anger fed nicely into her plan. Paul would expect her to be furious at this point.

He'd taken off his jacket and tie, and now wore a light blue button-down shirt, his rocky pecs bulging against the cotton material. His sleeves were rolled up, revealing super ropy forearms, and his top button was undone showing a peek of brown chest hair. Over the shirt was his black leather shoulder holster, 1911 Kimber semi-automatic firmly in place.

Paul gestured toward her. "You sure you don't want anything to drink?"

"I don't want anything from you," she said with as much hate in her voice as she could manage.

A nearly imperceptible twinge of hurt flashed through his gray-blue eyes. "Like I said, I'm not your enemy, Sam. I just saved your life. Saved you from those animals. And if you play your cards right, I'll save you from Tyrell, too."

Her heart rate went crazy and she broke out in a full body sweat. She examined every square inch of Paul's face and expression. What did he know? Was he taking her to Larry? Or would he use her as leverage against the big man?

She'd die before she let any of that happen.

"I showed him your picture." Strong's eyes glittered with knowing.

Her throat closed up, her chest tightened, and she pushed back away from him. "You fucking idiot," she whispered.

He locked his eyes on hers and leaned forward, assuming a power posture with his shoulders squared and his elbows on the table. He focused all his energy on her. "Had quite a strong reaction. Then he ordered me to bring you to him."

Her stomach hit the floor, and the plane's cabin swirled around her. She had to get out of there. She had to take over the plane.

He brought himself up taller in his seat and his face went harder. "Don't try anything, Sam, and don't move from that seat."

Gripping the arms of her chair, she studied him, too freaked out to cover her reactions. Let him shoot her. A much less painful fate. "He's going to kill me."

His gaze unwavering, he didn't flinch. "I know."

Hate poured from her center and her nostrils flared. "So why are we having this useless conversation?" If she could knock him out of his seat, she could get his gun. Didn't matter if she died, she was dead already. She'd crash this fucking plane.

Paul attention darted to her hands, her body posture, then back to her eyes in a split second. "You wouldn't even get two steps out of that seat before I'd take you down. Now tell me. Why does Larry want to kill you?" He leaned closer and leveled his blue gaze straight into hers.

She was so close to lunging for him, she had to wrap her arms around her body and hold onto her upper arms to stop herself. Nothing she could say would matter to this asshole.

Forcing her attention out the window, she argued with herself. Pros and cons of telling him? Pros, who knows? Cons? She was dead meat, anyway. Pretty easy decision. Besides, she sensed Paul might be an ally under that creepy Fed exterior. But she needed to know what he knew.

She turned back to him and looked into his eyes for the truth. "You don't know? He didn't tell you?"

His expression was open. "No. Not specifically. But he sure acted weird. When he saw that photo, his mouth dropped open, and his face went white as a sheet. He touched it and said, 'Cathy,'. I thought he was gonna start crying. Then he threw the picture back at me. 'Cathy's dead', he said. He demanded to know where I got the photo and who it was."

Her stomach scrunched into a small ball. "What did you say?"

"I told him that the picture was of a woman named Samantha Murdock, a woman who put her life on the line to get hold of that blackmail packet."

Sam put her hands to her chest to try to control the frantic beat of her heart.

Paul didn't miss one of her reactions. "Tyrell thought for a moment, then he gasped and looked like I'd punched him with brass knuckles. He started shaking and sweating. Then he got pissed. Really pissed. 'That little fucking bitch is still alive? Bring her to me. I want her here," he said, doing a spot-on imitation of Larry.

Her body temperature dropped like her blood had been flash frozen. It took all her strength not to leap out of the chair. Larry's dark eyes bored into her from her memory, full of menacing violence. Shuddering, she hugged herself tighter and rubbed her arms. "Christ."

"I've seen him rabid, but not that rabid. I asked him what you'd done, specifically. He made it very plain that it was his business. He also said to make sure you were unarmed. That you would lie to me."

Her stomach wrenching, she blew out a breath through her teeth. "Of course I would. I'm a lying whore."

Paul looked through her, like he was trying to read her mind. "He said your lies nearly ended his life once. That no one should know you exist. Once he got through with you, I'd have to make you disappear."

All the air left the cabin and she struggled to breathe. Her worst nightmare.

"Erase all records of your existence," Paul continued evenly. "The guy is pretty crazy. But I've never seen him more volatile, like he was spitting acid."

Sam steepled her fingers and pressed them against her mouth, working hard to hold back a long, soul-wrenching scream. She wanted to punch Larry's face in and then waste him with an Uzi. How dare he hate her like this! "After all he did to me. He's mad at me. Unreal," she managed to say in a very calm voice.

Paul moved closer and dropped his voice to a near whisper. "What did he do to you? What do you have on him, Sam?"

Maybe her story would tweak his heart. Either that or he'd shoot her right on the spot to make sure the truth never got out. At this point, either option was better than facing Larry alone and unarmed.

But if the guy even gave her a whiff he was taking her to Larry, she'd kill him and his whole band of merry men.

"You have nothing to lose. Tell me."

Somehow from telling her story to Burke, this seemed easier. Like she'd already removed the staples from her lips. She looked him dead in the eye. "When Larry was forty and I was fourteen, he seduced me and did many unnatural things to me for two years until my father caught us and threatened to expose the dirty secret to the world. So Larry shot him point blank in the chest, right in front of me."

Paul gasped and the color drained from his face.

"And then he turned the gun on me. He shot me in the leg, I dove into a river and held my breath. He emptied the gun into the river all around me and then threw it in and the pistol landed on my foot. When I sneaked home six months later, I found Larry in bed with my mother. A month after that, Mom killed herself."

Paul's eyes widened. "Fuck." He blinked fast and his brow furrowed hard over his eyes. "Are you serious? Do you have proof?"

"Yes and yes. Well, I hope so. I hid the murder weapon, the pistol, in the wall of a house. I hope it's still there. I'm not sure it is. That's why I wanted that information packet so badly. I wanted to blackmail Larry while I built the murder case."

He nodded, his attention dropped to the arm of his chair, and he twisted his mouth to one side. Slowly, he shook his head. "Wow." His gaze flickered to hers. "So you *are* Amanda Hutchins?"

She flinched and her stomach went hard. After all those years of training herself to forget her name, hearing it spoken aloud freaked her out. "How did you know? Did Larry mention my name?"

"Yeah. And I looked you up. You do resemble that girl. Your father was Robert Hutchins and your mother was Catherine?"

Stiffening, she took a deep breath. She hadn't said or heard her parents' names in years. "Y-yes."

"The Cathy in question. You do look remarkably like her."

Sam took a deep breath. "I know."

"So Larry set up a transient for the murders?"

"Old Tony," she said with a nod. "The local bum. Harmless. Dad used to give him odd jobs. I'm sure it took nothing to pin the murders on him. Larry always had it in for that guy, anyway. One of a handful of homeless people who lived in town. Larry hated him. Said he made the town look bad."

"Christ." Paul stood and paced the cabin. He rubbed the back of his neck, then his forehead. Covering his mouth, his attention darted around the plane and he muttered to himself. After a long few minutes, he stopped, then shrugged. Straightening his posture, he nodded and took out his cell.

Who was he calling? Would they kill her? He didn't seem like he wanted to kill her. The way his eyes kept straying to her tits said he still wanted to screw her. Which would win? His pocketbook or his dick? She'd bet his pocketbook.

Sam checked the door to the cockpit. While Paul was distracted, she could make a break for it and take the plane down.

But what if he wasn't going to kill her? Sam studied Paul's face and body language.

Brow furrowed hard, sweat glistening on his forehead, his hands twitchy, Paul was bothered. Clearly her story had affected him, but which way had it pushed him? Would he give her to Larry or let her go? Or neither?

Paul walked to the far end of the plane, turned away from her, and engaged in a heated discussion. He kept his voice low, but she caught her name and Larry's name. His voice got louder. "...we need to change the plan. Yeah, we do. He's too crazy, I'm not going down with him. And this just dropped in our laps. I say we jump."

You mean me. A buzz started in her belly. Promising. If he wasn't going to take her to Larry, then she had a chance. Even if Paul decided to keep her imprisoned and use her, he'd eventually make a mistake and give her an opportunity to escape. Then she'd hunt down and kill that horrible bastard before he sent someone else to murder her. Paul might want to change his plans, but Larry wouldn't.

After a long back and forth, Paul seemed to have convinced the person on the other end of the line.

Boo-yah! Sam didn't show any emotion to Paul, but inside, she did a little dance. Crashing the plane and dying hadn't sounded like much fun.

Paul sent her a guarded look, then turned serious. He returned to his seat and faced her. "Here's my offer. You help me recover that murder weapon and set up the case against Larry and I'll protect you."

While she fully intended to go along with whatever plan he'd devised, she wasn't going to make it easy on the bastard. She chuckled. "Why should I trust you?"

"Because you don't have a choice," he replied flatly.

This wasn't about his dick. This was about Larry. She was disappointed and happy at the same time. "You're gonna use me to take him down."

"Yes."

"I thought you were his go-to boy."

"I was."

"So what's changed your mind? Can't just be my story."

He made a noise with the back of his throat and sat back. "I may have sold part of my soul, but not all of it. Anyone who's capable of that kind of shit is too unstable. I've gone along with most of his depravity, keeping my eye on the ball. And on the money he paid me. But I finally see that I can't trust this guy for shit."

"Huh," Sam said, not convinced.

"You're right, aside from what he did to your dad and you, I received intel this week that he'd killed some friends of mine. I've been trying to get proof. His sickness goes all the way to the core. And he's escalating. Gotta get away from him before he brings us all down."

She fidgeted and her brow hurt from wrinkling. No way was she trusting this asshole.

His expression softened and his old self showed through. "But I'll tell you the truth, Sam—"

"Novel idea."

He barely missed a beat. "—your story affected me the most. I'm so sorry. I can't imagine how awful this has been for you."

She wanted to slap him. Now suddenly, he was on her side? *Bullshit.* "I don't want your sympathy. I want my freedom. I want to know where Burke is."

Paul's eyes went cold and his jaw clenched. "Honey, for a smart woman, you are really dumb. Burke doesn't care about you. Tyrell's the prize here, sweetheart, not you."

Ka-pow! Like a bullet between the eyes, his words pierced her. The accusation ricocheted through her skull, ringing loudly of truth. She dismissed the idea immediately. Burke loved her first, his job second.

Or did he?

"We can help each other." Paul leaned in, briefly grasped her forearm, then sat back. Turned up the volume on his charm dial. "And

I know you won't believe me when I say this, but I still like you. I meant what I said at our dinner. I wish we'd met some other time." He delivered the line with much sincerity.

She chuckled, but wasn't amused. "You'd kill me as soon as look at me. You were gonna sell me to Larry."

The line between his eyes went deep and he made a dismissive gesture. "No, Sam." Then he stopped and gave a hand shrug. "I'll be honest with you, I considered it during the first part of the conversation with Larry. When I still thought you might be a spy. But after he slipped your real name, I did extensive research. The date of Amanda's disappearance and the simultaneous appearance of Sam Murdock in 1994 accounted for your whole life. That's when my opinion of you changed, when I realized you weren't a professional. I figured you witnessed something Larry didn't want you to see, maybe the murder of your father. But I couldn't have imagined how bad the story would turn out to be."

Sam gave a snort. "Why did you think I was a spy?"

A brief raise of his brows. "First, the way you reacted to the gunfire in the forest. Not being surprised that someone was shooting at you. And the fact that you carried. But the topper was dinner at my place when you started bargaining with me regarding that packet. The hard way you looked at me and listed off that litany of weapons. I thought you might be a mole trying to infiltrate Rampart. Your knowledge of guns and urban warfare is far too extensive for a cocktail waitress. That part of you still surprises me."

Sam lifted one shoulder. "I had to prepare for the day I faced Larry."

"I see that now." His brows came together. "You were going to assassinate a Presidential candidate?"

"If I couldn't get him put in jail. You're damn right I'd kill him."

He rolled his eyes and shook his head. "Sam, you'd never even get within a mile of him."

"I've done all kinds of things that you and the Patriots haven't thought I was capable of."

"You have no idea how powerful he is now. You knew him a long time ago. Your plan is beyond crazy, it's fucking suicidal."

"What would you do in my position? Just let the guy get away with murder?"

Paul looked her straight in the eye. "First I'd want to live. I told you what I think about revenge. Granted, I don't know how anyone would let something like that go. But killing him wouldn't have done anything but landed you in jail."

"I was already in jail." Sam crossed her arms and legs.

His expression softened and turned earnest. "No, you had a nice life, Sam. Friends, a home. So many people who love you. You have no idea how lucky you are. I haven't stayed in a town long enough to make the kind of friends you have. All my friends are coworkers."

"Who all carry guns and whose loyalty can be bought by the highest bidder."

"Exactly," he said, sitting back.

"You chose that life."

He held his shoulders straighter. "No, I chose to serve my country. And they fucked me over," he said with force, his eyes flaring. "I get where Rampart—the Patriots— are coming from. They're all ruthless, soulless motherfuckers, but I get the need to break away from the power structure. It's a rigged game. But the Rampart fucks can't be trusted. You can't buy them. Their ideology is super narrow. They consider themselves righteous demigods."

Guy was so full of crap.

"That kind of passionate rhetoric and fundamentalism breeds false justice," Paul continued with a sharp gesture. "I may be for sale, but I have limits. And I cop to my greed. I own it. They lie to themselves and their supplicants. And women. Paint themselves as warriors for good when they have become what they hate. They're more than willing to have Larry stay in power."

"Burke said after they heard what happened to me, they wouldn't."

He laughed. "Bullshit. Carter Blackstone—or Captain as you know him—leads those guys around by their noses with his lofty, god-like, straight-shooter bullshit. Manipulative bastard. They're all delusional do-gooders who will never be able to face the truth that they're worse than the guys they put away. I have no respect for people who are blind to their own bullshit."

Sam's foundation wobbled. This guy made a little too much sense. Like if you were fighting for good, but playing with the bad guys and doing bad things, how did that make you different? And the Patriots were all true believers, that was for sure. They'd drunk the Patriot Koolaid. Beyond that, bathed in it, and injected it straight into their red, white and blue veins.

Sam understood how dangerous misguided passion could be. She and Emma had a crazy friend from college who'd ended up blowing up a chemical lab—and himself in the process—trying to save the animals inside. He was a true believer. Turned out he'd previously murdered a bunch of scientists because of their animal experimentation. And he'd been a really caring, passionate person. A total love.

Like all the Patriots.

Her stomach roiled. She hated Paul. How dare he put these doubts in her head? She mentally grabbed her mind and shook the bad thoughts out. Burke and Rollin's honor was beyond reproach, along with the rest of the Patriots. Maybe they were deluded, but they were the best men she'd known.

"I'm telling you the truth, Sam. You don't deserve their shit. Or Larry's."

"So I deserve yours?"

He smiled, his eyes twinkling. "I won't hurt you. I like you. You're a strong lady. Full of piss and vinegar. Spicy. But blind. I need to open your eyes so I can save you. And you can save this country. We can't let Larry become President. Trust me, Sam, and I'll make sure he dies in prison."

She studied his posture, and pretended to think about his offer. She'd lure this bastard in like a prized fish. And then kill him and mount him on her wall. Dickhead.

He grinned. Warm, genuine, easy. "Hold off on your final decision about me."

She sent him a *get real* half-smile. His gaze went hooded, a tinge of lust surged deep within them.

Sorry, buddy, once you have Kobe Beef, you never want McDonald's again.

He checked his watch, gave a quick raise of his eyebrows, leaned back, and withdrew her ulcer pills from his front pants pocket. "Here, time to take your meds." Putting the bottle on the table, he got up and moved to the back of the plane. He returned and set a bottle of water in front of her, then took his seat.

Glaring at him, she took a pill and chased it with the water. She'd had no idea how thirsty she'd been. She hadn't wanted to accept anything from the buttwad, and was happy for the excuse to hydrate.

She waited for him to take back the meds, but he left them on the table.

His attention went to the bottle, then he met her gaze. "Take 'em."

A peace offering. To show what a stand up guy he was. Snake. She snatched the container from the table and stuck it in the pocket of her hoodie.

After eying him for a moment or so, she briefly lifted her chin. "So what's your deal? Tell me the plan."

"You give me that murder weapon, testify against Larry, and let me protect you until the trial is over. This could be a long time, Sam. You'll need to stay with me or one of my friends. Only we can protect you. Larry has some very scary allies. Like the Patriots."

"No, they aren't."

He smirked. "Maybe they don't like him, but they sure want to control him. Carter Blackstone's been angling for this kind of power for a long time. I'm telling you, Sam, this isn't about you. This is about Tyrell."

"For you, too. You care fifty bazillion times more about Larry than me."

"Sam," he said with a pitying expression. "If I didn't care about you, I'd already know where the murder weapon was."

A chill went through her and the hair on the back of her neck stood up. He was right. He could easily torture her for the information. Sam's pain tolerance wasn't exactly very high.

And it was also a reminder of just who this guy was: a super big creep.

"And I could trump up some charges and force you to testify against Tyrell to save your ass." His features softened. "But I don't want to do that. I don't want to hurt you. I want to help you. And I want to start over and maybe explore a future with you, once this is all done. I like you, Sam. A lot."

And I will use every bit of that emotion for me against you, you douchebag.

"Where are you taking me?"

"My house in DC. Safe and you'll have your own wing."

"What? Wing?"

"It's a big house."

"Whatever. Alright, so you say you like me, but if I don't give you the murder weapon, you'll torture me, right?"

He frowned and waved his hands dismissively. "No, no, Sam. Jeez, no."

"So what if I don't give up the murder weapon?"

He didn't react much, but she got the feeling he had on his poker face. "Then it will be much harder to put Larry away."

"You really want him to go down."

"More than you could know."

She sat back, crossed her arms, and studied him. No way in hell would she trust this clown. He'd been using her from the start. "So in the forest? Did you know those guys who were shooting at us?"

"Yes, I hired them," he said with no apology on his face.

Gasping, she sat up. *"What?"*

A brief raise of his brows and shoulders. "Timetable got pushed up once we lost the trail with Joseph. I had to move quicker. I needed to bond you to me faster. Then Burke shows up out of nowhere. Some timing. He clipped one of my guys in the shoulder and shot the hat off the other. I would have never hired those Army grunts had I known a fuckin' SEAL would show up. We were all lucky Burke wasn't in a killing mood that day."

She didn't think it could, but her admiration for Burke leapt higher. He could have killed those boys. But he just scared them off.

And Paul was even more of a rat than she'd thought. If he was trying to seduce her, his efforts were failing miserably. Punching him would be so satisfying. A nice uppercut to that thick jaw of his. His head would snap back…

Strong shook his head. "Freaked out those kids. They called me, screaming, after I left you, and quit. But it all actually worked out perfect because I found out where the packet went. Much quicker than I'd planned."

Sam realized in that moment that no matter what she'd done—gone to Seattle and contacted Ursula or not—her life would have been blown apart through no fault of her own. Paul had found her before she'd decided to contact Ursula about the murder weapon. After that first date, everything changed. Eventually, Paul would have found out who she was and then Larry would have known.

Her stomach went hard, her jaw set, and her fists balled. "You're rotten. You would have ruined my life for a job. Terrorized me for some stupid selfish purpose. You *suck*."

His face reddened and he briefly looked at his lap. Seemed ashamed, anyway. "Sorry. I hate my job sometimes."

"You should. I didn't deserve that."

He met her gaze. "No, ma'am, you did not. But if you give me another chance, I'll do everything in my power to make it up to you."

She kept glaring and didn't acknowledge his offer. "You must have manipulated my Match.com results, too. I thought it was weird that only you and two Troglodytes responded to my ad."

One side of his mouth turned up. "Just doing my job, Sam. You were never in danger from me. Only from Burke."

She hated hearing this shit about Burke and no way did she want to agree with Strong about anything, but she had to manipulate him. She'd fight him for a while longer, then convince him she'd turned to the Dark Side. Maybe even con him into getting hold of that murder weapon.

Strong nodded and tapped his Bluetooth. "What? I thought we took care of that. No problem. I'll destroy them." He sent her a grave look.

Her stomach fluttered. "Now what?"

"Rampart has a tracking device on you. Did Burke feed you, by any chance? Something really tasty that didn't need much chewing?"

All her muscles gnarled at once. "A particularly succulent slice of peach this morning, why?"

Paul reached below the table and brought out a briefcase. He opened it and withdrew a small black box with a line of tiny green lights on one side. None of the lights were lit.

Paul said, "Sit up and face me."

She recoiled. "What are you going to do?"

He grinned. "Won't hurt. Come on." He made an upward motion with the ends of his fingers.

She hesitantly sat up.

He turned a switch on the gizmo. A beeping sound came from the device, the lights flashed a few times, then they went off. Holding the gadget a foot away from her face, he moved it downward. The sound got progressively louder and faster, and more of the lights lit. When he reached her belly button, the beeping hit a crescendo and all the lights came on. As he moved on past, the sound faded, the lights flickered out. He returned the black device to her stomach area. It beeped crazily, its LEDs shining at full force.

She punched the seat, wishing it were Burke's face. "Fuck! Are you kidding me?"

"No. A transmitter no bigger than a grain of rice."

She held her throbbing head. "Holy crap."

"Well, looks like that's where it will end up shortly. It's in your intestines."

Feeling nauseous, she made a face. "I'm going to puke."

He sent her a small smile. "Diarrhea would be much more helpful."

His joke caught her off guard and she actually laughed. A split second later, her stomach convulsed and her muscles tensed hard. She buried her head in her hands, and let out an agonized moan. The betrayal! Fucked her and then violated her body all over again with the tracking device!

"I'm sorry, Sam. I hate to do this to you."

Facing him, she waved a hand. "Don't apologize. You were right. How could I have been so wrong?" She shook her fists.

Strong sent her a sympathetic look. "Don't feel bad. You were vulnerable and he took advantage of you. And I think he does like you on some level."

"Bastard. I was so stupid." She punched her palm.

"Give yourself a break. Jesus, Sam, you've been through hell lately. Between what Rampart did to you, and what I did to you, I'm surprised you're not drooling in a rubber room."

She raised her brows in a quick move. "I'm almost there."

"Nah, you'll be fine. Can I check the rest of you for bugs? That might not be the only one."

"Please." She held herself up in the seat, arms extended to her sides.

Paul swept the rest of her body and found tracking devices in her shoes, the bottom seam of her jeans, and in the lining of the hood of her sweatshirt.

Her body trembling, her neck so tight it burned, Sam was practically foaming at the mouth. "Jesus Christ, why didn't he just tattoo me with a barcode? Implant a chip in me?"

"I'm sure he planned on that."

"Dick!" Sam fumed while Strong destroyed the tiny devices.

As she watched him pulverize the one from her sneaker, she got nervous. "What about the one inside me? Please tell me you don't have to hurt me to deactivate it."

He smiled. "No. It's so small, its signal is pretty weak. They'd have to be close by to track you."

She let out a sigh. Shaking her head, she massaged her aching temples with her fingertips.

"Really am sorry about all this, Sam. I didn't get you involved with Rampart, but I take full responsibility for my actions. I thought anyone in their circle had to be rotten. I was wrong. You're a hundred percent and didn't deserve any of this shit."

"I sure as hell didn't," she spat. She wanted to rip Burke limb from limb. Pour gasoline all over his fucking Versace and light him on fire.

Paul was right, Burke probably did care for her on some level. That's how she'd been fooled. And she was so damaged, it hadn't been that hard to use her emotions against her. Jerk!

Of course, she'd done all the same things to him. Used him. Betrayed him.

Life had gotten decidedly ugly. Her actions. His actions. Strong's actions. A cesspool of trickery and betrayal. So what else was new? Since she was fourteen, she'd been living in a self-created hell. And Burke was tailor-made for her damage.

That asshole had clearly lied to manipulate her. He probably thought she *was* a whore. Probably faked his reaction to her story. He'd just wanted more sex. He'd said exactly what she desperately wanted to hear. That her problems weren't her fault. That her father had been wrong. That she hadn't deserved everything that had happened to her.

The pit of darkness in her mind grew larger and sucked her further into its depths. Her heart, her back, her head, everything ached. She held her stomach, but wouldn't let herself cry.

This was all her fault. All of this pain, this horror. She'd brought it all on herself. If she'd never gone after Larry, never accepted his advances, she wouldn't be in this position. If she hadn't been morally corrupt, she wouldn't be suffering.

She'd be living in a house in Concord with her husband and two kids. Maybe married to Bob McCahon. Good ol' Bob. Boring, but he'd loved her. Followed after her like a puppy dog.

More importantly, her parents would still be alive.

The image of their smiling faces knifed her heart and a few tears escaped. She had to take responsibility for the situation. She wasn't the victim. She was the problem.

"Hey, Sam?" Paul asked gently.

She jerked, surprised to find herself in an airplane with Paul. She'd completely lost touch with her surroundings.

He sent her a very sweet look. "Don't want to piss you off, but I'd love nothing more than to hold you."

She shook her head and turned her attention out the window. "I'm cool."

"Listen, I don't want anything from you. But if there's anyone I've ever seen in more need of a hug, it's you."

His steel-blue gaze clear, his expression was warm and open. He'd reverted to Nice Paul. While she wasn't fooled for a moment, his arms and welcoming energy looked damned good. And he was right. She'd never needed a hug more.

Smiling, he stood, brought her out of her chair, and guided her to a large sofa along one side of the plane. They sat down and he held her close to his nice hard chest and wrapped his thick arms around her. Burying her face in his shoulder, she took in his warmth and scent, and a bit of the tension eased from her body. She hugged him harder. He felt really good. Very reassuring to have a big strong man's arms around her. She probably hated him. She certainly hated his world and job. But in that moment, she was happy to have someone comforting her. Even if it was yet another soulless bastard.

Really, Sam, we must do something about your choices in men.

No shit.

"Where are we going, Sam?" he asked softly.

She moved back from the crook of his shoulder just far enough to speak. "Concord, New Hampshire."

"Why am I not surprised?" He kept her tight to him, but touched his earpiece. "Lloyd? Deploy the guys to New Hampshire. Concord. And tell the pilot to stay the course to DC. Sam? Where in Concord?"

She pushed away to face him. "741 Beacon Street. Nearest cross street is Lyndon. In the basement. Five feet down from the ceiling, one foot away from the back wall on the adjoining wall that shares the staircase. Five, one, staircase wall. The gun is behind some sheetrock. Hopefully."

"You got that?" Paul asked to whomever was on the other end of the line. "Rampart is in Seattle? Why?" He looked at her. "Ursula Slonaker?"

A shot of adrenaline buzzed her, her muscles went taut, and she pushed away from Paul. "What about Ursula?"

Paul's features hardened. "Ursula is your old best friend, right? Does she know where the murder weapon is? You told Burke about her, didn't you?"

Molten lava surged through her veins and her face heated red-hot. She jumped to her feet and smacked herself on the forehead. "That bastard! He slept with me just to get that information out of me! He never cared about me, all he wanted was to protect Larry! How could I have been so stupid?" She turned to Paul. "You have to get to that house before the Patriots."

"Don't worry, Sam, we're on it."

Darkness claimed her mind and her stomach convulsed so hard, she had to swallow to keep from puking. "Oh, yeah, he loves me so much he's gonna make sure that the man who murdered my father will become President. How could he use me like that? Oh, that vulnerable look in his eye, the fucking tears, his stupid confession about his childhood. He probably made up the whole thing to sucker me in! What a liar! No wonder he can't sleep at night, he's a fucking demon!"

Raging, Sam grabbed her crutches and paced for a good ten minutes before she slumped next to Paul.

He arched a brow at her. "Remind me never to piss you off."

"Don't ever piss me off."

He laughed. "Come here." He brought her close to his iron-like body.

While she was feeling more angry than sad, being in Strong's arms was a nice *fuck you* to Burke.

Paul squeezed her. "Don't worry, Sam. I've got a good feeling about this. Everything will work out just fine. And pretty soon, you'll see that I'm not such a bad guy."

Whatever. Just hold me, you piece of shit.

Burke. Her chest hurt like her heart had been torn and shredded, but she wouldn't allow herself to cry. No way would she shed a tear over that lying asshole.

She'd been right all along. Burke was a duplicitous penis and she was alone.

And now she had absolutely nothing holding her back from taking down Larry. Use Strong to get the murder weapon, steal it from him, and then go after Larry herself.

Fuck Burke, fuck the Patriots, and fuck this guy Strong.

And fuck Larry Tyrell.

She'd take them all on and win.

This was *war*.

NINETEEN

Burke paced the center aisle of the Patriots' jet, his body pounding with adrenaline. He, Rollin, Catherine, Ty, Captain and Banana were en route to Washington DC to rescue Sam.

Catherine caught his arm as he passed her for the umpteenth time. "Burke, honey, calm down. She'll be fine. We'll find her. Roman's just about to grab the murder weapon, that will save her. Strong won't risk killing her with that out of his hands. He needs both the gun and Sam if he wants to take down Tyrell."

Burke shook his head. "I can't stand what they'll do to her. We know these people. We know what they're capable of. They've already tortured Joseph to death. And I can't believe I let Strong kidnap her. This is all on my head."

"Burke, stop."

"Listen to her, Burke," came Rollin's sleepy reply. Behind Catherine, Rollin lay sideways across two seats with his legs hanging off the end into the aisle. Eyes closed, he wore his iPod earbuds. Burke had thought he'd been asleep.

Catherine pulled him down on the bench seat where she sat. "Just sit down and relax. You're not going to be any use to Sam if you don't get some rest. We've got three hours before we reach DC. Take it easy. I've never seen you like this."

His mind swirled with horrible images of Strong beating Sam. His hands fisted. "I've never been like this."

She sent him a grin that warmed him to his bones. "While I'm sorry for the circumstances, I'm so happy you finally found a good woman. You deserve her, Burke. Don't worry, you'll get her back."

He smiled at the pug-nosed terror and tousled her short pink spiky hair, then hugged her. Since the beginning, they'd always had a special connection. None of the other Patriots knew, but there had been one night in Pakistan where he and Catherine had gotten sauced and woke up naked together the next morning. She'd been horrified; him, not in the least. Beautiful woman, and such a waste being a lesbian. They'd sworn each other to secrecy and three years later, their drunken encounter had only served to bring them closer. Aside from Rollin, Catherine was the only Patriot who'd truly accepted him back into the group.

And here she was comforting him when she'd just suffered a huge loss. Fluffy had meant the world to her. Burke had been with her when she'd rescued the gray tabby as a week-old kitten in Iraq, ten years before. Catherine always said outside of the Patriots, Fluffy was her only family.

He gave her a squeeze. "And I'm really sorry about Fluffy. I know how much you loved him. He was a great cat."

Her eyes filled with tears and she stopped them just as suddenly. "Thanks, Burke. He sure was. He was the best pal ever." Her gaze turned icy, and her jaw tightened. "I'm gonna hunt down the bastard who did that. And I'm gonna make him pay," she growled.

"Yes, you will. And if you need any help, you know who to call."

"Yeah, me," Ty said from across the aisle, his face stern. His eyes widened and quick sheepish look crossed his face. "I mean, and you. All of us." Red-faced and flustered, he turned his attention back to his iPad.

Ty had better watch himself, Catherine didn't like possessive people. And Ty had been acting far more like a jealous boyfriend than her partner of late. Of course, all the male Patriots had fallen in love with the girl at one time or another. Burke had had a terrible crush on her, especially after they'd made love. The feelings passed eventually.

Burke's Bluetooth beeped in his ear. "Yes, Bobby?"

"I got some good news and some bad news."

His heart rate jumped and he sat up straighter. "What? You've heard from Sam? Is she safe?"

"She's safe." Crunching.

The tightness in his neck eased. "Thank God. Wait, what's the bad news?"

Bobby swallowed. "Her being safe isn't the only good news. What do you want first?"

"For God's sake, just fucking tell me what's going on!"

"You really have gotten more demanding ever since Sam and y—"

"Bobby!"

"We got Danny embedded with Strong's security team at his house in DC."

"We did?" A rush of energy powered through him. "Thank God!" He let out a large sigh. "Wait. What's the bad news?"

"Strong turned Sam against us. She just gave him the location of the weapon. Strong's guys are headed to the same house in New Hampshire that Roman is."

Burke jumped out of his seat, his heart hammering his ribs. "Holy shit! Did you warn Roman?"

"Yeah, he's almost there. A minute ago he was ten minutes out from the target." A plastic bag rattled in the background, followed by more munching sounds.

He rubbed his forehead. "God, I hope he makes it."

"What?" Catherine demanded, kicking him lightly. "What's going on?"

Burke gave the group the news, with the exception of Banana, who was out cold in the very back of the plane.

They all whooped when he told them about Danny, but their faces fell upon the news that Sam had been turned.

Captain waved from behind Rollin. The silver-haired man was slouched in his seat, his feet in the aisle, holding his iPad. "Tell Bobby to let us know the second he hears from Roman."

"Will do," Burke said. He repeated the command to Bobby and paced down the aisle, stepping around Rollin's legs and over Captain's outstretched feet. "Does Danny know Strong's plan for Sam?"

"Yeah," Bobby replied. A long slurp. "Strong wants to use her and the weapon to bring down Larry. Cabal is breaking apart."

"Never thought we'd be on the same side as Strong."

"You can say that again," Captain said.

"Larry's gotten too dangerous for everyone," Rollin said with his eyes still closed.

Burke stood at the back of the plane and leaned against the bulkhead. "Bobby, are you sure Sam willingly told him the location of the murder weapon? He didn't drug her or hurt her?"

A loud burp. "Way Danny heard it, Strong waited until the best possible moment to show her the tracking devices you'd put on her. She wasn't happy. Then she got really pissed you guys went to see Ursula. Sam thinks you slept with her to recover the murder weapon and protect Larry."

Burke's pulse whooshed in his ears and pounded his skull, his temples throbbing hard. Pushing away from the wall, he stormed toward the front of the plane. "Holy shit. No wonder she believed him. Fuck!"

"Danny thinks Strong wants her for himself, too. Strong just got a big suite in his mansion all ready for her arrival. Really rolling out the red carpet. Orders are to make Sam feel welcome, like she's in her own home."

Burke went up and down the aisle of the plane, his body hyped up like he'd downed fifty cups of espresso. He wanted to rip Strong apart with his bare hands. "That bastard!"

But how could Sam believe he didn't love her? After all they'd shared? His heart cried out for her.

He collapsed next to Catherine. "Fucking Strong. I'll pull out his liver through his throat."

She grabbed his forearm and squeezed. "Sam will see through his lies, don't worry. But at least for right now, she'll be safe and well treated. Keep the faith, buddy." She gave him a quick kiss on the cheek.

His heart warmed and he leaned into her. As tough and tomboyish as she was, Catherine was the group's de facto mother. And she was a love.

"Hey! Gettin' awfully cozy there, aren't you?" Ty demanded from across the aisle, sounding and looking a bit hostile.

Happy for the distraction, Burke turned, grinned at him, and wrapped his arms all the way around the tiny fireplug of a woman. "Well, Sam's gone."

Catherine snuggled close and sent a cheeky smile to Ty. "We're getting married," she said in a comical, faux-dreamy tone.

Everyone in the plane but Ty laughed. He gave her a smirk, but sent a look to Burke like he'd like to gut him. Burke wondered if the Aussie had realized that he'd fallen for the lesbian cutie. Poor Ty. He'd have more luck dating a nun.

Chuckling, Burke turned away and instantly his mood took a nosedive.

Sam. He had to get to her and talk to her. Once he saw her, he could clear up the mess. Once she found out that he hadn't betrayed her, only tried to protect her, she'd come around.

He sighed and tried to calm. Catherine was right. He'd get Sam back.

He had to.

"Sam, wake up. We're about to land."

Sam became aware she was lying on her side on a couch. On an airplane. She blinked against the light and the plane noise grew louder. Paul's face came into focus.

Paul. Not Burke.

Her stomach convulsed and her aching heart felt empty. Burke had betrayed her. The asshole. She closed her eyes and groaned, wishing she could make reality go away. "Feel like shit."

"You've had some bad shocks today," he said in a soft voice.

She opened her eyes. Paul appeared different to her. Lighter. Happier. Shinier. Younger.

Weird.

She stretched and yawned. "I need more sleep. Pickles, I feel like crap. Like I ran a marathon, and an obstacle course, and then I watched my family die, and ran another marathon. And I didn't sleep for a week. Like ten minutes or something."

"Try two hours."

"Really? I should feel better."

Paul rubbed her shoulder. "We'll get you some rest."

"Good. Did you get the gun?"

Paul's expression fell. "We were twenty minutes behind them. Big hole in the wall, and it's gone."

Burning rage spewed from her center. She sat up and pounded the sofa cushion. "Those bastards! Not enough to ruin me, they want to save that murderer's life? I knew I shouldn't have trusted them! Emma hasn't been the same since that idiot came into her life. She's been kidnapped and tortured and—I can't believe I fell for their true blue act!"

"Sorry, Sam." Paul appeared thrilled by her anger, but by the deep line between his brows and the tight way he held his mouth, he clearly wasn't happy about the missing weapon.

"I kept getting lulled by these horrible jerks! I hate them. Oh, sorry. You don't need to hear all this." She rubbed the sleepiness from her eyes. "So where do we go from here?"

"We'll hole up at my place here in DC for a day or two and then I'm moving you somewhere safer. We're trying to recover the murder weapon from the Patriots. With or without it, you'll be an awesome witness on the stand. There are some people I want you to meet. People who can help us bring Larry to his knees."

"Your place, huh?" She eyed him, trying to figure out if he expected sex.

He chuckled and waved his hand dismissively. "You'll have your own wing, Sam."

"Wing? What the hell is this wing? You mentioned that earlier."

Shrugging, he shot her a grin. "Uh, yeah. My house is pretty big. Okay, it's a mansion."

"Huh. Mansion. You a rich boy?"

He seemed so down-to-Earth—aside from his creepy Fed side—she couldn't picture him in expensive digs. Not like Burke. Paul's ruggedness and beefy frame made him seem suitable for the outdoors, maybe running a farm.

"Guess you could say that. Not Trump or anything, but I have a few houses and vacation places. Some cars. Plane." He wasn't bragging, just stating facts. And from his tone, while he liked his wealth, he didn't seem to need the money for status, he just enjoyed having it. Didn't need the Mercedes and Versace labels as penis extenders. Unlike a certain metrosexual fashion-whore shithead she knew. Paul's power came from his belief in himself.

She felt like she was meeting the guy for the first time. He was much more relaxed. Easy in his skin. A completely different person. "Really?"

"Yeah. Housekeeper's made up some food for us, got your suite all ready. I took the liberty of ordering you some clothes. The housekeeper, Jenny, she helped."

"How'd you get my sizes?"

He smiled. "You'd be surprised what information is floating around out there about you."

"Okay, cool." Her stomach froze and all her limbs tightened. Wait. This was all too easy. Too good to be true.

She had to get the truth from him. The direct approach had always worked best for her. Taking him by the arm, she searched his eyes. "Are you giving me to Larry Tyrell?" She checked his expression carefully.

His eyes widened for a split second and his head jerked back. He shook his head. "No. Absolutely not." He took her hands in his large ones. "You'll trust me soon enough, Sam. You'll see. No more games. I'm on your side." She saw only honesty in his face.

But she'd been wrong before. Like earlier that day. Burke had certainly hypnotized her. "I hope you're telling me the truth. I really don't feel like dying today."

Pain lines appeared on his forehead and around his blue eyes, then softened into sympathy. He rubbed her hands. "Stop worrying. I'm here for you. And I'll prove it."

She stared at him, unsure. How the hell could she trust his new warmth? Dude had a dual personality: Dr. Jekyll and Mr. Fed.

As they drove to his house through the streets of DC, she'd catch him out of her peripheral vision, checking her out. Like she was a new toy. So bizarre. Like a switch had been thrown the second after he heard her story about Larry. Disconcerting, but definitely more pleasant.

The sun had just set when their black sedan pulled up at a huge wooded estate surrounded by a tall brick wall. An ornate black iron gate swung open upon their approach and they drove past a security guard standing in front of a guardhouse. The short, fat and bald sixty-something guard smiled and waved. Paul saluted back.

They continued down a winding driveway with blooming foliage on either side. Around a bend, the house appeared, looking remarkably like Monticello. Only bigger. A vast brick-fronted colonial masterpiece with white columns rising two stories.

"Holy bejeebus, this can't be your house."

"Why not?" He sent her a cocky grin.

"Why the Eichler?"

His smile softened. "I love that little place."

She admired the big windows and massive porch. "Wow, this is amazing."

"Wait until you see the interior. Built in the twenties by a crooked senator who dreamed it was the White House. Lots of nefarious history. And part of the reason I bought it." He shot her a wicked grin.

She had a millisecond of a sexual thought about him and smiled back. Unfortunately, she liked Paul's new persona, the honest rogue.

The driver parked in front of the house and a tall, thin older white guy in a formal black suit waited in the open front doorway. Two suited security guys stood on either side of the porch.

Paul chuckled. "That's James waiting for us at the door. I told him to go home. Came with the house. I keep trying to get him to retire, but he won't. He's going to be 75 soon."

They got out of the car and Sam walked up the staircase on her crutches and into the magnificent home. Strong introduced her to James and the elderly gentlemen welcomed her.

Sam was so blown away by the architecture she wasn't as responsive to the butler as she should have been. The immense foyer had a two-story-tall white ceiling with a winding wood banister that led to the upper level. High, arched doorways led off the grand entry hall. Every surface gleamed, from the hardwood floors to the polished tables and sparkling windows. Fresh flowers everywhere. Gorgeous dark wood period furnishings completed the twenties décor. Perfectly maintained in the original style, like his Eichler.

Paul gave her a tour of the main areas of the grand, twenty-room house. Downstairs had a bunch of living rooms with different names: drawing room, morning room, formal living room, blah, blah, but they all looked more or less the same to her: big, wood-paneled and magnificent. Kitchen was massive with two pantries.

Seemed like every room had its own guard. So far, she'd counted six guys inside the house.

Upstairs were two more guards, myriad bedroom suites, another library, and a den furnished with a large screen TV, a wet bar and modern leather couches. Clearly Paul's hangout.

Paul escorted her to her huge bedroom suite in the "east wing". The centerpiece of the room was a mahogany canopy bed in white and blue striped brocade. Adjacent was a sitting area with Victorian furnishings. Large windows lined two walls and overlooked the illuminated colorful, lush backyard and pool area. An adjoining en suite bathroom featured a massive claw-foot tub and a beautifully maintained vintage cream tiled shower.

After examining the bathroom, Sam joined Paul in the center of the luxurious room. "Wow, this is beautiful, Paul."

He seemed very pleased. "Glad you like it. Why don't you get settled in and meet me downstairs in the dining room in a half an hour?"

"Cool. And thanks."

He beamed. "You're welcome. I hope you'll be comfortable here."

"I'd have to be an idiot not to be. This place is astounding."

He sent her a sweet grin and left, closing the door behind him. After kicking off her shoes, she hobbled into the bathroom. She'd hang out for a day or two until she healed a bit more. Then escape. Had to be a weakness somewhere in Paul's security.

After a quick shower to wash the last of Burke off her, she dressed in a pair of comfy blue jeans and a nice pink cotton button-down shirt from LL Bean, gifts from Paul. The clothes fit perfectly and had been washed and pressed.

She found Paul in his expansive dining room. He lit up when he saw her and guided her to a chair at one end of the twenty-foot-long polished table, taking the chair beside her at the head of the table. Directly across from her was a huge, black-and-white marble fireplace that rose all the way to the tall ceiling.

Paul followed her line of sight. "If it weren't summer and I wasn't paying so much for air conditioning, I'd light a fire. Really makes this room homey."

"It's beautiful. Like the whole house."

"I'm so glad you like it here." He put his hand on top of hers and squeezed.

She resisted the urge to yank it away. *Must play the game.*

Jenny, a round motherly woman of sixty, served them tasty homemade chicken pot pies and a green salad full of fresh vegetables from the estate's garden. For dessert, Jenny brought out her special peach cobbler. To. Die. For.

Tired of masking her emotions while making small talk, Sam excused herself shortly after they finished. He walked her to her room and looked like he wanted to kiss her, but she just smiled, thanked him, and shut the door in his face. She kicked herself for the missed opportunity, but she was not ready to go there. Not yet. Hopefully the next day.

Sam downed her ulcer meds, threw on some new PJs with a cute retro kitchen appliance print, and brushed her teeth. After slipping between the cool sheets, she scanned the huge room. Her stomach went wonky and her limbs got jittery. Even with the canopy above her, she felt too vulnerable in the middle of the huge suite. Too exposed. Who knew what type of men Strong had hired? And how far did she trust Paul?

Searching the room, she settled on the closet. Her old reliable. Might work if it were big enough. She got out of bed, limped over, and found the space to be a huge, nearly-empty, walk-in affair. A few blankets and pillows were stored on the shelves above the clothes racks on either side, but that was it. The knot in her stomach eased. A perfect sleeping spot.

The bedding in the closet—along with the comforter and pillows from her bed— made a great makeshift mattress. She stuffed the bed with decorative pillows from the couch in the sitting area and pulled the sheets over the mass. Looked more or less like her sleeping form. While it wouldn't pass close inspection, she was sure she'd be awake before Paul came and got her. Shouldn't be a problem.

The floor squeaked outside her door. Her heart thumped hard. The guard. She couldn't let him know where she slept, it would defeat the whole purpose.

With her attention on the door to the hallway, she limped to the closet and quietly shut the door behind her. Despite the lack of a fully loaded rifle in her arms, she crawled into her new safe spot and went out like a light.

What felt like no more than two seconds later, Sam awoke to yelling.

Her heart pounding, she sat up and felt around in the darkness for her rifle, but couldn't find it. Adrenaline slammed her. Where was her gun?

Wait. This wasn't home. Shit! She was at Paul's. Burke had betrayed her. A wall of depression slammed her to the bedding. Groaning, she curled into a ball.

"How did she escape?" came Paul's frantic voice from her bedroom.

She almost called out to him, but thought better of it. Could her escape really be this simple? Could she sneak out while they searched for her? Maybe. She'd stay put until they left and then run for it. Where were her clothes? Damn it, in the other room. No worries, she could grab them on the way out.

"Men! Check the grounds," Paul barked. "Sam escaped somehow during the night."

"Impossible," came a gravelly voice. "We were right here. We would have heard her. And her windows are rigged to sound the alarm if they're moved."

Good to know. No exiting through her windows.

"Check to make sure," Paul clipped out.

"Danny, check it out," said Gravel Voice.

"Where is it?" came a different voice. Male but younger and higher.

"Thought I showed you," Gravel Voice replied. "The relays all lead to a central control right there near the curtain pull. Yeah, that. It's disguised. Flip up the plastic cover."

A high-pitched alarm sounded and was quickly shut off.

At least she knew where the alarm was located. Tuck that little piece of information away for later. She may be able to escape from the room yet.

"Damn. How did she get out?" Paul demanded.

"What if she didn't get out?" Gravel Voice asked. "Did you check the bathroom?"

"Yeah, first thing," Paul replied. "Shit, she's slippery. Should have figured she'd make a break for it. Any other ideas?"

"The closet. Pillows are missing from the couch and yesterday there was a comforter on the bed."

"You're right. How did I miss that?"

Footfalls on the hardwood floor increased in volume as he approached the closet door. Sam shut her eyes and pretended to be asleep.

The door squeaked open and light flooded inside.

Crap. There went all her hopes of escape for the moment.

Not only that, now Paul would know she slept in her closet. Tensing, her body flamed with anger. One method of self-protection gone. Sloppy, very sloppy. She should have set the alarm clock the night before.

"Thank God." Paul let out a huge sigh of relief. "Sam?"

She snored a teeny bit for effect.

"Jesus, she's dead asleep. Sam, honey?"

He touched her foot and she sat straight up with a yell, scaring him back a few feet.

She clutched her chest. "Where...? Where am I?"

"You're in a closet at my house." He turned to the three hulks behind him. "It's okay, guys, you can go."

"Okay, Paul." The large men left.

Leaving her facing a questioning Paul. "Why are you in the closet?"

"I'm not going through this again. I don't want to talk about it." She stood, her ankle and leg complaining loudly. Groaning, she grabbed the pillow and comforter.

He backed up and allowed her to pass. "Again?"

"Never mind." She limped over to the bed, threw the comforter on top and climbed in between the cold sheets. She lay down, ignoring his intense scrutiny. "What time is it?"

"Eight."

Even though she'd slept far past the time she'd intended to, this intrusion merited a glare. She couldn't have him breaking in on her. Not if she was going to escape. "Is there a reason you woke me up?"

"You slept ten hours. I was worried." No duplicity on his face, only concern. The Nice Paul again. He had no idea how hard it was for her to believe him.

Wait. *Ten hours?* Jesus, she rarely slept more than eight. She yawned. "I'm fine. I've been known to sleep for longer." Not. "Are we leaving?"

He walked over and sat on the end of her bed. "No, not yet. Tomorrow." He sent her a sweet smile.

The bastard had the audacity to look hideously lovely this morning. Wearing a blue polo shirt that brought out the deep color of his eyes and drew attention to his sinewy biceps, he looked and smelled wonderful. Fresh, showered and shaved. Jeans and sneakers completed his homey look. She might actually like him if he wasn't such a devious jerk.

"And where are we going?"

"I have to hide you. Larry is starting to ask questions."

Her stomach wrenched and she sat up, her heart pounding.

Grabbing her hand, he squeezed it. "Don't worry. He won't get you," he said with confidence. He let go and rubbed his brow. "He doesn't know I have you, but he will. This a small town."

She wanted out of there. She'd feel a lot safer alone. "So when do I talk to these people? When can we leave?"

He patted her leg. "Tomorrow. I'm setting up the meetings."

Biting her lip, her brow furrowed to the point of pain.

Paul sent her a nice, genuine smile and gripped her leg. "Take it easy. I won't let anything happen to you."

She settled back and pulled up the comforter. "I guess I'll have to trust you. But I am worried about testifying against Larry. Without the murder weapon, it's all hearsay. He could accuse me of killing Dad."

"You can still help me convince some very important people what kind of a guy he is. They're already on the brink of defection, they just need a push. Your story is very compelling, Sam. That and the other information that's just coming to light should sway them. We can't let Larry take the White House."

She wrapped the covers around her tighter. "So how can you hide me and have me convince these important people at the same time?"

"The two meetings I have scheduled tomorrow are at top secret facilities, but when we're off site problems may come, so I've got a solid plan in place to protect you."

A plan hopefully she could foil. She needed the details. Appeal to his vanity and get him bragging.

"Patriots know all about Paul Strong," he said. "And so do Larry and his buddies. But neither of them know about another persona of mine that owns a really nice place in Texas."

She smirked. "Sounds like an oxymoron."

Laughing, he said, "No. I think you'll like the house. Nice pool, nice spot. And once we settle you in, I'll arrange some more secret meetings to build the case against Larry. I'll make sure nothing happens to you, Sam."

Something about the look in his eye made her want to trust him. While Paul's broken nose, thick jaw and heavy brow reeked tough-guy, his energy was gentle, yet confident. Yes, his morals were ambiguous, but she got the feeling he could be loyal.

Not that she was going to hang around long enough to find out.

"Good," she said, relaxing back against the pillows. The mattress was fifty times more comfortable than the makeshift closet bed had been. "And no offense on the slag on Texas. I had a Texan boyfriend once and had the worst vacation of my life visiting his family. Left a bad taste in my mouth."

He smiled at her warmly. "Then I'll be happy to change that opinion and give you some better memories."

"You don't have a toxic, fat aunt who likes to pick on people until they cry, do you?"

Chuckling, he shook his head. "My family's all gone. Well, mostly, but none in Texas."

"Cool. Sounds great."

Super great, actually. Texas was much closer to Portland and Burke's weaponry than DC. Once in the land of beers, steers and queers, all she had to do was convince Strong she was falling in love with him, get him to drop his guard, and then she could disappear.

And bye-bye Tyrell.

TWENTY

Burke ground his toes against the bottoms of his Versace black leather half boots and kneaded his hands while Rollin drove a black Humvee through an upscale residential district of Washington DC. Banana snored in the back.

"Strong's mansion is in a swanky part of town, Forest Hills. Had a girlfriend once who lived out here," Rollin observed in an upbeat tone. "Rich girl who wanted to screw the bad boy. Never told her I had as much money as she did. Course, not as much as Strong. Did Bobby tell you? He found two more personas of Strong's. Total so far, the dude is sitting on almost a billion."

Burke's neck twinged. He massaged out the pain. Strong hit his competitiveness buttons hard. Bastard had even more money and connections than he did.

"Wonder why he still works," Rollin continued. "Why do something low level like infiltrating us through dating Sam? Excitement of the front lines?"

Burke's blood turned to fire and he dug his fingers into his thigh. Who knew what garbage Strong had filled her head with?

Rollin glanced over. "You okay, buddy?"

"I will turn him into pâté," Burke bit out through gritted teeth.

Rollin grinned, then shot him a look that said he was just about to tell a bad joke. "Be pretty *strong* flavored, don't you think?" As expected, he burst out laughing.

Burke sent him an obligatory eye roll. Sam laughed at her own jokes, too. He closed his eyes. He could almost hear her. Smell her. Feel her. Taste her. He rubbed his aching chest. His heart hurt like she'd blown it apart.

"Dude, no worries. We're on this one. Emma overnighted the note. We give that to Danny and Sam's out by tomorrow." Rollin turned onto a six-lane thoroughfare and merged with the mid-morning traffic.

"How would you feel if the tables were turned? I just found her, Rollin. She's my other half. She's the woman I've been searching for. And she's in the hands of another man. A man she kissed and—"

Rollin shot him a deadly cold look. "Yeah, got no idea how that feels."

Burke's face went hot and he winced at his stupidity. He'd been the other man kissing Emma. "Sorry." He sighed heavily and turned his attention out the window. "Karma is a nasty little mistress, isn't she?"

Rollin gave him a knowing smile and a small nod, then focused on the road. After a pause, he turned, splitting his attention. "You really liked her, didn't you?"

"Who?" Burke kept his expression neutral, feigning innocence. Those memories made him want to jump out of the moving car.

"Emma."

Burke waved his hand. "It's history, my friend."

Rollin shrugged. "Love's complicated. And technically, you met Emma first."

His gut contracted. "Yeah, and fucked with her head at a time she could least handle it. Stellar behavior."

"Hey, so did I. She had a fucking nuke, Burke. The torture thing was over the top, but you have to admit, it worked."

Burke grimaced. "Technically, it worked. But I hurt someone I cared about, and inflicted permanent mental damage on her. I know she still has nightmares."

"That whole thing was a mess."

"I fucked up. Fine, I would have brought down a small cell of al-Qaeda. But what I risked was not worth it. My life sucked without my friends. You're the only person who's stood by me all these years. No matter what knuckle-headed shit I do, you forgive me. You're a much better man than I."

Rollin sent him a big grin. "Awwww. Love you, too, big guy." He gave him a punch on the shoulder.

"I know what we do is important, but it's just a fucking job. I have to have some balance and I haven't in years. Since before I left home. I'm still shocked by what I did to Emma." He shuddered, his gut aching.

Rollin gripped his shoulder, tight. "Don't be hard on yourself, man. A lot of your crazy shit has worked. But no matter how smart you are, we're always blind to our own faults. I can't see my own shit for shit."

"Did anyone ever tell you that there's poetry to the way you speak?"

Rollin laughed.

Burke smiled and stared out the window, picturing Sam's slightly parted lips, the arousal on her face. He frowned. "You think Strong loves Sam?"

Rollin lifted one shoulder. "Don't know. He's a tough cat to read. I mean, I hope he likes her so he treats her well until we can spring her."

He had to focus. Sam's wellbeing was all that mattered. His heart didn't. His needs didn't. Get her to safety, then worry about their relationship.

He rubbed Sam's engagement ring in his pocket. He'd bought it for her three days before. As long as he held onto the ring, he had hope.

Rollin touched his earpiece. "Bobby, go ahead. Strong's moving her tomorrow? I hope that message gets here. Sam's not going to believe anyone but Emma. We're pulling up at the safe house now."

"Danny sent a message?" Burke asked.

"Yep. We have to act tonight."

"Good. Strong better not have touched her." Then he realized he'd spoken words aloud. His face warmed again, he raised an eyebrow, and focused his attention outside.

Luncheon was served in the dining room. Jenny served marinated skirt steak salads and homemade popovers with her special strawberry jam. Dee-lish. Sam tried not to be tempted by Paul's amazing life; she'd rarely been exposed to such luxury. She'd thought Burke had been rich, but his wealth couldn't compare to Paul's.

The vast hardwood-floored room seemed bigger in the light of day. Not to mention more beautiful. Dark wood paneling went halfway up the tall walls, with light-gold paint above accented with cream-colored crown molding. Five intricately designed wrought-iron light fixtures hung down the center of the arched ceiling. Several landscapes in gilded frames decorated the room. Two sets of French doors flanked the massive marble fireplace and led out to the expansive pool area. Gorgeous.

But the joint was still a prison. A mink-lined prison.

Sam pushed a radish around her plate.

"You done?"

At her nod, Paul pulled out her chair and escorted her to the morning room of the house. The sun shone brightly through the tall windows. The view of the superb gardens outside was spectacular. All the plants seemed to be blooming. An explosion of reds, blues, yellows and whites filled the yard, contrasting beautifully against the vibrant green foliage.

"Wow. Beautiful, Paul. Beats the hell out of the Eichler." Sam said, settling on a large overstuffed cream couch. She sunk down into its plush cushions. Money sure could buy a lot of nice things.

Like Burke's furniture and apartment. Her gut burned and she wiped the man from her thoughts. Betrayer.

"I really like the Eichler," Paul said, sitting next to her, a bit too closely.

The heat of his hard thigh pressed against hers made her want to move, but she needed to play the game.

"Reminds me of my house growing up," Paul continued. "My family didn't come from money. We all worked our asses off for what we got."

"Good for you. Me, too. I mean, my family, too."

His gaze was a little too intense and needy, so she shifted her focus to the glass-topped, carved mahogany coffee table.

"Your father built up that hardware store," he said.

Her father's face appeared in her mind. Sam closed her eyes to block out the pain.

He grabbed her hand and squeezed. "I'm sorry."

"No, please. Don't worry. I'm just not used to talking about them." She looked out the window at a purple hydrangea. "I had to eradicate them from my vocabulary. I couldn't think about them. I haven't even been back to the East Coast since I walked in on Larry and my mother. It's hard even being near New Hampshire. I haven't even visited my parents' graves." Her throat swelled and her eyes teared, but she couldn't afford to fall apart now.

Ever since she'd told the story, the sorrow had been getting more and more difficult to keep at bay. She'd kept an ocean of pain dammed since she was sixteen. Only small amounts had leaked through. Once the dam broke, she'd drown. And she couldn't allow that to happen until she brought down Senator Evil.

Swallowing hard, she regained control.

Paul put his arms around her and she leaned into him. She'd love to resist, but with the war going on inside her and the intense loneliness Burke's treachery had caused, she needed someone to be there for her. And Paul smelled really good this morning, and his arms felt wonderful.

But not nearly as wonderful as Burke's. Anger flared at her stupid emotions and she tensed her fists. Here she was being held by a hunk and all she could think about was that demon. Sick.

Needing to block Burke's face from her mind, she looked up at Paul.

His blue eyes twinkling, he smiled and nuzzled her. Better. Thank God, the man was a hottie. Pleasant symmetrical face, nice lips and heavy jaw.

And he was being very sweet with her.

Reaching up, she touched his slightly rough, but warm cheek and he leaned into her palm. *Well, look what we have here.* Looked like a giant hunky can of Burke-Away to her. She'd fuck that jerk right out of her head.

Moving forward, she gently kissed Paul. He ran his hand over the back of her head and deepened the kiss. Tender. Loving. Sweet. He tasted good and he was a fine kisser. Her body warmed and a small pulse went through her sex.

It wasn't licking-the-high-voltage-line like kissing Burke. But it was nice. And reassuring. To have anyone there at this point was a mighty gift.

Sam ran her hands over his bulging arms and up to his neck, then cupped his face. He groaned and his kiss turned urgent.

Warning bells sounded in the back of her brain. This wasn't right.

He broke it off, breathing heavy, seeming a bit stunned. "God, Sam." He sat back and blew out a breath, like he was overcome. His pants were tented, looked like he had quite the package.

Crap. She couldn't sleep with him. Paul might be hot, but no man who'd done this kind of shit to her passed through the Gates to the Pooty. He'd lied to her a million times, and crossed umpteen boundaries. No way would she whore herself out for her plan.

But she couldn't help but admit that as slimy and opportunistic as he was, she enjoyed his company. She smiled at him warmly.

"Sam, you are so—you're on fire, lady. Pure fire. But I..."

She patted him on the knee. "You're right. I don't want to go any further until this is all over. I can't do that to myself or you. I've already had my heart broken once where you're concerned." *Good one, Sam.*

He bought her lie and gathered her in his arms. "I'm sorry. How could I have known we'd click like this?"

Sorry, dude. You can't comprehend what I had with Burke. "You couldn't. I just think it's going to take time."

"You think you can forgive me?" he asked softly and ran his hand down her back.

"Sure. But first we have to take care of Larry. Or I won't live long enough to date."

Contrasting micro-expressions crossed his features. Curiosity, a slight flare of anger, a tinge of vulnerability, some affection, then he became guarded. "What about Burke?"

Ah-hah. Jealousy. Great weapon. "What about him?"

Paul carefully examined her face. "How do you feel about him?"

"He's a creep and I want to kick his ass," she said with no duplicity.

Paul's expression remained shielded and he squeezed her. "You still love him?"

He wanted her to say no. Damn, he really did like her. Good. Maybe she could lure him to his bed, use her tranquilizer dart, and sneak out.

Right. Past six guards. She wished she'd grabbed a handful of those darts when she'd had the chance.

His face fell and he let go. "That's okay, Sam, you don't have to answer."

Holy bejeebus, she'd completely forgotten to answer him! She grabbed his hand. "No, Paul. I'm sorry, I'm tired and I went off on a mental tangent about beating his face bloody. He's a malignancy."

He chuckled and his body relaxed. But there was still doubt on his face.

She had to tell him the partial truth. "Of course, I still have feelings for him. I don't shut off that quickly. But I can tell you one thing, I like you more. I always have. Since the moment I met you." She looked away and allowed a bit of pain to cross her face. "Even though you were using me."

He hugged her. "No, I wasn't."

She sent him an incredulous stare.

He reddened, looked down briefly, then met her eyes. But he didn't lessen his hold on her. "I mean, I was, but this job has crossed over to the personal for me. I knew you were a nice girl. I was hoping you weren't. But after our first date, I was smitten. No lie. I didn't feel good about setting up that sniper attack. But I had orders."

She pursed her lips. "You must have been overjoyed when you figured out I had the package."

"Pretty much." He laughed and released one arm, keeping the other firmly around her shoulders. "I'd been up in Seattle, too. Missed you by minutes."

She jerked her head back. "What?"

"Yeah." His gaze shifted to arm of the chair, the line between his eyes deepened, and his gaze went haunted. "That was ugly. I got to Joseph too late. I know you two were friends." Paul shook his head and appeared disgusted. "Made me sick."

Her belly tensed and sorrow tightened her throat. "He was a good man."

"Shouldn't have happened."

"I didn't think the Cabal cared about people."

He snorted. "Sure we do. Keep the populous happy and uninformed and productive so they make us tons of money. By the way? We call ourselves The Group, not *The Cabal*. That's the Patriots' crap. But the Group was never involved in such messy problems before Larry came to power. Our motto was always: *we don't kill, we legislate.*"

"You scare me."

He smiled, then shrugged. "Way the world works, and it's worked well for me. Until Larry. Larry's philosophy—well you know Larry— kill, maim, torture and blackmail."

She fought a shudder. "He's a gem, all right."

"But people are dumping him like a two-week-old hot dog."

"I hope so."

Paul rubbed her shoulder. "What do you think? Can we start over?" he asked with a soulful look.

A surge of victory was followed shortly by a jolt of shame. This spy game sucked. But since she didn't have lots of money and weapons, she had to use the resources at her disposal. She softened her expression and took him by the hand. "I'd like to."

Paul smiled and kissed her on the forehead, warming her. "From here on out, I won't lie to you. I want you in my life, Sam. I don't know what will happen, but I'll do my best to make it up to you. I'm sorry I put you in danger and I'm sorry I kidnapped you. Scared you. That's why you slept in the closet, huh? Because you're afraid."

She looked away to hide her true feelings. But maybe a bit of truth would hook him better. "Yeah. Just wish I'd had my rifle. Then I really sleep well."

His brow wrinkled and he brought her close to him. "You shouldn't have to live like that, Sam. Is it all because of Larry?"

"Yeah. All I care about is getting sleep, so whatever it takes is good with me."

"I want to make you feel safe, Sam. I won't hurt you and I'll protect you."

"Thanks, Paul." *Like I'd trust a bastard like you.*

He kissed her on the cheek, then pulled away and gripped her knee. "Listen, I have to do some work in my office. You read in here or whatever you want. I'll have two guards with you to make sure you stay safe and the Patriots don't kidnap you. They're planning something. Tonight apparently."

She gasped and her gut recoiled to the back of her ribcage. Scary news. "Really? They want me back? Why?"

He gave her a look like it was all so obvious. "Burke?"

Her nerves flamed, her muscles tensed and she wanted to scream. *"He's trying to get me back by kidnapping me?"*

"Apparently."

She punched her palm. "I'll kill him if he comes near me. That creep! Why won't they just leave me alone? They have the evidence. They have the murder weapon. They have everything."

"Tyrell wants you. He's probably figured out that I'm not delivering. The Patriots want to do business with him. Put it together."

Her body chilled and the steak salad felt like it curdled in her stomach. Would the guys really hand her over to Tyrell, knowing that he'd kill her?

Carter Blackstone was all about the greater good. One person's life versus the control over the entire United States of America? Patriots may hate giving her to Tyrell, but they did all kinds of horrible stuff in the name of protecting the country.

Burke might object to the plan, but Captain ran the group. She couldn't picture Rollin handing her over to Tyrell, either, but Strong had made an excellent point earlier: she'd only known the Patriots for seven months. Not long enough to make an accurate judgment.

All of them were damaged. They'd seen too much war and had lived through nightmarish horror. They were all twisted. And completely untrustworthy.

Paul could be making up the story to control her, but at this point, that was immaterial. She had to avoid the Patriots and escape the Fed.

Paul ran his fingers over the tight aching line between her eyes.

She jumped, her heart thumping.

He smiled. "Don't worry, Sam."

She let out a long breath and returned his smile.

Paul kissed two fingers and pressed them to her lips. "I'll see you in a few, okay?"

The look in his eye derailed her for a split second and she felt a tinge of guilt.

He stood, winked at her, and left the room.

She shook her head to clear it. Paul was a manipulative jerk. The enemy.

Her mind tuned to the challenge at hand: escape. She'd use the Patriots' attack to ditch out. Her pulse jumped higher. This was just the break she needed.

Getting up, she stretched and decided to "explore" the mansion. She'd pretend to be examining her future home while searching for escape routes. Freedom was a mere few hours away.

After studying every inch of the house—trailed by two guards— she had many ideas. Number one, getting rich someday. Wow, what a place. She felt like she was in an episode of *Lifestyles of the Rich and Famous*. The tour the night before had seem sort of surreal because she'd been so locked in her head. Now that she was really paying attention, she was astonished by the beauty and grace of the house. While it reeked money, Paul hadn't overdone it, the mansion was decorated tastefully. Perfectly.

More importantly, due to the many entrances and exits, there were several avenues of escape. No matter how the Patriots attacked, she had a way out.

She retired to her room "to nap" and avoid Paul. She was about to betray him. Strong and the Patriots might like playing with people's emotions to do their jobs, but these manipulative games weren't her style.

Sam flopped on the bed and stared up at the blue and white stripes on the canopy above her. Music wafted through the open window from a radio in the garden below. Gardener must be listening to it. Sounded like an oldies station.

A familiar song came on. *Midnight at the Oasis,* by Maria Muldaur.

Her belly hollowed, her muscles tightened, and everything went dark.

Mom and Dad's song. From the high school dance when they first got together.

Tears stung her eyes and her mood went into free fall.

Her parents disapproving faces glared from the reaches of her mind. *Why did you kill us? All we did was love you.*

She curled into a ball, and her face and stomach burned. She didn't deserve anyone being nice to her. She didn't deserve this luxury. She hadn't even deserved Burke's false love.

For the last sixteen years, she'd been in a bubble of denial: completely immersed in her fairy tale life in San Mateo. She'd buried her past. Never dealt with the deaths of her parents, nor faced her culpability. But all those old truths were surfacing now. The two people she loved most in the world were dead because of her weakness.

She had to ignore the voice deep within her that kept telling her she was the victim—the one Burke had exploited. No matter how hard she'd worked, no matter how hard she'd tried to make up for killing her parents by being a good person—the person they wanted her to be —she had failed. And no matter how much she wanted to foist the blame on Larry, she had to take responsibility for her actions.

In retrospect, she'd deserved Larry's gunshot. A part of her wished he'd had better aim. Anything to take away this horrid pain. The shame was unbearable.

But then Larry would have gotten away with murder. She wished she could bring him to justice through the courts so everyone would know the horrible things he'd done, but the Patriots had taken away the gun and the evidence. Leaving her only one choice.

Envisioning her future, she saw herself in a jail cell alone reading a newspaper. *Senator Lawrence Tyrell Murdered!* the headline proclaimed. The fire in her stomach diminished, surprising her. She realized she was no longer afraid of prison. Or death. In fact, she'd welcome both.

A soft knock came on the door.

She jumped and her stomach knotted. *Please don't be Paul.* "Yeah?"

One of Paul's security guards, a young blond hulk with a square head named Danny, walked into her room carrying a tray. On top sat two bottles of water and a plate of fresh fruit.

Sam relaxed into the bed. Good. She was too tired to deal with her Fed host.

Danny set it on the table next to her, sent her an intense stare, and moved his attention to the tray. Then back to her. "Read it in the bathroom, no cameras in there," he whispered without moving his lips. He gave her a brief nod, turned, and left the room without looking back.

Her heart rate leapt high and she casually perused the fruit. Beneath the plate, a small white piece of paper peeked out. She palmed it and chose a piece of nectarine. After eating the fruit, she swung her legs off the bed, and hobbled to the bathroom.

Her body vibrating with excitement, she opened the note.

Emma's handwriting.

She took a short breath and her heart beat faster. Then her gut hardened and her teeth gritted tight. Of course, they'd deploy her best friend against her. Dickheads.

Sam,

I hope you're okay, I'm super worried about you. And so are the guys. Burke is apparently out of his mind with worry over you. And so is Rollin.

Fire filled her and she crumpled up the note. How dare they use Emma! "If they think I'm gonna read these lies," she whispered to herself. She held the wadded letter over the toilet.

Just as she was about to let go, curiosity got the better of her.

"Pickles." She straightened out the paper and kept reading.

The guys are not on Larry Tyrell's side, they're on your side. They retrieved the gun for you, not to protect Larry. Burke knows you're mad about the tracking devices, but he said they were to protect you, not hurt you.

Sam had to clamp her hand over her mouth to halt the scream. What bullshit! Emma probably even believed the lies. "I should throw this note away. I shouldn't be reading it."

You have to trust me. You have to trust the guys. You have to let us help you. You know I wouldn't lie to you. I'm your soul sister, remember that. I would never do anything to hurt you and neither would my boyfriend.

"You love me, but you've been brainwashed, honey," Sam said under her breath.

Burke wouldn't hurt you either. I know he was an idiot to me, but I understand him more now. He's a really good man and he loves you. More than he ever loved me. (I hope Rollin doesn't see this note.) Rollin said he's been ranting and raving about killing Strong ever since he took you. And he's hurting. Rollin said he's never seen Burke like this.

"What bullshit!" Sam whispered loudly.

Anyway, here's the message: ignore the first attempt to rescue you which will come around eight o'clock tonight. Let Strong protect you. Do what he says. Make him think you're on his side. Just make sure you're in your room alone by one this morning. Danny will come for you. Do what he says and you'll be fine. I'll be waiting here for you. Please don't do anything stupid and run, okay?

"Ha. Running is not stupid. Letting those bastards near me is stupid."

I know you're confused, but check your heart. I know your emotions are clouding your judgment about Burke, but think about Rollin. About me. Would we really screw you over?

No. Confusion engulfed her and a sob caught in her throat. She wanted to believe Emma so badly. But she couldn't. Emma might be on her side, but she was deluded. The Patriots needed control over her to protect Larry. Couldn't have some murder witness running around loose, or worse, in Strong's camp. Patriots had to be manipulating Emma.

This is the truth: the guys are on your side and I'm on your side. Strong isn't. Love you. See you tonight. Flush this note now.

-Emma

Sam loved Emma, but her bestie had smoked a big Patriot fatty. And as a result was temporarily untrustworthy. And since Sam's life was temporary, she'd not only lost her parents and everyone else she loved, she'd lost Emma.

Tears rolled down her cheeks. An aching emptiness filled her. Horrible, but almost a cleansing of her fake life in San Mateo. A very final ending.

Samantha Murdock was dead.

And Amanda Hutchins had just risen from the grave.

TWENTY-ONE

When Sam joined Paul in the drawing room at five for cocktails, he was visibly nervous: tapping his hands at his sides, his eyes a bit too wide. Clearly upset about the Patriots' rescue operation. He kept looking to his men like he expected to be attacked and wanted to ensure he had back up.

"Looks like you're nervous about the Patriots' plans. Am I in any real danger?" she finally asked, leaning her crutches against the wall.

He sent her a worried glance and tried to cover his fear. "No. But I did just get confirmation. Your former friends are coming for you tonight at eight."

Just like Emma's note had said.

She jerked her head back in fake surprise. "So why aren't we taking off?"

His expression remained grave. "Because that's what they want. They're trying to flush you out so they can grab you. I can defend you best from here."

"Do you have a safe room?"

"I do. It's where you're going in a while, if that's okay with you."

"Fine." Even though, escaping from a safe room might not be the easiest thing. She'd been thinking she'd use the first attempt to ditch out on Paul and the Patriots, since the Patriots wouldn't be expecting her to run. But that might not work. She'd have to stay on guard and be ready to jump when the opportunity presented itself.

They made small talk and had an early dinner in the dining room.

After dessert, she grabbed her crutches and Paul escorted her to his wine cellar. On the way, she made sure to groan and wince a few times to fool him into believing she was still badly injured.

The wine cellar was immense. About thirty feet long by twenty feet wide, half of the back wall and one adjacent wall were completely covered in wine bottles. A hell of a collection. Sam began salivating. He walked to the middle of the long wall and reached through the shelving between bottles.

A whirring sound filled the air and the half wall of wine at the far end of the room slid to its left about six feet, revealing a solid steel door.

Her throat went tight and her feet itched to run. Was she to be entombed? Had she misjudged him?

He read her expression and said, "I can't lock you in there. Don't worry. Once it's occupied, it only opens from the inside."

Good, maybe she could slip out when he was upstairs defending his house.

She checked around the top of the wine cellar for cameras. Three were pointed at the safe room door from various angles. Not good.

He held his palm up to the identification pad—which illuminated —and the giant door clicked. Using his weight and some muscle, Paul swung open the foot-thick steel door. Looked like a vault. He stepped inside and flipped on the overhead lights revealing a surprisingly big and luxurious—although windowless—room with Berber carpet, two leather couches and an entertainment system with a plasma screen mounted on the wall. Bunk beds lay just beyond the couches, and a small but full kitchen was along the opposite wall. At the back of the cement room were shelves filled with canned and dry goods, and a fridge. Next to the fridge was a door.

"Bathroom is through there," Strong said, pointing to the closed door. "But if you hear a fight going on upstairs, don't flush, okay? That will alert them that someone is down here."

"Okay."

"And don't come out until I come get you. Let me give you a signal in case they have a gun to my head or something. I doubt they'll get this far, but those guys are dangerous and tenacious."

"So what's the word that lets me know you're being held hostage?"

"I'll say 'They're gone'."

She nodded. "Good one. They're gone. I can remember that."

He put a hand on her shoulder. "I don't have the men to spare to have one down here with you to protect you. And I'm sorry, but I can't trust you with your own weapon."

She gripped his forearm. "Paul, I understand. But I'm not running. I need you. I need your strength and your help to get Larry." She half expected her nose to grow.

He softened, brought her to him and kissed her.

One more stamp on her ticket to Hell. A few more and she'd have a full card.

He pulled away and his gaze turned vulnerable. "I really care about you, Sam. I hope you see that soon. I know you're shell-shocked, but…" He kissed her again, this time more passionately.

She allowed herself to enjoy the kiss. Why not? Might be the last one she ever got.

After Paul left, Sam checked the room for cameras and found four, covering the whole area. Bummer.

Ensuring that none of the cameras had a good shot at the screen, Sam settled on one of the couches with Paul's iPad. Nothing sensitive on it, he only used it for entertainment. But she couldn't believe he'd left it for her. First thing she did was go to Google Maps and study the immediate area. She quickly planned several escape routes from the neighborhood. But she needed a car. The residential area was high-end with large estates. No businesses or shops. She'd stick out if she were walking.

She wished she knew the Patriots' plan beyond using Danny to spring her.

Her stomach knotted. Even if she got away initially, escape would not be easy. Both the Patriots and Paul had access to satellite surveillance and facial recognition software. Paul knew she planned to assassinate Larry. He was CIA. He could call out the big guns on her. He could post her picture in the media.

Number one priority: she had to put as much distance between herself and DC as quickly as possible without taking public transportation. They'd be checking the airports, rental car places, buses, and trains. Had to watch out for traffic cameras, store cameras, and bridge and toll crossings.

So where could she get a fast ride out of town without drawing attention?

Truck stop. Chat up a nice trucker and leave with him that night.

And hope she didn't pick a fucking serial murderer.

Nice thought, Sam.

Once she got far enough away, she needed a place to hide where the people wouldn't ask questions. Sleazy motel? No, too creepy.

Battered women's shelter. That's right! One of her old plans. Genius! A little surge of hope rose inside her. Good one.

What about disguises? Paul might have something she could use. Even a hat and glasses would help.

Sam rubbed her arms like she was cold and searched the room. In a dresser under the bunk beds, she found a stash of clothes. Right on top was an old baseball cap and a big black Washington Nationals hooded sweatshirt. Perfect! Even though it was warm in the room, she put on the sweatshirt, careful to tuck the baseball cap into the front pocket, out of the view of the cameras.

After mentally running through several escape scenarios, she settled into the couch and tried to distract herself with a game of solitaire.

As eight o'clock approached, her tension rose with each passing minute and her foot tapped progressively faster. She hoped no one got injured in the "first" attack. Even though Burke, Paul, and the Patriots were her enemies—and they were all knuckleheads—she didn't want any of them getting hurt.

Of course, if they all annihilated each other, she could just walk out.

Niggling doubts began to annoy her. What if Emma had been telling the truth and the Patriots had recovered that murder weapon to help her? What if they *had* decided to bring down Larry?

No. *Remember what Burke did to you to get hold of that information packet.*

Besides, the Patriots had known all along that Larry had been sleeping with fourteen-year-olds and that hadn't dissuaded them from putting him in the White House. Neither had his other criminal behavior. But even a snake like Strong had been turned against Tyrell after hearing her story.

Sam flashed on all those barbecues and parties with the guys. Her long conversation about ethics and morals with Carter. Zane's story about taking down a corrupt Congressman. Stefan's love of Christ. The way Rollin cared for Emma. None of it was faked. They were all good moral men.

The note began to ring true.

Her reality slipped, and she lost her bearings. Disoriented, she lay back against the couch, a thousand questions bombarding her mind. What if Burke really loved her?

She slapped her face, hard. "Wake the fuck up. You are at war. You can't trust anyone." Jumping to her feet, she began pacing on her crutches.

"But I don't want to be blind. I have to look at this. I have to consider it. Okay, so let's just say Emma is telling the truth," Sam whispered as she walked the length of the room. "Suppose the Patriots are on your side now. What then? Like they're gonna let you take down Larry? Like Burke won't imprison you somewhere? And who knows? Patriots could change their minds about Larry at any time. No matter what, you can't trust them. Stay on point here. All are the enemy for now. Even Emma. You go this alone."

Larry's handsome evil face leered at her. She formed her hand into a gun, aimed at his imaginary face, and pulled the trigger. Ka-blam, she envisioned a bullet piercing his ugly forehead. Seeing that same surprised look that was on her father's face. The same shock. "Goodbye, Larry, and see you in Hell," she muttered.

Clock read eight fifteen. Sam strained to hear, but no noises came from upstairs. She was so jittery, she couldn't stop pacing. Why weren't the Patriots attacking?

Were they testing her? To see if she told Strong? Determine if she was brainwashed? WTF?

By nine o'clock, Sam was convinced that the Patriots had lied to Emma. Which just proved their untrustworthiness.

But why would they go to all that trouble of sending a note filled with misinformation? What were they up to? Hopefully, they'd been truthful about the visit at one in the morning. She had to get out of there.

At nine-thirty, a faint knock came on the door. "It's me, Sam, open up." Paul.

She hesitated. No safeword. Was the coast clear?

"It's cool, Sam. Unless you like staying in there. Safer than the closet."

She snorted, opened the door, and made a face at him.

He shot her an easy grin and seemed very relieved. "They didn't show. Just got word that they found out we were ready for them. Unfortunately, the world of the covert is actually quite small. And, damn, people who deal with secrets for a living sure have big mouths."

She chuckled. "Are you positive they're not coming?"

"Sure," he said with a definitive nod. "Just saw live feed of Hanson, Cherlenko, Blackstone and Powers getting on the Patriots' jet and I watched their plane take off. My source said they're responding to an attack on a friend in California. I'll know more soon."

Had Paul staged the attack to draw them away? Either that or the Patriots had lied to Emma.

Emma! Her heart rate accelerated and she hugged herself. "Did they say who got attacked? Was it Emma?"

"No, I think it was a Patriot, not her." He sent her an uneasy glance. "But you shouldn't worry about her, Sam. She's with them, she's not your friend anymore. They'll use her to get to you. Expect it."

Did he know? She chewed on her lower lip and looked down at the wheat colored carpet. "Disturbing idea."

He ran his hand down her arm and caught her hand. "You've been drawn into a lonely world, Sam. But I'm here for you." Pulling her to him, he hugged her.

Hopefully, she wouldn't accidentally get kidnapped by the Patriots. She didn't want to face Burke. Or Emma. Or Rollin.

She forced her mind to quiet. Escape was all that mattered. She'd worry about the future in the future.

He pushed away, checked out her sweatshirt and cocked an eyebrow. "Cold?"

She nodded. "I get cold when I get scared. Is it okay if I wear it?" She hoped he didn't notice that she was sweating. Nor that she had his baseball cap in the hoodie's front pocket.

His face etched with sympathy. "Of course, but you have no reason to be scared."

She squeezed him and picked up her crutches. "Thanks, Paul." *You fool.*

He walked her to her door and clearly wanted to come in.

Taking him by the hand, she said, "I'd love nothing more than to seduce you right now, but it wouldn't be fair."

"I know what I'm getting into, Sam." He moved a step closer, his expression full of longing.

She put her hand to his broad chest. "Yeah, but I don't. And I can't separate my emotions from sex. I sleep with you and I'm yours. I don't want to make that sort of commitment right now. Not when my head is so messed up. You're too nice. I don't want to hurt either of us."

A glow of ownership grew in his eyes. He thought he had her. All he had to do was wait her out for a few more days. Poor deluded idiot.

He kissed her, but didn't push. When he pulled away, dark lust and raw hunger steamed in his blue eyes. But he had amazing composure. He sent her a cute smile, kissed two fingertips and pressed them to her lips.

The gesture was so genuine, so him, so sweet, it tweaked her heart.

She hated using people. Even people who were using her.

With a wink, he left and Sam closed the door.

She quietly put her pjs on over her clothes. Then she stuffed a pillowcase with her ulcer meds, Strong's hoodie, his baseball cap, and the clothes, cosmetics, and toiletries Jenny had gotten for her.

After applying an extra ace bandage to her ankle, she slipped into bed to wait. As she lay there, she thought of Paul's kindness that day. The image of his gun in her face and the heap of bloody bodies at Burke's followed. He was a jerk, she shouldn't feel bad about ditching him. But he did like her. The twinkle in his eyes, the way he admired her. And he'd been incredibly sweet to her since he found out the truth about Larry.

Damn her stupid gratitude!

She grabbed the notepad from the nightstand and jotted down a quick note.

Paul, I'm sorry, but I don't feel safe here. Thanks for protecting me from Larry and not obeying his orders. But I can't trust you. But I do like you and have since the day we met. Jenny is a treasure, your house is amazing, and your hospitality was over-the-top. And I enjoyed your company (when you weren't threatening me with a gun).

Have a good one, Mandy Hutchins

She stared at the signature. Her real name. Signed it without thinking. Wow. That was weird and totally unintentional. Her mind and identity were changing fast.

After stuffing the note under her pillow, she lay down and waited.

Ten minutes after one, her door opened, and Danny gestured to her.

Adrenaline fired her body like a rocket. Yay! Escape! She ripped off the covers, grabbed her crutches and the pillowcase of stuff, and was at the door in a heartbeat.

Danny put his fingers to his lips and whispered, "Follow me and don't stop for anything. And, no, they're not dead, they're asleep. I drugged them. But I couldn't get Paul to drink the spiked coffee. So be quiet."

Her heart beating hard, her palms sweating, she carefully followed Danny out into the dimly lit hallway. As she moved forward, her right crutch hit something and she almost tripped. The leg of a snoring guard. Dude's pants were nearly the same color as the navy runner on the hardwood floor.

Maneuvering around the large lump of a person, she hightailed it after the Patriots' henchman while paying close attention to the floor.

Danny and Paul didn't know—and neither did the Patriots—she was right on the verge of not needing the crutches. Her ankle was tender, but she could walk on it. And hopefully run when the time came.

Danny led her out to Paul's six-car garage and up to a large, black Buick. He popped the trunk.

Eying the dark scary space, Sam broke out in a sweat and her limbs went rubbery. "I have to get in there?"

The large man nodded. "Couldn't drug the gate guard. Too obvious. And he always checks the back seat. We're meeting Rollin not a mile from here. Short trip, Sam."

"Okay." She searched for the emergency handle that released the lid and found it fast. This might work fine. She threw her crutches and the pillowcase into the trunk and climbed inside.

Danny shut the trunk. Blackness enveloped her. Her muscles tensed and her heart beat harder. Out of the darkness came the glow of the emergency handle. She grabbed it.

He started the car and pulled out of the garage. Sam was jostled by the movement, but kept hold of the release latch, careful not to activate it.

The car stopped and idled at the gate.

"Danny? What's up?" came a deep, gruff voice.

"Roommate just called, my dog ate a battery. Gotta get him to emergency."

"Shit! Go, man, go. I hope Roscoe's okay."

"Thanks." Danny drove out the gate and turned right.

Her pulse quickening, Sam waited for the car to stop at the intersection two blocks up. Popping the trunk lock, she held the lid in place.

The car slowed to a crawl. But didn't come to a complete stop. She'd have to make a run for it.

Her body juiced, her muscles hard, she grabbed the pillowcase, let go of the trunk lid, leapt out, and landed on the asphalt. Her ankle hurt, but held her weight. Screw the crutches. She ran for cover.

Tires screeched. She glanced over her shoulder. Danny flung open the car door and leapt out.

While running as fast as her tender ankle could carry her, Sam dropped the pillowcase, reached inside her bra and withdrew the tranquilizer pen. Flipping off the top, she palmed the device, needle down.

His footfalls came up fast behind her and he grabbed her by the shoulders, hard. She wrenched out of his grip, turned, and jammed the pen into his thick neck.

Danny cried out, grabbed her wrist, and jerked it away from his neck. She yanked her arm back and got one step away before he caught her in a bear hug.

A second later, his arms went limp and she shoved him away. He staggered backward, his eyes rolled and closed, and he crumpled to the ground.

Sam stared down at his lifeless body. "Wow, it really worked! Wicked cool!" She dove down next to him and relieved him of his wallet, cell phone and gun, but nixed the idea of the Kevlar vest. No time.

After stuffing her new treasures into the pillowcase, she leapt to her feet and raced, limping, back to the sedan and hopped inside. She spun a U-ie and sped the other way, knowing the Patriots had to be right up the road on Albemarle, waiting for her. She followed her plan and hung a left onto Linnean Avenue and another left onto Brandywine. Hopefully, she could hit Connecticut Avenue before the Patriots caught onto her scam.

When she reached Connecticut, there was no sign of the men anywhere. Sam took a left and headed for Rock Creek and Potomac Parkway.

After a few miles, a surge of victory powered through her and she did a fist pump. "I rock!" She turned on the radio and Sir Mix-a-Lot came on with *Baby Got Back*. Cranking the sound, she car danced.

Freedom at last.

Thank God, she didn't have to see Burke! Especially if Emma had been telling the truth. She shuddered. She couldn't think about him now.

Only one thing mattered.

Larry was about to get blasted by his past.

Burke's gut stewed with fear and worry. "Something's wrong."

"Where the fuck are they?" Rollin demanded. "Danny called me not ten minutes ago. Shit, I don't want to move and give our position away. Captain, you see anything?"

"Nope. They haven't driven by here," Carter replied over the com.

"I don't like this," Burke said. If Strong hurt her, he'd tie the asshole's intestines around his neck.

Ty said, "How 'bout Catherine and I take a look?"

"I'll cover your position," Captain said.

Ty's SUV drove past Rollin and Burke, heading left down the wide, tree-lined street.

"Nothing so far," the Aussie reported.

"Catherine?" Captain asked.

"Dark as hell out here," she replied. "Is that how the rich people stay rich? By cheaping out on streetlights? You'd think they'd want the place lit up for security reasons."

"Holy shit," Ty exclaimed. Tires squealed over Burke's headset. "I almost ran him over!"

Burke's heart rate went into triple-time. What the fuck had happened?

"Cover me! Danny!" Catherine yelled. A car door slammed.

Burke wanted to magically transport to the scene. Sweat dripped from his forehead. "What's going on?" he demanded.

"Danny's lying in the middle of the road. For fuck's sake," Ty reported, sounding worried and upset.

"Where's Sam? Do you see Sam?" Burke asked.

Sound of footfalls and heavy breathing. "No, only Danny," Ty said.

Burke's mind exploded with worry and his back and shoulders tensed hard. Where the hell was Sam? Was she hurt? Had Tyrell taken her?

"How is he?" Rollin asked.

"Breathing. Snoring—shit. Tranquilizer pen in his hand," Catherine said. "Looks like one of our custom jobs."

Burke's head nearly blew off his shoulders. "Sam! She raided my weapons closet. Damn it, I checked through everything she had with her. How did I miss that?" His worry turned to anger. The most exasperating woman he'd ever met. Just when he thought he had her, she slipped through his fingers.

"She's sneaky and determined," Rollin answered, his lips twisted. "But she couldn't have gone far. What's the car's license plate?"

Burke took out his Blackberry. "Bobby has it. Bobby? Sam took Danny's car. Does it have a GPS? Or a remote engine shut off?"

"Working on it," Bobby replied.

"We're headed to Connecticut," Rollin said, starting the car. "Only way out." He hit the gas and launched forward.

"Fuck, how much does this guy weigh?" Catherine grunted.

"Did she grab Danny's gun?" Burke asked.

"Let me check," Ty said. "Yes. Damn, cleaned him out. Wallet, cell and gun."

"She took his cell?" Burke nearly jumped out of his skin. "Bobby? You hear that?"

"On it. I got her car on GPS, too. She just turned onto Rock Creek and Potomac Parkway," Bobby said and then he burped.

Burke got a glimmer of hope. He'd catch her. "Danny should have anticipated she'd try to escape."

"She left her crutches behind," Catherine said.

Burke's ears went back and his jaw clenched. "She probably faked the pain to make us think she was weakened. Fucking wench."

Rollin smacked him on the upper arm. "Think about how Paul feels."

Burke's lips stretched into a wide smile. "Payback is a bitch."

"Wow, I haven't heard that much happiness in your tone all day, Burke," Catherine teased.

"Spank her for me, Ty, will you?"

Ty laughed. "I'd rather keep my arms, if you don't mind."

"Okay, we'll head to the safehouse and see if we can wake Danny," Catherine said. "And Burke, if you ever try to spank me, they'll be callin' you Burketta."

"I'd never spank you, Catherine, you'd enjoy it too much," he drawled.

Captain said, "I'm following you, Rollin. I have a feeling you'll need back up. Girl's a pistol."

"And she's got a pistol," Rollin added.

Burke rolled his eyes.

"She's a handful and that's a fact," Captain said. "You sure you still want her, Burke?"

"She's an incurable virus," he replied tartly. "And I'm still infected."

His friends chuckled. Ty and Catherine said their good-byes and wished the others luck.

Burke put his head in his hands and rubbed the aching muscles of his forehead.

"You okay, pal?" Rollin asked.

"She's aging me. You know, at the very beginning of this ordeal she told me that she was my Karma. I'm beginning to believe it."

Rollin laughed. "Bobby?"

"You're right behind her by about five miles."

"So where is she headed?" Rollin asked.

"Who knows? New Hampshire eventually," Burke said. "She might suspect we have equipment to track that car."

"I'd count on that. She'll ditch the car fast. We have to get to her." Rollin picked up the speed.

"What if I distract her with a text message?" Burke asked. "She has Danny's phone. Maybe I can get through to her."

"Worth a try."

Sam, please call me. Strong lied. We have the gun and want to help you. Please don't run.

His phone rang. Danny's cell. His heart raced. "That was quick."

"Put her on speakerphone," Rollin said.

"Will do. Sam? Are you all right?" Burke asked. "I've been so worried."

"Look, you guys need to back off."

Hearing her voice made his whole body sing.

Sam continued. "I don't know whether Emma was telling me the truth, but—"

"She was. Sam, please, where are you? I have to help you. Stop and let us pick you up. I have to see you. Are you all right? Did Strong hurt you?"

"No. I'm fine. Clearly or I just wouldn't have been able to pull that shit on Danny. Is he gonna be all right? What's in that dart thing?"

"A tranquilizer. He'll be fine in about an hour. Ty and Catherine are taking care of him. Listen, Sam. We're not the enemy. We're on your side. I know you're pissed at me about the tracking device, and I'm sorry, I was protecting you."

"Well, they didn't protect me much, did they? No. Because Strong found them."

"He found them the moment he captured you. He didn't reveal that until you were on the plane because he wanted to wait until the perfect moment to deliver the information. Anything to drive us apart. He played you, Sam. I didn't use you. I didn't do anything but protect you. Now please, come in, and we'll take down Larry together."

"Figures Strong was manipulating me. I thought the timing was a little too good. I did question why he hadn't found the devices sooner. I mean, hell, you had four on me."

"Sam, pull over, please."

"No way. I can't trust you guys."

His gut contracted and his jaw set. "We're not on Tyrell's side. Even Strong has turned against him. And we retrieved that weapon for you, Sam."

"Okay, fine, say you're on my side, it still doesn't change anything. You guys could easily change your minds. And even if you didn't, this is my job. I told you a long time ago that I didn't want you involved."

He made an exasperated noise. "Sam, you're talking crazy. We have resources you can't imagine."

"I know, you've been using them against me ever since I met you."

"I have not," he bit out. "I've been on your side since the moment I saved you in the forest."

"From Strong's fake attack. We were in no danger."

"You didn't know that and I didn't know that until—"

"You shot the hat off one kid and popped the other in the shoulder."

"Yes. Strong told you."

"Yes. He admitted everything. Look, tell Emma that I love her."

His body went to battle stations. He couldn't lose her, not when he was this close. "Sam, don't do this. You need us. Oh, fuck that, I need you, woman. I love you. I want to marry you."

Silence. "I can't go there now, Burke. I can't think about you. I'm totally emotionally overloaded."

"Sam, please don't shut me out. Please let me be there for you."

"Burke, don't make this personal. I've been upfront with you from the start. You and I have nothing to do with this."

His muscles hot and hard, he broke out in a sweat. "Bullshit. Right now I have everything to do with your decision."

"No, you don't."

A perfect argument came to him. He'd use her flawed logic against her. "Your whole mission since you were sixteen was to bring Larry to justice, right? Do we agree on that?"

"Well, yeah."

"All right, fine. So you're at a crossroads right now. You go on your own as planned or you allow us to help you. Right?"

"Well, yeah, but—"

"Let's look at this logically. Let's separate our emotions from the problem. Like you said, let's not make this personal."

"Burke, what—"

"Given your decision isn't personal, does it make sense to take on one of the most powerful men on the globe with the resources of one person, or a large team of law enforcement professionals with deep pockets?"

"Burke, you won't win this argument."

"Sam, this is bigger than you and Tyrell. His sickness affects the world. If you fuck it up and wound him or kill him, you'll look like the psycho and he'll look like the valiant war hero. Tyrell is what's important here, right? Well, you're turning down resources just because of our personal connection. You're running away from me, which is only puts you in more danger."

"You bet I'm running from you. You're crossed so many boundaries with me, I can't even sort through the mess. You violated my body with those rotten tracking devices—"

His face and body heated with anger. "I didn't violate you, I protected you. Don't turn that into a violation. Of course, I'm going to do everything in my power to protect you, including covering you in tracking devices. And yes, feeding them to you. I've been ingesting the transmitters myself. I always do during times of crisis."

"Don't lie to me."

"I'm not. All the Patriots take those capsules. It's standard procedure."

"Sam, he's telling you the truth," Rollin broke in. "We all eat those things when we're on dangerous missions. Besides, those orders came from us, not Burke. Don't blame him. I was a hundred percent behind the decision."

"I knew I was on speakerphone. Hi Rollin."

"Hi Sam."

"Look, whether or not you made the decision, Burke, you're still untrustworthy. I mean, you fucked me to get information out of me."

His pulse throbbed in his ears. "I did not. That's pure fabrication on your part," he countered angrily.

"You fucked me and used the information against me."

"No. I made love to you and protected you and loved you and retrieved that weapon *for you*."

She made a disgusted sound. "Whatever."

His blood turned to fire and he wanted to shake her. "Not 'whatever'. I've put my life on the line for you. I battled the fucking Cabal for you. These are not trifles, woman. You're mad at me, fine. Just don't disrespect me or belittle what I've done."

A moment of silence. "You are such a pain in the ass," she muttered under her breath. "Look, I don't want to disrespect you or belittle you, you big, dumb jerk! I just want you to go away! Stop messing with my mind!"

"Sam, I love you. Please pull over."

"No, you'll imprison me to protect me and do all kinds of knuckle-headed shit in the name of love."

"Do you love me?"

"Burke, I don't want to—"

"*Do you love me?*" he said louder.

A long silence, followed by a heavy sigh. "Of course, I do. I don't shut off that fast."

"Then pull the fuck over!"

She didn't reply.

Burke punched the dashboard. "Goddamn it, Sam!"

Rollin said, "Please listen to him. We all love you and want to help you. Please don't commit suicide."

"I have no intention of dying. Although, at this point, I don't really care. Not to be dramatic, but I've blown this life. Whatever bullshit you threw at me about my innocence, I do know the truth. I killed my parents. I brought Larry into our lives and if I hadn't slept with him, my parents would still be alive."

Burke's muscles were so tight, his body trembled. "Don't internalize that abuse, Sam. Don't let Larry win."

"Oh, don't worry, I won't."

He almost screamed, but knew that wouldn't help convince her. "Paul Strong and the CIA will kill you if you come within a mile of Larry."

Sam made a surprised noise. "Oh, pickles, I almost missed my turn off. Look, I know you guys are about ten minutes behind me. I know you're tracking me by this cell and by the car. I know you have access to facial recognition software. I know what your capabilities are. And you're wasting your time."

"Will you please save us the bother?" Burke demanded.

"Which way do I go? This airport is super confusing. Oh, here it is. One more final point here: the courts aren't going to convict Larry. He'll turn everything around on me. He'll say that I shot my father and he covered it up for me. My story is all hearsay."

"We're gonna make sure he goes to jail," Rollin said. "We have other evidence on him."

"We won't stop until he stays in prison for life," Burke added.

"Okay, see you guys."

Panic struck him and he wanted to reach through the line and grab her. "Sam, don't!"

"Burke, if you're still around afterwards—if there's an afterwards —I'll look you up."

"Sam!"

"And Rollin, will you please marry Emma?"

"Only when you can be maid-of-honor," Rollin fired back.

"Oh. Too bad."

"Sam!" Burke shouted.

Click.

Burke punched the dashboard in a quick series of lefts and rights. "This woman will be the death of me!"

"We'll get her," Rollin said, his expression hard and determined.

"We sure as hell will. Christ, she's the fucking Terminator. I'm going to have to imprison her somewhere. Blindfold her and drag her somewhere where she'll fight me until we can put that bastard away."

"Having any second thoughts?"

"No, God no. I just don't know why I don't count enough to stop her. I mean, if she really loves me, why won't she listen?"

Rollin burst out laughing. "How long has it been since you were in a real relationship, Burke? Two completely separate ideas: loving and listening."

"Being late to dinner and assassinating a presidential candidate are vastly different."

"True, but in Sam's mind, it's the same thing. Like she said: don't take this personally. She loves you. She's just gone absolutely bat shit crazy. Look, I didn't take you trying to kill me personally, did I? Sam will come back to herself. You did."

"All true. I just hate that she's out there, feeling as alone and crazy as I did. Rips my heart apart. Right when she needs me the most, she won't let me in. How did you get through to me, Rollin?"

"I don't know. I think I hit you. Or poured alcohol down your throat. You were pretty far gone in Colorado. I think by the time I tracked you down, you were ready to be saved, Burke. You always had a strong inner compass. Main thing, we need face-to-face contact. Once you get her back, you'll wake her up."

"Bobby? Have you located Sam on the cameras?" Burke asked.

"Car's still at Ronald Reagan airport. I just hacked into their grid. Sam left the car running in front of Baggage Claim for United Airlines. Cops are around the car, scratching their heads. No Sam."

"We're almost there," Rollin said. "We'll recover the car."

"We'll need the video playback from the airport, if I can't find her live," Bobby said.

"Captain can handle that," Rollin replied.

Bobby couldn't locate Sam on the cameras. After much back-and-forth, Captain finally got his contacts to convince airport security to let them view the footage of the drop-off for the baggage claim area. Not easy since he had to wake up his buddies in the dead of night.

Once they began examining the footage, it took them a full twenty minutes to trace Sam's movements on the airport cameras after she'd left the car, due to the huge crowds that had flown into the airport on the red eye flights. Sam had slipped inside the baggage claim area and ducked into a large crowd of people around a luggage carousel. After dropping to the floor and quickly donning a large dark hoodie and a baseball cap, she'd slipped outside and got into a cab.

The cabbie reported that he'd just dropped off Sam at a truck stop in Jessup, Maryland.

Footage from the truck stop security cameras revealed Sam getting into a long haul tractor-trailer with a male and female, presumably a trucker couple. After tracking the license plate, they learned that the truck's destination was Texas.

When Bobby finally managed to get a cell number for the driver, the truck was in Virginia. The trucker reported that he and his wife had dropped off Sam five blocks past the truck stop, back in Jessup.

Burke, Rollin, Captain, Ty and Catherine searched the area around the truck stop for hours, but found no trace of Sam anywhere. Finally, they decided to concentrate on Tyrell's location as the best chance of recovering her.

"So where the fuck did she go?" Burke demanded as he paced the jet en route to New Hampshire. "She didn't take a train, or a bus, or a rental car. A plane. Nothing. She couldn't just have vanished into thin air!"

"Jesus, Burke, sit down and take a nap," Rollin ordered. "You haven't slept in twenty-four hours."

"I can't."

"Okay, let me put it this way, I haven't slept twenty-four hours. So sit down and stop knocking into my feet."

"Yeah, please," grumbled the Captain. The rest of the gang was asleep.

"Sorry." He slumped on a bench. "I should ask Bobby if he heard anything about Strong finding her."

"He hasn't," Rollin said, sounding very annoyed. "At least not in the past five minutes. Just lie down. And I mean this in the nicest possible way: shut the fuck up. And leave Bobby alone, he's exhausted."

"Sorry. I know I'm driving everyone nuts, but she's out there and scared and alone and I just..."

"She'll be fine until we can recover her. And we'll get her. No way will she get within a mile of Tyrell without us knowing it. Go to sleep."

"I don't think that's possible."

"Well, then just sit still so the rest of us can."

"Okay. Sorry."

He had to calm down and focus. Taking a deep breath, he worked hard and managed to shake the doubts from his mind. He'd scour New Hampshire for her. She might be determined, but he was more tenacious.

He wouldn't stop until he found her.

TWENTY-TWO

Her hands shaking, her heart battering her sternum, Sam drove in the gate for Maple Grove Cemetery in Concord, New Hampshire. An old lady prayed on a bench beside a large mausoleum. An elderly couple stood in front of tall gravestone. But no one else was around. She took a deep breath.

She'd managed to evade the Patriots and everyone else for the past two days, but now she was in super dangerous territory. A place she'd have staked out if she were searching for her.

Hopefully, no one would recognize her. With a short brown wig, a baseball cap and a giant hoodie, plus baggy jeans, she looked like a teenage boy. She'd perfected the walk, the stance, and the voice. She had her character down.

Despite her preparations, she'd been freaked out the moment she hit the city limits of Concord. She hadn't planned on coming by the cemetery, but she'd probably be dead by that night. She wanted to visit her parents' grave at least once before she joined them.

She parked the rental car near the family plot and scanned the graveyard for threats again, but no one was in her immediate area. The thick, humid hot summer air caused her to immediately start sweating. But no way could she risk taking off the hoodie.

Her breathing shallow, her legs shaking like hell, she limped to her Dad's parents' gravesites. *Hutchins, William and Martha.*

She checked the grave right next to it and gasped. Felt like someone had thrown ice water in her face.

Hutchins, Robert and Catherine.

Below their names was another.

Amanda.

Not just her parents' grave. *Hers.*

Her chest tightened so fast and hard, she stopped breathing. She sank to her knees on the soft grass and stared at the headstone. Tears ran in rivulets down her cheeks.

Amanda. Beloved Daughter. 1978-1994.

Her vision tweaked and the grave moved far away. Like she was viewing it from the end of a long dark corridor. Surreal.

Despite the heat and humidity, she shivered and wrapped her arms around herself, chilled to the bone.

Here it was. Her future. If Larry killed her, there wouldn't be a gravestone for Samantha Murdock because there already was one in Sacramento with a baby buried under it. All there would be was: *Amanda, Beloved Daughter, 1978-1994.* Like the last sixteen years of her life hadn't happened. Like she'd never gone to California. Never met Emma. Never gone to college. Never bought her houses. Never met Burke.

She'd be nothing. No impact on the world except an empty grave.

Her friends from her past probably never even thought about her anymore.

No one would mourn her death this time. No one would know.

Robert. Catherine.

Mom and Dad's smiling faces popped into her mind. The way they looked at each other. The way Dad nuzzled Mom as she cooked. They'd had such a special relationship.

And Sam had killed it. Horrid pain blistered her interior and she held her stomach.

The gravestone was so impersonal and somber. Such a terrible marker of the life and fire and love that was her parents. Said nothing about who they were. What they'd given the community. How they'd live their lives. After all that work and sacrifice, all they had left in the world was two coffins filled with rotting corpses and this miserable chunk of granite.

While Larry lived high on the hog, raping little girls and ripping off people while living in luxurious surroundings. With people bowing and scraping to him.

Unreal.

Deep sorrow mixed with rage and fired up all her limbs. Her jaw set, and her mind quieted and focused. Standing, she wiped the tears from her eyes.

She had an appointment to keep.

Breathe. Focus. Relax.

Kneeling in the shade next to a giant, loud air conditioning unit on the roof of an office building, Sam peered through the crosshairs of her new high-powered sniper rifle. She ignored the gravel digging into her knees through the rough material of her coveralls. Ignored the sticky humid air and blistering heat. Sweat trickled down her face, but she didn't wipe it off. Her target was all that mattered.

Several dignitaries stood on a short podium next to the Soldiers and Sailors Memorial in front of the New Hampshire Statehouse. Even with the rifle's attached bipod, the shot was a tricky one. If her hands shook too much, she'd miss the shot. She couldn't let anyone but Tyrell die. Thankfully, the gun was loaded with hollow-point bullets designed to slow once they entered the victim. But this wouldn't be easy.

Larry stepped onto the stage and into her gun sight.

God, he'd changed. She barely recognized him. Old, pasty, bloated, with watery eyes and a bulbous nose. Red cheeks. Skin hanging off his once sharp jawline. Dressed in a white shirt with the sleeves rolled up and a tie, plus dark dress slacks, he looked nothing like the man she'd once loved. Almost too pathetic to kill.

But she knew his heart. That middle-aged paunch hid his darkness. His evil. She pictured Larry shooting her father and her rage centered her.

Taking off the safety, she aimed for his face. Fuck him. Hopefully, he'd suffer before he died.

Two men moved away from him slightly, giving her a clear shot.

One, two...

She put her finger on the trigger, remembering how far back she needed to pull to engage the firing pin. Slowing her breathing, she concentrated on her heartbeat. For perfect accuracy, she had to time the shot between beats.

Thump. Thump. Thump.

Go!

Her finger wouldn't move.

Larry dropped a piece of paper and bent down to pick it up, moving out of range.

She flipped on the safety and put her head down, breathing hard. What was wrong with her? Why didn't she pull the trigger? One shot and he was gone.

"Come on, Sam. You can do this. You've been picturing this moment for the last sixteen years. Kill the fucker," she whispered.

She took another deep breath and got back into position.

Larry popped up right in the middle of her crosshairs. She thought of his favorite dildo. His leer. Handcuffing her to that tree. Shooting her father.

Hatred coursed through her.

She took off the safety, put her finger on the trigger and held her breath. *Count your heartbeats. Time the shot.*

His fat forehead. Right in her sight.

One. Two. Three...

She let out her breath. Now.

Her finger stayed still, like it was encased in steel.

Fuck! She put the safety back on. "Goddamn it! *You wuss!*"

Why couldn't she do it? It wasn't that hard.

Tears stung her eyes. She'd failed. Utterly failed. Shit!

She slapped her face. "Stop it. You're not a failure because you couldn't kill someone in cold blood. For Christ's sake. Shows you're more human than he is. And we still have Plan B, girl. We'll go with that." She shuddered.

Her back-up plan was beyond tricky, it was suicidal. And it involved facing her worst nightmare. She'd need a miracle to pull off the complicated ruse. Plan Crazy to Plan Crazier.

Cold steel pressed against her temple. "Hold it, Sam."

She jerked and gasped and her heart rate revved to full. But she forced her limbs to freeze.

Paul Strong.

Her thoughts went dark and she almost collapsed. She hadn't heard him sneak up on her because of the noise from the air conditioner. *Son-of-a-bitch.* Not now! Not when she was so close! Somehow she had to keep going. Somehow she had to defeat the guy.

"No, you hold it," came another familiar voice.

Burke?

Worried about setting off Paul's gun, she strained to look out of her peripheral vision. Burke had his pistol pointed at Paul's head.

She wanted to scream in frustration and throw a huge tantrum. After all this work, she'd been caught by not one of the guys, but both!

"For Christ's sake!" she yelled over the din. "Put your guns down. I'm not going to kill Tyrell. I've been here for ten damned minutes and I haven't been able to pull the trigger."

Strong moved his gun a few inches away from her head, but kept it aimed right at her.

"Drop the gun, Strong," Burke ordered sharply.

"You first," Paul replied.

"Can we all put the guns down?" Sam bit out. "Can we not play out the last scene from *Reservoir Dogs*? Look, my hands are off the rifle. I'm going to stand up. Let's all be adults and calm down and no one should have to shoot anybody."

Her head throbbing with fury, she rose to her feet and the men moved with her. She turned and met Burke's eyes. Her interior hurt like he'd reached inside her chest, removed her heart and crushed it in his meaty fist. In person, his impact was fifty times greater than she'd imagined. Damn, she loved him. More than ever.

But now, she had to be very careful not to allow her feelings for him to cloud her judgment. She hardened her heart and downloaded her escape. The plan was ugly, but it would work. It had to.

She glared at the men. "Okay, I'm going to count to three and you two are going to lower your weapons. And then we can talk like adults. If that's possible. Okay? One, two, three."

Burke and Paul eyeballed each other like junkyard dogs about to attack and gradually brought their weapons down. Sam didn't breathe until they'd stowed their weapons in their jackets.

They turned to her with the same hurt, wary and concerned expressions. While she could care less about Paul, the pain and worry on Burke's face made her gut churn.

Be strong! Keep your head on straight! Tyrell now, Burke later!

And while Burke might still love her right then, after what she was about to pull, he'd more than likely change his mind. But he'd left her with no choice.

"Stop looking at me like that, I couldn't do it," she bit out.

"But you still put yourself in mortal danger," he snapped back, his dark eyes flashing. "A fluke you're still alive. I hope you understand that."

"Duh."

His ears went back and his eyes narrowed. "You still have another plan, I know you do. But you can go ahead and give that up, because you're done."

"She sure is," Paul agreed. "Where did you go after the trucker and his wife dropped you off a few blocks past that truck stop?"

"They didn't drop me off there, I was still in the truck when you both called. The woman took one look at me and knew I was running. So I told them a bit of truth, that an ex-boyfriend who was a very powerful government figure was trying to have me killed. Very nice couple. With some very interesting underground connections. They hooked me up with some paramilitary nutjobs who had a warehouse filled with more guns and military equipment than I've ever seen in my life."

Paul's brow furrowed and Burke frowned.

"You two shouldn't have worried about me. I was fine. I just can't believe I couldn't kill that bastard. After sixteen years of training and acquiring all those weapons and all this drama, turns out I'm not a killer. If you guys had arrived five minutes from now, I would have been gone. Look, I'm not gonna kill the guy, so I'm no longer a threat, so you can both turn around and leave. Burke, I'll give you the address in Oregon of the storage facility where your weapons and Mercedes SUV are stored."

Burke's full lips thinned. "You're crazy if you think we're just going to walk away and leave you here."

"Which one of us are you coming with, Sam?" Strong asked. "I can protect you better than he can."

"You know why I want you with me," Burke said. "Because we love each other."

Strong took a step forward, his chest puffed up. "Bullshit. Sam, you aren't buying his crap, are you? You know I'm the better choice."

Burke stood even taller and his gaze went fiery. "Fuck that. She loves me, not you. Don't you, Sam?"

She sighed and rolled her eyes. "Yes, I do," she said in a resigned voice.

"How the hell can you love this psycho? He'd fuckin' kill you as soon as look at you. If I hadn't arrived, you'd be dead."

Burke started to yell at him, but Sam held up her hand. "No, he won't kill me. I'm not sure about you, though."

Strong looked at her with pity. "You know how I feel about you, Sam. I'd never do anything to hurt you. But he already has. He's tagged you like a cow, imprisoned you, and manipulated you into thinking he loves you. All I've done is protect you."

"By kidnapping me at gunpoint."

What the hell was she doing taking sides? These idiots had just given her the perfect opportunity to get away. All she had to do was pit them against each other.

"But you do bring up some important points," she added. "Burke did tag me like a cow."

Burke's expression went flat. "We discussed this already. You know why I did that and I won't apologize for it. But this is all a moot point. You're coming with me."

"Wait a minute. I'm in charge here," she said. "I decide. And I haven't decided."

"I'm going to decide for you," Burke pulled himself taller.

Strong stood between them. "Touch her and die."

"Don't make me kill you," Burke warned.

"Will you two stop posturing?"

Burke glared at her. "Why are you doing this, Sam?"

"Because you're trying to take my power away from me."

"So's he," Burke said, his face flushed. "He wants what we want. To bring down Tyrell."

"Using me. I love both you guys." She looked between them with as much revulsion as she could.

Strong stepped forward. "I'm not just gonna let you go with him, Sam, not without a fight."

Burke squared his shoulders. "Clearly, neither of us is just going to let the other take her. The most logical choice in this situation—no matter how much I loathe the idea— is to join forces, Strong. I know you and your people in The Group jumped ship on Tyrell, so did we. We help each other, we can take him down together."

Paul crossed his thick arms. "And why would Rampart want to do that?"

"Lesser of two evils. We'd rather have you in power than him. Think of it as a short truce."

Paul stared at Burke for a long moment. "Why should I trust you?"

"Because we both want the best for Sam. And the best is making sure that Tyrell goes to jail for the rest of his life."

Paul nodded, but then shook his head and held Burke's gaze. "I don't like it."

Burke continued, "We recently discovered that Tyrell's behind the murders of David Gilroy of GiantCom, Judge Peter Warren and District Attorney Gary Street."

Paul's eyebrows raised high. "Warren? Shit. I knew about Dave, he was a friend of mine. Last straw for me. But I didn't know about the judge. And I wasn't sure, but I suspected Tyrell was behind the DA's disappearance." He blew out a long breath.

"Tyrell's empire is unraveling fast. This information is bound to get out, only a matter of time." Burke's focus sharpened on the Fed.

Paul blinked fast, pulled his mouth to one side, then met Burke's gaze. "You guys have the murder weapon."

Neither man noticed Sam slowly reaching into her pants pockets.

"Yeah, but we shouldn't discuss this here," Burke said, scanning the area. "I'm surprised the Secret Service isn't guarding this roof."

Paul nodded. "They should have been, but were short-handed today. Did an initial search, but couldn't post anyone. I told 'em I'd help 'em out. Thought I could get a good vantage point from here to look for Sam. And lo and behold."

"You watch her while I break down her rifle and then let's head to neutral territory to discuss a plan," Burke said with a quick glance her way.

"I'm still not sold. But I'll hear you out."

"Good." Burke picked up the rifle and began taking it apart.

Paul turned to her with a slightly wounded stare and moved closer.

"I may be pissed at you, but I meant what I said in that note," she said, hoping to disarm him. "And my feelings for you were honest in the beginning. I liked you a lot. And I was very hurt when I found out that you'd used me."

The line between his eyes deepened. "Can't go back and undo what was done, Sam. But I really wish I could."

"You're a good man, Mr. Strong." Which was a big fat lie. "But I'm in love with Burke." *Unfortunately.*

Paul smirked and gave her breasts the visual once-over. "Burke, I envy you and I don't. Truthfully, I'm not sure I could handle her. But I would have loved to give it a try. Things don't work out with him, Sam, give me a call."

Burke pointed at Strong. "That's enough."

Paul's smile widened. "So what's your plan on containing her when neither of us have been able to do that so far?"

She inched closer to Burke while the two men's focus was on each other.

"Only reason she got away from us before was because one of us helped her. If we're both on the same team, she won't stand a chance." Burke knelt down and snapped the disassembled parts into their plastic carrying case.

"Tyrell knows about your places. And mine. Where do you plan to take her?"

Sam took another baby step toward Burke. Now she was almost equal distance away from the men, but within reach of both. Perfect. She closed her hands around the two devices in her pockets. Her heart beat faster.

Burke glanced up at her, then met Strong's gaze. "A place Tyrell will never find her, and more importantly, a place she could never escape from." He returned his attention to her, and his expression became sympathetic. "Sorry, Sam, but I can't let you hurt yourself."

"Where?" Strong asked.

Burke pressed the last piece of the gun into the case. "I've bought an isolated property, built like a fortress, and only accessible by helicopter and a ten-mile- long dirt road." He shut the lid, flipped the buckles closed, and stood. "A hundred miles from the nearest town. Middle of the country."

Her stomach knotted, making it burn. This guy's arrogance was unbelievable. Whether she loved him or not, she couldn't wait to wake him up.

"She doesn't want to stay, she won't," Strong said.

"I'm going to take her there blindfolded so she has no idea where she is and keep her locked up until Tyrell's trial. She won't escape from me again."

She itched to punch Burke's smug face.

He closed the distance between them and stood next to her with a protective stance, a hard look on his face. "I'm sorry, but I couldn't stand it if something happened to you. Someday, you'll thank me."

"Highly doubtful," she said with a curled lip.

His brow wrinkled, but the look behind his eye remained strong and sure.

Poor deluded fool.

Paul said, "So where should we go? Wherever it is, we're going together. I'm not leaving either of you."

She waited until Burke turned his attention to Paul. "I've got a hotel room close by where we—"

Sam whipped out two stun guns and jabbed them into both men's backs at once.

They let out weird, agonized, strangled gurgles, jerked and hit the ground, curling into fetal positions.

Guilt turned her stomach to fire. Mitigating her pain slightly was Burke's disturbing tirade about imprisoning her.

She ran for her backpack. She'd leave the rifle because it was too heavy, and she had five more if she needed them. But she had to hurry, the men would only be incapacitated for a few minutes.

As she passed Burke, she found herself stopping. She dropped to the ground next to him. His whole body trembled and his eyes couldn't focus.

She kissed his shaking cheek. "Sorry, baby. I do love you, but I have to do this myself."

His face red, he made a loud grunting noise.

Forcing herself from his side, she swallowed her emotions and ran for it.

Burke's muscles finally obeyed him and he stretched out. His body still pulsed with pain. Felt like he'd been punched in every place at once. He was going to kill her. "Fucking bitch!" Groaning, he pushed himself into a sitting position.

When he turned to check on Strong, he found the barrel of a gun an inch away from his face. His heart beat jumped high.

Strong stood above him, his steely gaze mean. "Give me one good reason why I shouldn't kill you."

Burke figured he was bluffing, just trying to get a rise out of him, but responded fast, anyway. "I can find Sam."

"Good reason." Paul worked his mouth, probably pretending to think about it, the gun still trained on his face. He examined him carefully. "How do I know you won't kill me if I put this gun away?"

"You don't. But I meant what I said earlier. We're on the same side for the moment. Let's take advantage of it. We've got the murder weapon, and between you and us, we have a lot of people in his camp. And you're as motivated to protect Sam—and this country—as I am. We can't let Larry take the White House."

The hard lines around the Fed's eyes relaxed. "You're right. About the country. And Sam. Really gets under your skin, that one. Okay, I'm not promising anything, but let me talk to my guys." He shot him a deadly glare. "You fuck me and I'll ruin your life and the lives of everyone you love."

"Ditto."

Paul gave a short nod and put away his gun. He offered his hand to Burke, his razor-sharp focus noting every single move.

Burke took his hand and stood. "Where's your car?"

"Two blocks."

"Mine's below. I need to get Sam's rifle."

"Why'd she leave it?"

"I'm sure she still has plenty."

Burke grabbed the rifle case and they headed for the roof's stairwell. When they came to the door, they reached into their breast pockets at the same time.

Burke's heart rate jumped and he prepared to attack. Paul's body jerked back and he made a move for him. Then Burke saw the cell in Paul's hand and stopped. Paul noticed the phone in Burke's hand at the same moment and relaxed.

They both sighed. And then punched numbers into their cells.

"Bobby?" Burke said.

"Maria?" Paul said.

"Get me satellite on the area within six square blocks of the New Hampshire State House," Burke ordered. "Specifically around the structure on the southwest corner of Capitol and North Main."

Paul said, "Get me satellite coverage on the New Hampshire State House. Building on corner of Capitol and North Main."

They glanced at each other as they descended the stairs.

"Go back…" Burke checked his watch and took in a short breath. "Shit. Ten minutes ago. Check the roof of the building, spot Sam when she came out and tell me which direction she went and in what vehicle."

"What was she wearing?" Bobby asked.

"Look for a dark blue workman's outfit with a dark blue baseball cap. She probably came in a van."

Paul gave his contact the same kind of order.

Burke cleared the building, Paul on his heels, and they hustled to the Patriots' armored Cadillac Escalade.

As Burke climbed in, Bobby said, "She got into a white van and headed north from there on Main."

Strong got into the passenger seat and Burke started the car. Pulling out of the parking lot, he hung a right on Capitol, then took an immediate left on Main.

Paul buckled himself in and said, "White van, headed north. Take Main and—oh."

Burke shot him a grin.

Paul returned it. "Seems like we have equal capabilities."

"Let's see how it pans out. Bobby?"

A slurping sound came over the receiver. "Lost her momentarily…
oh, okay. Take a left on Bouton, which is 3."

"Take Bouton. Highway 3," Paul said.

"On it." Burke took the left.

"Turns into North State," Bobby said.

"I see that."

Bobby burped. "Turn into the Rite Aid on your left. Her van is
parked there on the north side of the parking lot. She got out and went
into the store, but on the tape, she hasn't come out yet. She may still be
in there."

"She's at Rite Aid. Oh. Damn," Paul said, scanning the area. "Why
am I bothering?"

Burke turned into the parking lot. "Highly doubtful."

"Doubtful, what?" Paul asked.

"That she's still there."

"Let's find out," Paul said.

Bobby said, "You're coming up on the van. Within a few feet.
There, right there, the white one by the blue truck."

Burke pulled up and blocked the white panel van.

Paul leapt out of the rental car and checked the vehicle. "No one
inside. But there's a note taped to the window." He ripped off the paper
and read it. His shoulders slumped.

"What does it say?"

Paul glared at him and shook his head. "It says: I'm not here and
I'm not in the store. Did you think I was this stupid? Go home! Signed,
Sam."

Burke's body hard and hot, he punched the steering wheel.
"Witch!"

"Let me guess, you didn't find her," Bobby said. "I checked
everyone as closely as I could as they came out of the store, but Sam
must be in disguise and must have changed. Go inside and ask for the
security footage."

"On it." Burke parked the car and got out.

"Checking the security feed in the store to see what disguise she used?" Paul asked as he followed Burke.

He nodded.

Ten minutes later, Burke and Paul left the store. Burke wanted to pummel something, and Paul's jaw clenched tight. Security cameras hadn't caught Sam. The day manager had forgotten to turn them on.

Paul walked briskly beside him. "We'll do better if we just track the governor. She can't be too far away from him."

"Bobby, where is Tyrell?" Burke asked as he reached the car.

"On his way to another glad-handing session."

"Where?"

"At the Library, right near the Capitol Building."

"We're on our way."

Burke and Paul shadowed Tyrell all day. But they didn't spot Sam anywhere.

Finally, after darkness fell, the governor led them back to his mansion in a rich country enclave. They parked down the street.

Burke worked his toes inside his Gucci boots, his body hot with frustration. Where the hell was she?

Paul's attention went to the impressive front gate. "She couldn't have gotten inside."

"Don't underestimate—wait," Burke said, snapping his fingers. "She told me about a secret tunnel that led inside the mansion from Tyrell's grandfather's bootlegging days."

They both looked at each other and nodded.

Paul's attention went to the mansion. "She's inside. Fuck. Pure suicide."

Burke's heart beat faster. "Agreed. Bobby? I need house plans for Tyrell's mansion off Shaker Road by Snow Pond."

"You bet." Crunching. Slurping.

"Call me when you have them." Burke clicked off.

Paul gave similar orders and hung up. "A secret tunnel?"

"Yeah. When his father was governor, Larry took her on a tour of the place for her fifteenth birthday." His phone beeped and he answered.

"Got 'em," Bobby said. "Nothing looks out of the ordinary. Normal big ass house. Way too many rooms. Where is the secret tunnel supposed to enter the house?"

"Through the master suite," Burke replied.

"Okay. No indication here of any tunnels. But the master suite is at the very north end of the house. If there was a bootlegging route, it would have to come out on another road. Old road goes…yeah, I see a faint line here, up a hill. Goes to Snow Pond Road. Keep going up Shaker and turn left on Snow Pond. Stop when you reach Graham Road and I'll tell you where to look. That has to be it."

"Okay." Burke turned over the engine and pulled out.

"Do you believe her story about why she didn't take the shot?"

Burke nodded. "Yeah, I never thought Sam was a killer. But it did shock me how far she got before she figured it out. And I still can't believe we let her get that close to Tyrell. How can a fucking cocktail waitress keep doing this to us? Aren't we the trained professionals?"

"Sure makes us look like a buncha rookies." Strong's attention went out the front window. "But if she's not gonna kill him, what's she doing here?"

"Confrontation of some sort. Probably wants to beat him up."

"Reckless idiot. Has no idea the danger."

"I think she does. But I don't think she cares." After a pause, Burke turned to Paul. "You really like her or were you just using her?"

"Using her at first. Not at the end. What about you?" Paul straightened his shoulders.

"I've never loved a woman more."

Paul held his gaze for a long moment. Blinked a few times, then nodded. "You still want to marry her?"

"Yes. Well, after I turn her over my knee and spank the fire out of her for tasing me."

Paul laughed. "She'd make you bloody."

Burke grinned. "It'd be worth it."

"I think we're both out of luck," Paul said with a raise of his brows. "I don't think she'll last the day."

"Not if I—we—have anything to do with it."

"Let's hope we find her in time."

"We will," Burke said with confidence he didn't feel. He came to a T-intersection. Snow Pond Road. He turned left and continued down the well-maintained country road. Area was sparsely populated with huge McMansions on five-plus-acre lots.

Paul examined him. "Heard your nuke stunt almost worked."

Burke grunted.

"Too bad your friends got in the way."

"They were only doing their job. I miscalculated."

Paul shook his head. "I think you were right not to trust that bunch. I still don't know why you joined them. I know we made you an offer."

"I don't agree with your politics."

"Come on. It's about the money."

Burke turned his face toward Strong, but kept his eyes on the road. "Not for me."

"Used to be."

Graham Road came up on his right. He pulled over, parked and shut off his lights. "Learned a lot from that."

"You'd make a lot more with us."

Burke settled back in his seat and pulled his neck to one side to stretch it. "Well aware of that. So is that the only appeal? The money?"

"Bet your ass. In this business, you have no friends."

"I disagree."

Paul turned to him, his amused, yet pitying expression bathed in the green glow from the dashboard lights. "You really think the Rampart guys are your friends?"

"Yes."

The Fed snorted. "Then you're more deluded than I thought you were."

"That's your opinion."

Paul watched him for a few moments. "I've been authorized to offer you another deal."

Burke held up his hand. "Not interested."

"You're making a mistake. Hell of an opportunity. Larry split the Group right down the middle. We need good people. We don't take the same kinds of risks as Larry. We're looking for sure pay offs with as little drama as possible. You'd be welcome. And you'd make far more with us."

"I've found your path is too lonely."

Paul made a disgusted face. "You're a sap."

"Apparently," Burke replied as his attention went out the window. A half moon barely illuminated the forested and hilly area surrounding them. As his eyes adjusted slowly to the faint lighting, more of the detail of the road and two driveways up ahead came into focus.

Strong frowned and gestured toward him. "And hey...I'm sorry for what happened to Joseph Reilly."

Burke's gut caved in and his face went hot. His hands fisted. "Did Tyrell order that?"

"Indirectly. That was a mess. I swear, I thought I was in charge and then I find out some jerkoff hired the Kowalski twins behind my back. That should not have happened."

Burke honed in on the man's eyes. Seemed to be telling the truth. Once a Marine, always a Marine. Semper Fi. "How did the Kowalskis get out of the asylum?"

Strong made a disgusted noise. "Larry got 'em sprung a year ago."

Heat filled his body and his trigger finger twitched. "Fuck. Did look like their handiwork. Fuckers. I'll kill them."

"I'll get you their address and phone number and help if you want."

"Why?"

"Because they're untrustworthy psychopaths who need to be put down," Strong said, his tone belying no duplicity. "Bloodthirsty motherfuckers. Scare the shit out of me. I got pissed when I saw what they'd done to Joe and they fuckin' turned on me. Almost didn't get out of there alive. I had to pull my gun on 'em and fire off a shot to hold 'em back. Blood-crazed whackos."

New information. Burke tuned all his senses into the man. "So you were there?"

Strong's face darkened and he looked down at his lap. "Yeah. But too late. Felt really bad," he said with what appeared to be genuine pain in his face. "Larry's fucked and perverted everything. Ordered the hits on Gilroy—then he decided to kill Dave himself—and ordered the attack on you guys. He wants anyone who saw or touched the evidence against him to be tortured to death. He wants to send a message to the world that he's the worst badass of the century and he's in charge. Our side wants him taken down before he brings the whole Group down."

"Why are you telling me this?"

"No reason not to," he said with a slight shrug. "We both know we need that gun to get a conviction. I just need to trust that you guys will do the job."

"We will," Burke replied firmly.

Doubt played across Strong's face. "We'll see. But without Sam, this is gonna be hard."

Burke studied his adversary. "So why did you infiltrate us through Sam? Like we wouldn't have figured you out?"

Strong sent him a salacious grin. "Sam."

Burke fought the urge to punch him. "You followed her around for a couple weeks and liked what you saw."

"Yep. I did have someone else. Sam changed my mind."

"Burke?" came Bobby's voice in his ear. "Look on your left for tire tracks."

Burke turned around and reached for his gear bag in the back seat. "Can't use a spotlight or we'll attract attention. Need night vision." He retrieved two pairs of glasses from his large canvas bag. "Here." He handed one to Strong and put on the other.

As he scanned the road for breaks, his phone beeped. But who was calling him? "Just a minute, Bobby. Hello?"

"Burke, it's me, Emma. Rollin said I should call you. A friend just told me he's been in contact with Sam."

His body tensed and his heart beat faster. "When?"

"Just a few minutes ago."

"Where is she?"

"He doesn't know. But he said she's streaming a show live over the Internet," Emma said.

He took in a sharp breath. "Holy God. So that's her plan. What's the website?"

"Here you go." Emma read off the web address.

"I'll tell Bobby. There's no way the broadcast will go out. Someone will shut it down."

"I don't know, my friend's pretty good. Apparently, Sam's been working on this plan for years."

"Shit. Thanks, Emma."

"Save her, Burke."

"I will." He toggled back to the Patriots' network. "Bobby? Here's a web address." He quickly repeated what Emma had said. "Find out all you can. Sam is streaming live on there now. Shit, we have to find her. He'll kill her."

"That's her plan?" Strong demanded, his eyes wide.

"Apparently."

Strong's brows raised high. "Gotta give her an A for inventiveness. But...God."

Burke spotted the overgrown road about twenty feet ahead. He slowly pulled onto the pothole-and-brush-filled dirt track and drove with his lights off. Fresh tire impressions grooved deep into the soil, and many branches lining the abandoned trail had been recently broken off.

"She was here," Strong said.

"Yeah."

About a hundred yards along, they found a small black beater Honda tucked into the brush alongside the road.

Paul said, "Entrance has to be around here somewhere."

They parked, got out, and inspected Sam's vehicle.

Strong pointed at the ground. "Footprints."

Burke studied the area in front of her car and spotted more. "Over here, too."

The men followed Sam's trail, which led to a large ivy-covered rock formation.

Paul pushed aside the green blanket of vegetation, revealing a six-foot-tall arched opening cut into the rock barred with an ancient rusty iron gate. It had been forced open and a pair of bolt cutters lay below next to a broken lock.

Sirens whined from far away.

Burke exchanged a grave look with Paul. "We have to hurry." He jerked his head toward the entrance. "Let's go."

Burke led and Paul followed as they descended into an inky tunnel, thick with moss and spiderwebs.

TWENTY-THREE

Still disguised as a teenage boy, Sam sat in the darkened bedroom suite, her heart beating so fast she could barely get a breath in her lungs. Why hadn't she eaten? Her stomach hurt like she'd swallowed a pint of sulfuric acid. Despite the meds, her ulcers were getting worse. If Larry didn't kill her, her belly certainly would.

She'd heard Larry arrive downstairs ten minutes before. His wife was still in Martha's Vineyard, thank God. The only people in the house were Larry, his two bodyguards, and her. It was only a matter of time before he walked through that door.

She'd had a lot of time to reacquaint herself with the luxurious room. Especially the emergency features that protected the jerk in case of attack. Larry's bedroom was half master suite, half panic room. Press a button and solid steel bars deployed across the door and locked into place. Larry had loved showing her the security protections. But he'd improved the system over the past sixteen years and added a remote control along with the original wall switch.

Sam squirmed in the corner in a large overstuffed chair, the remote to the lockdown mechanism in her left hand, a 30-shot Glock in her right.

The doorknob clicked.

A super-charged blast of adrenaline powered through her system and her muscles went hard.

Showtime. She flipped the recording switch of her video set-up with her foot. The red light said she was live.

The door opened.

Her mind went foggy and dark. A voice in her head nearly deafened her. *RUN!* Tightening her grip on the remote and the gun, she wanted to dive out the window. Tyrell was the summation of all her fears wrapped up into one hideous man.

She mentally beat the terror from her thoughts. This was no time to panic. One false move and she died and he went free.

You can do this. Stick to the script. You can handle this.

He flicked on the lights and didn't seem to notice her.

It was so hard to comprehend that this fat old man was Larry Tyrell. He didn't look as big as she remembered. And, damn, had he been beaten hard by the age stick: he didn't look fifty-eight, he looked four hundred and fifty-eight. Flabby, bloated, with a terrible comb-over.

What happened to the hunk? She searched, but she could hardly find any sign of the man she'd known. Everything that had been up top was now on bottom—his pumped chest had fallen around his waist. His healthy glow had been replaced by puffiness and rosacea. Instead of that straight, strong jaw line, he had piggy jowls and his regal nose was now crimson and bulbous.

She could smell the liquor from all the way across the room. Her already searing belly wrenched more and she fought a shiver.

He shut the door behind him and walked right toward her.

She stopped breathing and froze.

Larry waddled past without looking at her and went into his closet. Took off his coat and hung it up, and kicked off his shoes. She was just about to stop him. No way did she want to see his ugly naked body.

He walked back into the room, spied her, stopped and gasped.

She hit the button on the remote. A deafening cranking sound filled the room as the bars locked into place.

His eyes went huge and he made a beeline for his bedside drawer. Where his 44 Magnum used to be.

"Not there, Larry."

He wrenched open the drawer and his body jerked back and his mouth fell open. Narrowing his watery eyes, he turned to her, the folds of his face all twisted into an evil clown's snarl. "I don't know who the fuck you think you are, but you are one dead son-of-a-bitch, boy," he growled.

"Sit on the end of the bed, Larry," she commanded in a deep tone.

He didn't move.

"Do it before I tase you, you piece of shit. And don't think I won't."

He honed in on her face and squinted. "Who the fuck are you?"

"Sit on the end of the bed," she ordered more loudly.

"You're a woman?"

"Sit! Hands on your knees where I can see 'em!"

He slowly moved forward, his gaze now sharp. The cop took over and his attention went to her gun and taser. Then he took in every single aspect of her body: her position, posture, and her distance from him, every detail.

His gaze flickered back to hers. Freezing, deadly energy radiated from his core.

Sitting with his hands on his knees, he faced her. Larry was back. Seemed like he'd shed twenty years. Still old and fat, but now full of dark fire.

Without taking her eyes from his, she set the remote on her lap, reached over and flicked on the light next to her.

His brow furrowed hard.

With one swift move, she removed her wig and baseball cap, shook her head and let her hair tumble around her shoulders.

All the color drained from his face, he gasped and put his hands back on the bed to catch himself. "Cathy…" he whispered.

"Guess again, dickhead."

He sat straight up and his eyes went dark and demonic.

Her heartbeat jacked higher.

His face flushing a deep red, he looked like a pitbull about to attack. "How dare you look like her? You fucking little whore!" he spat, rabid.

Took her a long second to process his statement. "How dare I look like my mother?" She couldn't help but laugh.

"You don't deserve her looks. You're nothing like her and you never were. You stole her face and you stole her from me, you fucking bitch." Bits of spit spewed from his blubbery lips.

"Interesting perspective, Larry. Let me guess. You didn't miss me."

"You little...I am gonna love killing you. I'm gonna take it slow and fuck you up the ass like I used to until you cry. I loved making you cry. Then I'm gonna fuck you with my pistol and shoot your fucking cunt back to Hell where it belongs."

Her stomach convulsed and her pulse throbbed in her ears. Flashbacks to those horrible times in the backseat of his Sheriff's car flooded her mind and she battled for equilibrium. Hardening her body and face, she glared at him. "You already fucked me with your pistol, Larry. When I was fourteen. And you fucked me with your baton, flashlight, and every other goddamned thing in your patrol car."

His beady eyes narrowed. "You got the devil in you, girl. I was tryin' to fuck it out. But I see Satan got a hold of you in the end."

"You're the Devil, Larry," she spat. "You're Lucifer in the flesh. But you aren't getting a hold on me. I've got you."

He gave a smug toss of his head. "Think you can take me on." He laughed a rough, hate-filled laugh.

"Not think, am. I *am* taking you on, Fat Boy."

Muffled thumping came from nearby in the house. Thick walls shielded most of the noise, but she could barely make out someone shouting for the Senator.

"Hear that?" he gloated. "They'll be in here in a second. You let me go now and I may let you live."

She laughed. "They can't break in here and you know it. You showed me all the security features of this room on my fifteenth birthday, Larry. When you fucked me on that bed right there. They don't have access, they can't cut the power, all the controls for this room are in your master closet. And I'll reckon you never showed them the secret entrance to this room." She purposefully avoided mentioning its location, not wanting to reveal any information to his security detail. They had to be monitoring the transmission by now. "Remember when you told me that your Dad never informed his security detail about the secret passageway? In case his own men turned on him? And in case he wanted to sneak away for an affair he didn't want them knowing about? I'll bet you share his same philosophy, don't you, Larry?"

His mouth went even uglier. "You think you got all the angles covered, don't you girl?"

"I *do* have all the angles covered, you sack of shit."

"You're nothing. You may have your mother's face, but you're nothing like her."

She snorted. "How the hell would you know, Larry?" She let her hate show.

He sneered, venom oozing from his pores. "The moment you spread your legs for me, I knew what kind of a whore you were. Your mother was never a whore."

It was so weird. She heard his words, but they didn't hurt her like they once had. The man was clearly unbalanced. While he frightened her, she was having difficulty taking him seriously. She chuckled. "Oh, please. I was fourteen, Larry. I was a child."

"You knew what you were doing. You loved me. You loved me fucking you. I'm just glad your mother didn't have to see you grow up into this monster."

"Nice projection." *And thanks for admitting to child abuse on camera, you ugly creep.*

"So what the fuck do you want?"

"To destroy you. The way you destroyed me. I did love you, Larry. And you rewarded me by shooting my father in the chest and murdering him and then you tried to murder me."

He blew out a sharp breath through his lips. "Did a lousy job, didn't I? Where'd you go, anyway?"

Thanks for the confession, fuckhead. "I hid in the water, Larry. And then, you moron, after you emptied your gun into the river all around me, you threw it in and it landed on my foot. And you know where that gun is now? The one registered to you? The one that will match the bullets in my father's corpse?"

His eyes dilated and his shoulders hunched. Then his posture relaxed, he put on a cocky expression and smirked. "Like I believe that."

"You don't have to. I have the gun. So what did you do? Pay off the medical examiner? There were two kinds of bullets in my father's body, Larry. I know you set up Anthony McCoy for Dad's murder. Old Homeless Tony as the town knew him. You grabbed him, put one of your unregistered guns in his hand, and shot a few more rounds into my father's already-dead body. Then you forced Tony to leave his DNA everywhere and poured a pint of whiskey down his throat."

He sent her an arrogant grin. "Worked. And no one will ever prove different. Found out that someone visited him in jail recently and poked around in that case. Poor guy died right after that in a tragic kitchen accident. God rest his soul."

She took in a short breath. "You bastard. But I don't need Tony. I have the murder weapon. And you are about to lose your whole life."

His bloodshot eyes darkened with rage and his mouth twisted. "You won't live long enough to use that evidence against me."

"I won't need to, Larry. Besides, I wasn't stupid enough to bring it with me. If I don't return, a friend will send it to the police."

He laughed and he held himself taller, full of confidence. "I own the police, you stupid bitch."

"Not the local police, you dope. The FBI. Who you don't own."

He laughed harder and slapped his fat knees. "And you are still the most naïve little tramp I've ever met. Of course, I own the FBI. And the CIA. I own them all. I'm going to be President, you little cunt. Not only will I wipe you from the face of the Earth—handy you're already

dead and buried, isn't it?—not only will I eliminate you, I will throw
you down a well on my property here and no one will ever find you.
You'll die slowly and have all the time in the world to realize how
stupid you were by taking me on. You'll rot down there. The
cockroaches will consume your slut flesh. You'll scream and no one
will hear you."

Her blood chilled, her stomach contracted, and she fought a shiver.
He meant every word. Fucker was insane. "Have you ever thought
about trying your hand at fiction?"

"Fuck you, you little whore. I'm getting bored with this." He
stood.

Her heart beat so fast and hard, she couldn't breathe. Working hard
to keep her face and body free of obvious reaction, she motioned with
the gun. "Sit down, Larry," she ordered loudly.

"Or what? Little pipsqueak like you? I'm not afraid of you."

She didn't move. "You should be."

He looked at her gun, then at her. He was just about to make a
move.

Gun had been a bad choice. No way would she shoot him in front
of the world, she needed the taser.

As quick as she could, she dropped the gun and grabbed the taser.

As soon as she moved, he lunged for her.

Panic fueling her muscles, she brought the end of the taser up, fast,
and pulled the trigger. The spikes landed on his chest and he jerked
and shook and made a weird strangled sound. Staggering backwards,
he fell to the floor and curled into a ball. She yanked the wires back,
threw the taser aside, reached for her extra stun gun and pointed at
him.

Took a good long minute for her to start breathing again. Her
whole body shaking, sweat trickling between her breasts, she stared at
the ugly lump of inert human, seriously considering killing him and
being done with it. That was too close. Way too close. She should have
had the taser in her hand to begin with.

After a good five minutes, he sat up, pulled himself onto the bed and wiped his eyes. Then he sent her a look that chilled her to the bone. "Forget the well, I'll fuckin' bring you to my killin' shed and kill you like I killed Dave Gilroy. Slowly. I'll start with your kneecaps and shoot every part of your slut body until you beg me to end your miserable tramp life."

Bile rose in her throat and she tightened her grip on the taser, but forced all emotion from her face. She couldn't let him see he was scoring any points. "I'm glad you've found such a healthy outlet for your anger, Larry."

His expression turned imperious. "I'm more powerful than you can imagine, you little whore." His face reddened and his features hardened. "And I hate you more than I hate anyone on this sorry excuse for a planet. You fucking ruined my life. Your mother was mine! Mine!" He jabbed his thick thumb into his flabby chest.

"Yeah, and she killed herself to get away from you."

He laughed. "You idiot. You stupid fucking little idiot." Shaking his head, his face was full of pity.

"I caught you two screwing, by the way. I came home six months after you killed my father and found you on top of my mother."

He straightened his shoulders and held his chins higher. "Damned right I was. She was mine." He screwed up his face. "And you took her from me! You and your fucking diary! I told you not to keep a diary!" He shook his finger at her dramatically.

She'd forgotten all about it. "I did have a diary, didn't I?"

"And your mother found it! Everything was great! Everything was finally working out! I knew I'd get her back someday."

Taser must have busted something loose in his brain. He was making no sense. "What the hell are you ranting about? She was never yours. She met my father in high school."

"Hell, she wasn't! Your fucking bastard father stole her from me."

"When?"

"Senior year in high school."

Sam felt bashed across the skull. Her mouth dropped open. *"You dated my mother in high school?"*

"You bet. For two years. We were gonna elope. Then your no-good father stole her from me," he seethed. "I should have killed him then. Didn't know how easy it was. I should have made him disappear. Then you woulda been my daughter. Think about that."

A sharp wave of nausea roiled her gut and she shuddered. "I'd rather not."

"And I wouldn't have had to fuck you, wishing the whole time you were her."

Sam had the sensation of falling. She was glad she was sitting or she would have keeled over. He'd wanted her mother? He'd loved her mother? "Whoa. Whoa, wait... Okay, now my mind is totally blown. No wonder you looked at me like that when we first met. My mom's and my freshman pictures were almost identical."

Larry nodded. "I couldn't believe it. When I walked into that classroom and saw my Cathy sittin' there, the spitting image of the day I fell in love with her. You were even wearing a red dress like she had on that day."

Sam fought to comprehend the news. "Holy shit. You never wanted me."

"Hell no. But if I could get you to shut up, I could make believe I was with her again."

"It was never about me." The information was so big, she could barely fit it into her brain.

"Course not. You're nothing. You're half him. Your flesh is tainted with his no-good blood. Now Cathy, she was my world. Always had been. And finally, I got her back. Took killing you two fucks, but I got her. I knew I would. She wanted me something awful. I was so much better in bed than your rotten father. She loved what I gave her. Begged me for it." His face flushed red and he pointed at her. "And then, you little whore, you fucked it all up by leaving that goddamned diary behind!"

Every time he opened his mouth, he blew her thoughts apart. "She found it?"

He nodded, sending ripples through the flesh hanging from his neck. "I was gonna propose to her that day. I waited the whole fucking proper six-month grieving period and then went to her house to propose and found her in your room on your bed, crying her poor eyes out. Looked at me like I was some kind of devil," he said, seeming genuinely perplexed.

"Fancy that."

"And then she went crazy, screaming at me and punching me. I let her get away with a little bit of that, but she wouldn't calm down. I mean, so what if I fucked you? I did it because I loved her. And that's what I told her."

Sam took in a sharp breath, stunned to her core. "Oh, I bet that went over well." Her poor mother! His audacity was mind-boggling. She'd thought he was a crazy fuck before.

"She got hysterical. Started throwing things. Then I don't know how she figured it out, but she accused me of murdering the two of you. She knew Bob had gone after you and your boyfriend. Surprised me. She was much smarter than I thought. Then she went for the phone to call the police. I had to stop her," he said in a defensive tone. His brows angled hard toward his misshapen nose and his face twisted with anger. "But that blood is on your hands. You killed her."

The room contracted and waved around her. She pressed her toes harder into the carpet to keep upright. He wasn't saying what she thought he was saying, was he? Gesturing with the taser, she said, "Wait. Back up there. Mom didn't kill herself?"

He sneered. "You fucking idiot, think you're so smart. Well, everyone was fooled, because I'm good. Doesn't matter now if you know the truth, you won't live long enough to tell anyone. Yes, I killed your mother, I had to."

Sam recoiled and gasped, her thoughts vaporizing like a bomb had gone off in her mind.

Larry's fleshy face drew down with pain. "I didn't want to! Hell, I cried and cried while I was killing her. I loved her. But she was gonna tell. She made me kill her. I gave her a chance to live. I told her if she just kept her mouth shut everything would work out fine. I mean, she had me. We were meant to be together. We could just forget she ever married Bob or had you and we could pretend we'd been married right out of high school."

Sam couldn't believe the words that were coming out of his mouth. "And that's when she realized you were fucking crazy."

"Crazy? Hardly. But I could tell she wasn't gonna go along with it. She gave me no choice. All because of you. She was mine and you made me kill her! It's your fault for looking like her, for fucking me and not being her. Your fault for that fucking diary. If it weren't for you, she'd be alive today. And I swear, I will torture you to death for taking her from me."

"You killed my mother," she whispered, the idea finally hitting home. Her body heated so hot and so fast, she almost melted with rage. His image contorted in front of her and she had to fight to keep from shooting him. "You killed my mother, you fuckin' piece of shit!" she blasted at him, her whole body shaking. "You seduced me when I was fourteen, you murdered both my parents and tried to kill me *because my mother dumped you in high school?* Are you this pathetic?"

"No, you killed her, you little tramp. And now you're gonna die and no one will know the truth."

The pressure on her stomach vanished, the straightjacket of guilt disappeared, and it felt like the Earth had been lifted from her shoulders. Larry didn't know it, but he'd switched the channel on her self-image. From guilty horrid slut to innocent teenage victim. All her memories shifted. She saw herself as she was. A good healthy girl who was victimized by a psychopathic sadist. "It wasn't my fault."

"Hell it wasn't. You killed me in that moment. When she died, I died. There isn't a day that goes by that I don't grieve for her. You don't have the right to live! Not with her face. And I'm gonna shoot it right off your skull."

All at once, Sam centered. Her shoulders squared. The ground solidified underneath her. Her body flooded with self-confidence, fury and vengeance. She felt like an adult for the first time in her life. She was the matriarch of the family now. For her and her parents, it was time to bring this dirtbag to justice. "That'll be a little hard, Larry. Because you're going to jail."

Sirens sounded from close by.

"And here they are, ready to arrest you," she finished with a satisfied grin.

"Ha, jail. Only one going to jail is you. But I'm more hopin' for the morgue. That extra taser of yours will only work once and then I'll kill you," he said with a menacing grin. "I own these local cops. Once we get out of here, they'll let me take you. And I got a special soundproof room built in a warehouse just for the purpose. My killin' shed. I love watching my enemies die. But you, I am going to make you my special event. You little slut. You loved being used. You loved it when I hurt you. You'd probably love it if I fucked you to death with a baseball bat."

Her gut twisted and roiled. "Okay, I'm done with your torture porn bedtime stories and I'm sure America is, too. And now, I'd like to draw your attention to something, Larry."

"What?"

"Do you see that little black thing attached to the lamp?" She jerked her head toward the porcelain lamp on the table beside her. "It's a camera. And there's one behind you pinned to the drapes that's pointed at me."

Using the end of the taser, she flipped up the tablecloth on the table next to her, revealing the computer, and spoke to the camera over Larry's shoulder. "Ladies and Gentlemen, I'm your host, Amanda Hutchins, and I'm coming to you live from the Tyrell mansion in Concord, New Hampshire," she said in a radio announcer voice. "And now I'd like to introduce to you, that sadistic creep about town, that serial killer we've all come to know and love, presidential candidate Senator Larry Tyrell. Take it away, Larry."

He didn't believe her and gave a nervous laugh. "You're bluffing. You're not getting out of here alive."

"Yes, I will. I'll have a police escort."

While holding the gun on him, she flicked on the screen. "I'll bet we're live on CNN."

Her friend Hans' website display was split into three screens. One featured the camera feed on her, one showed Larry, and another was the CNN homepage. A still photo of Larry sitting on his bed was featured on the popular news site. Underneath the picture, the caption read: *Senator Confesses Live to Torture/Murders. Click here to watch.*

Joy surged through her and her body bubbled with wild energy. She wanted to jump up and dance. It worked! Her insane plan worked! Whoo-hoo! *Thank you, Hans!* He'd done it! She could barely believe it was true. After all this time, the truth was out. Told in the fucker's own words. Sweet!

A huge smile on her face, she said, "Say hello to the people, Larry. And say good-bye to the Presidency and hello to a nice jail cell for the rest of your miserable life."

Larry's mouth dropped open, his jowls hanging like a bulldog's.

"In your face, Tyrell. Gotcha!" she said, feeling happy for the first time in sixteen years. She burst out in delighted laughter.

Larry leapt to his feet, screaming in an unintelligible string of expletives. Almost like he was speaking in tongues. He wailed, crying, and collapsed to the bed. Then he sat up, howled, and pounded his knees.

She could only stare at his crazy outburst.

He made a lightning quick move with his hand—shoving it between his legs to the mattress—and a gun magically appeared in his hand.

Screaming, terror firing her limbs, Sam fumbled with her Glock.

He stood, sent her an evil vengeful smile, and shot her square in the chest.

The concussion to her sternum was so painful, so intense, it felt like someone had pounded her heart with a baseball bat. She couldn't breathe. Her ears rang.

A loud explosion and her right hand erupted in agony. Her gun flew across the room, hit the floor, and slid out of reach. Blood poured from a hole in the heel of her hand.

When she turned back to Larry, the smoking barrel of his pistol was inches from her face. Gunpowder burned her nostrils. Her pain was so overwhelming, the shock to her system so violent, the horror so outrageous, her thoughts froze.

"You fucking rotten cunt. I don't have time to torture you to death, so I'm just gonna kill you. You don't deserve an easy death, but no one does this to me and lives."

She expected to die, but still moved her left hand, trying to locate the taser.

Larry stared at her and the barrel of his gun shook. His expression went pained. "Fuck. I cannot shoot the face of your mother. I'd love nothing more than to blow your fucking head off your slut body, but I can't in deference to your mother. Fuck you and see you in Hell, Mandy." He dropped the gun to her chest.

Blam! Like someone fired at her with a missile launcher.

Blam! Like a battering ram impacted her.

Blam! Like a tank drove right into her.

A gray shield dropped over her eyes. No breath. The whine in her ears deafened her.

Then it felt like the Hulk reached inside her body and tore her stomach in half. The most horrible pain she'd ever felt in her life, then nothingness.

She awoke to Larry bellowing and ranting his head off. Her chest and stomach hurt like she hadn't been wearing the Kevlar vest. She could barely get any air in her lungs, each intake of breath sent searing pain through her. She had no idea how long she'd been out. Couldn't have been more than a few seconds because Larry was stomping on her computer.

Blood dripped onto the floor from her useless right hand. She reached into her pocket with her left and slowly withdrew her back up weapon. A Beretta 380 Tomcat.

While Larry was turned away, she stood.

Excruciating pain attacked her belly. She bent over and weird bright patches of color and light zigzagged in front of her face.

Summoning every last bit of her will, she straightened. Then, with everything she had, she kicked his knee with her steel-toed boots. Fire seared her interior.

He screamed and crumpled to the ground.

Despite the agony it caused her, she kicked him in the head as hard as she could. Yowling, he brought his arms up to protect himself. Sam pulled her leg back as far as it would go, then swung down and nailed him right in the balls. He let loose with a hi-pitched squeal and grabbed his crotch. She kicked him in the head, then the ass, and alternated between the two, again and again, until she couldn't take it.

Bleeding and crying, Larry curled into a ball and cowered at her feet.

Bent over, she stood above him, holding her belly with her right arm. She pointed the barrel of the gun at his ear. "And now, fucker," she groaned. "You will die. And since you did me the favor of breaking off the live webcast, everyone will think I'm dead. They won't be able to see me shoot you. And I will leave here and disappear and start a life elsewhere."

If I live that long. Her stomach hurt like a rabid badger was trying to tear its way out. A wave of nausea nearly made her collapse. Her hand dropped a bit, but she took all her remaining strength and focus and forced the gun to his head.

"Go ahead then, you dirty whore!" he wailed.

She drilled the barrel into his temple. "Let me savor the moment." The room went blurry and her legs felt like they'd turned to Slinkys. "Bye, Larry."

A loud crashing came from the closet and Burke, of all people, burst into the room. "Sam, no!"

"Sam, put the gun down." Paul Strong came from behind him with a pistol trained right on her.

"He killed my parents," she grunted. The pain in her stomach built so high she heard a buzzing in her ears along with the whine from the gunfire.

Burke came one step closer. "Sam, don't, you'll never get him out of your mind. You'll be connected to him forever."

"I already can't get him out of my mind. I'm already connected to him forever." Her stomach hurt so badly, she couldn't breathe.

Now or never, Sam!

She cried out, her hand shaking, but she kept her aim on his head. "He has to die," she rasped.

"Dead people don't suffer," Burke called out.

His words reverberated through her head.

Her hand shook so badly, the barrel tapped Larry's temple. She pictured Larry's fat dead body and realized how disappointing it would be. How anti-climactic. Burke was right. She wanted Larry to be humiliated. Wanted him to go to jail. Wanted him to lose everything.

"Good point." She pulled the gun away and staggered back, holding her stomach and trying to stay conscious. Pain was excruciating. The gun dropped to the floor.

Burke rushed to her side, put his arm around her, and held her up. "Are you okay?"

"No," she croaked.

"Bobby, get me an ambulance!" he shouted.

Sam panted, trying to control the agony. How could she hurt this much and still be alive?

Larry spotted Paul. "Strong! Shoot her fucking head off!"

"No, Larry. You depraved sick fuck. I just heard your whole confession over my phone. You'll be lucky if I don't take you on a trip to your 'killin' shed'. Dave Gilroy was a good friend of mine, you bastard. I'll make sure you get the death penalty for murdering him. And Sam's parents."

"I own you!"

Strong gave a harsh chuckle. "You haven't owned me in a long time, Larry. And now that your story is all over the web, you have no collateral. You're dead in the water. They'll execute you for this."

Larry laughed. "You little pissant! I'm Larry Tyrell! I'm going to be President! I can discredit this fucking whore with my hands tied behind my back. Now shoot that fucker and shoot this nasty cunt and that's an order!"

Strong stepped forward holding handcuffs. "Larry Tyrell, you are under arrest for the murders of Catherine and Robert Hutchins, and David Gilroy, and for the attempted murder and assault of Amanda Hutchins. You have the right to remain silent. Anything you say can and will be used against you in a court of law. You have the right to an attorney. Since you can afford one, be prepared to empty your bank accounts in your defense. Stand up."

Larry shook his fists, his stomach jiggling, his chins wagging. "You're making a mistake! I will take you down! I'll throw you in a well and let the rats eat you alive!"

The pain in her gut increased and Sam began salivating. A cold sweat broke out all over her body. She was going to puke. The contents of her stomach came up violently all over the floor.

Blood. An ocean. A flood. Followed by a pain so severe, it felt like she'd swallowed a running chopsaw.

"Sam!" Burke shouted, his voice tinny and distorted. She became aware he was holding her by the shoulders.

"Fuck! Will you look what's she done to my rug?" Larry exclaimed. "That cost me fifty grand! Move that bitch into the bathroom, will you?"

"Shut the fuck up, Larry," Paul snapped.

"Hang on, Sam, the ambulance is almost here." Burke rubbed her back.

The men's voices sounded like they were coming out of tape recorder being played back in the next room.

She puked again and fell to the ground on her hands and knees. Horrible anguish ripped through her. Was she dying? She wanted to stop throwing up. But couldn't. Fuck, she *was* dying! Panic set in and she broke into sobs.

Heaving, more bright red liquid poured from her.

The intricate pattern of the Turkish rug, colored in red, swirled in front of her eyes. The room tilted and the side of her body got hit hard with the floor. She stared at the crack between the bedspread and the carpeting, trembling.

This was it. Bummer. Larry had killed her whole fucking family. At least she'd brought the bastard to justice. But she'd never have that life with Burke. "Burke. Love…you...sorry…"

"I love you, too, Sam, and I'm here. Just hang on."

She groaned, but had to get out her last words. "Tell Emma I love her."

"Sam! You're not dying!"

"…sorry…" She tried to get up, but collapsed into the carpet, which bowed like a giant rubber sheet until it snapped. Falling through, she hurtled downward.

From far up above her, Burke screamed, "Sam! Don't leave me!"

Blackness.

TWENTY-FOUR

Pain in her gut awoke Sam. Horrible, awful. She let out a weak raspy moan. "It hurts. It hurts so bad." Nasty cleaning smell. Bright lights. Agony.

A woman's voice came from the void surrounding her. "I'm giving you more morphine. You'll be fine, Amanda."

A rush of warmth and golden light washed through her. The pain faded. She closed her eyes and crawled back into the comforting darkness, away from the blinding fluorescent lighting. Regular beeping thrummed in time with the throbbing in her belly.

Shit. Hospital. Car accident?

She moved and her stomach hurt. Groaning, she cracked open her eyes again. An IV stand was on her right, the tubes hooked up to the crook of her arm. Behind it, a screen displayed her vitals.

Damn it. Rotten hospitals. She hated them.

Her throat was super parched. The room wobbled. Her eyes were gritty like she'd washed them with sand and her eyelids felt like they weighed four pounds each. Sam blinked until her eyes lubed up. But her hospital room still appeared contorted. She made a giant effort to awaken.

Last thing she remembered was…

Larry shooting her.

"Am I dead?" Her voice came out in a croaking whisper.

"No," came a man's voice.

Very familiar. She turned and a guy was sitting in a chair in the corner of her room, holding a book. His face came into focus.

Burke?

Sure looked like Burke.

But why? She cleared her throat. "Burke?" Her voice sounded like it came from the end of a very long tube.

He sent her a warm smile. "Yes, Sam." He stood, walked over and took her hand. His skin was smooth and warm.

She instinctively moved her other hand to grasp his, but found it bandaged. She wanted to ask why, but he distracted her.

He looked so beautiful. Those sparkling dark brown eyes, straight white teeth and that strong jaw and generous mouth. His dark buzz cut speckled with gray, that sexy scar along the left side of his cheek. Healthy and clean-shaven. She caught his cologne and a wave of calm spread through her.

The image of Larry's bloody cowering body intruded into her thoughts.

A slight jolt of fear shook her, but her body reactions were so disconnected, it was like someone else was afraid.

The scene in Larry's master suite played like a disjointed movie trailer through her mind: short clips, but not very linear. And fuzzy toward the end. She could see herself holding the gun at Tyrell's temple. Why didn't she shoot him? Burke. Burke had stopped her. *Dead people don't suffer.* That's right. Paul Strong had been there, too. Right? Her thoughts were so jumbled.

But if Burke was in her hospital room it meant she was going to be okay, right? "Am I safe?"

"Yes, you're safe. Tyrell can't hurt you any longer. Your plan worked."

She shifted in bed and a searing, jabbing pain came from her stomach. Reaching down to her belly, she found a large bandage and cried out, "What the hell is this?"

He moved her arm away from her stomach. "Don't. You have a hell of an incision there."

"I…" She coughed. Horrible agony. But located more on the skin of her stomach and the top, less on the inside. "Owww, man, this hurts. What do you mean by incision? How did I cut myself? I was wearing Kevlar. Oww." He was making no sense.

"Let me get the nurse. You need morphine. Hang on, darling." Burke disappeared.

Darling. Her heart went warm and fuzzy.

After a few moments, the room pixilated then faded out. An instant later, sharp pain awakened her to an empty hospital room. The walls undulated and blurred.

Had Burke been in the room? Or had she hallucinated him?

She tried to get up and her stomach hurt so badly it felt like she was run through with a sword. She cried out. The machine next to her beeped faster.

The nurse rushed into the room, followed closely by Burke.

"What the fuck happened to me? Why do I have a giant bandage on my belly?"

The nurse, an African-American woman in her late fifties, took her by the shoulders and gently pressed her to the bed. "Now calm down, honey, you're fine. You had an operation."

Sweat beaded on her forehead. "What kind of operation?"

Burke came up on her other side and took her hand.

The nurse patted her. "One that saved your life. The doctor will come in soon and explain it to you."

"Just tell me what they did," Sam demanded.

"They had to stop the internal bleeding," the nurse said, rubbing her shoulder.

"You'd lost a lot of blood, but you're fine, Sam," Burke said with a squeeze of her hand. "Your prognosis couldn't be better."

"But why did they have to operate?"

Rubbing her free hand between his big strong ones, Burke replied, "When Tyrell shot you, even though you wore the Kevlar vest, the concussions of the blasts were powerful enough to rupture your ulcers. And crack your sternum. You're very lucky to be alive, Sam."

The beeping increased along with her tension. "I almost died?"

His brows furrowed and he tilted his head slightly to one side. "You don't remember any of our previous conversations?"

"Well, yeah. But I haven't talked to you since we were on that roof and—"

His worry lined deepened. "You don't remember anything from the previous seven days?"

A super-injection of adrenaline blasted through her. *"I've been here seven days?"* The beeping machine went crazy.

Burke and the nurse gently pressed her down onto the bed. "Sam, stop," he ordered.

The nurse said, "Honey, calm down, no need to shout."

Sam wanted to run out of there, back to a time when none of this had happened. "They cut my belly open, I've lost a week of my life—I still can't believe that Larry killed my mom—and you tell me not to shout."

The nurse shook her head and chuckled. "Here, I'll help you. Nearly time anyway." She grabbed a long cord draped over the side of Sam's hospital bed and pressed a button at the very end.

A cloud of warmth slammed Sam back against her bed and her pain and concerns vanished. "Oh, that was fun. Do it again," she slurred. Her whole body pulsed with pleasure.

The nurse laughed. "Girl, you are a devil. You were right, Burke. Go ahead and feed her some ice."

Everything became happy, shiny and pretty.

The room swirled around her, then Sam floated away on a cloud.

A piece of ice was in her mouth. The ice melted and was like manna from heaven for her throat.

"Open up, Sam."

She opened her eyes and Burke stood there. Burke was feeding her ice. How lovely. He was so fun to look at. He spooned another ice chip into her mouth. Ice was the best invention known to man. She loved ice. And she really loved Burke. "More."

He grinned and fed her several more pieces.

A bit of the haze in her mind cleared. Had he forgiven her? Where was Emma? She wanted to ask him, but the ice was too divine.

Finally, she held up her hand. Which took a lot more effort than it should. Felt like her arm had weights attached and moved in slow motion. "Is Emma here?"

"She and Rollin are on their way."

"Cool. Where ish here?" She cleared her throat and tried to speak more clearly. "Where *is* here?"

"Concord Hospital."

"We're still in New Hampshire?"

"Yes."

"What happened to Larry?"

Burke grinned so widely she couldn't help but smile back.

"What?"

"In jail without bail. They exhumed your father's body. The bullets from Larry's gun matched. The case is solid. And of course, your stunt worked. There is a circus of media downstairs. Every time I walk out, I get mobbed. I had to hire a PR person for you. You've been all over the front pages for the last week. You're a hero."

"I'm a *what*?"

Patting her arm, he said, "I shouldn't overload you."

"Hey, I'm messed up on morphine. Best time to tell me everything. So my plan worked? People saw the video? How many before they shut it down?"

"I think there's one Yak herder in Outer Mongolia who hasn't seen it, but everyone else on the planet has. Went beyond viral. And because you stepped forward, you empowered twenty-five other young women to do the same."

A shot of pure joy cut through the fog of the drug. "I hadn't even considered that part. Wicked cool."

He sent her an admiring smile. "Most of their cases are beyond the statute of limitations, but ten aren't. Also because Tyrell confessed on camera to torturing his enemies to death, they found his killing shed, as he called it, and two skeletons in old wells on the property."

Sam shuddered. "I was afraid he was telling the truth about that. Just when I thought the guy couldn't get any creepier, he out creeped himself."

Burke gave a grim nod. "So far he's been charged with eight murders—including your parents—your attempted murder, and eleven cases of rape and twenty-two for statutory rape. Plus myriad counts of sexual assault with a foreign object, sodomy, child endangerment, racketeering, tax evasion, the list goes on and on. He tried to commit suicide in his cell, but failed."

"Cool. I hope they keep him alive forever. I want him to suffer."

"He's suffering, all right," Burke said with a quick smile. "They said it will be years before they're done prosecuting him for all his crimes. Him and his friends. He's turned on all his buddies and tons of guys will be going down with him. It's a mess."

"Is Paul one of the casualties?"

"No. He's helping build the prosecution's case. He was here earlier, checking on your progress."

"So he's not an evil spy?"

"He is, but not that evil. He's helped you—and me—cut through a lot of red tape. He's stood up for you and protected you. You won't be facing charges for trespassing or false imprisonment or tasing Larry. Strong convinced his superiors that you were working for him on a secret sting operation. Plus the powers that be realized that there wasn't a jury in the world that would convict you."

"Thank God. I'm glad Paul turned out to be a good guy."

Burke nodded, but the coldness behind his eyes and the slight twist to his mouth told her that he still didn't like the Fed. "Here, have another ice chip." He pushed one in her mouth.

Sam closed her eyes and let the cool moisture trickle down her throat.

"When you're up to it, you should give an interview. Diane Sawyer's people have made contact, Barbara Walters, Oprah's people, plus thousands of newspapers, all the big magazines, TV stations."

A dull shot of anger flared through her, her fists made a weak attempt at balling, and she opened her eyes. "I don't want to talk to anyone about that asshole. I'm done. I don't want to relive any of that crap." Again, the machine beeped faster.

"You can decide what to do when you get better."

"Damn, my intent was to reach everyone on the planet with that stunt. I just didn't realize the aftermath. Once I flipped that switch, I not only put Larry out in the public's eye, I put myself. Holy shit, they're gonna feed on me and my past like piranhas. This sucks. This is probably the most juicy, salacious story that's hit the news in awhile. I totally screwed myself and my privacy forever."

By the look on his face, her worst fears were confirmed.

She let out a sigh and wondered if it was time for more morphine. Like maybe the whole bottle.

Burke rubbed her arm. "We'll come up with a plan to protect you. The Patriots are good at that. All you have to do is heal. Just try to relax and realize that's it all over. Larry's in jail and you're safe."

"Thank God."

Sam fell quiet while Burke fed her ice chips. From absolute anonymity to absolute exposure. Unreal, surreal, freaky and no way could she get her head around it. Especially on morphine.

After a few minutes, she focused on Burke. His gorgeous deep brown eyes radiated caring. His calm, strong quiet presence was so comforting. And he was taking such great care of her. Did that mean he loved her? Why hadn't he brought up their relationship?

She frowned. After tasing him, stealing from him and all the other stuff, how could he still want her? Emma was probably busy and he was just standing in for her. "I never found out, are Banana and David okay?" she asked instead of asking what she really wanted to know.

"Both healed fine."

"Thank God."

He offered her another piece of ice, and sent her a nasty look. "And so did Strong and I from your attack."

She winced and wished she could hide. Okay, no, he hadn't forgiven her so they probably weren't together anymore. But why wasn't Emma here instead? And why was he being so nice?

He narrowed his gaze. "You're still in huge trouble. Not only did you subject me to thousands of volts of electricity and horrendous pain, you stole thousands of dollars worth of weaponry."

Making a little grimace, she glanced down at the IV.

He leaned in closer. "And you stole my custom Mercedes SUV, sideswiped it on something gray and metallic, then dumped it four hundred miles away."

Sam fiddled with the covers even though her fingers didn't work so well. "I didn't sideswipe the Mercedes. Technically." She glanced at him for his reaction.

"Technically." He rolled his eyes. "I can't even imagine the excuse. Have another ice chip." He stuck one in her mouth.

She sucked on the ice and tried to collect her thoughts and come up with an apology that she actually meant. While she loved the guy and wanted him more than anything, she wasn't lying to him. Nor would she grovel. "Dude, if you hadn't imprisoned me and kept me from using my own weapons and equipment, I wouldn't have had to steal yours. You're at least half responsible."

His mouth tightened and his eyes flashed cold, but he fed her more ice chips. Clearly still waiting for that apology.

"Uh, sorry I tased you." Not much, but it was best she could come up with.

He arched a brow. "That's it? You're not sorry for anything else?"

He wasn't nearly as mad as he should be. In fact, he looked like he was fighting a smile.

"No." She shrugged, which hurt. "Ow."

"Pain serves you right. Brat. Can't imagine what it's going to take to win my forgiveness. But I'm sure I'll think of something," he said with a wicked glint in his eye. His old warmth showed through.

Her body buzzed with hope. That meant he still loved her, right? She wanted to ask him point blank, but she wasn't sure she could handle it if he said no. But he was there. Didn't that mean something?

He raised a brow. "Yes?"

"What are you doing here?"

"Taking care of you, what does it look like?"

"Don't you have to work?"

"You're my job right now."

"On orders from the Patriots?"

"No, on my own orders." His expression was completely unreadable.

"Good." So what did that mean?

A cell phone rang from somewhere nearby. He looked down, reached into his pocket and withdrew his iPhone and checked the screen. "I have to take this. If you'll excuse me." He put the phone to his ear and walked out of the room.

"Great timing, Burke." She sighed and closed her eyes.

After a few moments, the monitor's beeping faded out.

When she awoke, Burke's chair was empty and the older African-American nurse was checking her vitals. He'd probably taken off. She wished she could start over with him, but until time travel was invented, that was an empty desire. And if he didn't want her, she hoped he stayed away.

"Hi," she said to the nurse.

"Hi, there." The nurse smiled and read her blood pressure.

Before she could stop herself, she asked, "Where's Burke?"

"I kicked him out to go find some food. That man never thinks of himself, only you. You got yourself a good husband there, Amanda."

"Call me Sam. And I think you misunder—"

"I've never seen a more dedicated man. We brought in a recliner so he could sleep in your room in ICU because he refused to leave. He pulled some strings, too, because that was against hospital rules. He's only left your side when someone made him go eat. He's been a pest, too, making sure you got top-notch service. You're lucky, honey. Wish

I had a husband like that. Now you take care, Mrs. Cherlenko. Be proud of that name, honey. He's worth a million." The woman walked out.

Mrs. Cherlenko echoed through her mind. Adrenaline powered through her and her fists balled. Another one of Burke's rotten tricks. She was going to kill him.

Unless she'd married him in the previous few days without remembering.

But what the hell was that dick doing, marrying her when she wasn't even lucid? She loved the guy, but she was kicking his ass.

Wait a minute. This made no sense. What possible reason could he have for marrying her while she was incapacitated? What was his motivation? Clearly it wasn't because he loved her or he would have brought up the subject already. Probably had something to do with her being unconscious and not being able to make decisions about her care. Emma probably hadn't gotten there in time and he'd lied so he could handle the emergency.

Whatever the reason, if he didn't want her anymore, could he have devised a more exquisite torture? *Let's pretend we're married right before I dump you.*

As if on cue, Burke walked into the room.

"Oh, look. It's my *husband.*"

Burke winced.

Her shoulders tightened. Not a good sign. "We didn't have a hospital wedding I don't remember, did we?"

He chuckled. "No. We didn't."

"Did you forget to tell me something, Burke?"

All the apology and reticence left his face and he assumed his power pose: shoulders squared, arms crossed, head and chin held high. "It was the only way to take care of you properly. With the current health system, if you don't have an advocate, your needs aren't always adequately addressed."

Her mood plummeted, but she kept her expression neutral. "So Emma didn't get here in time, huh?"

"Not only was she in California when you almost died, since you have no listed next of kin and you never filed an Advanced Care Directive, Emma couldn't make any decisions for you. They only allow spouses in the ER and ICU, so I lied. Play along."

Yeah, *play*. Real fun playing the part of his wife with no hope of actually marrying him. Where was that morphine? To cover her feelings, Sam raised her eyebrows and grinned, like she was amused by the whole thing. "Mrs. Amanda Cherlenko. Serves you right, being my husband for a while."

He sent her a sparkling smile. This guy was a master at mixed signals. Did the fucker love her or not? "Brat. You're lucky I pretended to be your husband. After what you did to me."

"I apologized."

He made a face. "For the *tasing* only."

She caught his hand. Even though her heart was breaking, before they parted ways she had to at least give him credit for what he'd done for her. She owed him that much. "Look, Burke, I honestly hated that whole scene. I felt like crap for hurting you. And God bless your soul, no matter what I did to you, you kept coming to my rescue. I know your job overlapped with what you did for me, but I saw the intent in your heart. And it was pure, the whole way through. You were loyal to me and I didn't make it easy on you."

"No, you didn't." While her words seemed to make the look behind his eyes happy, his expression still remained guarded. No way to tell what he was thinking.

"But the biggest thing I need to thank you for was saving my life. Not just by calling the ambulance, but stopping me from killing Larry. Killing him would have ruined me. You knew exactly what to say to get me to stop."

His expression softened and he squeezed her hand. "Completely understandable, Sam. Horrific what he did to you and your family."

A flare of anger made her center hot and she gripped her sheets. "I still can't believe he murdered my whole family because Mom dumped him in high school. Have you ever heard of anything more lame?"

"That quote really made the rounds. That and many of the things you said to him." His phone rang. He answered it and grinned at her. "You're here. Good, just come up, I've already given your names to the security detail. We're in 214. Great." His face sparkled with shiny, golden energy. Looked like he was about to burst. Adorable. But why? "There's someone here to see you. A couple of people."

"Emma and Rollin?

"No." Still with the bubbly anticipation.

"Who?"

"You'll see," he said with a sly smile.

A large woman in a garishly printed shirt appeared at her door. In her mid-fifties, she had a big red hairdo. Behind her was a man about Sam's age with auburn hair and a red beard.

"Mandy?" the woman asked. Tears streamed down her face.

It took Sam a long second to recognize the woman.

Aunt Belinda. Her mother's sister. Her favorite aunt in the universe. Bigger and older, but as flamboyant as ever.

A tsunami of emotion swept through her and her eyes filled with tears. Sixteen years of longing ripped her apart. "Aunt Belinda?" Sam held out her arms.

Sobbing, Belinda rushed to her bedside and embraced her. "I can't believe you're alive. I can't believe I didn't lose you."

She clung to her plump aunt, her familiar scent sending Sam flying back through time. Felt so good to be in her arms. "I'm so sorry I didn't come to you. I was so afraid. I didn't want him to kill you."

Belinda pushed away to point at her. "You stop, Manders." She wiped the tears away and pointed at her again. "No apologies. If it's anyone, it should be me who's apologizing, I should have come looking for you."

"No, then we would have both died. I should have let you know I was okay."

She shook her head, making her big red hairdo jiggle. "No, you were afraid for your life. I saw the video. Oh, my God, you poor thing. What he did to you! I wanted to kick his balls right up into his throat. Wait. Before I blather on, was that you who called on the day of your mother's funeral?"

Her heart shredded and burned and she took a deep breath. Most horrible day of her life. More tears flowed and she nodded. "I wanted to warn her. I finally couldn't stand it. Then when you picked up instead of her and I heard all those voices in the background, I thought she was having a party. And I was pissed, like she'd forgotten me and Dad so soon and was celebrating? Then you revealed that not only wasn't Mom there, she was dead, and the party was her funeral reception."

Belinda's face fell and she took her in her arms once more. Cupping the back of Sam's head, she cradled her as best she could around the tubes and wires. "Oh, honey. I prayed it was you. And that you were safe somewhere. And taken care of."

Sam wiped her eyes and nodded. "I was. A woman and her daughter rescued me and took me in within a few hours of arriving in California. I found good people who loved me and I built a great life for myself."

Belinda glanced at Burke and then back at her. "And you found yourself a great husband. We love him," she said to Sam. Then she turned to him. "We love you, Burke."

He blushed. Actually blushed. His dark eyes crinkled, he flashed a white-toothed grin, and briefly looked at the floor in an aw shucks move.

Husband. She hated the deception. Hated the whole thing. *Here's the husband you want, but can't have.* Sam turned back to her aunt and her heart warmed again. But Belinda still didn't feel real. Nothing had seemed real since she'd woken up. "Seems like years and minutes since I've seen you, Belinda. This is all so overwhelming."

"For me, too. I can't get over how much you look like your mother."

Sam's attention went beyond Belinda to the man standing behind her. She saw the child in his face. Her cousin, Gerald. "Holy bejeebus. Gerry? No way. Look at you! Facial hair. You're a man. No more beanpole, dude. You filled out."

"Hey Manders. Didn't think you'd remember me," he said, stepping forward.

"Dude, you are the Ho-Ho King, how could I forget that?"

His grin touched his ears. "Never puked that much in my life. Oh. Mom wasn't supposed to know about that."

"What? What did you kids do?" Belinda said in a teasing tone as she looked between them.

Sam stared at her long lost family, unable to grasp the enormity of it all. "I've missed you guys so much."

Belinda burst into tears once more and hugged her. "I thought I'd lost you all." After a moment where they cried and held each other, her aunt pulled back, but took hold of her hand. "But I have you back. Finally. And you're not going anywhere, right?"

"I'm back for good, Belinda. If you guys will have me. After what I did to everyone. I should have never slept with that creep."

Belinda's brow furrowed. "Don't tell me you're blaming yourself for that."

"I always did, Belinda." Sam looked down at the bandages on her right hand.

Belinda tucked her finger under Sam's chin and met her gaze. "Don't let Larry win, girl. That was all him. You were a good girl. No matter what shit your Dad shoveled on you, you did nothing wrong but grow into a beautiful young woman. Your father was an asshole." She put a hand to her formidable chest and looked toward the ceiling. "God rest his soul." She broke her reverent pose and her features darkened. "Bob freaked out when you grew breasts. He actually felt betrayed. All those Hutchins, they were throwbacks. No wonder you hooked up with a father figure."

"You're kidding me. Everyone loved my dad. Wasn't he a God or something to the community? A paragon of virtue?"

Belinda's face screwed up into incredulity. "Bob? Are you kidding? No one liked him. He was a total controlling prick. All those Hutchins men were and are assholes. I never wanted Cathy to marry him."

Sam's foundation shook and she fought for center. "Really?"

"Really. I know you've been eating yourself alive—those ulcers aren't a surprise—but you let all that go. You were the best daughter anyone could want. The best. Cathy loved you until the day she died. She blamed herself for not stopping Bob from coming after you. He lost his mind when he overheard you making plans to sneak out. He wanted to catch you and rip you a new one."

"He got his wish. He called me horrible things, Belinda. He called me a whore."

Belinda's face blackened with anger and her eyes narrowed. "Bastard. All you did was become a woman. Sometime soon, we'll stay up late and have a few bottles of wine and I'll tell you all about the Hutchins boys. Bad news, whole lot of 'em. Abusive, self-centered jerks. Your mother, she sure could pick 'em: Tyrell and Bob. Just like dear old Dad. Thank God, I broke that tradition when I married my Hugo."

Sam's mind took another jog that hurt. "Wait? Grandpa Billings was an abusive jerk? I thought you and Mom worshipped him."

"Worship, ha. No. Old bastard. We hated him. We did a secret little jig, just the two of us, at his funeral."

"This is the craziest stuff I've ever heard. Really? My grandfather and my dad were jerks?"

"Yes. Way beyond jerks. I know Bob was good to you when you were a kid and I'll always be grateful to him for that. But after that he went downhill. It wasn't just you, he turned on his friends, on Cathy. Your parents' relationship was on the rocks when the whole tragedy happened."

Sam's mouth dropped open. "You're kiddin' me. I thought it was me. I thought I turned him into that man."

"No, his dad was like that and so's his brother, your uncle Fuckhead—I mean, Phil. Sorry, we always called him that."

Sam stared into space, trying to reconfigure the memories to fit the new truth. "You are blowing my mind."

"We got a lot to talk about, girl. And I want to know every single little thing about you. How you met this hunk here. About how you bought all those properties? In California? I knew you were goin' places."

Sam's consciousness seated and the tension eased from her body. She felt centered for the first time since she was eleven. All the misinformation that had conflicted with the reality was finally being reconciled. *Your father loves you.* The shame and anger on his face when she wore her first bikini. *Your father adores you.* How he couldn't make eye contact with her the day she bought her first bra. *You're the light of his life.* His remote, dark coldness when she got her period.

Damn! Her father was the one in the wrong, not her! Wow! No wonder she had all these conflicting feelings. Dad kept telling her how much he loved her and then he'd treat her like shit. Just like Larry. "Belinda, I think you just single-handedly cured me."

Her aunt burst into a huge happy smile.

Over the next half hour, Belinda caught her up on the rest of the family news. It was so wonderful being reunited with her relatives. After all this time of being alone. So awesome. She'd finally come home. Overwhelming.

After a nice visit, Belinda and Gerry left.

Leaving her alone with Burke. Her interior burned. Out of the fat and into the fire.

Sam wanted to know once and for all if he still loved her, but wasn't sure she could take many more emotional shocks. And she could not tell what he was thinking. She smirked. "Husband. You are too much."

"Think about me. You as a wife? Please." But the look in his eyes radiated love and affection.

Damn it, why wouldn't he just say how he felt?

He stepped up to the side of her bed with an expectant look on his handsome face.

Excellent. *Now say it, Burke!*

"While you're still awake, I wanted to ask you something."

"Yes?" *Yes, I love you, too! Now kiss me, you fool!*

"I'm trying to locate all the things you *borrowed* from my weapons locker. Banana removed some items around the same time you did and didn't keep track."

Her heart sank. Of course. Where was his precious stuff? She was beginning to hate this jerk.

"To confuse matters, you acquired another small arsenal with many duplicates of my own weaponry. So far, I've recovered my sniper rifles, the Kevlar vests, the Tasers and grenades. I don't want to know what you had planned for the grenades. Is the storage unit in Portland the only other place you stored the weapons besides the Toyota and motel room in Seattle?"

Sam sighed. "You must have found the storage facility receipt and everything else in my Battle Bra, right?"

"Yes. So is that it?"

"Yep."

He shook his head, sent her an exasperated look, and sighed.

Screw this. She was done waiting. "Look, I appreciate everything you've done for me, but I don't want to keep you. Seems like I'm getting my brain back. I can make decisions for myself from here on out. If Emma's around, she can help me get a place nearby. Or I'll move in with Belinda for awhile. I have to hang around until Larry is brought to trial, right?"

The line between his dark eyes deepened and his mouth twisted to one side. "Yes, the FBI mentioned that. Not that you'll be on your feet anytime soon. As soon as they release you—probably in the next couple days—you'll be facing a long recovery. You'll need a long-term rental around here. And someone to care for you."

"Okay. That shouldn't be too hard now that I'm reconnected with my family. Honestly, Burke, you've been amazing, but I don't want to keep you. You probably have a million things to do."

His gaze hollowed and his expression drew down with pain. "I'll go if you want me to, Sam."

"It's not that I don't enjoy your company, I just don't want to inconvenience you any longer."

"How do you feel about me?"

"I'm grateful." But she had an idea that's not what he was asking. She prayed he wanted the same information as she did. He sure looked like it. Her insides buzzed with hope. *Say you love me, you big idiot!*

He frowned and rubbed his mouth. "Is that it?"

She played dumb. "What do you mean?" No way. Him first.

"I want to know if your feelings for me have changed." He moved forward and took her hand. "Sam, I have to know, despite all that's happened, do you still want a future with me? Please say yes." His grip tightened. "I love you, Sam. And I can't live without you. Please tell me you still love me." His voice strong and clear, his eyes were wide with vulnerability and sincerity.

A three-ton weight lifted from her. "Thank God!" Her shoulders slumped with relief. "Now that wasn't so hard, was it? For crying out loud, that took you forever!"

His brows furrowed. "What the hell are you talking about?"

"You've been torturing me ever since I woke up. There was no way I was asking you if you still loved me because I'm stuck here in this bed and I totally utterly screwed you over. What if you said no? I can't get up and leave, I can't cry without tremendous pain, and I can't kick your ass if you piss me off. I can't do anything but lie here."

He narrowed his eyes and pursed his lips.

She smacked his arm. "And you, you bastard, wouldn't say a goddamned thing. We talked about everything—the weapons, your stupid Mercedes—everything but what mattered. Then you devised this nasty awful marriage thing and tortured me more. Sent in some relatives to enhance the pain of the lie. Thank God for the morphine or

I would have expired from the anguish already. All you had to do was tell me you loved me. Idiot."

Shaking his head, he snorted. "You really are a wench. So let me guess, you still love me."

"I love you so much I feel like my heart—hell, my whole body—is about to explode."

He burst into a brilliant smile, his shoulders relaxed and he leaned in and kissed her. A tender light touch of the lips quickly turned into a possessive declaration of love.

Felt like the morphine flooded her body through a fire hose. She clung to him and fought back the tears. "I thought I'd lost you."

"No. Never."

"Thank God." It was over, finally over. And she'd won. Not only had she beaten Larry, she got to keep Burke. "This is so sweet. For the first time in sixteen years, I can be myself and I don't have to run, I don't have to hide. And I'm finally free to just love you."

Beaming, he kissed her again.

Her heart cracked open wide. Tears welled in her eyes. She pushed away to face him. "You know our lives are going to be completely different."

"They'd sure as hell better be. No more drama, woman," he warned with a finger jab her way.

"I'm done." She held her hands up in an I-give-up gesture. "I can just go back to living a normal life. Even though I have no idea what normal is. Are you sure you won't get bored with me if I'm not trying to run away from you all the time? Are you sure you didn't just love the chase?"

His brows came down hard over his flashing brown eyes. "Are you out of your fucking mind, woman? No. I didn't love the chase. I hated it. I hated every moment you were gone from my side and in danger. No one has ever put me through this kind of hell. Sam, I know who you are, I know how you normally live your life. Believe me, we're very compatible."

"I just don't want to disappoint you."

He laughed. "Not possible."

"Well, this is all a moot point, anyway, huh? Because we're already *married*." She chuckled.

"Speaking of that, I have a confession to make."

"What?"

"Since I was concerned about impersonating your husband—lots of legalities with signing forms for your care, the PR person, all the access I needed to your personal accounts to make sure they were taken care of—"

"Yeah. And thank you, by the way."

"I, uh—you're welcome—I took some precautions."

"What kind of precautions?"

He looked away and rubbed the back of his neck. Looked like he thought of and rejected several answers. Clearly worried.

"What did you do?"

"Bobby hacked the San Francisco records department and..."

"Burke, spit it out."

He looked her straight in the eye. "We are legally married."

It took a long few seconds for the meaning to penetrate her brain. She burst out laughing. "Ow, ow, ouch." Gasp. "Ow, can't laugh. That's rich. You poor bastard. So he can just undo it, right? After I get out of here?"

"Uh, yeah. No. Maybe."

What was he getting at? "Burke?"

He sent her an undecipherable look. "I was going to wait. But so be it. I've been carrying around this thing for the past two weeks. Samantha Murdock, Amanda Hutchins, I love you with my whole heart and soul, and I want to be by your side forever." He withdrew his hand from his pocket and presented her with what had to be a four-carat pink diamond ring. Looked like the fucking crown jewels. "Will you please do me the honor—shit, I wanted to get down on one knee, but then you couldn't see me—"

She laughed, in complete shock.

His grin widened. "Samantha Murdock, will you please do me the honor of not divorcing me?"

She knew everything about this man. All his warts. Especially his warts. And despite his past and flaws, she'd never met a better fit. She thought of their relationship so far. The fights. The fucking. Oh, the fucking. But all she could really think of is how he'd cared for her since she'd been in the hospital. No one had ever loved her like this. And she'd never loved anyone this much, either.

Sam sent him a huge grin. "I promise to love, honor, cherish and not divorce you, Burke Cherlenko."

He burst into a bright smile, slid the ring on her finger and kissed her.

Despite the drugs and unsexy circumstances, all she wanted to do was be naked with him. When he pulled away, she said, "Once I heal up, I am going to fuck you until you cry."

His eyes lit up and his smile turned wicked. "Promise?"

"Promise. Now come here and give me another one of those, Mr. Cherlenko."

"With pleasure, Mrs. Cherlenko."

EPILOGUE

Lying on a chaise on the upper deck of Burke's yacht, Sam adjusted her cell phone so it wasn't pressing on a sensitive part of her ear, and absently gazed at the Lahaina Boat Harbor. "I swear, Emma, Burke knows every square inch of this planet. And if there's a town of three people and there's a restaurant, Burke knows the chef. And in every damned restaurant he takes me to, some foreign guy comes rushing out of the kitchen and speaks some weird-ass language—to which Burke responds in the same language—I swear he knows 750 fucking languages—ending in Meester Burke, you try! Then the chef hands him some eyeball-on-a-stick or Yak nards and Burke bites into them with sublime bliss on his face and offers the crap to me and I go: 'Uh, so you guys got a burger?'"

Emma went into peals of laughter.

"I'm serious, this guy has favorite foods everywhere. It's crazy." Sam scanned the sunny Maui harbor for Burke's ski boat. Fishing vessels and yachts bobbed on the blue-green sparkling waves, but no sign of the husband. "Speaking of which, I have to get off the phone soon, I want to make Rice Krispy Treats and if he catches me befouling his precious granite kitchen with marshmallows, he'll lose his mind. He's out shopping for some shirt he had to have—probably cost fifty grand—and he's due back any minute."

Sam rolled sideways off the chaise, her belly twinged with pain and she winced. With a grunt, she heaved herself to her feet, careful to stay bent over.

"What was that noise for? Are you healing okay?"

"Yeah, overdid it yesterday. I was feeling good so I stupidly dove off the boat— even though Burke ordered me not to—and hit the water hard and pulled something. I was in so much pain I almost drowned. Then after he dove in to save me—fully clothed, mind you—and hauled me out of the water, I lost my footing and slipped on the deck and brought him down with me."

Emma laughed delightedly. "He must have loved that."

"Yeah, he's a got some very attractive bruises. I think it was the first time he's yelled at me since I tased him. But, shit, today I woke up in more pain than I've felt in weeks. This healing process is a bitch. I wanted to walk everywhere in Europe, but couldn't handle it. We had to drive or be driven. So annoying."

"Does Burke take as good of care of you as he did here?"

Sam slowly straightened out, breathing through the ache in her gut. Finally, the pain dulled and she slowly made her way across the deck, headed for the stairs that led to the middle deck and the galley. "Yeah. So patient and tender and kind. Even yesterday, after he yelled at me, he carried me into our cabin and took care of me. I feel like his million-year-old mother he's carting everywhere."

"Well, you may be hurt, but at least you get to heal on a bazillion dollar yacht in Hawaii."

"Yeah, it's really nice. Except I can't wear a goddamned bikini anymore with this fucking zipper down my belly." Sam reached the staircase and leaned heavily on the railing.

"Oh, honey, I'm sorry. You poor thing."

"I'll be fine." Sam descended the stairs one step at a time. "Just have to adjust to my limitations so I can heal. And deal with all this newfound crappy notoriety. Did I tell you that the tabloids keep finding us? Even in obscure places. We were in…shit…somewhere where they spoke French. Belgium, maybe? I don't know. Anyway, we're at one of Burke's favorite cafes and some woman comes up to me and says, 'I always hated that bastard, can I have your picture?'" She slowly walked through the expansive living room area with its luxurious leather couches and mahogany dining table for twelve.

"That sucks. They finally stopped waiting around your house. Vultures. I've had to shoo them away from the store a bunch of times."

"Assholes, I hope they don't find me here, and stay away when we get back home in a few weeks." Sam pushed through the swinging stainless steel galley door. Grabbing her sweaty ice tea glass, she took a swig. She leaned against the butcher-block kitchen island and caught her breath.

"That will be so cool! Finally get some girl time. So how is the relationship going between you and Burke? I mean, when you're not making him dive fully clothed into the water? You guys getting along still as good as you were?"

Sam chuckled. "Hell yeah. He's the most normal, non-drama dude I've ever hooked up with. We don't argue—well, except for yesterday. And we don't have to entertain each other. We spend hours reading and not talking. Never been with a guy who wasn't needy and didn't require babysitting."

"Finally. He's so different than I thought. So nice."

"Don't be fooled by all that niceness. He still has an edge. Once in a while, the Burke you first met rears his ugly head. While we get along great, it's because I don't take his shit and I stand up to him."

"Sam the Burke-tamer." Emma laughed. "Rollin just walked in the door—hey honey, I'm talking to—what the HELL happened to you? Jesus Christ! I hate it when you come home bloody!"

Sam frowned and her heart beat faster, but Emma didn't sound as concerned as she should be, more annoyed than anything. "Rollin's bloody?"

"Yeah. I wish I could say this was an unusual occurrence," Emma replied in a withering tone. "Now he's going to give me some stupid lie about how he fell on his motorcycle or hurt himself surfing. This man drives me nuts. You wait right there, mister! No bleeding on my new rug. That one, the one you're bleeding on! Stop! I'll get the disinfectant and Band-aids. Sam, I have to go. Love you, I'll call in the next few days—not that towel, Rollin! Bye, Sam!" Click.

Chuckling, Sam hung up the phone, withdrew an All-Clad saucepan from a cupboard and put it on the eight-burner gas stove. Rice Krispy Treat Time!

Burke turned the rental Jeep from Front Street onto Canal Street, heading for the harbor. His phone buzzed. Rollin. "Hey buddy, how are you?" he asked over his Bluetooth.

"How's it goin' with you?"

"Never been happier."

"No, uh, issues yet?"

"No. Sam's the least needy woman I've ever met. I feel like we've been together much longer than we have because we fit. She's helpful and sweet and caring. She's perfect. Well, except for yesterday when she decided she was healthy enough to dive off the fucking boat even though I ordered her to stop."

"Uh, oh."

"Yeah, she almost drowned, I had to dive in and save her—ruining my new fucking Gucci shorts and shirt, thank you very much. First idiot thing she's done since the deal with Tyrell. But she learned her lesson. She can barely move today."

"I'm glad Sam hasn't completely changed."

"As much as I'd never admit it to her, I agree. That woman has spark and fire that no one could diminish or control."

"Damn, Burkey old boy, your relationship sounds so, uh, normal."

Burke pulled into the parking lot for Lahaina Harbor. "I know. Really, I've never had more fun with a woman, never had this much fun in my life, nor have I ever been this much in love. I...I'm happy, Rollin." He parked and turned off the car.

"And I mean this in all honesty, it's about time, Burke."

"My sentiments exactly." He retrieved his packages from the passenger seat. "So we're all set for tomorrow. I have your cabin all ready and Sam still hasn't discovered our secret. She'll flip when she sees Emma in downtown Lahaina."

"Uh—"

Alarm bells went off in his head and gut, his heart rate kicked up, and his muscles readied for action. "What? What happened? Are you alright?"

"How can you tell all that from one 'uh'?"

Burke climbed out of the Jeep and locked the doors. "Because I know you too well and if you're canceling it means something happened. What?" He walked onto the dock and moved past a few fishing boats and a pleasure boat.

"Uh, something weird."

"Weird, how?"

Rollin sighed. Then grunted with pain.

Burke stopped walking. All the hair stood up on his neck and arms. His friend was hurt. Also, normally, Rollin just gave quick concise reports. If he hesitated, it meant he was scared. And if Rollin was scared, it meant the world was about to end.

Rollin cleared his throat, probably to cover another groan. "Someone slipped me a roofie at Peet's Coffee. I woke up in the back of a van on my stomach with three dudes trying to undress me."

Burke's gut roiled and he fought a shudder. "Yikes."

"Yeah. So I bust their asses—man, I was half out-of-it, fuckin' roofies—I get free of them—"

"Who were they? Cabal?" Burke made himself continue forward to his boat.

"No, I don't think so. But they wore ski masks, so I'm still not sure. One guy's mask came off, never seen him before—I drew a sketch of his face—but since they'd relieved me of all my weapons, I was more focused on getting away from them than figuring out who they were. So I broke out of this van—fuck, they'd taken me all the way into the City into an industrial zone—but in the struggle, I ended up with a piece of paper with a list of names on it. Mine's on it and Emma's on it and six other people. Two of the names were crossed off and I'm guessing it means they're dead. Bobby's going to do a search for me."

Burke climbed into the back of his boat. "Do you know why you and Emma are on the list?" He laid his packages on a padded side bench.

"Yeah. I recognized all the names."

"From where?"

"Childhood. Kids of my dad's and Emma's dad's crime crew. Looks like someone's decided to find the jewels. You know the story."

A shot of adrenaline fired through him and the need to protect Rollin grew strong. "Yes, your father and Emma's father plus six of their cohorts were murdered by the Mob because they'd stolen umpteen million dollars worth of jewels from them." He sat down at the controls instead of untying the boat and leaving. If he turned on the motor, he wouldn't be able to talk to Rollin.

"Actually, just snaked them on a job." Rollin's breathing hitched. "Dad's crew stole from a jeweler's conference in Sacramento. But yeah, in effect they stole from the Mob. Which is why the Mafia wiped 'em all out." He grunted again.

Burke searched his mind for the details of the story. "But before they died, your father and the rest of the gang hid the jewels, right?"

"Yeah."

"Then tattooed their children with a map to the gemstones' location. So the list you recovered is of all the children who were tattooed with the map?" Burke wiped water stains from the chrome trim of the dashboard with a forefinger.

"Yeah. And I think we're being killed one-by-one for the tats. They were undressing me and I was on my belly. My tat's on my back."

"And all of them are required to solve the code."

"Apparently. None of our experts have come up with anything solid from Emma's and my tattoos. But that's only a fourth of the information. Best guess is that the code reveals the longitude and latitude of where the jewels were hidden."

Burke grabbed a towel from the seat next to him, stood and began wiping down the windshield of the ski boat. "*If* the jewels were hidden. The Mob still could have recovered them. All they would have needed was one of the men left alive. Extracting information is one of their fortes."

"I heard they didn't find the jewels."

"And someone else obviously heard the same story."

"Yeah. I thought all these people were dead. I've done some research since I found Emma, but hadn't been able to locate any more of the tattooed kids. And we've been a bit busy with other things."

"Yes, we have." Burke sat in the leather bucket seat and threw the towel onto the floorboards of his boat.

"This new guy has their old names and all their new aliases. I don't know how he got this information, but he's good."

"Maybe from the Mob."

"That's what I'm thinking. The goon that I beat up in the back of that van looked Italian."

Burke straightened his back and shoulders. "Alert the Patriots."

"Love to, but no one's in the country right now. Zane's the only one, but he's under deep cover. Finally penetrated the crime syndicate that the Cabal uses to do a lot of their dirty work in the Bay Area."

The need to protect Rollin and Emma overwhelmed him. He had to get to them and right that moment. Then his mood plummeted. *Sam.* "I'll come home."

"I can't ask you to do that when Sam still isn't well."

He kept his voice strong, making sure not a shred of regret seeped in. Rollin didn't need guilt on top of his fear. "She's well enough to care for herself with a bit of help. I can hire someone here to care for her. But I'm not going to allow her to come home now, because if Emma's in danger, Sam's going to want to be involved. She's impossible to contain."

"You sure she'll be okay without—"

"Yes. I'll be there by tomorrow night. I can rent a house or Sam can stay here on the boat. Have you told Emma yet?"

"Yeah, she's running around packing. Poor kid's pretty shook. She didn't tell me until now, but yesterday, she said some guys in a white van were following her, same license plate as the guys who grabbed me. She thought she was just being paranoid, but ditched 'em all the same. License number comes up on a stolen white van, taken from Los Angeles last week."

"Good thing Emma was alert."

"Yeah. And now we have to get to one of the safe houses before these bastards attack again."

"We need more people. You and Bobby and I aren't enough. I'll call Banana back from Tahiti. David's with Captain, Ty and Catherine in Kuwait, right?"

"Yeah."

Burke clenched his jaw and shook his head. "Shit. And Dino, Roman, Stefan and Greg are in France protecting the oil company whistleblower. Great fucking timing." He punched his palm. "I wish the Cabal hadn't compromised all the other local security companies."

"Me, too. This just proves we're too short on people. Captain's looking for new recruits."

"Are you okay?"

"Yeah," Rollin said in an unconvincing tone. "More worried about Emma. I have training, but she…"

"Is much more resourceful than you give her credit for. Like how she handled herself yesterday?"

"Yeah, but honestly, do you give Sam any credit for being resourceful now that you're married?"

His stomach tightened. "Point taken. I'll call you as soon as I get in."

"Let's take a rain check on this vacation. I'm glad we didn't tell the girls."

"Me, too. And I'm holding you to the rain check. Just stay alive until I see you and keep your lovely fiancée alive, too."

"Will do. Thanks, buddy. You're a pal." Click.

Rollin's normal cheery tone was faked. He was worried. Which made Burke worry even more. His neck and back hardened. He stood and untied the powerboat from the dock.

So much for a happy vacation with his best friends.

As good as the Patriots were, taking on the Mob with a skeleton crew would be a challenge. Almost a suicide mission.

Fuck.

Hopefully, they'd all live long enough to cash in on that rain check.

The End

Sam's Kobe Beef Sloppy Joe's

1 pound ground Kobe beef
16 oz chopped tomatoes
1 4 oz can tomato paste
1 medium onion chopped
6 cloves of garlic chopped
¾ cup cabernet sauvignon (make sure it's expensive)
2 cups sliced Morel mushrooms
3 cups diced zucchini
2 tbsp olive oil
1 ½ tsp Italian Herbs
1 tsp salt
1 package whole wheat hamburger buns
grated Parmesan cheese
1 can black beans (optional)

Chop onions and sauté in olive oil until translucent. Add chopped garlic, sauté for one minute. Add Kobe beef and brown the meat. Add chopped tomatoes, tomato paste, wine, mushrooms, Italian herbs, garlic powder and salt. Cook twenty minutes. Add zucchini and cook another ten minutes until zucchini is tender but still slightly crispy. Open a hamburger bun flat on plate, put a full scoop of mixture onto one side. Top with Parmesan cheese and serve immediately. Yield: 10 servings.

MARKED EXCERPT

Chapter One

Standing over his victim, the assailant kicked the large, overweight mass of drugged plumber. No reaction. A surge of happiness warmed him in the cool, foggy San Francisco night air. Rohypnol rocked. Idiot didn't even know what hit him.

He heaved the man over onto his stomach. Lifting up the back of the fallen man's bowling shirt, he took out his digital camera and took a picture of the tattoo of random letters and numbers on the victim's back among the folds of white, hairy flesh.

After checking to make sure that the photo was good, he scanned the deserted dirty back alley. Two-thirty in the morning. No one around but rats.

He looked down at his victim once more. Dude was more still than he should be. He knelt next to him and checked his pulse. Nothing. Must not have the right place on his wrist. He felt up and down the man's arm. Still no beat.

What?

He flipped the man onto his back. No movement.

Dropping to his knees, he put his head on the man's chest. Silence.

Gasping, he leapt to his feet, his heart pounding. "Whoa!"

The street wobbled beneath him, blood whooshed in his ears and he had to use both hands to hold his head steady. Sweat broke out all over his body. He'd killed someone!

His attention darted around the alley. Nothing moved, no one was around, but the place looked different to him. Darker, more grimy somehow.

Shit, how many people had spotted him in that bar? Fuck, this was sloppy.

He gazed down at the large dead human. Guilt wrenched his gut and he held his belly. Anguish roiled through him. Just a half an hour before the man was telling stories about plumbing mishaps and bragging about his kids. Shit. He'd just killed a very stupid, very loyal, very union plumber, who'd done nothing wrong but be born into the wrong family.

How much more could he have fucked this up?

Must have used too much Roofie. The dosage on his first two victims had been right, but he hadn't used enough on that Rollin Hanson asshole. Fucker had come alive in the back of his van, beat the shit out of him and the three guys he'd brought with him, and escaped before he could get a photo of his back. He was damned lucky his ski mask had stayed on.

He stared down at the lifeless lump and nudged it with his toe.

A tear rolled down his cheek. His body stiffened and he wiped it away quickly. His face heated. God, he was glad he'd been alone on his first kill. If Pops or Jimmy knew he'd cried, they'd beat the hell out of him.

Oh, God, Pops couldn't find out! He'd never live it down. Killing a guy by Roofie? He'd get laughed all the way back to grad school.

He figured at some point he'd end up killing someone. But he never saw it happening like this. He pictured his first kill in a huge blaze of glory. Guns, blasts, smoke, blood. Not dumping powder in a boilermaker. Like, who drinks boilermakers, anyway?

But this couldn't be real. People didn't die that easy.

Kneeling, he listened again to the man's chest. Nothing.

He sat back on his heels and stared at the empty shell of a person, unable to grasp the reality.

A lightning bolt of panic struck him, his heart rate ratcheted high, and his whole body shook from the blast of adrenaline. What the hell was he doing, just sitting there? He jumped to his feet, flew out of the alley and sprinted for his car.

Halfway home, he began to calm and form coherent thoughts. No more Roofies. He had to get the information a different way. He was smart, he'd come up with a plan that would neither alert the victims, nor kill them. Some kinda *Mission Impossible* thing.

Then he'd find the jewels, hand them over, and watch his brothers' and father's jaws drop. Not only would he be bringing some serious bling to the table, he'd have accomplished something Pops couldn't.

Then Pops couldn't dismiss him and would see the truth. That he was the man to head the family business, not Jimmy.

He didn't have to mention he'd accidentally killed one of his victims. He had to start his reign off right. Set a good example.

He smiled. He'd take his family in a new direction. A much more profitable business and one that flew under the radar. Like Uncle Marco did with his identity theft ring. If they'd taken Grandpa's advice and done something like that, Mom would still be alive.

He'd always suspected that Pops clung to the old ways just to prove his father and little brother wrong. But now Marco was making a hundred times the money they did with little risk to personnel or property. Pops always said it wasn't manly, what his brother did, sitting in front of a computer screen instead of the "honest" work of drugs, gambling, and prostitution. What BS. Their family needed to change to survive and he was just the man to make it happen.

After pulling up in his driveway, he took out his list. Only six people stood in his way now. Next on the list? *Frances Gilotti.*

He thought back to the plumber lying dead in the alley. His stomach contracted and his face burned. Fuck. He forced the emotions away. At least his murder cherry had been popped. And while he'd do his best to avoid killing his victims in the future, he couldn't let anything come between him and his rightful place.

Not even his morals.

*   *   *   *   *

"Mom, I told you to stop stealing from old people. I can't sell this crap," Fritzy Gilotti snapped into the phone. Sitting on her stool behind her tiny store's tall wooden counter, she crossed her legs and adjusted the zipper on her faux leopard fur boots.

"Not listening," her mother cheerfully replied. "You should be grateful I'm supplying you with high-end jewelry."

"I'd be grateful if you'd let me go legit and sell stuff I buy," Fritzy muttered.

"Bite your tongue, young lady."

"I'm not young, Mom, I'm thirty-three. Going to be thirty-four in about a minute."

"That's four whole months away. And besides, you'll always be my little girl. Look, I have to go and send this Fed Ex package to you. Wait 'til you see what I fleeced off this golfer guy. Platinum golf ball cuff-links with one carat diamonds. Toodles!" Click.

"Yeah, those'll just fly off the shelves." Fritzy grumbled as she set the receiver back on her vintage Art Deco phone.

Her gut burned with frustration. She'd never be free until that woman was too old to fight her. Probably about a minute after she died. The store was supposed to be Fritzy's way out of The Life. She should have known better. Every time she tried to escape her mother's grasp, somehow she ended up playing right into her hands.

Sighing heavily, she straightened her fishnet stockings and checked the traffic on 16th. Pretty quiet for a Wednesday afternoon. Time to take ten. She put the break sign out onto the U-shaped counter that lined her tiny store, grabbed her latte and sat back to read the paper.

As soon as she opened the front page, customers came into her store. Too bad. They'd just have to wait until she was done. She'd learned long ago that San Francisco customers who demanded her attention immediately rarely bought anything. Besides, her small shop was packed floor to ceiling with high-end "pre-owned" and vintage accessories. Took a long time to sort through.

The people approached her. Fritzy bristled, irritation flaming her already exposed nerves. Couldn't they read? Her sign stated clearly: *I am on break. Don't bother me. Buying something is the only way to get my attention. Put the money on the counter. I'll see it.*

However, these inconsiderate morons not only didn't put any money on the counter, they tapped their feet and cleared their throats.

"Excuse me," came a female voice.

This merited a glare. The first warning. Peering viciously over her cat-eye glasses, Fritzy leveled a Def Con 2 fiery stare at the two miscreant/would-be-patrons. The male looked like a rock-and-roller with long dark hair and a black leather jacket. The female, with short dark hair and green eyes, looked like some generic Peninsula rich bitch in her boring Nordstrom's wear. Odd pairing, but still not worth a second glance.

Fritzy returned to her paper.

"What the hell am I doing?" the rocker suddenly shouted. "Look, you're in danger, we're in danger, look up from that stupid paper, we don't have time for this, woman!"

Danger. *Riiiiight.* Danger from stupidity. From crazy people. From freaks.

Fritzy let out a long, drawn-out sigh, but wouldn't look at the man. Pushing her glasses further up her nose, she let her jaw twitch. The jaw twitch normally scared the daylights out of her only employee, currently at the dentist.

"Lady, I'm not kidding!"

She refused to react. After a pause, she held the male's dark and surprisingly volcanic glare. She dropped her eyes briefly to the sign, then she met his gaze once more before returning to her book.

"Jesus Christ." The male advanced on her and pounded his fist on the counter. "Are you or are you not Frances Gilotti?"

Rage fired through her body and her hand twitched for the baseball bat she kept under the counter. "Back off," she warned through gritted teeth.

She turned every brain cell to the man. Hooked nose, dark vibrant intelligent eyes, carved cheeks, obligatory goatee. Not terrible looking. But it was his intensity that scared her. What was his game?

"When you were a kid, your dad's friends tattooed you in a basement late one night," he said in a rush. "The tattoo's comprised of numbers, letters and a name, but makes no sense. Well, we were there with you and we both have the tattoos, too. I think together all the tattoos make up a treasure map."

Goosebumps sprouted on every part of her skin. Her belly froze and her limbs stiffened. How the hell did he know about the tattoo? She tuned her senses into his fiery dark eyes and read him. His gaze radiated truth and conviction. And fear. He believed his story.

But there was another whiff of something coming off him: military. Cop. Fed.

Her core froze to sub-arctic winter temps. Adrenaline slammed her body. She placed her Escape Kit—closest one was in the car—and planned her route. She'd head to Canada.

Muscle memory took over: her face became its usual immovable mask and she slowly moved her lower body into a position to run, while keeping her eyes tight on the man's face. She'd been through this routine more times than she could count. Should have known seven years in one place had been pushing it.

"And now someone is killing us, one by one, for the tattoos," the rocker continued. "I was drugged and woke up in a van, but managed to escape. I got hold of a list my attacker had in his pocket. My girlfriend Emma here was on the list, I was on the list and you're on the list."

Suuuuure. Nice story. She had to give the guy credit, he was inventive. But why wasn't he just coming out and arresting her?

Because he wasn't convinced she was his unsub. He'd found out about her old tat somehow and was trying to use it as a positive identifier to capture her.

Thank God, Fritzy'd had the weird numbers and letters—*H2JONES59*—covered by an elaborate Japanese Geisha. Some weird alcohol-infused ramblings of her now dead father. The old asshole.

Fritzy suddenly recognized the female. Miss Perky Butt. A newbie antique dealer from a few blocks away who tried to hook up with her once upon a time to form a women's Mission Delores shop owner group. The last thing Fritzy had needed was some do-gooder asking questions about where she got her stock. Of course, Perky Butt's "antique store" turned out to be a money-laundering place for her husband's gang. So what the hell would PB want with Fritzy now? And what was PB doing with a Fed?

Bounty hunters. Perky Butt had lost money on her store and now was taking side jobs. Fritzy had to get out of there. Her spine turned to steel. Time to do some mind control. *I am not the droid you're looking for. Move along.*

Rocker Boy's expression turned graver. "Frances, you are in danger. I can't state this more plainly. You have to shut down this store and come with us or they will kill you. Three others have died that were on the list. We're next. We're not kidding, you have—"

The door to her shop burst open and four large men—who looked like extras from a gangster film—burst inside.

Mr. Rocker spun, yelled and advanced on the men. The shop exploded in violence. A blur of fists, legs, arms and screaming faces.

Adrenaline ramped her system, she flattened to the floor behind the counter and scrambled through the doorway to the storage room, heading for the back door.

Just as she reached the steel back door, fists thundered on the other side.

Fritzy screeched to a halt. Okay, it was time to fight. All she needed was her gun—shit! The Beretta was at home. Fuck! Of all days to do a full cleaning, why today? Hopefully, not a fatal error.

Grabbing a large baseball bat, Fritzy charged for the front of her store.

Miss Perky Butt's purse came zooming at her, Fritzy ducked, it slammed the wall above her.

Fritzy launched onto her tall counter.

Below her, the melee intensified. Three creeps battled the rocker: a large Hispanic guy, a black chunk of muscle, and a blond human tank with a crew cut who looked like a WWF escapee. The rocker's fists were a blur. Guy was good.

A thug with greasy black long hair carried Miss Perky Butt kicking and screaming out the door.

Fueled by rage and terror, Fritzy went the full animal. Swinging the bat, she aimed for skulls. The Hispanic guy ducked and leapt for her legs. Just as he touched her faux leopard fur boots, she slammed down on his head and a sickening thud rewarded her. He staggered backwards, holding his bleeding head and howling.

The blond WWF jerk, wrestling with the rocker, yelled at her attacker. "Grab her, you pussy!"

"Get out of my fucking store!" Fritzy bellowed.

Stalking down her counter and swinging the bat as hard as she could, she nailed her victim again. He cried loudly and stumbled out of the shop.

She advanced on the group attacking Mr. Rocker. She brought the bat down on the head of the black guy, he wobbled and fell to his knees. Mr. Rocker pounded the blond thug in the face. The skeevy dark-haired jerk who'd taken Miss Perky Butt pushed his way back into the store and attacked Mr. Rocker. She swung at the goon, but the man was too far out of reach.

Mr. Rocker fought like a wild man, clearly practiced at hand-to-hand combat. The big blond guy landed a fearsome punch to his jaw and he barely reacted. The black thug held a vintage wooden radio over his head.

"Watch out!" Fritzy screamed.

The black asshole slammed the radio down on the back of the rocker's head and he crumpled to the ground. The three guys quickly removed him from the store. The door closed behind them.

Fritzy raced down the counter toward the back of her store, dropped to her knees, reached underneath and pressed the silent alarm. She couldn't believe she was resorting to actually calling the police, but at this point, jail sounded better than death.

The shop door slammed open with a crash. Holding the baseball bat high, she jumped to her feet on top of the counter and let out a bellow that would wake the dead as she faced her attacker.

A chill went down her back and tension gripped her belly.

A Goth giant twice her size ducked his head under the doorway and stood before her, dwarfing her store. Dressed in a black leather jacket, with long black hair, a goatee and searing green eyes, she'd never seen a scarier dude, yet weirdly handsome, too. His shoulders were as wide as a bus and his combat boots had to be a size 20.

But that didn't matter.

Gothzilla was going down.

Zane Black stood in the doorway of the shop and gasped. The cutest woman he'd ever seen stood on the tall counter of the tiny store, her dark eyes wild behind her cat-eye glasses. Wielding a baseball bat, her white teeth bared behind perfect red lips, the purple-haired beauty wore a leopard print t-shirt, a black leather skirt, black fishnets and leopard skin boots. A punk wet dream. He didn't know if it was the savagery of her expression or her hot looks, but he wanted her instantly.

Advancing down the counter, she came at him, swinging the bat.

The sight was so adorable, this pint-sized tiger of a girl, daring to take him on, he couldn't help but laugh.

"Die asshole!" she screamed and came down with the bat.

He reached out quickly, grabbed the wooden weapon and ripped it out of her grip. Her adorable face twisted with rage. Her mouth open in a crazed yell, she dove for him, blood red nails first.

She attacked him like one of his Siamese cats in a mousie-induced frenzy. All teeth and nails. She'd pulled his hair, bit his hand and punched him in the eye before he could catch hold of her wrists. Finally, he immobilized her.

But that didn't stop her mouth. An incredibly deafening noise came out of her, making his ears ring. At first her words were unintelligible, like an animal's battle growl. Then her sounds became words. "I'll kill you! You'll die for this!!"

Confident he had her contained, he carried her out the door.

"Wait! Shut the door! Don't let the homeless steal me blind!"

Zane sighed, flipped her over his shoulder, locked the door and shut it. Turning away, he carried her across the sidewalk to the waiting van.

He sat on the bench back seat and wrestled her into place on his lap. A true pleasure. She smelled wonderful and her curves made his mouth water. "Go!" he yelled to Bonk, the skinny, dirtbag, red-haired driver. "Follow the other van!"

Sirens sounded from a few blocks away.

"And hurry!" he added.

Bonk nodded. "I'm there, man."

"You big dumb piece of shit! Let me go!" Leopard Girl yelled.

He squeezed her shoulders hard. "Calm down. And hush. You're hurting my ears."

"Like I fucking care about—ow!"

"I don't want to hurt you, but I will if you don't behave."

"Behave? You big nasty giant, what the hell—"

He deployed his deepest, harshest tone, one that made his chest rattle and his enemies wither. "I said, *hush*."

She stilled. Good. Didn't want to hurt this little thing. On the contrary, he wanted to take her somewhere and buy her a cup of coffee. Then drive her back to his house and make love to her from one end of his place to the other.

But unfortunately, these circumstances didn't exactly promote romance. But it did complicate his job. He'd known this would be a bad scene from the onset, but not this bad.

His gut twisted and anger seared his nerves. His temporary boss said nothing about kidnapping women. Zane had been told they were going after a rival gang who had information they wanted. He hadn't seen the first two victims because he'd arrived late. He hoped there were no more women involved. This sucked.

Fucking deep cover. Associating with these kinds of low-life pukes made him sick. But this job could be big payoff for the Patriots.

The girl shifted on his lap. He thoroughly enjoyed every millisecond of her movement.

This little hellion was lucky he was there. If Walsh hadn't called him, Leopard Girl might have gotten real hurt. But he'd protect her. And her friends.

And get his hands on that treasure.

Look For *Marked* To Be Released Soon!

www.janetperiat.com